PATH
OF THE
TAKER

WORLDSEA BOOK 1

By

Simon Grund Sørensen

Copyright

Copyright © 2024 Simon Grund Sørensen
All rights reserved.

No part of this book may be reproduced in any form or by any electronic or mechanical means, including information storage and retrieval systems, without written permission from the author, except for the use of brief quotations in a book review.

ISBN: 978-87-974688-3-8
First Edition
March 2024

Cover design by Katarina Prenda
Developmental Edit by Claudia Craciunoiu
Line and Copy Editing by Gareth Clegg

The Lord gave,
and the Lord
hath taken away

Book of Job, 1.21, The Bible

Prologue

Flint's knuckles were white from his tight grip on the rudder as another wave slammed against the boat. He had been certain they could make it to the docks before the storm hit and had kept at sea for too long. *It will all be my fault if we don't make it back...* He shook his head, rejecting the thought. The black sky was torn by yet another lightning strike and he dared release his grip from the rudder for just a moment to pull his oilskin cloak tighter, his fingers stiff and bordering on useless. Freezing rain drenched every inch of him, not to mention the towering waves that crashed over the boat, threatening to capsize it. From what he could make out, the wind had carried them around to the south of Fero Island, where the Iron Peaks jutted straight up from the ocean. There would be no chance of landing the small boat here, and he knew they had to outlast the storm.

"She won't hold!" John called from the mainmast, where he was fighting a losing battle, taking down the sails to save the mast from snapping.

"She will! She has outlived bigger storms than this. Give it time and the winds will relent," Flint replied, defiant to the last, trying his best to hide the bitter fear that slowly but steadily drowned his hope. He had never seen a storm like this.

"Perhaps we can swim ashore?" Katja called from somewhere further up the boat. "It can't be far. Can it? I can't see—" A wave drowned her words as it crashed over her.

"Are you there, Katja? Katja!" John called. He clung to the mast to stay on his feet, yelling into the darkness with a voice drenched in desperation.

"I'm fine. But I think we lost the fish," she called back after a moment of lamenting silence.

Flint sighed. "To hell with the fish. Just hold tight to the boat and we—"

His words were interrupted as an enormous wave hit the side of the boat. The terrifying sound of splintering wood was unmistakable as the hull shattered. He was torn off his feet by the mighty blast and barely managed a last breath before the ocean engulfed him. Icy waves tossed his body around like a rag doll. *Air! I need air!* He forced his eyes open, the salt water stinging but revealing no sense of direction or light to guide him. The water pressed against him, adrenaline drowning the cold but intensifying the fear. For the blink of an eye, lightning illuminated the darkness, and he spotted floating wood. He kicked and fought his way upward till he finally broke the surface and sucked in a desperate breath, inhaling as much ocean as air.

His whole body shivered as he could no longer ignore the tormenting cold. He had emerged into the chaos of a roaring thunderstorm, and fragments of the boat slammed against him while John and Katja's faint calls reached him from somewhere in the distance. Their voices were enough to ignite the tiniest spark of hope in his heart.

Desperate, he reached out for a passing piece of lumber; anything to help him stay afloat as wave after wave came over him, like wild animals tearing him down into the icy darkness. It was a struggle he could not win... The ocean was too wild, and there would be no salvation. John and Katja's calls were whispers compared to the roaring forces of nature that wished nothing but death upon them. Fear and cold tore at him, filled him. But then—it came—that tingling feeling he always experienced when he needed help and someone was near. It nagged him, begged him to use... To use them. Images flashed through his mind, images of how he could reach out with his spirit, suck the strength from Katja and John, and use it to save himself.

No! Not this time! Not them! He forced the images away and swam through the darkness towards their voices instead. It seemed like ages in the icy cold water before he finally found them, clinging to the side of a barrel. He caught hold too, and for a moment, they all just hung on, gasping deep gulps of air, their teeth chattering in miserable unison.

"Are you all right?" Flint called, his voice weak against the roar of the wind.

"That would be an overstatement," Katja called back.

"What do we do, Flint?" John asked, in a voice coated with fear.

Flint tried to gather his thoughts and ignore the tormenting cold. *If only Kathrine was here. She would know what to do.* Then he chastised himself for the thought: of course she shouldn't be here. If he died, at least Aaron would have one parent. Meanwhile, Bria—John and Katja's daughter—would be alone. He stared at his two dearest friends' faces, shivering and painted with fear and pain. Most likely, none of them would make it home to their kids, and they all knew it. *What will Aaron's life be like without a father? Will Kathrine find someone else and be happy?* His mind swirled with images of her in the flowing yellow dress she always wore on the first day of spring and of Aaron playing in front of their house... He snapped his mind back to reality. It was too early to give up! They had to try. For Aaron, and for Bria. And all the time, there was that feeling in the back of his mind, begging for his attention. Begging for him to save himself at the cost of his friends.

"We swim towards the rocks." Flint tried his best to sound confident as he pushed the words past his chattering teeth. "Hold on to the barrel. Stay close and afloat. When we reach the rocks, we will figure something out."

In the distance, the waves crashed into the mountainside where they would land, if they somehow made it that far. Surely, the ocean would suffocate them before that, if the cold didn't get to them first... He kept his bleak thoughts to himself.

They started kicking their legs side by side, wave after wave crashing over them, pushing and pulling. Flint felt dizzy, and the depths below became a tempting escape from the hell above. Too cold to feel, he hoped the rocky mountainside was getting nearer. And all the time, it was there: the urge to draw the strength from John and Katja. He knew he could do it. He had done it before, in desperate need. His nature screamed for him to Take. Take their heat, their strength, everything they had to keep him alive. Images of Kathrine and Aaron flashed before his eyes again as he fought the urge. How long could they keep going? He couldn't see their faces, but his strange ability to sense others told him they still held strength. Strength that he could use... the effort of holding back was nauseating.

His dark thoughts abruptly halted as a wave pushed him under water. He swallowed a gulp of ocean before he found the surface again, and his heart thundered as he heaved for air, throwing up ocean water, and screaming out in frustration. At least the barrel was still there, and he clung to it. Alone. He glanced around and screamed for John and Katja. No response. But he still felt them. Their force was still there, and the urge to Take was stronger than ever. *Surely, none of them will survive if I don't do it,* he thought. *At least I can live and at least, Aaron will have a father. John and Katja are already drowning and there is nothing I can do for them. I might as well...*

And in a moment, it was done.

Within seconds, Flint's body bulged with strength, vigor, intelligence, and an unbreakable will to survive. He had Taken all he could from John and Katja, and he knew it, even if he didn't understand how he did it. With his newfound strength, he swam onward, holding the barrel in front of him. Finally, the approaching mountainside rose before him. Katja and John did not scream or cry as they drowned behind him; he sucked the life from them before the ocean could end them. *A merciful way to go in these circumstances,* Flint thought, driven by the raw intelligence he drew from them. Nothing but surviving mattered now.

With long strokes of his arms, he finally made it to the side of the mountain. The barrel rolled back and forth for a moment, before a wave dashed it against the rocks, sundering it with a loud crash. He pushed pieces of splintered wood aside and reached up from the frigid ocean. The wet mountainside was smooth, worn by millennia of exposure to the waves, and his stiff fingers slipped again and again. He screamed into the night as he drew even more force from his drowning friends in the ocean. Finally, he caught a grip—however precarious—and grasped it with unnatural strength. The rock cut deep into his fingertips, but he felt no pain over the numbing cold as he pulled himself up and reached for the next handhold. Then another, ignoring the screaming voice in the back of his head. A voice reminding him that somewhere in the ocean, John and Katja were still drowning. Somehow, still living for him to Take more of their strength. They would only survive a few moments longer, a minute, if he was lucky. Determined, he climbed further. His bleeding fingertips dug into even the tiniest of cracks, and his frozen feet found a hold where there was barely any. Just another ten yards and he would be there.

Five yards.

One yard.

He pulled himself onto a small ledge and collapsed. He threw up sea water again, and then he could no longer ignore the pain. Freezing, cold and broken, he screamed into the night, cursing the sky, the ocean and himself. But his screams were nothing against the roaring thunder and the raging winds, and misery overcame him as his Taking vanished. The realization he had killed his best friends hit him like a sledgehammer: there would be no answer to his screams. No sounds apart from the brutal winds and waves slamming against the cliff face. For a moment, Flint considered jumping down and joining John and Katja. Memories flashed through his mind—of Kathrine and Aaron, together with Katja, John and their little daughter Bria—they had... They had always been there! Images of them as kids, climbing the big oak trees in the heart of the village, flowed through his brain like a dizzying fever dream. He almost passed out right there and then, but came to his senses just enough to pull himself away from the ledge. Slowly, he crawled under a small bush that stood pressed against the mountainside. His entire body shook uncontrollably, as he desperately prayed the bush might lend him enough cover to survive the night. Surely Kathrine would know what to do. Somehow, all would be well.

Part 1

Great Oaks

Chapter One

The wind came all the way from Meridian—the great island at the center of the world, far to the east—across islands and towns, large cities, mountains and forests. It carried with it the smell of life: bonfires and cooking, incense and spices, and the salty smell of the ocean. The whole Worldsea had shaped the wind as it finally crossed the Iron Peaks, picking up a scent of pine before it reached the marketplace of Great Oaks; a small village at the foot of the mountains.

The breeze tussled Aaron's hair as he moved his weight from one foot to the other, impatiently waiting for Mom to finish trading with the merchant. The spring sun had finally triumphed against the grip of winter, and there was too much adventure in the air to stand still. Birds sang in the three tall oak trees, and their song mixed with the sound of hammer strokes ringing out from Ruben's smithy. Despite it being early in the day, and not at all cold, Aaron could smell smoke from the hearths in the houses. Most likely, people celebrated the arrival of the first merchant since the long winter by preparing the finest foods they had left in their winter storages.

The smell of wood smoke blended with the fresh mountain air. This would have been a great day to take the sheep up to the fresh, untouched grass on the higher plains. Mom, however, had insisted they joined her at the market—both him and Bria. Bria looked equally impatient, repeatedly braiding and unbraiding the end of her long, blonde hair.

"May the blessings of King Eldrik be with you, and may he keep you safe from the Takers."

Aaron sighed in relief as the merchant shook Mom's hand and handed her a basket of colored wool before they finally turned to make their way through the crowd of gathered villagers. The market around the three oak trees bustled with life, and the merchant himself, a plump, bald man with a purple tunic, was almost overrun by curious townsfolk, eager to buy, sell, and—first and foremost—hear stories from across the sea. Aaron had been curious too at first, but the merchant had sternly refused any requests for stories at the market. Instead, he had directed all impatient ears to join him in the tavern that evening, where he would let the whole town know his tales.

"Looks just like a tiny Flint! How old are you now, kid?"

A burly fisherman rustled Aaron's uncombed mahogany hair, so it fell down and covered his dark brown eyes. The fisherman continued to pat him on the back with a force that almost knocked him over.

Bittersweet pride rose in Aaron, as always, at the mention of his father. He had been five when Flint died, and only remembered faint images of him now. He took a step forward to stop from falling and brushed the hair away from his eyes. "Thirteen."

"Thirteen! My gods. Kathrine, when will you let these kids come fishing with us?"

"Aaron and Bria herd the sheep, and help me with the herbs and treating the sick," Kathrine answered, her eye twitching slightly in the manner Aaron knew signified danger. This was a discussion they had already had too many times.

"It's been eight years, Kathrine. We will take good care of them, go on a day with no wind," the fisherman objected. He grew silent as Kathrine raised her finger and her voice.

"Let's climb the oaks," Bria whispered, tugging on Aaron's shirt sleeve.

Aaron nodded, glad to escape what looked like the beginning of a fiery argument. The two quickly snuck away, the sound of Kathrine yelling at the fisherman dying out behind them as they tunneled their way out through the crowd of people and onward to the three oaks. The trees stood majestically in the middle of the market, with spring leaves already sprouting from their branches, creating a cover that only allowed the most determined rays of sunlight to pass.

"Last to the top is a Taker!" Bria laughed and jumped ahead of him, giving him a push as she passed, so he lost his balance.

"Hey, no pushing!" he called, as he set after her. She was taller and—although Aaron would never admit it—stronger than him, too. Mom had asked that she wore a dress that day, which to Aaron had sounded like a fair handicap, but she had successfully refused and worn her brown linen pants and loose-fitted black shirt. She easily scaled the lower branches of the largest oak before Aaron even reached its base.

They had climbed these trees at least a thousand times, and Aaron's feet easily found the grip of the old metal spikes that stuck out from the trunk. Legend had it these spikes remained from a time when The Central Rule liberated Great Oaks from the control of a gruesome Taker and pinned him to the tree. Now, they served as footing for children eager to climb.

"Come on, keep up," Bria called. She was already pulling herself up on the thick branches, where one could sit and look out on the merchants and villagers trading.

"You started before me!" Aaron called back, trying to launch himself up to the branches. "It's not fair and I—" The frightening realization he had lost his grip sent a gut-wrenching shiver through his body. He reached out and desperately grasped for something to grab onto, but caught nothing but air.

"Aaron!" Bria screamed, and he felt the strange sensation of falling backwards and out of control. The world spun around him, the ground hurling towards him—

His fall stopped abruptly. Not from the expected painful encounter with the rocky earth underneath, but because he had been caught in mid-air.

"You okay there?" Tobias, the blacksmith's son, asked.

Aaron's legs were shaking as Tobias carefully placed

him down on the ground. "I... Thank you, Tobias," Aaron stuttered.

Despite Tobias only being a year older, he was already more than a head taller than Aaron, and several pounds of muscles heavier. He had even outgrown Bria, who was another year older, and who had always been taller and stronger than either of them. As always, his blonde hair and face, as well as his blue tunic, were partly covered in soot from working with his dad in the blacksmith's workshop.

"Anytime!" Tobias answered, looking up at Bria. "Did you push him this time?"

"Shut up, stupid. You know very well that Aaron doesn't need a push to fall. He does that just fine on his own." Bria jumped down from the tree with taunting ease, landing next to them. She picked some leaves out from her long blonde hair, which had ended up in a state of unbraided freedom.

"You started before me!" Aaron protested again, fuming over her mockery.

"Let's call it a tie," Bria said, and winked at Tobias.

Aaron hated how Bria seemed to get better and better at getting Tobias on her side, no matter the subject. She had all the unfair advantages, and Aaron was just about to object further when Kathrine interrupted him.

"Aaron, Bria, time to go." She had emerged from the crowd, her brown hair braided, hanging over the shoulder in decorative contrast to the yellow dress she had picked especially for this first merchant visit of the year.

"See you in the tavern later for stories then," Tobias said with a skewed smile as he turned and headed into the crowd of people waiting to trade with the plump merchant.

"Come on in, close the door, before the candles start dripping," Innkeeper Peder rushed them into the crowded room and closed the door behind them. He was a slender, middle-aged man with gray hair and a brown apron he wore on all occasions. He usually yelled at kids when they got too rowdy on the marketplace, and Aaron had never liked him much. For once, all the candles in the old wooden chandeliers were lit, and lazy flames danced in the fireplace at the end of the room. The air brimmed with the sound of talk and laughter, and the thick smell of beer, roast and wood smoke, hit them like a wall the moment they stepped into the lively room.

Aaron looked around for a place to sit. Sometimes he forgot that so many people even lived in Great Oaks. Luckily, Tobias was at a table in the corner, waving them over to sit with him and his family. Aaron happily set into motion, but Bria was faster and pushed past him, sitting next to Tobias, leaving him to sit between Mom and Ruben. Usually, he would have objected, but he was distracted as he caught the eye of the merchant who sat in the middle of the room, half a bench reserved just for him.

The merchant raised his voice and his slurred speech quickly drowned out the eager villagers. "I suppose even King Eldrik and his armies cannot protect the entire Western Sea." He burped as he gulped another sip of beer. "I'm telling you, the pirating out here has picked up. Loathsome bastards. Some fancy fella named The Raven, hair black as the night they say, attacks innocent merchants in his ship of cursed blackwood. Wouldn't happen in the Inner Sea where the king keeps order, but I suppose out here, The Rule leaves you folks very much to yourselves."

The merchant gazed around the room. A group of farmers nodded. He took another gulp of beer and apparently decided it would take more dramatic stories to rouse this crowd. Aaron loved stories of pirates, but dared not disturb by asking for more stories about The Raven.

"Not to mention the purgers," the merchant continued. He looked around with a daring smile as general unrest spread across the tavern. Children pushed themselves closer to their parents, and parents looked at each other, worry etched on their faces. All knew of the purges: emissaries and soldiers from The Central Rule arriving in ships, then killing animals and people at random.

All were silent as the merchant continued. "How long has it been since The Central Rule came here with a purging ship? I've heard they purge more seldom here in the Outer Sea. What, every five years or so?"

"Ten. It's been ten years since they have been here," Ruben answered on behalf of the crowd.

"The Takers be damned!" the half-drunk merchant sputtered. "Ten years? I suppose you should expect a visit here anytime."

"There is no need for such stories here. We follow the laws, and we have no quarrel with The Central Rule." Ruben crossed his arms, muscles bulging. The tone and look of the giant man would have brought most men to silence.

Not the drunk merchant, though, who barely looked up from his beer mug. "I bet you haven't had any reapers here either, searching for hidden Givers, like they did on the Southern Islands?" He dramatically shook his empty mug.

"Everyone knows they hid a Giver among them on the Southern Islands. We would *never* do that," Peder said as he placed another beer mug in front of the merchant.

"You never know, Givers could be hiding right here among you without you even knowing." He sent a gaze around the room. "That's why the reapers have to question people so thoroughly."

Peder said, "We are not like the southerners. We would never—"

"They were people just like you and me!" The merchant slammed his mug on the table, beer spilling over the edges. "Just like us. Living their lives, until some day The Rule realized someone was hiding a child with the power of Giving. Just *one* child was enough for The Rule to send their armies and enslave entire islands. I've seen it with my own eyes. Still now, forty years have passed, and they are still slaves, the Silverhand family running the whole thing with a tight grip on behalf of King Eldrik."

The tavern was silent, except for a child crying somewhere in the back. Aaron had always hated the stories about the War of the Lost Child, which concerned the whole enslavement of the south. Mom sometimes used it to scare him if he didn't behave, telling him that The Rule would come and kidnap him. He pressed against her and looked around at the adults. Ruben's usual smile was replaced with a serious gaze, his thick brows low over his eyes.

"We have nothing to fear here," Ruben said, his deep voice cutting through the tavern. "We have no quarrel with The Rule, and we don't harbor Givers. We live peaceful lives."

Nods of approval from around the room supported his statement.

"Well, I heard The Central Rule purged Burrow's Keep just a week ago," the merchant said casually. "From my knowledge of geography, this could be their next destination."

Gasps filled the room, and Aaron looked around as the adults exchanged glances. *Surely, purgers won't come to Great Oaks,* he thought. He had never even seen a Central Rule ship, at least not while he was old enough to remember it. To him, King Eldrik, The Rule and all that, was the stuff of stories and legends. Not something that would show up at Great Oaks and attack people. *But what if it did?*

Clouds obscured the moon, leaving it almost pitch dark as they left the tavern to walk the few hundred yards up the lower slope of the Iron Peaks to their cabin. A light drizzle filled the air, and Aaron pulled his long sheepskin jacket close around him, shielding himself from the icy wind that whistled down the mountainside. The gusts carried a scent of frost, the sound of sheep baaing, and Luna barking—the sounds of home.

"Will The Central Rule really come and purge here?" Bria asked.

"I cannot be sure. But if they do, it will be mild," Mom answered. "You have nothing to fear."

Aaron felt his heart sinking. It sounded like it could actually happen. He took Mom's hand, hoping Bria wouldn't notice and tease him for it.

"But why do they even do it?" Bria continued.

"To instill fear and avoid riots," Mom replied. "The Central Rule simply doesn't have enough soldiers to station them on all the islands, especially here in the Outer Sea. Instead, they make sure we stay afraid of them by occasionally showing up and making an example. But Great Oaks has no Givers and no bad history, so they will be mild with us."

The clouds separated, and the moon reflected from the small windows of the cabin, shedding a silvery glow onto the gray stone surface that made up the walls. In contrast, the tall grass covering the roof seemed to emanate darkness, and Aaron could barely see the little chimney that peeked through. The sheep stood like white clouds in front of the cabin, surrounded by a low garden wall of stones similar to those used to build the house. Kathrine opened the small gate into the garden, and Aaron let go of her hand to nestle in the fur of the nearest sheep, while Luna barked and jumped around them in joy.

"Easy girl, relax, will you?" Kathrine said, and continued into the cabin, while Aaron and Bria stayed outside and petted Luna.

"Do you have to let her lick your face like that? It's disgusting!" Bria said.

"What do you mean? The other day I saw you and Tobi—"

Bria punched him hard in the stomach, and he fell forward with a moan before he could finish the sentence. Luna continued licking his face, thrilled to be part of this new and exciting game.

Morning light streamed in through the windows, filling the bedroom with warm shades of orange. Dust hung lazily in the air, and Aaron spent a moment listening to Luna and Bria's breathing before he got up. His movement woke Luna, who stretched and nestled her face against his hand. He petted her lazily while he pushed the door open to the large living room. The front door was open a crack, and Aaron could hear Mom in the garden, probably gathering water from the narrow stream that ran by the house.

Herbs dangled, drying in front of the fireplace as usual, beneath Bria's hunting bow which hung decoratively over the mantel piece. A large cooking pot bubbled over a small fire; porridge, Aaron concluded with dismay. He spotted a chunk of bread and a leg of cured meat in the kitchen next to a lump of cheese, showing that Mom had already prepared lunch. His stomach growled; he'd choose bread with cheese and meat over porridge any day. On the dark wooden table in the middle of the room stood two baskets, packed to the brim. He looked up as Mom stepped into the cabin, shutting the door behind her.

"What's all that for?" Aaron said with a yawn and nodded towards the baskets.

"You'll take the sheep up the mountain today."

"Sure, but why do we need all this?"

Aaron preferred walking with his hands free, and he could easily fit lunch in his coat pockets and drink water from the clear, icy streams.

"It's going to be cold today," she replied as she packed another blanket into the already full baskets.

Aaron looked at the sunny sky outside the window, but knew it wouldn't help to object.

"I can take some of yours if it's too heavy for your poor arms." Bria stretched her arms as she walked past him and sat down at the table. Aaron growled and sat next to her, while Mom placed bowls of porridge in front of them.

He ate slowly, the thick solution clogging his mouth, making it hard to swallow. Porridge really was the worst food he knew. In contrast, Luna seemed to love it, so he fed her a few spoonfuls under the table whenever Mom wasn't looking.

"Off you go then," Mom said as soon as they had finished. "And please, don't come home early today. I have a lot of work, and it's better that you do not disturb me. Perhaps you should go higher up the mountain today and look for fresh grass."

"But it's spring, there's plenty of grass!" Aaron objected, growing increasingly annoyed. Why couldn't they just take the sheep up to the low meadow as usual?

"Come on, little brother. The Takers snatch the lazy."

Bria opened the door, grabbing her herding stick and the bigger of the two baskets. Luna ran out the door, and the sheep in the front yard baaed as she happily jumped around them, her gray fur contrasting their white fluffy coats. Aaron sighed and followed, grabbing his coat, the other basket, and his walking stick. There simply was no arguing with those two.

After all, Aaron loved herding sheep, and he put great honor on his and Luna's ability to move and control the flock. They made their way up the hill, making sure not to lose any of the animals, and soon, the path grew steeper. The pine trees stood close on either side, and the frozen grass crackled under their feet. The sun, however, was rising fast, and soon the frosty grass would melt and become a delicious sheep breakfast.

Bria was unusually quiet, walking a few steps up ahead.

"So, is Tobias your boyfriend now?" Aaron said, breaking the silence.

"Of course not. We just like to spend time together. And it's nice talking to someone other than the sheep for once. You should try it."

"I talk to you and Mom all the time! And Luna, too. And the sheep are good listeners." Aaron patted the nearest sheep on the head, which responded with a 'Baa'.

"Well, he isn't my boyfriend... He is just... Tobias. You know?"

Aaron had no idea what that meant, and was about to ask when Bria continued.

"Is this grass good enough for your beloved fur balls?" She pointed to a stretch of tall grass that stood untouched after the long winter. Some sheep were already gnawing at the nearest patch, while others waited politely for Luna to lead the way into the meadow.

"This should do, yes," Aaron replied after a moment of pretending to carefully inspect the vegetation, and together with Luna, they guided the small herd onto the grass. It was a beautiful day, and they had made it up high enough to have a clear view of Great Oaks. Smoke rose from the two chimneys in Peder's Inn, and another darker pillar of smoke rose from Ruben's workshop. The fishing boats were already setting nets just a few hundred yards off from the coast. Meanwhile, villagers set up stalls in the market around the three oak trees. It would be a lively day in the town.

Bria and Aaron sat and let the sun's rays warm them, while Luna rested her head in Aaron's lap. *This is why I love being a sheepherder*, Aaron thought, as he closed his eyes and settled into a nap.

"Wake up!" Bria shook Aaron, and he woke up with a startled shock. Luna whimpered and stretched her legs with a yawn. The sun was already high in the sky. How long had he slept? He blinked to get used to the sharp sunlight.

"Look!" Bria pointed down the hills towards Great Oaks.

"Look at what?" Aaron rubbed his eyes. Then he saw it. Three large ships in the harbor, clearly distinguishable by their red flags, with a golden circle and a four-tipped star in the center. Had she really woken him up so aggressively just to show him some fancy boats? Sure, they were a bit bigger than usual, but...

"Central Rule ships!" Bria clarified.

"Central Rule?" A chill ran down Aaron's spine. Now he understood, and his heart sank deep into his chest, thinking back to the merchant's warnings in the tavern the night before. "Are they here to... to purge?" He couldn't believe that someone—*anyone*—would do something like that here in Great Oaks.

"Maybe. That would explain why Mom sent us up here today. She must have suspected something and wanted us somewhere safe."

"But... Shouldn't we fight them? What happens now?"

"No one fights The Rule, stupid."

He looked closer, his eyes widening as he saw a new pillar of smoke rising from the row of houses at the front of the harbor. Red and orange flames danced at the root of the smoke; at least one house had been set on fire. They were too far away to see it clearly, but it looked as if people were running around now. The wind had turned and it carried the smell of smoke—and the sound of alarm bells and screams.

"But we have to do *something*! Don't we?" Aaron tried to stop his voice from shaking. *Surely Bria will know what to do. She always does.* Luna barked, jumping up and down in anxious impatience, while Bria got to her feet.

"Let's move closer. Perhaps there'll be something we can do without getting into a fight... If nothing else, we can help people hide in the hills."

Aaron nodded and they ran down the hillside, leaving the flock to graze on their own. Soon, Luna was far ahead of them, racing home towards the cabin.

As they got closer to town, the screams grew louder, and smoke clouded the air. Crying villagers ran up the hills, and Bria and Aaron directed them onto the safe path, up towards the sheep. Some of them had burn wounds, others had cuts and bruises, and all spoke of the fires by the docks, and of soldiers and interrogations. Apparently, an emissary with the power of Giving had come with the soldiers, and he used his powers to torture people for any information about hidden Givers. Melany, a middle-aged woman with frail legs and white hair, stuttered that two soldiers had specifically sought the town healer.

Mom!

Bria and Aaron looked at each other and dashed towards home without hesitation. From a distance, they could see two soldiers enter the cabin. A scream from Kathrine followed, and Aaron froze in fear.

"Move!" Bria pulled him forward, and he snapped out of it.

Surely Bria knows what to do, Aaron thought again, his guts clenching up in bitter fear as they kept moving.

Something lay on the ground in front of the cabin, and Aaron squinted his eyes to see clearly through the smoke that choked the air. *Luna!* The dog lay sprawled in a puddle of blood, and Aaron gasped at the sight and ran to her side, falling to his knees. She didn't move. She was... His heart sank, and tears burst forth and streamed down his cheeks. All the surrounding chaos seemed a world away as he touched Luna's ear. It was still warm. She was still... He touched her paw, held it in his hand. She still didn't move. Usually, she would never let him hold her paw this long without moving.

"Come on!" Bria jumped over Luna and continued directly into the cabin without hesitation. A crash and another scream from the cabin pulled Aaron to his senses. All of him longed to run away and hide, but he forced himself back to his feet and followed Bria into the cabin instead.

Inside, the cabin was a wild chaos of people and shattered furniture, clouded by thick smoke from the fireplace and the chair next to it, which had caught fire. Bria was hanging onto the back of one soldier, while the other soldier leaned over Mom, choking her with one hand and laughing at his comrade's frantic fighting. Mom didn't move, Aaron noted, his heart dropping. *Those monsters killed her!* Anger mixed with the desperate fear that clenched his heart. He searched for a weapon, ignoring the voice in the back of his head telling him to run. Bria's bow and arrows were all the way across the room above the fireplace, and there was nothing useful by the door. They had even left their herding sticks on the mountain. He turned and looked at the smoke from the village outside. And Luna. She lay there so still.

It reddened before his eyes. *They killed Luna! And they will kill Mom and Bria!* With a determined roar, he charged forward, punching and kicking at the soldier choking Mom. For just a second, the soldier seemed surprised. Then he regained control and pinned Aaron against the floorboards with the powerful grip of his iron-clad hand. He let go of Kathrine and moved to sit on top of Aaron's chest, legs heavy on his arms, making it impossible for him to move or get away. Aaron could barely breathe under the weight. Meanwhile, the other soldier had thrown Bria to the ground next to him. She was bleeding from a wound on her forehead.

"Remember the power of King Eldrik and The Central Rule," the soldier on top of Aaron hissed. He spat in his face and pressed his blade against his neck, so the sharp steel sliced into his skin. Looking to the side, the other soldier slowly carved the tip of his blade into Bria's chest. A trickle of blood ran down as she screamed and tried to kick herself free. Aaron could do nothing but watch, feeling the blade against his throat. Tears streamed down his face, while rage boiled inside him, and burned like a raging fire, blinding him. He tried to wriggle free. Every inch of him longed to break loose and save himself, Mom, and Bria. He didn't know if he was screaming or crying, when suddenly a wave of energy rolled over him. Like a tidal wave of power, it filled him, drowning everything but fury and a cold, calculated knowledge of how to fight.

Aaron surprised himself as he wrenched one of his arms free. With the free hand, he took hold of the sword pressed against his throat and pushed it away, ignoring the pain of the blade cutting into his palm. The soldier near Bria glanced over just in time to see Aaron pushing his comrade aside.

In a single motion, Aaron was on his feet and facing the guard that had been stabbing Bria. "Let her go," he hissed in an unnatural voice, hoarse like a whisper, but as loud as a yell.

The soldier stared at him, clearly confused by the sudden turn of events, but didn't move the blade from Bria's chest. The rage inside Aaron took over, and he grabbed the soldier by his leather armor, picked him up, and hurled him across the cabin. The man smashed into the wall next to the door and slumped to the ground in a heap. Meanwhile, the first soldier was back on his feet. It was as if everything happened in a dream: Aaron saw the soldier lunge towards him, blade first. He easily moved out of the way, countering with a punch that sent the soldier soaring across the cabin. Aaron leaped after him and slammed both of his fists into his chest before he even landed. The man smashed against the floor with a loud moan and lay still.

"Aaron?" a voice called, barely piercing the furious haze in Aaron's mind. He was just about to land another blow against the lifeless soldiers, when he saw Tobias and Ruben at the cabin door, dragging his mind back to reality. They sported cuts and bruises, carried hammers in their hands, and both stared at him, worry painted across their faces. Finally, Aaron looked down at himself and saw his arms bent in weird directions, as if they had both snapped just before the wrists.

"Are you... okay?" Tobias asked, taking a step towards him.

The overwhelming sensation of power dissipated and was replaced by another sensation: a wave of pain and exhaustion beyond anything he had ever felt before.

"My arms," He stuttered and sank to the ground.

Chapter Two

Bria woke up in Tobias's arms. *How romantic,* she thought, until she looked around the cabin and remembered what had happened. Tables and chairs laid shattered, glasses, herbs, everything was everywhere. One chair even seemed to have caught fire, and the room reeked of smoke. Mom coughed and talked to Ruben next to... To Aaron! He lay on the ground, his arms bent in directions they shouldn't bend. She suddenly remembered images of Luna bleeding on the ground, and of Aaron, screaming and fighting the two soldiers. It was blurry, like a distant dream.

"Are you okay?" Tobias asked, disrupting her attempt to recall the battle.

"Almost." She attempted to sit up, but aching pain shot through her head.

"Here," Tobias said, and carefully laid her down with a pillow under her head. Warming rays of red sunlight reached into the cabin, telling Bria it was already late afternoon.

"Where are the soldiers?"

"Dad and I gave them each a good knock on the head, for good measure. Then we carried them down to their ship and told their mates that we found them tumbling down the mountain. Brought a good laugh as they dragged them aboard the ship and headed off. They've all left now."

Bria nodded and looked up at him, noticing the cuts and bruises across his face. "You're hurt!"

Tobias grinned. "Builds character, I've heard. But don't worry, I'm okay."

"It does look kind of warrior-like, I suppose... And Aaron?" Bria felt like crying as she turned her head to look at Aaron: he looked so weak and broken. *It is all my fault for jumping into a battle we couldn't possibly win.*

"Broken arms, but your mom says he will be fine."

Bria sighed. She couldn't make sense of what had happened. Somehow, Aaron had been brave enough to follow her into the cabin, which was already surprising. Next thing, he had stopped a soldier from pushing a sword blade into her chest. But how? She moved her hand up and felt the cut just below the collarbone. The blood had dried now, and no longer ran down her chest, but the wound was there. It had been real. *Something* had happened, and it didn't make any sense.

Kathrine used teas and herbs to keep Aaron asleep for several days. During those days, they dug a grave for Luna, although Bria protested, knowing Aaron would want to be there for the burial.

"We cannot wait that long. She will rot before he

wakes," Mom argued, so they held the little ceremony without him. It was a gray morning, just her and Mom in the backyard, saying goodbye to the gray furred dog. Luna had been there ever since she joined the family, and Bria couldn't stop the tears from rolling down her cheek. She would miss waking up with Luna next to the bed every morning. And who was going to look after Aaron now when he went up the mountain with the sheep? She felt miserable at the thought of what her little brother would say when he woke up. *I should have kept Luna and Aaron safe up there on the mountain.* Then again, she couldn't bear the thought of what might have happened to Mom if they hadn't shown up. Or rather, if Aaron hadn't shown up.

Despite the many wounded after the purge, Kathrine reserved most of her attention for Aaron's arms, which she had to re-align in a gruesome procedure. Bria insisted on assisting, but soon had to capitulate and leave the cabin for fresh air before she fainted. Of course, she promised herself to never admit this to Aaron, who stayed asleep for several more days until he finally woke.

"Took you long enough," Bria said as he blinked his eyes open. Mom had forbidden her to wake him up, but in her boredom, Bria had carefully placed a glass so rays of sunlight reflected into his left eye. He lifted his arm to block it, but instantly stopped, letting out a squeak of pain.

"Easy, my dear." Kathrine rushed over from across the room.

Bria felt a sting of remorse as she saw Aaron's face contort in pain. Sometimes she didn't know why she kept teasing him, when she really wanted to cry and hug him.

"Here, drink this. You will need a day or two more in bed, I'm afraid," Mom said, giving him a cup of ill-smelling herbal liquid.

"But... What happened?" Aaron asked after gulping down the mixture. Bria held her nose from the stench. Thank goodness she didn't have to drink that stuff.

"You majestically saved us all by kicking around a lot, and somehow breaking both your arms in the process," Bria said, still holding her nose. She just couldn't help herself, and Mom gave her a stern look.

"The soldiers broke your arms, but we are all okay," Mom said, putting a hand on Aaron's head.

"I remember... I think I was actually kicking around a lot," Aaron responded slowly.

"That's what I said! Honestly, I really think you kicked those soldiers well and good."

"Don't tease me," Aaron protested.

"I'm not!" Bria objected, although it admittedly sounded like she was making fun of him. And after all, she barely remembered the incident herself.

Days came and passed, and Bria was fully occupied with cleaning bandages, restocking herbs, and assisting injured townsfolk. She both pitied and envied Aaron, who slept through most of it. Somehow, there was always something for her to do, and she never had a moment to go down to the town. Most of all, she missed Tobias, and kept worrying if he was okay. He had carried several wounds and bruises when she last saw him... If only they had been together during the attack, surely they could have beaten up those soldiers without Aaron getting hurt. And she would have loved to help him rebuild the burned houses at the dock, if only Mom would give her a moment of free time.

"Bria, can you please tell me again what happened that day? I mean, when you returned to the cabin and fought those two soldiers," Kathrine asked as they were alone behind the house, hanging bandages to dry. It was a warm spring day, and Bria could feel the familiar wind coming down the mountain, bringing the scent of pine trees and the sounds of birds.

"I know, I know, we shouldn't have come back when you told us—"

"It's okay, my dear. I am grateful you saved me. I just... I just need to know more about how you and Aaron defeated the two soldiers."

"I did nothing, really. I mean, I jumped on the back of one of them. But he was surprisingly strong. I am too used to fighting with... Well, with Aaron I suppose, and it has made me used to fighting someone who is a lot weaker."

"Please, Bria, keep focus. Do you remember any details about what happened?"

"Oh, yeah. So, I was going for a choke, or maybe just a powerful punch. But the helmet got in the way. So, he slung me around and stabbed me. I think I hit my head then, 'cause I can't remember much after that."

"Please dear, try," Kathrine encouraged, a worried expression painting her face. It seemed like she was fishing for *something*... But what did she want to hear? That she had failed and Aaron succeeded? She had already said all that, even though she wished it had been the opposite.

"Well, I had been thrown on the floor and Aaron was lying next to me, held down by the other soldier. So, we were in trouble. But then, Aaron did something. Broke free somehow and got up. Next thing I remember, he was jumping through the air and punching the soldiers, dodging their swords and everything. I've never seen anything like it. So I guess I must have hit my head pretty hard."

Kathrine paused her work, and just stared at Bria for a long moment.

"What?" Bria said. "I know we shouldn't have come into the cabin, and I'm sorry."

"I think you're the reason we are still alive," Kathrine said.

"Me? But I did nothing!"

"Perhaps... How much do you know about Giving?"

Bria felt confusion rising in her. "Like the monsters from The Central Rule, and from the old stories?"

Kathrine nodded.

"Only what I've heard in stories, I guess. But why is that relevant?" Bria's stomach tingled with the strange feeling of something being wrong. Something bad.

"I think you might be a Giver, and that you Gave Aaron the power he needed to fight that day."

The warm spring breeze suddenly felt cool to her skin.

"But... How? What does that mean? Am I... Is it like a disease?" Bria felt dizzy, and she carefully leaned herself against the pole of the drying rack. The ground felt much less stable than usual.

"No, my dear, no," Kathrine put a comforting hand on her shoulder and the dizziness waned a bit. "You are not wrong or evil or sick. You may very well have saved both my, Aaron's and your own life that day. But, Giving is a... dangerous skill to have. And therefore, we have to know for sure."

"But... How? I don't want to be a Giver!"

"We will wait until Aaron is up again. Then, I'll send him to the village while we do some tests. Nothing dangerous. Just to be sure."

Tests? Givers were servants for The Rule, far away at Meridian, not normal people like her, living in Great Oaks. It just didn't make sense.

"But please Bria, don't tell *anyone* else about this. Not even Tobias and Aaron. The Rule has ears everywhere, and if they hear anything, they might send their reapers to search for you," Kathrine pulled her into an embrace but Bria was too distressed to reciprocate the gesture. *Reapers would come for me? But surely I can trust Tobias... Though he might not like me anymore if he knew about all this nonsense.* Her heart dropped at the thought, and a silent tear rolled down her cheek.

Finally, Kathrine announced Aaron's arms had healed enough, and she sent him down to the harbor to pass some hours and buy himself a new shirt for the upcoming Tides Turn festival. His old one was torn during the battle, and it was a perfect excuse to get him out of the cabin for a few hours. Bria knew what this meant: finally, she could get some answers about this whole Giver business.

Kathrine had covered the windows, and it took a

moment before Bria's eyes got used to the dim light in the cabin. In the meantime, Kathrine sat down in front of her, a stern look on her face. The atmosphere gave it all a touch of mystery, Bria thought. She was excited to prove she wasn't a Giver. Still, a small voice in a far corner of her mind kept asking: what if she was? She ignored the voice, as she had for days.

"What do you know about Giving?" Kathrine started.

"Givers are people who temporarily give their own powers to others. Giving is transferring your strength to someone else," Bria suggested. Although Giving was somewhat of a taboo, she had certainly heard stories here and there. And she had spent several days condensing that knowledge in her mind.

"That's correct. Givers can temporarily send any power or feeling from themselves to someone else. It can be used to help others when they need strength, or even aid in healing them when they are sick. Stuff like that."

"Help others? But Givers are evil, aren't they? The people from the village told us about the Giver that came with the soldiers during the purge, and how he used his powers to hurt people."

"Yes, Givers work for The Rule now, and they are trained to use their powers for evil things, such as giving people pain. But, many generations ago, Givers were healers and helpers, supporting the people around them."

"But that doesn't sound bad at all?" Bria said in mild surprise. She had always learned to fear such powers, and anyone that might have them.

"No, Giving can be a beautiful thing," Kathrine said, a faint smile tugging on her lip. "But, The Central Rule has decided to use Givers instead for their own malicious intents." Her face darkened. "Many, many years ago, King Eldrik Evermore gathered enough Givers to claim power over all the islands of the Worldsea. He himself is even said to be an incredibly powerful Giver. Or perhaps even a Taker... Anyhow, that is why he has the reapers. The reapers search for any sight of Givers and bring them to a school called Roak to be trained to work for him. After all, a Giver can impart incredible power, turning even a young boy, like Aaron, into a soldier much faster, stronger, and more skilled than a normal human."

"Even Aaron?" Bria giggled. "But that doesn't make sense. Why would Givers work for The Central Rule then? It sounds like the reapers kidnap them?"

"Many Givers are born in families that serve The Rule willingly. For the ones that are reaped, I have heard The Rule has ways to break the mind and turn them into tools whether they want it or not." Mom's voice shivered ever so slightly, and for a moment it looked as if she might say something more. Or cry?

Uneasy, Bria decided to change the subject. "So, how do we know if I am a Giver?" It felt weird saying it out loud. "Oh, and if I am, then what? Will the reapers claim me to work for The Central Rule? You know I would never do that!"

"Easy now. No one will come and take you away, because no one knows about your powers. Who knows, perhaps one of your parents was a Giver and passed the power to you. That is how secret it must be, so that even your children and your partner cannot know."

"My parents? That cannot be!" Though, on second

thoughts, sometimes she barely remembered them. *Could it be?* Her heart sank a bit at the thought of her mom and dad. She only had a few memories of them, but surely none of them included Giving or any weird stuff like that.

"My theory is that you must have Given Aaron your strength during the fight. So, I suggest we try to test your ability to Give strength to me. Since Giving includes temporarily losing whatever power you give away, we can measure the success by how well you can lift the cauldron here." Kathrine pointed to her biggest cooking pot, which stood filled with water next to the fireplace.

Bria nodded, a smile tugging at her lip. She loved physical challenges and usually excelled at them, with Tobias being the only person stronger than her among the youngsters in the village.

"Okay, so try to lift the cauldron and tell me if it's heavy."

Bria grabbed on with both hands and lifted the cauldron from the ground. It was heavier than she expected, but it moved.

Kathrine patted her on the shoulder. "I had to have Ruben carry that one for me. You're strong!"

Fortunately, Kathrine didn't seem to notice, as she almost fell over when putting the heavy pot back down.

"Now, let's see if you can give some of that strength away. During the stress of the battle, you must have Given over some distance and amplified your strength severalfold to make Aaron strong enough to fight the soldiers. Giving, however, becomes weaker and more challenging over distance, so for now I will hold on to your arm."

Bria felt a strange, warm sensation of pride.

Amplifying her own strength and Giving it to Aaron sounded... Awesome? To her own surprise, she smiled as Kathrine gently took hold of her arm.

"Here comes the tricky bit. Visualize a flow of strength running from you and into me. Imagine yourself feeling weak while you do it, and wish for your strength to be given to me."

She tried to do as instructed, but wasn't sure if anything was happening. Perhaps there was a slight tingling where her hand held her arm, but it could easily be a trick of her mind.

"Now lift the cauldron again."

Bria grabbed the wooden piece of the cauldron's handle and pushed against the floor with her feet. Again, the cauldron lifted from the floor. It felt even heavier, but maybe her arms were just getting tired? She put the cauldron back down, keeping her balance this time.

"Well done, my dear,"

"Wait, did I do it? I felt nothing. And I didn't... you know, pass out, like I did when we fought the soldiers."

"Well, Givers don't usually pass out when they do their craft, my dear." Kathrine laughed.

Kathrine insisted they repeated the exercise again and again, while Bria felt increasingly frustrated as nothing seemed to happen. Her arms were definitely getting tired now, and her palms were sweaty and slippery. Meanwhile, Kathrine kept making up new ways to visualize power flows, or whatever nonsense. At the end, Bria's hands, arms and back were sore, and her mood low.

"How do we even know if this is how to Give or not?" Bria asked, crossing her arms and sitting down so forcefully that the chair squeaked under her. The test wasn't working, and Mom just kept making up new, stupid ways to try Giving! Why did it all have to be so mystical and secretive?

"My mother was a Giver. She... told me a lot." Kathrine said after a moment of silence. Bria gasped. Her adoptive grandmother had been... One of those? She had passed away several years ago, but Bria remembered her as a normal and kind old woman. Nothing like those monsters from The Rule.

"I... I am sorry. Why did you never tell me? You know I'd never tell anyone."

"Secrets like these are not gifts to give to others, although they might seem so at an initial glance. Keeping such a secret—whether it's your own or someone else's—is hard, but essential. I probably shouldn't even have told you... But then again, I think she would have wanted you to know, given our situation here." Kathrine showed a strained smile.

Perhaps she had been ashamed of her mother's powers, Bria wondered. In some ways, that would make sense. No matter how 'good' she said that Giving could be, it was hard to imagine how people would react if they knew what they were practicing in the little cabin. And that a Giver had already lived in the village. They had all heard the story of the War of the Lost Child, which left the whole Southern Islands enslaved for hiding a single Giver, and she doubted that the villagers would see kindly to a Giver living among them.

They repeated the exercise, again and again, day after day. The flow of strength, if any, remained incredibly weak, and Bria's mood grew more and more grim. Perhaps she could only Give under the utmost stress and dire need, Kathrine offered. At least, they couldn't provoke any reaction during the experiments. After a few days, they also tested Bria for the Giving of powers other than strength, but nothing seemed to work. Bria couldn't feel anything, no matter how much she reached out and imagined all kinds of flows and energies.

"I'm not a Giver, and that's just how it is! These stupid experiments are a waste of time!" She finally burst out after almost two weeks of trials. She was fuming with frustration. *Why won't Mom see it is hopeless?*

Kathrine finally sighed and agreed. "At least we know now. And to our luck, Tobias and Ruben were there to take care of the two soldiers, before they got any good ideas about what might have been going on. It appears that, whatever happened that day, was a strange coincidence. Who knows, perhaps Aaron was simply lucky, and the soldiers unfocused—maybe even drunk. Anger can make anyone stronger, and I suppose Aaron has been growing since he started helping Ruben and Tobias down at the smithy…"

Bria wasn't entirely convinced; from what she remembered, Aaron had moved much faster than what should be possible. Still, she could not understand or explain it, so she nodded in agreement. At least she wouldn't have to stay in the cabin and do Mom's stupid tests and exercises.

Chapter Three

Aaron blinked his eyes open. A ray of sunlight hit him in the left eye, and he tilted his head away from it. His body felt stiff and—

He shrieked in pain as he moved his arm.

"Morning, sleepyhead. You won't believe what horrors Mom and I have gone through to fix your arms!" Bria said. She was sitting next to the bed looking as confident as ever, with a wry smile and crossed arms. "I did a lot of the bloody parts myself, you know. You owe me. We even had to realign your bones."

Aaron shuddered at the thought and considered himself lucky he had stayed asleep through the procedure. Then he remembered the vision of Luna on the ground.

"Is... Is Luna okay?"

"I... We buried her two days ago." Bria stared down at the floorboards.

Tears welled up in Aaron's eyes, and a drop trickled down his cheeks. It hurt too much to move his arms to wipe it away, so he let it stay. He couldn't think of anything but the feeling of her ear. It had still been warm. He had hoped she would make it.

"I am sorry," Bria said. "We sent the sheep to stay with some of the larger flocks until we have a new dog and the time to look after them again. Mom and I are busy with all the wounded from the purging."

Aaron didn't reply, just gulped down a big cup of tea that Mom had brought. The taste was disgusting, but the discomfort waned compared to the pain he felt in his chest. Luna was dead. Soon, he faded back to sleep.

Aaron's arms healed fast, and soon he could go around the garden and visit Luna's grave. He picked a small handful of flowers, ignoring the pain in his arm every time he picked one up. Then he sat by the grave for a long time. It felt weird. Luna had always been there. When Dad disappeared, it had just been him, Mom and Luna. Then, Bria came as well. But Luna had always been there. The sun had long gone, and it was bedtime before he finally got up and left the grave, his body cold to the core despite his heavy sheepskin coat. It felt weird going to bed without Luna on the little blanket between him and Bria, and he felt silly for being so sad. He was too embarrassed to tell Mom and Bria how he felt. Still, it seemed Mom somehow knew, and every night she would patiently sit next to him as he fell asleep. During the days, Mom's tea, however disgusting it was, helped ease his mind, and before he knew it, she even allowed him to go down to the village. In fact, she demanded he stay outside, getting exercise and fresh air. Apparently, it would help the healing, although Aaron found his arms already felt good as new.

Aaron had been eager to talk to the people in the village and hear what else had happened during the purge. To his surprise, people preferred not to talk about it. Most adults dismissed his questions: 'It's better to move forward,' they said. In the end, Tobias was the most informative person, as he let Aaron know that The Rule soldiers had burned down five houses, killed tens of chickens, goats, and dogs, and a single horse, but no people. There had been an emissary among the soldiers, and he apparently used Giving to question people for any signs of rebellion against The Rule or hidden Givers. According to Tobias, adult men had cried in seconds. Most had begged for mercy and given any information they could, however irrelevant or even untrue. Anything to stop the emissaries' mystical attacks. Even Tobias seemed uneasy talking about the subject, and Aaron let it go. At least no people had died, although this knowledge did little to relieve the deep pain in his chest for the loss of Luna.

Without the sheep to tend to, Aaron spent his days by the docks, talking to the fishermen and looking at the boats arriving and leaving. This was a privilege he would usually have begged his mom for, but now he couldn't stop thinking of the sheep, and Luna. Still, it was better being by the harbor than having to help around in the cabin, and he enjoyed watching how small trading ships came and went. Most traders came to buy Ruben's metalworks, but many also bought wool and clothing, praising the quality and the pure white color. In return, the traders brought spices, paper and books, and all kinds of tools and equipment, much of which Aaron could not recognize. Most of the wares were sold at the market in Great Oaks, but sometimes the merchants paid for carriages to take the goods to the smaller farming villages south and north along the coast of Fero Island, Weathertop two days' ride north, or Greenhedge a single day to the south.

"Aaron, can you help us?" Ruben called as Aaron walked by the workshop.

"Sure!" Aaron replied, too fast to consider what kind of work he might be getting himself into.

"A merchant ordered a load of raw iron bars delivered to his ship. Could you help Tobias take them there?"

Tobias came out from behind the workshop, carrying a bar of iron in each hand and placed them in a heavy wheelbarrow. Like always, he had black smears of soot across his face, and Aaron could see the muscles tensing in his arms as he lifted the heavy bars.

"Thanks," Tobias grinned, collecting another set of bars and handing one of them to Aaron. It was much heavier than it appeared, and Aaron nearly dropped it before he got a proper hold and placed the iron bar on the wheelbarrow. He wished he could lift the bars as easily as Tobias did.

"Just another few rounds, and it's loaded." Tobias smeared a hand across his forehead, leaving another black trail of soot. "How are your arms now?"

"Good," Aaron answered, lifting one of the heavy iron bars to demonstrate, trying his best to make it look like an easy task. At least Tobias never teased him like Bria always did.

Tobias grinned and grabbed four. "And Bria? How is she? I haven't seen much of her lately," Tobias asked as they walked back and forth from the stack of metal bars to the wheelbarrow.

"She's good too. Mom keeps her at home for lessons these days."

"Strange," Tobias said, scratching his nose so that it too became black from soot. "Tell her I said hi, will you?"

"Sure," Aaron replied, as he placed the last iron bar on the cart. He would say 'hi' from Tobias, though he was happy to spend time with him without Bria. Lately, it seemed like the two of them had their own language, and he couldn't keep up with their jokes. Many of them aimed at him, it seemed.

Tobias grabbed the wheel barrow handles and set it rolling, while Aaron helped steer and pulled it over any small potholes in the road. They went through the marketplace, past the bakery, Peder's inn, and down to the dock. Here, a middle-aged man with a white beard, a long black robe, and a red turban was waiting for them. The black robe had lustrous silver embroidering running along the edges and looked more valuable than any piece of clothing Aaron had ever seen before.

"Ah, Fero iron. Perfect. I've come a long way for this." The merchant squinted in the midday sun, ordering his own men to move the heavy bars onto his boat, while keeping his attention on Aaron and Tobias. "So, you're the boy who broke his arms in the purge?" he asked, looking at Aaron.

Apparently, some people were telling stories of the purge after all, Aaron thought. "I suppose that would be me, yes, sir," Aaron replied, wondering if that was how one was supposed to talk to important people. He nervously shifted his weight from one foot to the other. Something about this man felt strange...

"I heard stories of how you and your sister fought off the soldiers. Not a small feat for a young man. Where's your sister, if I may ask?"

"Bria is back in the cabin, up the mountainside, with my mom," Aaron said. Somehow, he felt an urge to help the white bearded man the best he could. Answer his question as honestly and completely as he could.

The man smiled and shook his head, as if to regain his focus after something had distracted him. "That's great. Both of you take good care of yourself, and be careful with fighting soldiers like that. No use in you young people breaking your arms. If you do, old people like me will be forced to carry the iron ore ourselves," the man replied with a kind smile. "My name is Karim, and what are your names, if I may?"

"Tobias." Tobias stood upright, two heads taller than Aaron.

"And I am Aaron." Aaron stretched as tall as he could as well, and even felt the urge to make a formal salute, as he heard soldiers did when face to face with superiors.

"Very well." Karim smiled and handed Tobias a pouch heavy with coins, then turned and left. Aaron noticed he felt uncomfortably warm despite the cool mountain breeze. In fact, he was sweating as if he had just been running. The two boys looked at each other, but said nothing as they drove the wheelbarrow back to the smithy.

Ruben counted the money, then gave each of the boys a golden coin. An incredible sum for the little job, and easily enough for Aaron to forget everything about the strange man at the harbor. Aaron marveled at the gold in his hand. People in Great Oaks usually only traded in silver, and he was certain his mom would never let him have a whole gold coin, no matter how hard he worked. With such wealth he could buy... Well, *anything*. His heart lifted as thoughts and ideas for things to buy ran through his mind.

"Hard work deserves good pay." Ruben laughed at the amusement in the eyes of the two boys. "Spend it on something worthwhile."

Aaron and Tobias headed back towards the marketplace. If they were fast, they could still trade with the traveling merchants before they shut their stalls for the day.

"What are you going to buy?" Aaron asked as they passed the inn. He was still holding the coin in his hand, enjoying how the golden surface reflected the sun's rays. Such a treasure! But he already knew what he wanted to buy with it.

"Er... I might think a bit before buying something. What about you?"

"I want to buy a map!" Aaron replied with excitement and went straight to the cartographer, leaving Tobias gawking at a metal vendor. Ever since a sheep ate his mom's old map several years ago, he had dreamed of getting his own map of all the places from the stories of the wide Worldsea.

"What will it be, then?" the old cartographer asked in a frail voice. His eyelids drooped heavy over his ash-brown eyes, and his bushy gray eyebrows covered half his forehead.

"A map."

"Indeed, but a map of what?"

"The Worldsea, of course." Aaron put the golden coin on the table, and the cartographer looked at it for a moment. Then he grabbed a rolled-up parchment from somewhere under the counter, while mumbling something about 'ambitious younglings'. He rolled out a scroll, revealing a crude map with various lines, words and smudges. The map was rather small, and it looked as if Fero Island and Great Oaks had been added recently by a rough hand. Still, it showed all the way from the Silent Sea in the west, to the Inner Sea and the western edge of the enormous Meridian. It even included parts of the islands to the north and south of Meridian.

"For a coin, I can get you all the Western Sea," the cartographer said. "And believe me, you won't need any more than that. The north is too cold for travelers, the south is enslaved. And the Eastern Sea is empty, no land as far as any man can go. As for Meridian, it would take a much bigger map to show all the roads and cities there, so including it on a Worldsea map would be no good at all. The Capital would need a separate map on its own as well."

"I see," Aaron replied, his eyes fixed on the map. So much ocean and so many islands, his stomach tingled with excitement. *So many places I could go!* He had heard there were places much bigger than Great Oaks, with many more people, and he had seen merchants in all kinds of strange clothes and with accents from far away. He wanted to see it all.

"Dreaming of adventures, are we?" The cartographer asked, a smile widening on his face.

"Yes!" Aaron blurted out.

"Curiosity is the start of any adventure! Sailed a lot, lad?"

"I... no, not really," Aaron said, his heart sinking as he recalled sailing with his dad. Before the ocean had killed him. The thrill of adventure vaned, and he felt stupid for dreaming of sailing off like that. Mom would never let him sail onto the Silent Sea. Even the fishermen stayed close to Fero Island, their boats too small to reach the other islands.

"Well, if you ever go on an adventure, you will have to find a spot on a ship. And if you go, please note this map here is a little off scale to the west." The cartographer pointed to a discolored smudge that marked Fero Island. "I added your island myself just this morning. The actual distance from here to the nearest island," the cartographer moved an old bony finger to a nearby sludge denoted 'Tidun', "Is in fact five days' sailing on a proper ship."

On the map, Tidun was only an inch or so away from Fero Island, and Great Oaks was written just below the city called Burrow's Keep, which apparently lay in Tidun.

"What about the distance to Meridian?" Aaron asked,

pointing to the western edge of the big Island, which took up the whole right side of the map.

"Oh, that would be a month to the Inner Sea, and another month through the Inner Sea till you reach the western coast. Of course, depending on how close you dare sail to Roak Island, and whether you want to keep out of the pirated waters here north of Tidun." The cartographer pointed to an island on the border between the Outer Seas and the Inner Sea.

Aaron squinted to see the island more clearly on the map.

"Avoid Roak? What is Roak?"

"Rule's island. Used to be the most secure prison in Central Rule. I guess, at one point, they decided prisoners were easier to kill than to guard, so they converted the island to a sort of school designed to teach Givers. The entire island is like a fortress. Ships from The Rule are known to stop anyone coming too close, and they don't take kindly to the curiosity of a young adventurer."

The cartographer looked from side to side to see if anyone was listening. Then he leaned forward and lowered his voice. "The Rule may not be doing much as far west as Great Oaks. Here, even the pirates roam free, more or less. But as you get closer to the Inner Sea, you will find The Rule keeps a firm grip on things. Better keep your adventures out here, if you ask me."

Aaron shivered. Fero Island wasn't too bad after all, with only one purge every ten years or so. He thanked the cartographer and rolled up the map, excited to get home and show the precious possession to Mom and Bria. First, he found Tobias, who stood pondering at a merchant displaying various jewels.

"What are you buying?"

Tobias gave a little jump. "Oh! Er... Just some silver for... A project in the workshop."

"That's great! I bought a map!" Aaron said, too excited to care about Tobias's answer, as he was already unrolling the map to show it to his friend.

Chapter Four

Bria stepped out of the cabin with a sigh of relief and took a deep breath of the fresh air. It was the middle of spring now, and the sun came down with warming rays, dissipating the last remains of the morning fog that had rolled down from the mountainside. How she had missed the freedom to go wherever she wanted! Mom had finally given up on that nonsense idea of her being a Giver and allowed her to return to the village. She couldn't help but feel a slight sting of disappointment, that she was, after all, just a normal person, with no mystical powers. Or perhaps she was just disappointed that she had wasted almost a month trying to reach out with 'her inner powers' with absolutely no results to show for it. Either way, the fresh air was already helping clear both her mind and her heart from the frustration that had filled her for a while.

First things first: she ran down to visit Tobias, rays of sunlight reflecting in her long blonde hair, which she had let loose for once. As she neared Ruben's workshop, she was met by the familiar smell of coal, smoke and iron. The workshop had only a roof and two walls—the other sides left open for ventilation, and the hammer strokes rang out long before she could see Ruben and Tobias busy at work.

"Hey!" she called as she slid to a halt in front of the workshop, where Ruben occupied the anvil and Tobias worked the bellows. They both looked up in surprise, a wide smile spreading across Tobias's soot-covered face. *Why can he never stay clean?* They had kissed once, and she remembered it had tasted like a bonfire. She had complained back then, but now even the taste of bonfire might be worth it, to relive the thrilling sensation of kissing him. *I have really been with Mom in the cabin for too long!*

"Hi," Tobias replied.

Bria smiled and did her best to look graceful, despite feeling dizzy from the fast run.

"Hi, Bria. Long time no see," Ruben added. "How is work up in the cabin? And how is your mom? Must have been a busy time with all the wounded."

"She is good! And yes, busy, busy, busy. But now all is well. I..." Bria said between panting breaths. "Are you free today, Tobias?"

"I am sorry, it will be a few more hours before Tobias is available," Ruben replied. "Come back when the sun reaches the peaks of the mountains, and Tobias will be free to go. I'll even insist he washes his face." Ruben looked at Tobias with knowing eyes, and heat rose in Bria's face.

Bria could barely stop herself from singing as she left the workshop and walked through the village. The day was beautiful, and she felt like she could burst with joy. She wasn't a Giver, and all was well. A tiny fear in her, almost too small for her to notice, kept reminding her that perhaps The Rule would come back and search for her. She drowned that voice with Mom's words: If that was the case, they would already have been here by now. She sat down by the three oaks and waited. What should she do? Actually, she hadn't thought of anything else than wanting to spend time with Tobias. So, she waited patiently. *After all, patience is healthy*, she schooled herself.

The hours dragged along infinitely slowly. Now and then she'd fall into conversations with passing villagers, but the sun seemed too stubborn to move. Perhaps this was the day, when it finally got stuck in the blue sky.

She tried to think of all the nice things they could do together... Go for a walk, and he could tell her all about the fight. But slowly, the nice thoughts gave way to worry: perhaps he had forgotten her? Found someone else? After all, Bria could name at least a handful of girls in the village who would happily kiss Tobias, bonfire taste or not. *Well, if that was the case, then he just wasn't worth the trouble anyway!* Bria told herself as she restlessly braided and unbraided her hair, her stomach filling with an unpleasant tingling—until finally, the sun reached the tip of the highest mountain peak. It was time!

Nervously, Bria walked back up to the workshop while the sky slowly darkened. Tobias sat waiting in front of the furnace. He was wearing a clean, blue tunic which she loved, and he had even washed his face, only missing a few spots. Bria sighed, her nerves relenting a bit.

"Hi," he said.

"Hi," she replied.

"I'm sorry you had to wait."

"Oh, that's alright. I was busy with errands and tasks and talking with people across the village." *No reason for him to know that I spent half a day staring blankly into the horizon while thinking of whether he had found someone else to kiss,* she thought.

"That's good. Do you want to go for a walk?" Tobias got up and Bria felt a tingle of excitement. She had felt this before when she was around Tobias, but it was much more intense now they hadn't seen each other for a month. It was strange to think that just a year or two back, he had been nothing but Aaron's annoyingly strong friend. The only one who could, occasionally, beat her in a foot race or arm wrestle.

They walked beside each other, through the village and down the path towards Greenhedge. It ran parallel to the coast, and it was just far enough inland that they didn't have to walk in the sand on the beaches. The sun was completely hidden behind the mountains now, and the chilly evening air prickled her skin. The birds no longer sang, and she became uncomfortably aware of the alarming silence between the two of them. *What did we usually talk about? Perhaps he is upset... But he seems so calm. He probably appreciates the silence after a long day's work.* His arm was moving back and forth with each step, his hand so close to hers. *Should I reach out and grab it?* But... *perhaps he wouldn't want that. Why doesn't he just take my hand? And why doesn't he—*

Tobias cleared his throat, interrupting her flood of thoughts. "Nice evening, no?"

"Yes. Yes, it is very nice," Bria replied. "Cold, isn't it?" Perhaps he would catch on, and put his arm around her. He didn't.

"I think this is the perfect temperature. The workshop gets hot like a furnace during the day. It must be lovely working in the fields instead, having the fresh air like this."

"You want to work in the fields? Like a farmer?"

"No, no. I just mean. It must be nice."

They continued walking. Then Bria was the one to break the silence. "Thank you again for being there after the soldiers attacked us at the purge."

Tobias halted his walk and looked at her. "But, I wasn't. I was too late! I... I wasn't there when you needed me!" For a moment, it sounded as if Tobias was about to apologize.

"But it all went well, remember? We didn't need you after all. Aaron took care of them. I think. But I was so happy when I woke up and you were there."

Tobias turned and continued to walk in silence, while Bria wondered if she had said something wrong. She didn't want to hurt him, and now it felt like his warm hand was moving further and further away.

"Is that why you didn't come and say hi until now?" Tobias asked without looking at her.

"What? No, I told Aaron to tell you, Mom wouldn't let me leave! She had, er... some very important lessons for me and—"

"So, for a month, you had to stay up there? Yes, Aaron told me."

"Well, it's not like you made any effort to come and visit me either!" Bria protested.

"I thought you wouldn't want me to! You even sent Aaron to make sure I knew to keep my distance."

"I... No! Why would I want that?" Bria felt the tingling feeling in her stomach turning to frustration at an alarming rate. She fiddled with her hair, braiding and unbraiding the ends.

"Well, how was I supposed to know that? I mean, the first week or two made sense with all the wounded, but then even Aaron left the cabin. What could possibly be so important?" Tobias pressed on.

Bria clenched her teeth, pressing her lips together to not say anything rash. She wished so badly that she could tell Tobias the truth, but she had sworn to Mom to keep it a secret. Specifically, she had sworn not to tell even him, and she wasn't going to break that promise just because he was being stupid and stubborn.

"I can't tell you, okay?"

"But... Why not? I would tell you anything!"

Bria felt her heart beating fast. "It's... private. And it has nothing to do with you," she bit back, her tone harder than she had intended.

"Does Aaron know? What is it?"

"No! No one knows. And... It's between me and Mom, okay?" Bria hadn't even noticed they had stopped walking. She took a deep breath. The air no longer felt cold, and she let go of her hair and composed herself. This wasn't how she wanted this to go, and she had to make it right. Unfortunately, as she found out when she finally opened her mouth, her mind disagreed. "You're just being stupid, and I think we should go back home now."

＋

Bria lay restless in bed. *I really wish I could just tell Tobias the whole thing about Mom thinking I might be a Giver. And after all, I wasn't a Giver anyway, so why can't he know? Then again, he needs to accept that I don't have to tell him everything.* Her heart beat fast, and she stopped herself from punching the pillow. And to make matters worse, Aaron snored like a bear. How could he snore so loudly when he was so small and whimsical?

As morning finally came, she had barely closed an eye. Then, she spent the whole day in the cabin with Mom, helping, but mostly just complaining. In the end, Mom insisted she go down to the town and let off some steam. Bria refused, as she couldn't possibly go near Tobias now. What would she say if they met? Another sleepless night, another day of grumpiness. Even Aaron kept his distance, and Bria knew she had to do something. Finally, she gathered her courage and went down to the workshop. It was early in the morning, and the village was draped in fog and silence. She had to make up with Tobias before she lost her mind entirely, and it was all too late.

Determined, she knocked on the door of Tobias's family house, next to the workshop. Her knocking felt awkwardly loud in the quiet morning, and for a long moment, she felt the urge to spin around and run away. There was no answer at first, and she found herself wishing that no one would open. Her wish did not come true as she heard footsteps and the door opened. Tobias peeked out, looking as if he had just woken up.

"Bria?"

"Good morning."

"I..." he stuttered.

"I came to say that I am sorry that we misunderstood each other the other day, and I would like to invite you to come with me to the Tides Turn festival next week."

Tobias rubbed his hair. His curls looked a bit like sheep fur. "Everyone goes to Tides Turn, so of course I'll be there," he responded, his voice drowsy.

"No, I meant, with me. As in, we go together."

"Oh."

Gosh was he slow witted!

"So, will you go with me? Even if I cannot tell you what Mom and I were doing in the cabin?"

"I... Of course. I would love that. And—"

Bria cut him off before he could say anything more. "Good. So, see you next week then." She turned on her heel and walked home, feeling a slight bit proud, but mostly just worried if it had been the right idea. Still, any move was better than no move, she told herself.

※

The following days, Bria realized how stupid she had been. It was another six days before Tides Turn. And what was she supposed to do until then? Ignore Tobias? Avoid him? Aaron, in contrast, seemed to get along with Tobias splendidly. He came home from the workshop every evening, more soot and dirt than clean skin, and Bria caught herself longing to ask him about Tobias. But she couldn't take the humiliation, so she bit her tongue and focused on her tasks in the cabin.

Finally, after six long days, it was time to celebrate Tides Turn—a traditional festival that marked the annual change in the ocean current—a change that always led to large catches for the fishermen. The entire village prepared food, wines, and put up tables around the big oaks. Bria helped Kathrine make pies while she nervously waited for what would happen. She wasn't actually sure what it meant to go 'together'. Would she pick up Tobias on the way? Would he pick her up? Her nerves grew thinner and thinner until she capitulated and turned to Kathrine. "Mom, I need help."

"With what, my dear?" Kathrine was taking out a pie from the oven, and the smell of herbs and broth filled the cabin.

"With... Er... With Tobias."

"Oh, I see." A smile tugged at Kathrine's lip as she put the pie down. "And what is the problem?"

Suddenly, the words streamed from Bria's mouth, faster than she could stop them. "I asked Tobias to go with me tonight. And now I don't know what that means. What should I do? Should I wear something special? Maybe it's best that I—"

"Easy, child. It was a wonderful idea to invite him to go with you. He is a nice boy, and you seem to get along well." Kathrine put a hand on her shoulder.

"Well, we used to get along, but... I don't know. It feels different now. It's like we cannot talk anymore."

"These things can be hard. I remember when Flint and

I just started seeing each other, we barely knew what to speak of either."

"What did you do then?"

"I guess we just didn't speak that much." Mom winked.

"Mom!" Bria protested. This wasn't helpful at all! Still, she felt relieved to have said her worries out loud. Perhaps it really wasn't all that bad? Perhaps—

A knock on the door interrupted her thoughts. She opened the door and gasped. Her heart dropped, and she felt dizzy. In front of her stood Tobias, washed and in a dark blue vest over a white shirt and brown cotton pants. Meanwhile, she was still wearing an apron, and was covered in flour. Blood rushed to her face like a tidal wave, and she barely stopped herself from slamming the door on his face.

"Oh, am I here too soon? I can come back later?"

"Come in, come in," Kathrine called from the stove. Bria took a step to the side, allowing Tobias to enter the cabin. Her mind raced through thousands of things to say, but came up with nothing even close to as funny and relaxed as she would have liked. Her thoughts finally converged to, "I'll get ready!" which she stuttered and ran to her room.

Her mind tumbled with thoughts, but she forced herself to stay composed. *Oh how I miss the days of foot races and arm wrestling!* Quickly, she put on a red dress with birds and fish embroidered in decorative patterns. From the living room, she could hear Kathrine and Tobias talking. *What could they be talking about? About her? Good gods.* Bria's heart was beating fast, and she nearly tripped over her own legs as she put on her shoes and stumbled back into the living room. "I am ready. Let's go!" Without thinking, she held out her arm, and Tobias obediently wrapped his arm around it. *So far so good*.

"See you there darling," Kathrine called as they left the cabin, and Bria felt like she was on the brink of dying from the humiliation. Luckily, the cool evening air freshened her up. She took a deep breath and a long exhale. They would survive the night. Probably.

"You got some flour right here, and here," Tobias said, and brushed some flour off Bria's face and hair. His hand was rough and warm, and smelled of coal.

"Thank you. And, thank you for coming with me today."

"Well, I was going anyway," Tobias said.

Bria sighed in hopelessness, but she gave him another chance. "It is nice to walk there together, isn't it?"

"Oh, yes. Yes, very nice." His voice shivered slightly, and Bria felt the familiar tingling in her stomach wake up again.

The rest of the walked passed in silence till they sat down next to each other at one of the long tables, next to Tobias's family. Aaron was already there, and Kathrine joined them soon after. Somehow, the conversations ran smoother when they were around more people and soon they fell into their good old routines of making clever comments and trying to tease Aaron without him noticing.

"I bought a map!" Aaron bragged for the thousandth time.

"Have you decided which sheep to feed it to this time?" Bria asked.

All the while, fish were being cooked over open fires around the market square, and Peder had brought the lute from the inn. He played songs for all to sing along while barrels of beer were opened. Once the food had been served, a bard took Peder's place. All fell silent as the bard blew a wooden flute, marking the start of his story.

"My story unfolds seven hundred years ago, at the early days of King Eldrik Evermore's rule, back when Takers still wreaked chaos and spread fear across the world. King Eldrik and his army had freed all the islands and included them in The Central Rule; but the sailing people—the Tiranin—refused to yield their savage ways.

"Prince Tua Tiranin ruled his people and their fleet of more than a hundred blackwood ships from the far Kirrin Isles. They never set anchor, never furled their sails. No, they stayed forever at sea, forever adrift. The Tiranin were mighty sailors, living their whole lives on deck, from birth to nautical grave. And Prince Tua Tiranin was the mightiest, for he had the evil power of Taking.

"Prince Tua had a wife, a dangerous but beautiful woman named Luana, who was said to be a Giver of great power. Together, they were unstoppable, and even The Central Rule army kept its distance when the Tiranin fleet filled the horizon. They were a thorn in King Eldrik's side, so he thought up a plan to defeat this great enemy.

"First, King Eldrik sent a ship to Prince Tua, filled with gold, and an offer of peace if the Tiranin would give up their fleet and exile themselves to the Kirrin Isles from where the blackwood for their ships came. Tua laughed and burned the ship without even unloading the gold. It sank to the bottom of the sea, along with King Eldrik's offer of peace.

"A second ship was sent, much bigger, and built in metals so that it would not burn. Aboard was the mightiest force the world had ever seen: savage fighters from the frozen marshes of Orgrim in the far north and expert bladesmen and rangers from the scorching deserts of Kazam to the south, in joined forces with King Eldrik's own legion of powerful Givers. A vessel and a crew which could take down whole empires! But again, Tua laughed, and together with Luana he jumped aboard the steel ship. Side by side, they fought seven days and seven nights with no break until every warrior from The Rule was slain and the steel ship was left to float like a ghost on the sea with no crew to man it.

"Enraged, King Eldrik wished to fight Prince Tua himself, but an advisor stayed his hand. Instead, a third ship was sent. Aboard the ship were one hundred children, sons and daughters of the men and women that Tua and Luana had defeated. The children were starved and close to death when they reached the Tiranin, and when Tua saw this, he wept. He wept, because a Taker can never mend or heal, only Take, and he could do nothing for the children. Helpless, he watched as his wife Luana Gave all that she had to save as many as she could, but she Gave too much and lost her life.

"This was when Prince Tua realized his mistake, and the Tiranin surrendered. The prince handed himself over to Eldrik Evermore, and was chained and never seen again. His people, however, performed a last act of defiance. They did not leave their blackwood fleet behind and settle on

Kirrin, as King Eldrik had ordered. Instead, they ventured east where no islands exist, their black ships disappearing into the Eastern Void, never to be seen again."

During the story, Tobias had moved up close to Bria, and she felt the heat radiating from him. Although the story was sad, it was also romantic, and she couldn't help but imagine herself fighting alongside Tobias, like Tua and Luana. *If I had been a Giver, we could have fought against the purgers and protected the village.* Her heart sank at the thought. Were they really doomed to a life of waiting for the next purge? Life was good in Great Oaks, but wasn't there more than that? She drifted off for a moment, daydreaming of adventuring together with Tobias, her being a powerful Giver and him being a warrior with a great sword. Perhaps they would even have their own ship...

"Are you okay?" Tobias whispered, his head so close to hers that only she could hear.

"What? Oh, yes," she replied. "Just thinking."

"About what?"

How she wished she could tell him. It gnawed at her to keep this secret from him. But she had sworn... "Nothing. Just silly daydreams."

Soon, laughter and voices rose from the villagers, as they cheered, drank and ate. Bria and Tobias laughed as Aaron danced after the first half hour. Half an hour more, and they danced as well. The night was long, playful, and Bria's stomach was bursting with pies, fish, sweet rolls, and joy as she took a break from the dancing and sat leaning towards one of the old oak trees. Tobias sat next to her in a motion closer to falling than sitting, and Bria laughed while he pulled himself back to an upright sitting position.

"Graceful."

"I know how you love my acrobatics," he said with a laugh.

"Quite."

"I'm sorry I tried to make you tell me what happened in the cabin. I should have listened when you said it was private and... Well, I am sorry."

And finally, he took her hand. A shockwave rippled through her, and she leaned against him. He was warm, as always, and he smelled of smoke. Not too much, but enough that she could recognize him in the dark. Recognize him anywhere. The bonfires still burned along the edges of the marketplace, casting long shadows from the people dancing and singing, but they were nothing but distant silhouettes in the darkness now, painted against the flickering flames. Peder sat humming while strumming his lute by a nearby table, but other than that, they were completely alone in the center of the marketplace.

"It's okay. I wish I could tell you, I really do. But I promised Mom," Bria said in a low voice.

"Well, I don't want to upset your mom, I've heard she can poison people," Tobias said with a grin, squeezing her hand.

"Thank you." She leaned against him, resting her head against his collarbone. He was as sturdy as the oak behind her, and she could hear his heartbeat from this position.

"Mom thought I was a Giver," she whispered before she could stop herself. It had been on the tip of her tongue, and somehow it just slipped out.

"That you were a Giver?" he burst out.

"Shh!"

"Oh, sorry. But, what do you mean? A Giver?" he whispered back.

Bria felt her heart pounding. She had broken the promise! She had told him, even though she had sworn not to! "Please, don't tell anyone. And, I'm not a Giver. It was just... After the battle at the purge, Mom thought maybe I had somehow made Aaron stronger so he could fight off the guards. But, we checked everything and I am completely normal."

Tobias sat for a moment, while Bria waited desperate to hear what he would say. Would he be angry? Pull away from her? Her heart was beating fast, and felt her hands becoming sweaty.

"Well, that makes a lot of sense, I guess."

He didn't pull away, and Bria sighed. "But, please, I promised Mom not to tell anyone, not even you. You have to keep it secret, okay?"

"Of course. I'll keep it secret, even if my life depends on it." He swore, stroking her hair with his free hand. "You must have been terrified, but luckily it turned out to be nothing. Thank you for telling me..."

Bria felt a sting of pain. "Yes, luckily I'm all normal." *No adventures or epic fights for them...*

The next morning, she woke up in her bed. She had fallen asleep against the oak next to Tobias, and, according to Aaron, he had insisted on carrying her all the way to the cabin instead of waking her up. She blushed and threw a pillow after Aaron, while hiding the tears that came to her eyes. *Why all these stupid feelings?* At least they were good feelings now. Somehow, it all felt right, and real, and very, very important. And she couldn't wait to see Tobias again. A part of her felt guilty for telling him about the whole story of maybe being a Giver; but she shook it off. She wasn't a Giver, and it seemed right that he knew what she had gone through. Now he knew, and it had changed nothing, so she could relax.

From that night on, she and Tobias went somewhere almost every evening, when they had finished their respective duties. It was no longer hard to find topics to talk about, and when they didn't know what to say anymore, they would kiss. Tobias always washed his face, Bria noticed, but in reality, she didn't mind the soot anymore. She associated him with the smell of fire, iron, and coal, and he actually looked cute with soot on his nose. It was strange, Bria thought, to feel this way for another person.

It was the end of the summer when Tobias suggested they hike up the Iron Peaks. They started early in the morning. He had gotten a day off from the workshop, and she had spent days persuading Aaron to take her place at Mom's side during the daily duties as a healer. So, they set off at sunrise and started hiking. The cool morning air soon gave way to a warm breeze.

The birds were only just waking up, as they followed well-known trails from the cabin up the foot of the mountains. Eventually, they ran out of path and continued along small trails from passing animals. At lunchtime, they stopped at a patch of grass with a magnificent view of Great Oaks. People were tiny as ants down there, and the great height made Bria dream of flying. She stood as close to the edge as she dared, feeling the wind playfully pull her loose-fitted shirt as she spread her arms.

"Please, don't stand so close," Tobias objected.

"It's fine, I am careful." Still, Bria took a step back from the ledge, and Tobias visibly relaxed. They ate bread and cheese, drank fresh water from a stream, and gathered blueberries for dessert. "We could live here," Bria suggested. They were lying on the mossy grass looking up at the sky, too lazy and full to walk onward.

"It's very isolated, don't you think?"

"That's okay with me. We would be here."

"Would you like that?" Tobias asked from beside her.

"I would."

"I would too then."

Bria felt light as a feather. This was their world. Their mountain. She found his hand without looking. It was big, warm, and coarse.

"I have something for you," Tobias said. He sat up, his head covering a chunk of the sky above her.

"What is it?"

"Close your eyes."

Bria did, and she felt how Tobias gently placed something cool around her wrist. She shivered at his touch and looked. Around her wrist was an intricate silver bracelet made from little rings and threads knitted together in a complicated pattern. She gasped and looked up at Tobias.

"Did you..."

"I made it. For you."

Bria felt tears coming to her eyes as she dragged his face down to hers. His weight against her body and his lips pressed against hers. That feeling was enough to live for.

Chapter Five

Aaron spent the summer helping Tobias and Ruben with the hard work in the workshop, now that the sheep had been joined with the larger flocks from the farmers. Eventually fall came, and the leaves reddened, crumbled, and fell from the trees, leaving the three great oaks naked in the middle of the town. The market surrounding the oaks grew quiet, as fewer merchants made the long trip to Fero Island. Soon, no one would come at all, as the winter storms were too dangerous for the boats to make the journey.

So it was to Aaron's great surprise when he saw a large ship approaching the docks one gray morning in late fall. It was bigger than any merchant's. It wasn't until it was quite near that he could discern the flags of the ship: red with an outer ring and a star in the center. *The Central Rule.* Aaron felt a cold chill run down his spine. *Is it time for another purge already?*

"Mom, come and see," he called, his voice shaking slightly.

"What?" Kathrine stepped out of the cabin, wiping her hands on her apron. The sky above looked like it might rain soon, and a strong breeze blew her brown hair into a mess.

Aaron pointed to the big ship that lay still well off from the harbor. "They are back... The Central Rule. But, just one ship." Kathrine looked where he pointed. "What are they doing here? It's too soon for another purge, isn't it? Should we hide?"

"It's... It's probably nothing. Maybe they're searching for pirates, maybe they're just here to restock on supplies. It's not a ship for soldiers, this one," Kathrine answered hesitantly. In the distance, the great bell that hung in front of Peder's inn rang—the bell that meant for all to gather as fast as possible—and Aaron instantly felt his heart drop. He looked up at his mom.

Kathrine's lips were pressed together in a firm expression. "I will find Bria. I sent her to gather herbs before the rain picks up. You go down there, let them know we are on our way," she instructed, and turned towards the mountain.

Aaron nodded and ran down to the town, trying his best to ignore the gnawing fear in his chest. His legs were shaky, and mental images of Luna bleeding on the ground kept flashing before his eyes. *Not again,* he thought to himself. *Not again.*

At least half the villagers had already shown up, and stood side by side before the wooden dock. There was a strange atmosphere of anticipation in the air, as if everyone was waiting for someone to say something. The Rule ship lay anchored around a hundred yards into the ocean, like a silent mountain reaching up from the dark blue sea. Rain pattered down around them now, a prelude to the storm that the dark skies above prophesied. The wind had also picked up, and Aaron pulled his coat tight around him as he pushed through the crowd to stand next to Tobias and Ruben. From here, he could see sailors scurrying across the ship's deck and hear how they called to each other in various strange dialects.

"Where's Bria?" Tobias whispered.

To Aaron's surprise, both Ruben and Tobias were carrying large hammers, as well as heavy gloves and aprons from the workshop. Looking around, Aaron noticed that many other villagers had brought weapons, ranging from shovels to pickaxes and even a long knife here and there.

"She's on her way. With Mom. She was gathering herbs."

Tobias nodded.

Several minutes passed, the murmuring villagers scuttled together in the icy wind and increasing rain. A rowboat lowered into the sea from the side of the large ship, and it lazily made its way towards the harbor with no signs of alert over the fact that more than a hundred people stood waiting. As it got closer, Aaron saw there were only eight men and women aboard: half rowed the boat, one was steering, and three sat down. As the boat reached the dock, the three sitting figures stood and stepped out: a young man followed by two women. They each wore long blue robes, with the sigil of The Central Rule in a silver brooch on the left side of their chests. An overwhelming anxiety rolled over Aaron, and his legs started shivering. Strangely, the sensation mixed with a nauseating eagerness to do as the young man said, whatever it may be. The cool wind and rain drilled against his skin, pinning his attention and suppressing the growing queasiness.

"Fair greetings. Thank you all for coming here to meet us." The young man spread his hands in a welcoming gesture, a wide smile spreading across his face, which was paler than any Aaron had ever seen among the villagers or any of the visiting merchants. "I am emissary Leonis and I am here on behalf of King Eldrik Evermore, king of the Worldsea, immortal leader of The Central Rule. And on behalf of Roak School of Giving. I greet you all."

Aaron took deep breaths, but the nausea wouldn't relent. Meanwhile, the young man glanced at the faces all around him. A sting of pain rushed through Aaron as he met Leonis's gaze, as if needles had pierced the skin all over his body. It came and went almost before he realized it, and he let out a gasp. Several other villagers made similar sounds around him, but still nobody said anything, and only the sound of the rain against the rooftops and the ground accompanied Leonis's words.

"I am here because of the Giver in your village. It is time that she came to Roak for training. The Central Rule thanks you for your offering and promises to continue its protection of Fero Island and its inhabitants in return. I am here to collect Bria of Great Oaks."

Murmurs interrupted the heavy silence among the gathered villagers. *Bria?* Rain mixed with cold sweat and dripped into Aaron's eyes. *What does he want with Bria? She isn't anything special!* The nausea grew stronger, and he swallowed the spit building up in his mouth to stop himself vomiting. He felt Tobias's warm hand on his shoulder and realized he had been holding his breath.

Ruben interrupted the murmurs of the villagers and took the word. "You have come in vain. There are no Givers here in Great Oaks, not in all of Fero Island. So, you must have been ill-informed."

Leonis looked at Ruben with a sly smile. "Would you care to step forward?"

Ruben looked around. *He seemed... afraid?* Aaron had never seen him show any expression other than his familiar calm and kind smile, least of all fear. The giant man stepped forward and made his way until he stood before Leonis. Aaron felt Tobias's strong, warm hand let go of his shoulder, as he stepped forward as well, stopping two steps behind his father. Both were taller and much stronger-looking than Leonis. And each carried a large sledgehammer, heavier than what any normal man could handle.

Out of nowhere, Ruben's body twitched, and he gave a shriek of pain. Just a moment, then it was gone. No one moved, but Aaron's heart dropped at the sight.

"We don't want your tricks here, Giver," Ruben said, teeth clenched and his voice trembling as if he was fighting against something. He spat on the ground in front of Leonis. Then collapsed, silently. Tobias lifted his hammer and looked like he was about to launch himself at Leonis—before he too fell to the ground, letting out a scream as he fell. Aaron stood, frozen in horror, looking at the two.

Leonis gently nudged Ruben with his foot. No reaction. Aaron couldn't believe his eyes. He looked around, considering if he should run away. Every inch of him longed to escape.

"Does anybody know where we may find Bria?" Leonis scanned the crowd, his wide smile unyielding. Silence.

Then a roar from Ruben, who was still lying on the ground, but had his sledgehammer in his hand, moving at an incredible speed towards Leonis' knees. With sundering power, the hammer hit the young man's legs in a sideways swipe. Leonis fell forward, losing his balance—but only for a moment before he caught himself. Surely his legs must have been broken; destroyed from the magnificent blow of the heavy hammer. Aaron got pushed aside as villagers had seen their cue, and now charged towards Leonis with weapons raised. They were yelling, blades, axes and hammers drawn, the anger from the purge still fresh in their memories. In the middle of it all, Aaron would have sworn he could see Leonis smiling.

And then, screams.

Screams from Ruben and the men who had charged, all of them collapsing onto the ground like rag dolls. Screams of desperate agony that cut into Aaron's mind, no matter how hard he pressed his hands against his ears to keep them out. His whole body was shaking, fear flooding his senses like an overflowing river. He wished to be anywhere else, anywhere but here, but he couldn't move. He cried in desperation. If only he could hide! Hide forever, curled up in a dark corner. Anything to escape Leonis and his pale smile.

Aaron didn't know how long he stayed, crouched on the ground, but when he finally looked up, Leonis and the two women were in the rowboat, departing from the dock.

"We will come back tomorrow to pick up Bria." Leonis's voice rang unnaturally loud, drowning the sound of crying villagers. Slowly but steadily, Aaron felt the grip of terror ease as the boat drew further and further away. Around him, people climbed to their feet, sobbing and holding each other for support and comfort. No one was hurt—even Ruben had no injuries to show. People started murmuring until Peder's voice cut through the rain and the cool morning air. "I guess we better find Bria."

Ruben stumbled over to Aaron.

"Aaron, go. Go tell your mom what happened. Tell her to hide Bria."

"No need." Kathrine's voice sounded from behind Aaron. "We saw what happened."

Mom stood next to Bria whose face was as pale as Aaron suspected his own was. Mom, however, looked like herself, and her voice was firm as she turned to face the villagers. She spoke loud and clear, like Aaron had never heard her speak before. "That man was a Giver. A servant of The Central Rule. One of those we call reapers."

Aaron felt a wave of peace spread and dissipate the terror still echoing in his mind. It was as if Mom's voice brought a level of order and sense to the chaos that had existed all around him. The villagers stopped and listened as she continued.

"The reaper is not here to offer us any peace. No. He is here to claim one of ours. A child. To be tormented by The Rule."

People around them nodded in agreement. Somehow she seemed bigger at that moment, and Aaron felt an urge to follow her. Do as she ordered. She nodded to Ruben.

His voice was deeper and even louder than Kathrine's. "I suggest we do what is right, and fight to protect our children."

Several villagers cheered and clapped as he raised his sledgehammer. Many followed the gesture, raising their own weapons, and Aaron felt his heart rise. *They would fight, and they would win!* He raised his hand and was about to join the cheers when a voice cut through the crowd.

"You cannot be serious, Ruben. A single lad just defeated you as if you were nothing." It was Peder, who stood with a stern look on his face, and his arms crossed over his chest.

"But he wasn't alone," Ruben replied. "Those people with him, they were all Givers. All trained to cause us fear and pain. Surely we could have done better if we had been prepared. I don't know how Leonis could still stand on his legs after I crushed them, but please, these monsters are not gods. They can be defeated!"

"And what about Bria? How do we know she isn't like them? We cannot have someone like that here. No one is safe if she stays! They will turn us all to slaves like they did on the Southern Islands!" Peder replied. His voice brimmed with bitter anger. Aaron stared at him with all the spite he could muster; how dare he suggest Bria was like those monsters?

The docks grew loud with arguments, people shouting their opinions across the open square. Kathrine stepped forward again, and people grew quiet. "This is *not* like what happened on the Southern Islands, because Bria is no Giver. And when they realize this, the reapers will return to

Great Oaks. Back for someone else they can show to their lords and ladies back in Roak. They will keep taking children until they have found *someone* to deliver. They will not rest until they find a Giver among us. Even if they have to kill every one of us before they realize that we don't have Givers here... We don't have a choice."

"Also, what happened at the Southern Islands was many years ago. And one shouldn't trust *every* story they hear from a drunken merchant," Ruben added. "So, let us vote. Those in favor of defending ourselves raise your hand." His own hand, as well as that of Sofie and Tobias flew up.

Aaron, Bria, and Kathrine joined, along with most of the fishermen. *The people who had known Bria's parents the best*, Aaron thought. He glanced over at Bria, whose own hand was raised, her other holding Tobias's free hand. Her teeth were clenched and her face pale, but her eyes were filled with determination. Aaron felt his legs shaking, and he pressed against Mom, who put a comforting arm around him.

"Those in favor of delivering Bria to the reapers," Ruben continued after counting.

Peder's hand, along with those of his most regular customers and most of the farmers, rose. Aaron sighed, as the outcome was clear to everyone.

"Fighting it is!" Ruben roared.

They would defend themselves. They would defend Bria.

Chapter Six

Bria gripped Tobias's hand with all her strength. *It isn't fair! The reapers had come, after all this time!*

"Bria." Tobias's voice sounded as if it was far away.

And the fear... It had been so terrible...

"Bria, my hand, you're squeezing really hard."

"Oh, sorry." Bria's mind finally snapped back to reality as she looked down at their hands and eased the grip. Then she looked up at Tobias. His face was pale and serious.

"I... I will help my dad sharpen blades and arrows," he said. "We will keep you safe. I will keep you safe, no matter what. They won't take you." His voice was trembling.

"I know you will, and I will fight as well," Bria said. It felt good to talk about it, as if it was a fight. It implied she had some autonomy over her own destiny. She was about to ask Tobias if they had a proper sword she could use when Kathrine interrupted them.

"You will hide in the cabin together with Aaron."

"But Mom!" Bria protested. That wasn't fair at all! There was no way she would let Tobias and the rest fight for her while she went into hiding. In fact, she could imagine nothing sweeter than cutting down every last person from The Central Rule. They would come to realize their mistake.

"No objections. You are children!"

"But so is Tobias!"

"And he will also stay behind," Ruben said, placing his hand on his son's shoulder.

Tobias also protested, but finally agreed, as they decided he, Bria and Aaron would stay together in Kathrine's cabin. If the worst came to be, he would have his hammer to protect Aaron and Bria. And Bria would have her bow.

Aaron didn't insist on any level of fighting or weaponry, just nodded. His face was pale, bordering on green, and Bria pulled him into a hug. "It's going to be okay. I will stay right here."

"Please. Please stay," he whispered. "Are you really a Giver?" he stuttered.

Bria looked at Kathrine before answering, who looked nothing but happy as she nodded.

"No. I'm really not. I... After the purge, we thought maybe I had been Giving you the strength to fight the soldiers, so Mom and I tested it. But I am no Giver."

Meanwhile, the rest of the village had set into motion, ignoring the rain as they prepared for the coming battle. Even the people who had voted to surrender Bria seemed determined to make it a proper fight, and soon the harbor was full of piles of weapons and even an improvised shooting range where villagers practiced their aim with bows that hadn't been stringed for years. Bria felt like a stranger among them all. These were the people she had known all her life, but now they looked at her as if she had some strange disease. *There will be a lot of explaining to do after all this*, she thought to herself. For now, she thanked everyone for their efforts and tried to put on a humble face. To anyone brave enough to ask, she explained how they suspected she might be a Giver, but that they had completely ruled it out long ago. The more times she said it, the clearer it became to her: it was all a big misunderstanding. She even suggested to Mom that they simply sailed out to the big ship and explained the situation. Mom declined, arguing they would eventually have to convince Leonis that she had no Giving powers. But, to begin with, they would be better off giving Leonis a good reason to give up the fight. And that good reason might just be a village with hundreds of people fighting against the crew of a single ship.

Bria's heart lifted as Tobias came to the cabin early the next morning. The sky was gray, and a light rain danced against the windows. Mom had already left, and Bria was sitting with Aaron at the table, half eaten bowls of porridge before them. She had barely closed an eye all night, tossing and turning at the thought of The Rule coming to kidnap her, taking her to some terrible school for Givers. It looked like Tobias had been up all night as well, his wet hair and face particularly dark with soot from the workshop. He shook off the rain, sighed and sat down at the big table, his presence filling the cabin with the comforting smell of furnace and iron. It all felt better now he was there, and Bria felt a rush of confidence and happiness run through her. She barely stopped herself from kissing him. Instead, she smiled at him the best she could and laid her arm on the table so he might notice she was wearing his bracelet today.

"Do you think we will win the fight?" Aaron asked. Bria turned and looked at him; he looked so small at the end of the table. Her tiny brother, who had lost Luna.

"Of course. We are hundreds of people. They have thirty soldiers, perhaps even fewer." Bria tried her best to sound confident. Tobias nodded in agreement, though Bria suspected he was as uncertain as she was.

"What's that?" Aaron asked, his eyes fixing on her bracelet.

Bria stared at him in confusion. Then she realized this was the first time she had worn the bracelet at home. Somehow, it seemed more of a private thing. She used to share everything with Aaron, but somehow, she had forgotten to tell him about this, and her cheeks heated. "Tobias made me this."

"Dad helped me," Tobias said, equally blushing.

"It's very nice. Good job," Aaron said, looking closely at the jewelry, apparently more interested in the quality of the handiwork than the romantic connotations of such a gift.

"Yes, we spun the silver down to the second-thinnest measure and—"

"Nerds," Bria interrupted, barely hiding the smile that

tugged at her lip. She loved how much Tobias cared about his craft, and he and Aaron had worked so much together over the summer.

"Well, I'll show you how we did it later," Tobias offered, and smiled.

It seemed as if his smile warmed up the entire cabin. Together, they could definitely beat up a few emissaries, Givers or not. It made no sense that they weren't allowed to fight... Tobias was stronger than most adult men, and she was a better archer than half the village hunters, not to mention faster and probably stronger too.

Slowly, a plan took shape in her head. Tobias would never accept her getting into danger, but perhaps they could move just a little closer? "So, they said if someone comes up here, I can shoot them with my bow, right?"

"I suppose so," Tobias answered. "And I brought my hammer, just in case."

"Well... A bow isn't much use inside a cabin. Perhaps we should position ourselves a bit more tactically for safety reasons? Somewhere we can see if anyone approaches, and where I can shoot at them from a distance."

"But Mom told us to stay here!" Aaron protested.

"Still, you make a good point," Tobias acknowledged.

"I was thinking we could go to the house by the mill and climb up on the roof. From there, we will be well hidden, and we can see all the way down to the harbor. It would be easy for me to shoot anyone coming our way, and you would have plenty of space to swing around that big hammer of yours if it should come to that."

"I'm not sure..." Aaron said, his voice weak.

"You can stay here, Aaron. They're not after you

anyway," Bria offered. In fact, a part of her plan was to split up from Aaron. She couldn't stand the thought of him getting hurt fighting for her—again.

"No, if you go, I will join," he replied and picked up one of Mom's cooking knives. To Bria's surprise, he insisted, and so the three of them went out into the gray morning rain and made their way down the hill to the house by the old mill.

Here they climbed up on the slippery roof and hid just under the edge. It was like being children again, Bria thought for a moment. Then she remembered they were actually still children, and it hadn't been more than half a year since they had been competing in climbing the oaks. But that had all been before the purge, and it now seemed like a lifetime ago.

She placed her bow leaning against the spine of the roof, ready to aim and shoot if she needed to. Her hood was pulled deep over her head to keep the drenching rain from reaching her eyes, which she kept locked on the big ship that lay anchored in the harbor, half covered in mist. This wasn't a game, and she would shoot to kill if she had to, she told herself.

From their perched position, they spotted other men and women with bows lying atop the roofs of the houses nearest to the docks. Likewise, several groups of armed villagers hid in the narrow streets. Still, no movements could be seen on the ship, and minutes felt like hours in the freezing rain. Only the wind rustling the leaves of the great oaken trees made a sound; it seemed even the birds had stayed hidden on a day like this. An occasional cough, or the cry of a baby, pierced the heavy silence in a way that felt unreal. Great Oaks had never been this gray, never this silent. Suddenly, another sound pierced the air. The whistling sound of an arrow. It shot all the way from the ship and made a distinctive thumping sound as it burrowed deep into the woodwork of a house by the harbor. Chills ran down Bria's spine. Such a long shot, it shouldn't be possible. She dragged an arrow from her own quiver. Just to be ready. Just in case.

Ruben stepped forward and detached a note from the arrow. He looked around and yelled, "Stay hidden!"

Three more arrows broke the silence. Each flew through the cold air with a whistle. This time, there was no thumping sound from hitting a house. Instead, each arrow hit a person, sending them screaming. Bria spotted just one of them: a young woman who tumbled down from a nearby roof, an arrow protruding from her shoulder. *Such precision!* Bria clenched her teeth and wiped cold sweat from her brow. She felt the roof shake ever so slightly from Aaron's shivering.

"Stay still," she hissed. Her focus was entirely on the situation in front of her, and she couldn't worry about Aaron right now.

Three more arrows whistled through the crisp air, followed by another set of screams. Another minute passed, another set of arrows. More screams. Again and again. The villagers on the ground ran further away from the harbor, and archers hid deep behind the roof spines. But somehow, the arrows kept finding targets. Person after person fell, and Bria's heart sank. *What can we do against such an enemy?* It ached in her to hear the villagers screaming, all because they wanted to protect her. Should she stand up and let them have her instead? She looked to the side and made eye contact with Tobias. He gripped his hammer, a fierce and determined look on his face. Together, they would make it. More arrows. More screams.

Finally, Peder stood up from his hiding place. His coarse voice rang clear through the air. "This is insane. We surrender!"

Leonis's voice rang equally clear across the sea. "I was hoping for more fun, but well."

"Damn it," Bria growled. She didn't dare think what this meant; and she readied her bow. *They might surrender, but I won't. I can't.*

The rowboat lowered into the sea just like the day before, and Leonis and his crew took the brief passage towards the docks. This time, the boat also included a small group of soldiers. As they got closer, she felt the fear again. Unnatural waves of terror and nausea rolled over her, pulling her towards a state of despair. It was mild compared to yesterday, but it hinted at something worse to come. *These Givers are monsters, no matter what Mom said!* But there were only three... If she could hit just one of them, it might be enough to give the villagers the courage to fight. At this distance, it would be a lucky shot, but worth the arrow.

"What are you doing?" Tobias hissed, putting a hand on her as she readied an arrow on her bowstring.

"Killing Leonis, I hope."

For a moment, Bria thought Tobias would stop her.

Then he nodded and released her. The silver bracelet glistened in a rare ray of sunlight that made it through the gray clouds above as she pulled back the string. It was hard to pull the bow all the way back without rising too much from the roof and she would have to wait till Leonis was at the harbor. That was the absolute furthest her arrow would fly. She kept her eye on her target, waiting as he slowly came closer and closer... The waves of fear increased. Still, she could tolerate it. Shut it out... Leonis stepped out of the boat and walked towards the houses. This was her chance. With a deep breath, she pulled the arrow another inch towards her ear and released. The bow flexed, its force sending the arrow flying over the houses and the shivering villagers. The steel-tip moved straight towards Leonis. A one in a thousand shot, and just at the right time! It would hit! It would—

Leonis didn't even flinch as the arrow flew past him, missing by inches. From Bria's perspective, it looked almost as if it had shot through him. She swore and readied another arrow. Aaron's shivering had intensified, and even Tobias was breathing alarmingly fast now.

"Rude." Leonis called as the arrow flew by. Even at the great distance, Bria could see a perverted smile widening on his pale face. Then, to her great horror, she saw Kathrine step out in front of him. Bria gasped as two soldiers stepped up and bound shackles around her wrists and started walking her back towards the boat!

Bria filled with desperate fear. She had lost her Mom once. Lost everything once. *Not again! And it will be my fault if they hurt her!* Determined, she clenched her teeth and made a decision. Without hesitating, she rolled sideways and down from the roof, a pile of hay softening her landing, and allowing her to go straight into a run.

"Bria! Stop!" Tobias and Aaron called after her, but she had no time to explain. No time to waste.

I have to get closer, make them stop. They can't take my mom! She had her bow ready in hand, and she drew an arrow from her quiver as she sprinted down to the harbor. Finally, she reached the docks and stopped just close enough to see Leonis's face. She longed to shoot an arrow, pierce his smile, and make the waves of fear and nausea stop. Her teeth were clenched as she pulled back the bowstring, the arrow vibrating with force. Finally, Kathrine turned and saw her, her eyes opening wide.

"Bria! No!"

"Ah, so this is the famous Bria." Leonis's smile was even more disgusting than she remembered. Everything about him reeked of malice.

"Let my mom go!" Bria growled, holding the bow fully drawn and ready to shoot. She could hear Aaron and Tobias arrive behind her, and she sensed how Tobias took position next to her, his hammer raised.

"She's not a Giver!" Kathrine cried, turning towards Leonis. "Take me! I... I am the Giver!"

Bria focused too much on the arrow to fully take in what Kathrine was saying. Could she somehow shoot past her? Hit Leonis by surprise?

"But how would you know she isn't as well? It is not easy to evoke such powers. Believe me, this is to be handled by us at Roak," Leonis answered calmly.

"She is my daughter. I would know if she was a Giver. Whatever you've heard is wrong."

"Daughter. Perfect."

In the flash of an eye, Leonis had a blade in his hand, and he turned Kathrine around to face Bria, pressing the knife against her mother's throat.

"Let her go, or I will shoot!" Bria screamed.

"Can you shoot without hitting your mother?" Leonis asked rhetorically.

To Bria's surprise, a wave of confidence, strength, and calm rolled over her, almost drowning out the terrible fear. Hitting Leonis without harming Kathrine suddenly seemed the easiest thing in the world. "Yes," Bria answered bluntly, and released the string.

The arrow whistled through the air at incredible speed, directly at Leonis face. It passed less than an inch from Kathrine's right ear. Leonis, however, simply plucked the arrow out of the air, stopping it at the exact moment the steel tip touched his skin. A drop of blood trickled down his cheek.

"More than one Giver here I see," Leonis said. He dropped the knife from Kathrine's throat, who slumped down onto the ground in front of him as if she had passed out.

Bria felt the overwhelming confidence, strength and calm leave her, and waves of fear slammed against her like tidal waves. Out of the corner of her eye, she noticed two soldiers holding Tobias, who was on his knees. Behind him, Aaron lay on the ground, shivering. *They... They couldn't do it. There was no way to win. No other way than this...* A tear rolled down her cheek as she turned and made eye contact with Tobias. "Take care of Aaron," she whispered.

Then she turned her face and looked at Aaron. He still

needed his mother. "I love you, little brother." Finally, she faced Leonis. "I am no Giver, but I will go with you. Just leave my mom, and I am yours." She could barely believe her own words. Fear turned to sadness. Or madness. *I'll never see Tobias again. I'll never see my home, Aaron, Mom... But I have to save Mom.*

Tobias screamed for her to stop, his roar like a wounded bear as a blue-robed woman stepped forward and touched Bria's forehead. She did nothing to stop her, then everything went dark.

CHAPTER SEVEN

Bria woke in darkness to strange sounds and a sense of swaying from side to side. It took several moments before she realized she was on a ship, and yet another to realize that it must be Leonis's ship—the ship that would take her to Roak. Carefully, she sat up and started feeling her body: she was unscathed but shackled by the ankles. It seemed she still wore her own clothes and, thank goodness, the bracelet from Tobias. Apparently, she was below the deck of the big ship, since a few rays of light reached down between the wooden boards above her head.

"Easy, my child," Kathrine's voice sounded from behind her.

Bria spun her head and saw her mom's face through a ray of light. Her eyes were swollen, and her lip and one eyebrow had been split open. Her hair was a mess, and her voice trembled.

Bria's heart plummeted, and she felt as if the air in her lungs had been punched out of her. "You shouldn't be here, Mom! I came with them!"

"I know, dear. I know."

"No, you don't! I traded myself for you! Aaron needs you! It's not fair!" Her voice got louder and louder as desperation gripped her. *This has to be a nightmare! It cannot be true!*

"Bria. I am a Giver. They found out, and so they took me as well. It isn't your fault. There was nothing you could have done once they found out."

"What? So you are a Giver?" Bria pinched herself to see if she might wake up. No effect.

"It has been a secret all my life. I thought maybe... Maybe they would take me and leave you once they found out. I should have known The Rule knows no such kindness. They will do anything to collect their precious Givers."

"But I'm not a Giver," Bria protested.

"I know. And once they know it too, I am sure they will send you back home."

Somehow, Bria doubted this. Great Oaks must already be far away. Great Oaks with Aaron, Tobias, and her whole life, drifting away further and further as they spoke. "How long did I sleep?"

"Hard to say from down here. Half a day, I would guess. It has not been dark outside yet, but it was much brighter earlier."

Half a day? And we're trapped below deck, on our way to gods know what kind of place? Bria's heart beat fast, and she fought to control her breathing. Her sacrifice had been for nothing, and how many in the village had been hurt, or maybe even died? She tried to think back... She remembered how she almost pierced Leonis with an arrow.

How she felt confident in the middle of all the fear. "What happened back on the harbor?"

"Well, I... I tried to use Giving as a weapon and attack them, but they were much too strong. I am not... experienced in that kind of Giving," Kathrine said, sadness in her voice. "Then, when you attacked, I tried to Give you the strength and technique you needed. For a moment, I thought you had actually done it. Shot Leonis."

"I wish I had. Those bastards, may the Takers have them."

A knock on the wooden deck above them interrupted her. "I can hear you, you know." *Leonis*. A hatch pulled open, and Bria blinked as the sharp sunlight blinded her for a moment.

"Good to see that you're awake," Leonis said with an innocent grin, as if he was waking them up after a casual afternoon nap. "We want you both to be in good health and strength, so we have prepared some food for you. A proper feast to start your journey."

Suddenly, Bria could smell food, as clearly as if it was cooking right next to her. Then the scent was gone, leaving her stomach rumbling.

"Will you behave if I bring you to my cabin for dinner?"

He didn't wait for an answer, simply picked Bria up by the neck of her shirt and pulled her up on deck with surprising ease, then followed the same procedure with Kathrine. "Right this way, ladies."

They were on the deck of the large ship, four masts reaching far into a blue sky, each mast carrying several sails and the red flag of The Central Rule. The open waves stretched as far as Bria could see in either direction, and the ship was moving gently across a calm sea. Apparently, the gray clouds and rain had finally relented, or perhaps they had already moved far enough to escape the grim weather that had covered Fero Island. Bria took a few steps to conclude that the chains on her feet were loose enough for her to walk freely. *Not that there is anywhere I can walk to,* she thought, looking around at the confinement of the deck amidst the ocean. Still, her heart calmed in the fresh air, and panic slowly gave way to anger.

"Sorry about the metal." Leonis looked down at the rattling chains. "It is a precaution. Should you jump ship, they will be heavy enough to pull you to the seabed in moments."

Bria considered asking if they generally had problems with people jumping into the ocean to escape, but preferred not to know the answer.

They walked the length of the deck towards the ship's quarters, passing scores of men and women pulling lines and cleaning the deck—many more than she had imagined—and of various skin colors and sizes: some much darker than the people of Great Oaks, others as pale as Leonis, most of them much shorter than her, but a few of them taller; though she doubted any were as tall as Ruben and Tobias. All of them sweated from the hard work in the afternoon sun, and seemed too busy to pay them any attention as they passed. Bria smelled their sweat as they walked by, and couldn't help but wonder if they were slaves or workers. *Surely not Givers?* A group of soldiers sat further down the deck playing cards, apparently not expected to participate in the handling of the vessel.

At the end of the deck, they walked through a door and down a small staircase. Here she could smell the food again, along with woodwork and tar. It smelled like the Great Oaks docks in spring, when the fishermen pulled their boats up on land to repair them. They continued onward, through a hallway, and finally passed through a door into a large chamber.

Bria could barely feel the ship rocking here, and the sound of the ocean was reduced to a gentle whisper, giving the chamber a sense of serene calm. Luxurious gold-framed paintings and small shelves, filled with lavish gold and silver artifacts, lined the walls. Light streamed in through large windows filled with colored glass, forming playful hues and shapes across the room. In the middle of it all stood a large black table, neatly arranged with silverware and plates for three people.

"Sit." Leonis pulled out a chair for each of them, before he sat at the opposite end of the table.

Bria's stomach rumbled in defiant celebration at the various birds and roasts, along with gravy, potatoes and vegetables Bria had never seen before. She even felt an urge to thank Leonis. The feeling lasted just a moment, then the hatred returned, and she fought hard not to scream at him, as she imagined throwing her fork at his eyes. Mom, however, sat still, and Bria did her best to copy her.

"Please, eat. Drink. Let's be merry. We have a long trip ahead of us." Leonis gestured to the foods and wines, and servers began to fill their plates and goblets. Kathrine sat and used a napkin to clean blood from her face, then collected her hair in a knot behind her head. She was bruised, and her lip and eyebrow swollen where they had split, but she showed no sign of pain or even fear as she calmly tasted the wine. Bria put up her hair and sipped the wine as well. Mom ate, so Bria ate too. It was delicious, and Bria hated herself for liking it.

"You two gave us an interesting fight at the pier," Leonis said, while placing a napkin in his lap. "Or rather, you did." He pointed his knife towards Kathrine and stared at her with his wide smile.

"I am the Giver you want. Bria has no Giving."

"Well, we will see about that. Our informant was very specific about Bria, you are just a bonus. But since these things are often inherited, it only makes sense that you'd be a Giver too." Leonis cut a piece of steak, juice running from it, and filling his plate.

Bria stiffened: *Informant? Surely no one from Great Oaks would have ratted us out... And Tobias is the only one who knew!* The sight of the bloody juice leaking onto Leonis plate was sickening, and she felt dizzy with the weight of it all. *An informant in Great Oaks...*

"Well, I am not Bria's biological mother. And I've used my Giving to test Bria, she has no power." Kathrine's words interrupted Bria's thoughts, and she felt a fresh sting of pain as always when this subject came up. She didn't know if it was because it reminded her of her biological parents, or because it reminded her that Kathrine wasn't her mom from birth.

Leonis raised his eyebrows, and for a moment he paused his eating, holding his hands steady, a lump of meat halfway from the plate to his mouth. "Never mind. One too many won't hurt. She will serve another purpose, even if she is not a Giver," he finally said and placed the meat in his mouth. "Eat."

They ate in silence.

"You are valuable cargo, you know," Leonis continued, looking at Kathrine. "It is incredibly rare we find a Giver of capacity with no real training. Where did you get your skills from?"

"I learned it long ago from my mother," Kathrine said, her tone neutral and her posture confident and strong. Bria felt infinitely grateful she was there with her. Still, she would have given everything for her to have been left behind in Great Oaks with Aaron...

"Really? Your mother? Did we get her? Sloppy work by my predecessors to leave her daughter behind if we did," Leonis said calmly. "I'm not making that mistake," he said, and winked at Bria with a smile, as if this was all some kind of merry joke among friends. "And you have no biological children, then? Two boys seemed quite upset about you leaving?"

"Bria's friends," Kathrine said. "I have no children. I adopted Bria when her parents passed away."

A moment passed before Leonis nodded. "Very well. I believe we shall be pleased with you at Roak."

"Why did you lie about Aaron?" Bria asked as they sat on beds in a small chamber assigned to them. It was a nice upgrade from the hole under the deck, and the bed was invitingly soft.

Kathrine looked at her with a glimpse of horror. "Never mention him," she hissed.

"But we are alone!" Bria objected. "I just—"

"They can enhance each other's senses! I fear Leonis can hear anything that happens on this boat if he wishes," Kathrine whispered. "And I fear they would return for him as well. You heard Leonis. These things pass in the family. I... I don't think it did though. He never showed any of the signs."

Bria put a hand over her mouth. How dumb she had been! At least she hadn't burst out with such stupidities during the dinner.

"It is okay. And they will learn that you are not a Giver and send you home to him." Kathrine moved over and sat next to her, untying her hair. Bria had a throbbing headache from clenching her teeth for so long; she had focused all day to stop herself from screaming, biting or clawing at Leonis. She let out a sigh and relaxed. Somehow, she felt safe. Almost safe, at least. Kathrine put her arms around her and held her like a child, gently rocking back and forth.

It had been a long time since Bria had cried, and even longer since she had allowed anyone to see it. But now, she let the tears stream freely. "I *won't* leave without you," Bria said, her voice quivering.

She barely remembered losing her parents, but she remembered the feeling. The hollow spot within her that so easily filled itself with sadness. A sadness that she could never quite shake, because it was all so unreasonable. She couldn't take any more of that, and would rather fight than cry, and she wouldn't leave Kathrine now. They were in this fight together.

"You *can*, and you *will*, as soon as you get the chance, dear."

"I'm serious, Mom! I won't leave you!"

Kathrine didn't object, just continued to stroke Bria's hair.

They woke to the sound of a bell and a voice announcing through their bedroom door that it was time for breakfast. Bria pressed the door open and found a tray loaded with fresh bread, meats, porridge, and tea. Her mouth watered at the sight, and her heart lifted as she noticed a stack of brown robes in soft wool and a bucket of water for washing that stood beside it.

They washed and ate in the room, dressed, and went up on deck. It felt weird, and wrong, to wear the long robes, but Mom did it, so Bria copied. She couldn't deny that it protected well against the cool morning breeze on deck.

The gray morning held stains of rain in the air, but not enough to make them wet. The sailors adjusted the lines here and there, and several of them glanced up and greeted the two women as they passed. Even the group of soldiers nodded in their direction. *It all seems much more relaxed when Leonis isn't around,* Bria thought. Her notion was confirmed as she heard his voice behind her, and all the workers picked up their pace.

"Ah, you're awake. Are you feeling better?"

His tone had the same sickening friendliness as always, and she wondered how long she could restrain herself before she lost control and attacked him; although a growing voice in her begged her to hide, rather than fight. She drowned that voice. Anger was much preferable to cowering in fear.

"Certainly. Thank you for the food, the robes, and the beds," Kathrine replied, maintaining her proud posture and polite mannerism. *He won't break Mom*, Bria concluded with a smirk.

"Excellent. Now, your teaching will start in Roak, of course. But, there is no reason to waste time. You can even help aboard the ship! After all, Giving really is about helping each other, isn't it?"

Leonis led them down the stairs to where a large group of rowers pulled oars. Bria hadn't even noticed this before, but the ship wasn't moved only by sails. The rowers were large, bulky men who grinned as Bria and Kathrine descended. Their grins quickly disappeared when they saw Leonis following behind them.

"Perhaps we would be better suited as aids in the kitchen, or on deck?" Kathrine suggested.

Bria was as tall as most of the men, and strong, but her strength would be nothing compared to these experienced rowers. And Kathrine was slim, and both shorter and weaker than Bria.

"Perhaps so, but I don't have the creativity to imagine how that would improve your Giving," Leonis answered. "Take a seat."

He pointed Bria to a free oar, but stopped Kathrine as she was about to follow. "You sit here and watch her working."

Bria was puzzled. Kathrine was perhaps not as strong as

her, but this still seemed ridiculous. Rowers working two and two occupied all the other oars.

"I need the girl to row, so her oar moves as fast as the others, understood?" he instructed Kathrine.

Why is he talking to Mom and not to me? Anyhow, rowing twice as hard as these bulky men is obviously impossible.

"A Giver like you should multiply the strength you give by at least a fewfold, right?" Leonis continued.

Kathrine's lips were tightly pressed together. She nodded and Leonis smiled.

"A bit of motivation. If you do well, I will keep treating you as our fine guests aboard this vessel. If the girl rows too slowly, she will be whipped."

A bald, middle-aged man with a leather strap in his hand stepped up to them and placed himself behind Bria. She could smell his sweat and hear his breathing. Paralyzing fear gripped her, just for a second, then she felt normal again, and her sense of smell faded.

"Begin," Leonis said.

Bria picked up the oar. The wood was coarse against her palms until she found the grip where it had been worn smooth by the movements of hundreds of hands before hers. She looked up at Kathrine, hoping maybe she knew what to do. After all, Bria had never been allowed on the boats. At least not since her parents died when she was five.

"Go in circles," Kathrine instructed.

A wave of understanding came over her. Was Mom

Giving her... technique? At least she now understood how to row. She pushed and pulled the heavy oar in the right pattern. But it was incredibly heavy, and she couldn't tell if she was helping or if the oar just floated in the water outside.

"I'm sorry, I... I haven't Given much strength before," Kathrine stated. "I am going to—"

A loud crack and intense pain flooded through her as Bria felt the leather strap cut into her back. She screamed out in surprise and pain.

"Faster!" The man behind Bria yelled, spit flying over her.

She couldn't see the man, but she could hear as he rolled up the leather strap for another lash. Desperate, she looked up at Kathrine, who sat in front of her pale and wide-eyed. Behind her, Leonis wore his familiar perverted smile. *I would love to tear that smile off his face. If only I had my bow or a knife, I'd—*

Another lash interrupted her thoughts and sent her bending over, screaming in the sudden rush of agony. She looked back up, trying to hide the tears springing to her eyes. Leonis didn't deserve to see them. She wouldn't give him the satisfaction. She rowed as fast and hard as she could, but it barely changed anything. Sweat dripped from Kathrine's forehead now. Her lips pressed tightly together, and she seemed fully focused on something Bria couldn't see.

Suddenly, waves of sensations rolled through her. Bravery, fear, sounds became incredibly loud, smells overwhelming, her movements felt slow, then fast, then... the oar felt like air in her hand. She pushed and felt how it plowed through the water with ease. Then the feeling was gone.

"It was there, Mom!" Bria exclaimed through gritted teeth, too afraid to stop rowing.

Kathrine looked like she was going to be sick. "I know. I just have to keep that channel open. I... I just have to find out exactly how it felt, I—"

Another lash. Bria almost managed not to whimper this time, and she pushed on. Kathrine's face tightened again. Another wave of emotions rolled through Bria, but quickly the wave turned to a calm flow. To strength and speed. Bria felt light as a feather and strong as an ox. The oar now moved with incredible ease, and she no longer lost any breath, and the lashing had stopped. She barely even noticed the pain from the earlier lashes, just felt so incredibly strong that she couldn't help but laugh. Several faces turned to look at her, voices murmuring.

"Slower," the man with the leather strap instructed in a low voice. "Or the ship will lose its course."

Bria looked around for a second, awakened from the stirring feeling of strength, and realized she had been going at full power. She slowed down, although it felt ridiculously slow and weak compared to what she could do. In front of her, Kathrine sat with a strained look on her face. Leonis looked satisfied, though less so than during the lashing.

Eventually, Leonis interfered and stopped Bria's rowing. The sensational feeling of speed and strength left her, and the lashes stung with sour pain.

"Impressive. Now, exchange positions."

"But I'm not a Giver!" Bria protested, her face paling.

"We will see about that," Leonis said with a wide smile.

They exchanged seats, and Kathrine picked up the oar. Bria's mind raced, as she started rowing. *I can't Give! Mom is too weak for this work!* The rowing was incredibly slow. Too slow. Bria screamed in astonishment as the leather strap struck against Kathrine's back. However, her mom didn't even flinch, just continued with the slow rowing. Another lash. Kathrine stared at Leonis in silence, but Bria couldn't help but cry. The burning from her own lashing was nothing compared to watching Mom being whipped.

I have to do something! But what? I cannot Give! Bria dismissed her thoughts; she had to try. She put a hand on Kathrine's leg and tried to ignore the sound of the leather strap cracking against skin again and again. Tears rolled down her cheeks as she tried all the things Kathrine had taught her—visualized passing strength into her, tried to feel her presence, to channel. Anything! The whipping continued. Bria kept pushing and pushing, trying more and more desperately. But there was...

Nothing.

As the lashes kept falling, Kathrine remained silent, but her rowing grew slower and slower. Her brown robe was drenched from the inside, and blood spattered from the fabric with every lash. She grew pale, but she still didn't whimper. Not a sound.

Finally, Leonis stepped forward, and the whipping paused. "Ready to see a little trick, Bria?" he asked, smiling.

He put his hand on Kathrine's shoulder, and suddenly she screamed uncontrollably. She wriggled like an animal trying to escape capture, her entire body twitching and bending as if she tried to break her own spine.

"First, I overwhelm her with impressions and confusion to make her break her channeling of pain so that she cannot pass it on to others. Then I Give her sensitivity," Leonis calmly explained, keeping his hand on Kathrine's shoulder.

Bria screamed and threw herself towards him to push him away. Leonis pushed her back, his free hand as unrelenting as a mountain. It continued for just a few seconds, but it felt like an eternity. Finally, he stepped back, and Kathrine sunk into a sitting position, crying and gasping for air.

"See, the real challenge is to keep the person from passing out. That is one of my specialties." He smiled and wiped his hands in his own blue robe, with a satisfied expression as if he had just finished a good day's work. "I will come back and do that every twenty minutes," he said calmly, and left.

Bria found she was crying as hard as she ever had. *I can't save her. I can't help her. I can't do anything.* The thoughts repeated themselves in her mind, over and over again.

The process went on for days, then weeks. Bria continued to row with ease, while Kathrine was whipped again and again to provoke any sliver of power in her adopted daughter. Bria didn't remember ever crying so much, not even when her parents died, and more and more she longed to disappear, to jump into the ocean and end Kathrine's suffering. When they weren't rowing, they'd huddle up in their small room, shivering and crying together. Leonis forced them to eat with him every night; forced Kathrine to eat and both of them to live on. Slowly, Bria lost track of days, until finally a call sounded across the deck.

"Roak in sight!"

Chapter Eight

Aaron sat motionless at the end of the pier. Leonis's ship had sailed around the southern edge of the island, and he could no longer see it. Now, he just stared into the horizon, where the sun pierced through the gray sky. It hung lazily, mocking him with its life-giving rays. The ocean was still now, and a breeze prickled his skin, which was wet and cold from the rain and the cold sweat of fear. He focused on that and nothing else. Tried not to think of what had happened. As Leonis had left, so had the paralyzing waves of fear. And so had his mom and sister. Just like that. He didn't dare to think. What would he think of? Where would he go now? There was no answer. No one to answer for him.

"Come, son." Aaron felt Ruben's heavy hand on his shoulder. He nodded and followed, all the time focussing on the feeling of the wind against his cold skin. No thoughts, just focusing on that one feeling until his skin was dry, and the feeling disappeared.

Ruben and his wife Sofie took care of the things that had to be done. They moved Aaron's stuff from the cabin to their house, where they set up a bed for him in Tobias's room. Tobias said little during those days, but Aaron often heard him whimpering in his sleep and calling for Bria to turn around. They didn't talk about what had happened. Actually, Aaron didn't talk much to anyone about anything. Somehow, talking felt wrong. Living felt wrong. How could he live when his mom and sister were taken away to be tortured by The Rule?

Mom never even told me... No one told me this could happen. And was Bria really a Giver? And Mom too? All the time, they knew it, but never told me. The thoughts fought for space in his mind, and sadness mixed with bitterness and anger. Some nights he would dream of chasing after the ship, attacking Leonis and saving Mom and Bria. Most nights, however, those dreams turned to nightmares of Leonis's wide pale smile, as Bria and Mom were carried aboard his ship like sacks of potatoes, while he lay on the ground, paralyzed by fear. He hated himself for the fear and despised himself for not fighting. For not doing anything! After all, he had been the one who had beaten up those two guards back at the purge. Perhaps he could have done it again, if he hadn't been such a coward? But any thought of that day on the dock sent his gut clenching and his body shivering. The fear had been beyond anything he had ever imagined possible.

"How about you boys make your own project?" Ruben suggested.

For the first time in the four weeks since Kathrine and Bria were taken, Aaron felt a glimpse of excitement. They never made their own projects, not even Tobias.

"I've got a lump of iron waiting to be crafted, and I noticed how well you two work together. Also, I could use a break to help restore the inn."

The inn had partly burned down, ignited by a burning arrow during Leonis's attack. Four people had died that day... Another thing that no-one talked about.

"How about a war hammer?" Tobias suggested.

"What is it with you boys and weapons?" Ruben said with strained laughter. He and Sofie were always trying to be overly happy, and Aaron felt guilty for not appreciating it. He just couldn't...

"It's just... You know, for next time they come from The Rule," Tobias answered.

There was a moment of silence as Ruben and Sofie glanced at each other.

Sofie put a hand on Tobias's arm. "They are not coming back."

Aaron's heart sank. He didn't dare think of the possibility that Leonis would bring Mom and Bria back, but then again—why not? If they weren't Givers, maybe they could come home?

"You can make a weapon if you like. And it is good to learn how to defend yourself. But don't fear attacks from The Central Rule. The entire... incident with... Well, it was out of the ordinary. You boys are safe," Ruben added.

The two boys quickly agreed on the design of the war hammer. Pointy on one end, flat on the other, and it should be heavy. Heavy and big, and then they would simply have to grow strong enough to wield it. Tobias had forged many hammers with his dad, and they agreed he would do most of the smithing, while Aaron would focus on the bellows.

Tobias stood waiting to put a lump of iron into the furnace. "Are you ready?"

"Ready," Aaron said.

It felt good to make a weapon, thinking of how they could use it to fight against The Rule.

Tobias put the iron into the fire pit, and Aaron started pumping the bellow, which had used to be almost too heavy for him to handle, but now seemed almost light.

"Break." Tobias pulled the iron to the anvil and started hammering.

The lump elongated slightly under the heavy blows until Tobias returned it to the forge and Aaron resumed pumping.

Break. Hammering. Break. Hammering. Break.

Slowly, the hammer took shape. It would be big, even bigger than they had planned for. Tobias curved it to make the pick like one on a pickaxe, long enough so the weight countered the large, flat hammerhead on the other side.

They worked for hours, hammering and pumping. Sometimes they switched places, Tobias guiding Aaron as he hammered. Other times, Aaron held the iron while Tobias hammered. Their muscles ached as they finally punched the hole through the center using a cold steel cone, where they would insert the wooden shaft. Aaron felt a tingle of excitement. The head of the hammer was done.

The boys sat back against the wall, the hammer resting on the anvil. There was still work to do, polishing and making a handle, but they had done the bigger part. Aaron had lost track of time, but looking out the door, he could see they had worked through lunchtime and well into the afternoon. His entire body was numb and tired. Then, to his own surprise, he laughed. After a moment, Tobias joined in. It was a strange feeling to laugh together, and to feel... Happy? For so long, they had silently shared pain, and now that they shared a sliver of happiness, it was almost overwhelming.

"You know, my dad has been arguing with the other villagers that they should sail after your mother and Bria," Tobias said as their laughter died out.

"He has? Do you think they would do that?" Aaron asked in surprise. No one ever left Great Oaks, not to go far at least.

"My dad would do it himself," Tobias answered. "But my mom thinks it's a bad idea. I heard them discussing it."

Aaron thought for a moment before he replied. "I don't want you to lose your parents. He... He shouldn't go."

"But someone will have to go. Even if they release your mom and Bria, they'd have no way to come home," Tobias objected.

"I... I will go," Aaron said. The idea had been forming somewhere in his mind ever since the kidnapping but he had never dared say it out loud, or even believe in it. Now it seemed right though. He could spend the rest of his life cowering, or he could do whatever he could to save his mom and sister. It felt both good and frightening to confess it to Tobias, as it suddenly became more than just a dream. It became a plan, in all its terrifying reality.

"I have been thinking about the same thing... I could come with you, and we could save your mom and Bria together."

Aaron felt like an iron grip on his heart released. A grip that had been holding on for so long that he had forgotten how it felt without it, and he sighed. Tobias was almost as tall and strong as his father, which would help him save his mom and sister. For a moment, he really believed they might be able to save them.

"We have to wait until the spring," Aaron said. They would never make the voyage through the winter storms. "Once a merchant ship comes along, big enough for the trip to Roak. I have it on my map."

"Deal."

Aaron felt a sprout of hope. Somehow, they would find his mom and sister.

As expected, the head of the war hammer was incredibly heavy, and normal wood wouldn't be strong enough for it. So, they had to wait several weeks until a woodsman brought a staff of blackwood from one of the rare blackwood trees that grew in Northwoods, up north of Weathertop. Ruben refused to let them know the price, as he bought them a staff big enough for a long handle and made them a buckle for the bottom of the shaft to balance out the heavy hammerhead. And there it was, finally—a magnificent war hammer, too large and heavy for anyone except Ruben to wield properly. The boys were proud, and took turns carrying it around the city, although Tobias was the only one of them who could actually swing it. Aaron could barely stand properly when it was sheathed on his back.

Meanwhile, the last leaves fell from the big oaks, and the days grew short. Aaron turned fourteen and noticed he had grown taller, although he continued to look tiny next to Tobias, who was now almost as tall as Ruben. Sofie often complained about the challenge of feeding the household of what she called 'a pack of boars, both in manners and hunger'. Occasionally, Aaron overheard whispers in the inn regarding the kidnapping, and now and then, people would mention Kathrine when a sheep or child got ill, and there was no one to help. But people seemed to avoid any mention of Bria and Kathrine whenever Aaron was around.

So, the weeks passed, then the months. The icy wind carried frost from the mountains, and snow covered the roads in Great Oaks. Sometimes Aaron would look up at his old home, the cabin now lifeless and cold on the mountainside. A soft blanket of snow covered the roof, and the windows were lightless and without life. Even the sheep were gone, all given to other farmers to look after. He always felt a sting of pain when he looked towards the mountains, and he tried his best to keep busy with work instead. If he was to stand any chance of saving Mom and Bria, he would have to be strong, and the work in Ruben's workshop was the perfect recipe for it. Slowly but steadily, his muscles grew and the war hammer felt lighter. He was still a long way from wielding it in battle, but it felt good to improve his strength, like he was preparing for the great quest ahead of him.

As the snow melted and winter ended, Aaron had become part of Tobias's family. They all had their responsibilities, their routines, and their part of the work around the house and in the workshop. Because of this, that sadness filled his heart when he saw the first merchant ship approach the docks that spring. Aaron knew it was time to leave. He had spent months thinking about the quest, and concluded he might not survive, let alone succeed. Because of this, he had made a hard decision. He would go without Tobias... Tobias still had parents, a life, and Aaron would not let him throw that away, no matter how much he wished to have his friend along with him.

Aaron waited another few weeks before he took action. A merchant had fallen ill in town, and he and his crew stayed at the inn until he recovered. Meanwhile, their trading vessel lay in the harbor, ready to go. Aaron didn't remember much about sailing, but he knew the winds blew out from the harbor every morning and turned back east in the afternoon. So, if only he could raise the sails, he could leave Great Oaks in the morning and let the afternoon wind take him past the island and east toward the Inner Sea. Easy enough, he hoped. Now, all he had to do was get onto the boat without anybody seeing him.

He waited until it was the middle of the night, his heart beating fast with adrenaline. Finally, when he heard snoring from all around the house, he pulled out his bag from under the bed. During the day, he had packed a satchel with food, water, a knife, and the warmest clothing he had. His heart was heavy with guilt for taking the things, and even more so for leaving without a proper goodbye to Tobias and his family. He had tried his best to thank them all at dinner, in what had been an awkward monologue. It had ended with Ruben asking him if he was okay, and patting him on the back in an understanding manner. *They probably assume I have finally gone mad,* Aaron thought, as he silently snuck through the living room towards the door. The door opened with a squeak, and he felt a gush of cold air against his face. The street was quiet, but the light of the moon and stars was plenty to make his way down to the pier. He pulled the satchel onto his back and left as silently as he could...

"Psst... Hey," a voice sounded from behind.

Aaron spun around, his eyes wide.

"I'm coming with you," Tobias said, satchel already on his back and the great war hammer in his hand.

"No! Go back to bed!" Aaron hissed.

"Hey, we had a deal, remember? We save your mom and Bria together."

"Yes, but you have a life here! What about your family?"

"Well, honestly, I think my dad suspected this. He... He gave me this just a few days ago." Tobias opened his hand, showing a pouch of coins and what appeared to be a small compass. "And I've had this satchel packed for weeks. I've just been waiting for you to make up your mind and leave." Tobias grinned. "Didn't expect it to be in the middle of the night though, but at least your loud footsteps woke me up."

Aaron couldn't decide if he should laugh or cry. Surely, he was happy to go with Tobias. But also afraid. What if they didn't make it?

"I know the dangers," Tobias said, reading the doubt in Aaron's face. "I've always wanted to sail. So, about time I try it, I would say!"

Aaron was about to object when he heard a voice coming from a nearby house. "Who's there?"

"Fine. Let's go," Aaron hissed and turned back towards the road. This might be their only chance. The two boys snuck from house to house till they reached the dock. Aaron led them onto the merchant ship and began unfurling and raising the sails.

"You... You're going to steal a boat?" Tobias asked in disbelief.

"Well, what did you expect? To your apparent surprise, I don't have my own ship," Aaron whispered while pulling the lines. It had been nine years since he had set sails with his dad, and he only had vague memories of how to do it, but he had been observing the fishermen as well as he could.

"Here, hold this one tight."

He handed a line to Tobias, who looked baffled but obliged. As the sail rose, the rope tightened in Tobias's grip, and he caught on with his other hand to keep it steady.

"Tie it there," Aaron instructed while he tied lines and knots here and there. In reality, he wasn't quite sure what he was doing, but there was no reason for Tobias to know that. The only important thing was to get the sail up. The breeze was already rolling over the mountain, and he would prefer to be beyond the horizon before sunrise. His stomach tingled with both excitement and fear at getting caught. *Mom will be so angry once she finds out I stole a boat! She'll probably scold me for days just for going sailing,* he thought.

The chilly winds took proper hold of the sail, and the silence was cut by the sound of the fabric stretching. Still, the boat didn't move. Confused, Aaron looked around. *Was the ship anchored?* Looking over the railing, he finally noticed how several heavy lines held the ship attached to the wooden dock. Quickly, he untied them one by one. *Were they supposed to go on the dock or in the boat? Well, too late,* he thought, as he dropped the ends that held the ship into the cold ocean. And off the two boys went, their boat slowly lulling towards the horizon, the dark night lit up by the stars and the moon.

Finally, he was heading to Roak.

Part 2

Across the
Western Sea

Chapter Nine

Aaron and Tobias sailed much further out than the fishermen ever went, hoping no one would see them in the stolen boat. Then they furled the sails of the two masts and let the boat stay in the open sea, bobbing up and down on the gentle waves while the sun peeked over the horizon. Land was so far away that they could only see the tops of the Iron Peaks. Tobias sat, seasick, at the end of the boat, looking towards home.

"We can take you home if you want," Aaron offered. He himself felt quite nervous now they were on the open ocean. The ocean was calm, but frighteningly big, its deep blue shade hinting at the vast depths beneath them.

"No, it's... It's alright," Tobias answered, his face currently going through a strange shade of green. "We come back after we've picked up Bria and Kathrine."

"Right."

"And we can give back the boat then," Tobias continued.

Luckily, Tobias had to empty his stomach into the

ocean again before Aaron had to come up with an answer: he couldn't imagine the merchant would take lightly to them borrowing his boat for such a trip; let alone that he would still be around when—and if—they returned.

The sun lazily crept further up the horizon to the east, as Tobias slowly got used to the movements of the boat. Meanwhile, Aaron rummaged through the cargo hold, where he found barrels of water and wine and several satchels of dried meat. There were even jars of honey and a small chest of coins—which they agreed to spend sparingly, and only when they had to. Finally, the wind turned: Aaron turned the ship's wheel, pulled and turned the sails as he saw fit, and steadily they set into motion, making a big loop around Fero Island.

They journeyed east for days, simply furling the sails during the first half of the day and setting them again in the afternoon. This way, the eastward wind led them in the right direction in the evening and during the night. Aaron loved the feeling of wind in his hair and the rhythmic bobbing of the boat under his feet. He soon felt safer surrounded by the deep blue, and the ocean kept relatively calm, even as the wind picked up on the third day. Occasionally, seagulls would provide company, and once they even saw the water give way to the back of an enormous fish. It was much larger than anything they had ever seen the fishermen bring in, and Aaron feared for a moment that it would capsize the boat.

Now and then they passed tiny islands covered in green and gray, small mountains shooting up from the ocean.

None of them showed any sign of villages or people, and they passed without attempting to land the boat. These islands were too small to be on Aaron's map, they concluded, and they continued onward, hoping they were on the right course. The freedom and sense of adventure were arousing, and Aaron's heart filled with confidence that they would make it as they spent their days playing cards, talking, and trusting fate and luck to make up for their lack of sailing skills. At least Tobias's compass confirmed they were going in the right direction, and according to Aaron's map, they should be headed towards Tidun and the town called Burrow's Keep.

Finally, they spotted the coast of a large island with visible towns along its coastline. Guided by a gentle breeze, they drifted closer to land, revealing the outline of a large town, much bigger than Great Oaks.

"Should we go to land?" Aaron asked. They still hadn't dared such challenging steering of the ship, but he knew they'd have to learn eventually.

"Well, I guess we can't stay on the ocean forever," Tobias answered. "And I could use a break from your rambling, and these terrible waves."

The two boys aimed for one of the smaller docks, clumsily navigating the boat. Many single-masted boats lay harbored along the long wooden docks, and Aaron prayed they would not make too much of a fool of themselves. Or worse yet, crash into the dock or one of the other boats. As they were just a few yards from the dock, a man came running, calling for them to throw the landing lines. The two boys looked at each other for a moment, before Aaron realized what the man was talking about.

"Er... I'm afraid we lost those lines."

"Lost them?" the man responded, pulling a saggy brown hat off his head and scratching a bald spot on the top of his crown. "Wait, how old are you two? Where is the captain?"

"Nineteen," Aaron said. "And we both captain this vessel." He held his breath, hoping the man wouldn't question them further. Both he and Tobias had begun to grow signs of a beard, but perhaps nineteen had been a bit too optimistic.

The man looked at them, confusion painted on his face. "But this is a merchant's vessel... Er... Well, let's get you some landing lines first, so you don't just sit there blocking the harbor." The man turned, then paused and spun around again. "Can you pay?"

"Certainly, sir." Tobias shook his satchel of coins.

"Good, good," the man said, his confused expression turning to a grin as he walked to a small house on the harbor, returning a moment later with two ropes. He threw them onto the ship's deck, and Aaron and Tobias clumsily attached them where the old landing lines had been, and threw the other ends back to the man on the dock. The man had assembled a few workers who helped pull the ship tight to the bridge and secure it, while the two boys stepped off the ship, across a gangplank that the workers put in place for them.

The man wiped his hands on his shirt, took off his hat again, and approached. "Good day, young sirs, and welcome to Tidun Island, the town of Burrow's Keep.

Name's Ruddy, pier master, and may I ask the name of the captain?" He took out a wooden board from a large front pocket of his long red tunic and began scribbling on the paper attached to it.

"Er... Aaron."

Ruddy looked up from his paper. "And last name?"

Aaron thought for a moment. No one used last names in Great Oaks. It was uncommon that two people shared the same first name, so it seemed unnecessary. Still, many merchants had last names, and so did the people in the stories... One came to his mind.

"Silverhand. Aaron Silverhand."

At these words, Ruddy looked up again, this time with wide-open eyes and gaping mouth. He quickly performed a deep bow, dropping his hat on the ground in the clumsy maneuver. "My apologies, young sir. I did not recognize you, good sir Silverhand. It is a great honor to have you and your servant here. How long might we be graced with your presence?"

Aaron's heart sank as he realized he had carelessly chosen the last name of an affluent lord. "Just a night or two." He felt a sudden urge to leave again, before anyone realized the false name. Surely, faking a noble lineage would be a punishable crime.

At least, Ruddy seemed to believe the story, and he bowed again, this time carefully holding on to his hat. "Certainly. That will be three gold coins for the ropes, and five silver coins per night to be paid upon your departure."

The boys both gasped. This was beyond any price Aaron had ever heard of. Luckily, Ruddy seemed far too busy bowing and scribbling on his paper to notice anything. Tobias quickly produced the coins from his pouch, as Aaron concluded they would likely have to use the money from the merchant's chest after all. Ruddy bowed again and returned to a small office building on the landside of the dock. Finally, they had a chance to look around the bustling town that lay in front of them.

It was a beautiful spring afternoon, and the sun reflected golden in the windows of the white-chalked houses that stood side by side, lining the harbor. Far behind the first row of houses, a large stronghold stood in dark stone, overlooking the town and the sea. In front of the houses was a lively dock area with everything from well-dressed merchants, workers carrying stones and wood logs, beggars in dirty rags and small groups of guards. The guards wore brown leather chest armors, red pants, spears, and helmets—and all had the shining silver sigil of The Central Rule on the left side of their chest. At first, Tobias and Aaron tried to avoid them, but soon they realized the guards paid little attention to the two young newcomers. They also realized that the front row of houses was mostly taverns and inns, with drunken yells emanating into the harbor. The boys marveled at the many impressions, their noses full with the smell of everything from food to trash, urine, old fish, and spices. This was the first time either of them had seen a town other than Great Oaks, and they had never imagined a harbor could be so big or busy.

"Are you new here?" a shrill voice asked.

Aaron looked around in confusion, then down to where a young boy stood looking up at him with a dirty face, brown eyes, and a wide grin. The boy looked not a day past ten and wore an overly-large tunic made of coarse brown fabric held to his body by a thick cord wrapped around his waist.

"Er... Yes." Aaron replied, exchanging a glance with Tobias, who shrugged.

"Let me show you the town then!" the boy exclaimed, grabbing onto Aaron's sleeve and pulling them forward. Aaron was too surprised to stop him, and before he knew of it, they were walking away from the dock through a slender passageway that cut between two inns and further into the town.

"Here to trade? Or perhaps to visit the shrine to King Eldrik?"

"No, actually, we are just passing through," Aaron replied, increasingly uneasy with the situation. This passage was even dirtier and smellier than the harbor.

"Great! You'll want the blessing of the Well of Fortune then? Lucky that you met me, surely you'll need a guide to find your way here. I'm Luca by the way," the boy said without missing a step.

Tobias cut in. "The Well of Fortune?"

"Yes! Throw in a coin, and you will have good luck for days!"

The passageway opened up into a wider street, with fewer people than on the dock. Here the air was cleaner, and the guards fewer, causing Aaron to relax a bit. Luca was probably right, they needed help if they were to find their way around in this big town. A scent of spices and food sent his stomach rumbling; they should find a place for dinner soon.

"It's over here! What are your names?"

"Tobias."

"Aaron."

"Welcome to Burrow's Keep." The young boy took turns and passages in a confusing pattern, and Aaron soon lost his sense of direction, as he spent most of his focus marveling at the impressions of the town.

Aaron was about to object that they really had to get back to the docks, or at least somewhere that served food when Luca finally stopped. "Here it is." He had led them down a narrow side street and into a small square, where there was a simple well, built in gray rocks perched atop another in the center. A hooded beggar sat leaning against the wall of the well, with a long cane in his hand, but seemed to ignore them; other than that, the square was empty.

"So, we throw a coin in the well and get a blessing?" Aaron asked.

It sounded weird, and the well was nothing out of the ordinary. In fact, it looked a lot like the well back in Great Oaks behind Ruben's workshop.

"Indeed," the boy nodded, a wide grin on his face. Aaron looked at Tobias for advice, but he just offered another shrug. Aaron sighed. What a strange world. But, why not? After all, the money wasn't theirs, and they'd need more luck than wealth where they were going. He fished out his satchel full of coins and picked a single silver coin from it, trying not to feel too guilty for spending the stolen money. Then he leaned over the well, looking down into the murky depths.

"Just like this?" He asked, holding the coin stretched over the middle of the well. Suddenly he felt a pull from his other hand as the boy tore the pouch of coins out of his grip and set off at a sprint.

"Hey!" Aaron yelled, pulling back from the well. Tobias was faster and had already set into movement, but the beggar's cane locked his legs, and he tumbled to the ground with a grunt. Luca had already disappeared into a side alley faster than Aaron could set after him.

"Oh my, oh dear," the beggar mumbled in a frail voice, pulling back his staff. "My humblest apologies, good sirs, I was being careless with my walking stick."

Aaron's heart was beating fast as he helped Tobias to his feet. "He took the money! That little—"

A yelp came from the alley where Luca had escaped. "Let me go! I didn't do anything!"

From the alley, three guards marched, holding Luca by his tunic. Next to them walked pier master Ruddy, a wide smile on his face. "Knew I'd better keep an eye on you, good sir Silverhand," he grinned, walking up to Aaron and handing him the pouch of coins. "Saw this little one drag you off, and I figured I'd better keep track, along with some guards. These streets are full of vermin, and can be dangerous for someone of your honorable family."

Aaron let out a relieved sigh as he took the pouch from Ruddy's hand. Then, his gut clenched as he watched the guards force Luca to his knees.

"Do you want the honors yourself?" one of the guards asked, a stern look on his face. He was young, Aaron noted, not much older than himself. Aaron returned his gaze, hoping his confusion wasn't too obvious.

"Er, thank you for bringing back our money and—"

"Please, sir, it was a mistake! I wouldn't have never stolen from you if I knew you were a noble and—"

A guard slapped the boy across the face. "You shouldn't steal at all, rat!" he hissed.

"The punishment for stealing from a noble is death, of course," Ruddy added. "So yes, you had been wise not to steal from a Silverhand."

Aaron's heart dropped as Luca looked up at him with pleading eyes. Should he reveal he wasn't actually a Silverhand? Tobias stood uneasy next to him, but offered nothing but silence. Surely they would be punished if he admitted to having lied about his title. He cleared his throat and tried his best to speak with confidence. "The boy must have misunderstood the gesture when I pulled out the pouch of money. I cannot allow him to be killed for such a minor error." His voice was frail; surely they'd see right through it. Cold sweat gathered on his forehead as Ruddy and the guards looked at him, surprise painted across their faces.

"But, sir—"

"I insist," Aaron added, his voice a bit firmer this time.

"I... Very well," the young guard in front stated. "We will take him to the prison then to serve sentence."

"No! I—" Luca exclaimed, before another slap silenced him.

The guards dragged him to his feet, setting off towards the keep Aaron could see over the top of the houses, further away from the harbor. Aaron pressed his lips together, forcing himself not to object, although he was squirming with bitter guilt. The pouch of coins felt heavy and wrong in his hand, and he longed to throw it away. His lies would cost Luca dearly, and even if he was a thief, he didn't deserve such a fate. *He was just a child...*

"Perhaps you two would like me to show you an inn more befitting of your house?"

Pier master Ruddy's voice pierced at Aaron's thoughts, but didn't make it through; his gaze still locked on the alley where the guards had dragged Luca. Tobias forced him back to reality with a pull on his sleeve as he accepted Ruddy's offer and set them in motion back towards the docks. They left the beggar behind, still sitting motionless against the well where he was when they arrived.

Aaron's subconscious begged him to come clean. To stop the madness and somehow save Luca. But he knew it was too late. He was far too deep into the lie and, after all, Luca had stolen. Even if he revealed his lie, Luca would still be punished, right? But somehow, that thought didn't calm the bitter guilt that slimed its way through his mind like a slug, leaving a trail of nauseating remorse. His feet moved him forward, but his mind was full of dark thoughts and an overwhelming urge to do something. He just didn't know what...

Chapter Ten

Aaron remained silent as Ruddy led them back through the streets of Burrow's Keep towards the docks. Tobias walked defensively next to him, giving him a sense of calm in the free fall of self-loathing that filled his mind. The setting sun was uncomfortably warm, and he felt sweat running down his forehead. His palms were wet, and his tunic stuck to his skin. A gentle breeze carried the stench from the docks, and Aaron tried his best not to breathe in too deeply as the reek of old fish, trash, and urine canceled out the delightful smell of cooking that persisted further into the town. Finally, they reached the dock. Ruddy turned left and led them forward until he stopped in front of a tavern called 'The Lady and the Pig'. The four tipped star sigil of The Central Rule was carved deep into the wooden door.

Ruddy, who had been talking the whole way without Aaron registering a word, opened the door, and led them inside. "This is scarcely befitting a Silverhand, but it is the finest establishment in town I can assure you." He bowed deeply, holding on to his hat so it didn't fall off. "Mary! A table for the lord and his servant!"

A tall woman with short red hair and arms almost as thick as Tobias's stepped forward from the bar and said, "Lords? I'll be damned, Ruddy, if there are any lords in all of Tidun!"

"Relative of Lord Silverhand," Ruddy interrupted in a low, urgent tone, sending her eyes wide open.

"Very well," she said with a skewed smile, directing an attentive gaze at Aaron and Tobias.

Aaron realized he had been staring, his mind still occupied with Luca's fate more than the present situation. Tobias grabbed the pouch of coins that still rested in Aaron's hand, handed Ruddy a gold coin, and thanked him for his aid. The man bowed deeply and thanked them many times as he made his way back out of the tavern, leaving them in Mary's care.

"You are the lordling, I presume?" she said, directed at Aaron. Tobias yanked an elbow into Aaron's ribs, finally returning him to his senses.

"Oh, er, yes."

"We would like a drink and a meal now, and a bath and a bed later, if possible," Tobias added, taking charge.

"For a lordling and his handsome servant, such things can be arranged," Mary said with a smirk, turning to the bar.

"Andy! Two beers and roast!"

A grunt sounded through the open door that led to a room behind the bar. The grunt could almost be mistaken for an oink Aaron noted, suspecting the origin of the name of the establishment. Mary pointed them to a table, and

Aaron sank into a chair with a deep sigh, taking a look around the room. He had to focus; it was bad enough that he had caused Luca such a fate, but if he didn't start acting properly, he and Tobias might find themselves as cellmates with the young thief.

The room was sparsely populated, well-dressed people sitting two and two or in small groups at the round hardwood tables. The last rays of red sunlight shone through the windows, illuminating the room, while a bard on stage played a slow melody on his lute. The harmony of discussions and the bard's music created a comfortable hum of noise, making it hard to make out any particular conversation despite the proximity of the tables.

"You look like a corpse. Are you okay?" Tobias inquired.

"I... We should save Luca."

"We can't do anything for him," Tobias replied, though his droopy eyes revealed he didn't like this conclusion.

"But, if I hadn't lied about my title, he would—"

"He would still have stolen from us, and no one would have been there to get our coins back. In some ways, we could consider ourselves lucky. I agree with you though: he is just a kid, and he doesn't deserve a life in prison. At least we stopped them from executing him."

Mary placed two beers and a large platter of roast pig, potatoes, and a thick gravy in front of them.

"Eat and you'll feel better," Tobias suggested.

Aaron looked at the roast, his stomach rumbling, but his mind rejected the idea of such delicious food after what he had done. Instead, he took a deep swag of the beer. It was strong, stronger than the mild ale they served in Great Oaks, and he coughed. The bitter taste was almost repulsive, but he felt like he deserved no better, so he took another gulp.

Soon Aaron's mind gave up on self-loathing, as the beer slowly gained influence on his mind. The room had filled up, and the chatting had grown louder. Here and there, they heard loud laughs and drunken outbursts. A man and a woman, who were talking loudly at the neighboring table, caught his attention.

"...ever more thieves and pirates, may the Takers have them! The Rule should do something," the man said.

"Yes, at this rate, no merchants will come this far west. It's cutting off our whole business," the woman replied.

"I heard Rolando hasn't returned from Fero. Probably got taken by The Raven," the man responded.

Aaron stiffened. Was Rolando the name of the merchant from whom they'd stolen the ship? Perhaps...

"Best to take the southern passage now. Chubby sea, but pirate free."

Aaron shivered at the idea of being attacked at sea, imagining being swallowed into the icy depths he had looked on so often. As a child, he had nightmares about drowning. About Dad drowning...

Mary quieted his thoughts as she brought two more goblets of beer.

"They say The Raven sails a blackwood ship, like those from the Tiranin in the old stories," the man continued.

"Yes, so they say... But I doubt it. I've seen a blackwood ship once or twice, but never in the hand of a lowlife pirate. They are worth a fortune, you know and—"

"Cheers!" Tobias swung the heavy mug against Aaron's, sending beer splashing over the edge and distracting him from the conversation at the neighboring table. Tobias seemed to have had enough beer to forget about Luca as well.

"Shhh!" A nearby patron hissed at them. The bard had just begun another tale. Aaron and Tobias exchanged glances, then leaned back deep in their seats and listened.

"This is the story of the Southern Rebellion," the bard introduced, dramatically pulling his patchwork cloak to the side as he sat down on a chair placed on the center of the stage. His white hair and beard reminded Aaron of Peder back in Great Oaks. "A story also known as the War of the Child." The bard's voice finally drowned out the last conversations around the room. He cleared his throat and began his tale.

"On Muta, the middle of the three Triplet Islands in the far Southern Sea, a boy was born into a family of simple farmers. His mother and father soon realized their boy was not ordinary by any means. No one could stay sad or angry around him, and it was said his mere presence could heal the sick. Soon, people told stories of the amazing boy who spread happiness and health, stories that spread all the way to The Capital on Meridian Island, and to the emissaries of The Rule."

The bard strummed three chords in succession, creating a sad ambience. Aaron's full attention was on the bard, any thought of Luca or pirates drowned in the mental images of the far Southern Islands with their deserts and exotic warriors.

"The Rule sent a ship from Roak School of Giving to visit the boy and learn of his powers. And true enough, the child was a Giver with natural powers far beyond what the emissaries had ever seen before. This first ship never returned to Roak; some say it was attacked and brought down by the southerners, others say the boy himself persuaded the emissaries to stay and ally with him."

Another set of chords, these gave Aaron a feeling of discomfort; they signaled that something was wrong.

"King Eldrik heard of the lost ship, and he ordered Lord Silverhand to deal with the situation."

Aaron shivered at the mention of Silverhand, and he looked around the bar. Everyone watched the bard... Hopefully, only the pier master and Mary knew about his fake name.

"Lord Silverhand brought his army and a party of Givers to claim the boy. As you all know, all Givers must serve The Rule. And so began the War of the Child. What should have been an easy reaping, turned into a full-blown rebellion against The Rule."

Three dramatic chords built intensity in the story.

"Southerners attacked Lord Silverhand's army, and countless lives were lost. Eldrik's Givers and their soldiers easily outmatched the southern swordmasters. But still, the southerners hid the boy, moving him from island to island, forcing Eldrik's army to pursue, and luring them into many traps and dead ends."

More dramatic chords.

"So the battle lasted for years, as Lord Silverhand

slowly gained control over all the islands in the Southern Sea. Whenever he got close to the boy, though, the child used his magnificent powers to enhance the fighting skills of those who protected him, so that Silverhand's soldiers couldn't touch him. Finally, King Eldrik grew sad and tired with the war and offered a treaty: if the boy surrendered, he wouldn't kill the southerners for their rebellion. And so, the child gave and his protectors gave up the fight. The boy was delivered and brought to Roak to be taught to serve King Eldrik, in return for peace on the Southern Islands."

Three calm chords released the tension in the room.

"As promised, King Eldrik ordered Lord Silverhand not to kill the southerners. Instead, he ordered the land pay in sweat in place of blood, and ruled that the southerners must work for The Rule for a hundred generations to repay the debt for their wrongdoings. And thus ended the War of the Lost Child."

Aaron had grown increasingly uneasy during the tale. He had heard the captivating tale before back in Great Oaks, and it was the reason he thought of the name 'Silverhand'. Was it simply a coincidence that the bard brought this particular story? Or had he, or anyone else, overheard when Ruddy told Mary of his false title? Aaron wondered as he looked around the room, and let out a relieved sigh as nobody returned his gaze—

Except the bard, who stepped down from the stage and approached their table. "May I sit, lord?"

"Of course," Aaron answered, feeling cold sweat on his brow. *He knows...*

"How did you like the story?" the bard asked, his face widening in a grin revealing several lost teeth. His white beard contrasted a golden hued tan, and he wore a simple black hat made of fabric.

"It was great," Aaron answered, his voice weak. He wished he hadn't drunk so much beer, and he sent Tobias a glance, hoping his friend would know what to do and say.

Tobias cleared his throat. "It was a great performance, sir, but we must ask you excuse us. It's been a long night."

"Certainly, my Lord. You look unwell. Perhaps a lungful of fresh air will do you well? The cool night air refreshes the mind and heart both," the bard offered and grabbed Aaron's hand. Aaron, too confused and dazed by the beer to object, found himself following the bard out of the tavern before he could stop.

"Sir, please, we haven't paid our bills," Tobias objected, hastening after them.

They stepped out of the door, and a cool breeze hit Aaron's skin. He inhaled deeply and was about to agree with the bard on the healing sensation of the fresh air, when he heard a heavy thump behind him. Tobias sunk to the ground, and a hand covered Aaron's mouth before he could scream.

Next thing Aaron knew, he was dragged down an alley next to the tavern, and further across rough cobblestones through garbage-filled side streets. The smell of urine and garbage, along with pain and adrenaline, sobered his mind, and he looked up at the bard who dragged him violently forward.

A woman's voice sounded behind the bard. "A Silverhand? Are you sure it was him?"

"Aye," the bard replied without slowing his pace. "This is far enough. Let's be done with this before any guards interrupt us." The bard released Aaron, sending him stumbling forward and against a wall.

"I am not a Silverhand," he mumbled, his voice barely audible, and panic igniting deep in his stomach.

"Shut up, you filth! You burned our home, condemned our people to slavery, and now you took our son too."

The world spun around Aaron as the bard lifted him by the hair, before a kick in the groin sent him to the ground, vomiting.

The flash of a dagger reflected the moonlight. "Don't kill him quite. After all, he spared Luca from the execution." the bard hissed.

Instead of the stab of a dagger, punches and kicks rained down on Aaron as he desperately tried to crawl away. He lost sense of what was up and down as he shivered and cried out. He wanted to beg for mercy, but couldn't form the words between the blows and the mind numbing fear. For a fraction of a second, he remembered the power he had back in Great Oaks when he fought against the soldiers in the cabin. He searched for it inside of himself... but found nothing. He coughed blood, while another punch emptied his lungs and sent him to the ground, heaving for air. *This is it. This is the end.*

A roar interrupted his thoughts, followed by a crash. A yell, and another crash. The kicks and punches stopped, and as he blinked his eyes open, he saw the bard and a woman lying on the ground next to him. Above them stood Tobias.

"Are you... Are you alive?"

Aaron inhaled deeply and coughed up as much blood as he could, while Tobias lifted him to his feet. His entire body was shaking and he was crying, flinching in pain with every step, barely comprehending what was happening as Tobias led them through the dark, labyrinthine streets. It seemed like forever until Tobias laid him in his bed aboard the merchant ship, and cleaned his wounds, washing away the blood and vomit from his body and face. He was too weak to protest as Tobias undressed him from his ruined clothes and covered him with clean blankets, and finally let him drift off into dreamless sleep.

Chapter Eleven

It took a moment before Aaron could recall what had happened. He stared up at the wooden planks and felt waves shifting the boat up and down. Tobias must have set the sails alone and somehow made it back onto the waters, because they were definitely sailing. His head felt like it might explode, and it hurt all over as he carefully moved each limb, one at a time. Legs and arms were unbroken, and even his ribs seemed to have miraculously survived. Then a meek realization hit him like a sledgehammer: they had barely left Great Oaks, and he had almost been killed. Killed on the street for his own stupidity. Not to mention that he had gotten a kid thrown in prison. How would he ever save Bria and Mom like this? His heart sank as hopelessness filled his mind and heart. It took him a while before he finally forced himself out of bed, ignoring the pain as he dressed in fresh clothes and climbed the few steps to the door leading up to the deck.

"Good morning," Tobias called from the helm where he was navigating the boat by compass. The sails were set on both masts, two on each, and were all full of wind. The ship set a good pace, bobbing up and down on the passing waves.

"I... We should go back to Great Oaks." Aaron fought hard to get the words past the lump in his throat, and kept his gaze on the wooden deck to avoid Tobias's judging eyes. Shame of his own cowardice gnawed at him, but what else could they do? He was useless, and Tobias would be more than occupied just keeping him alive, with no chance of saving Mom and Bria.

"Giving up already?"

"What do you mean? We barely made it out of Burrow's Keep, and we already got a kid sent to prison. We cannot save Mom and Bria like this," Aaron protested. His headache reached a sickening level as blood rose to his head. He looked at the railing, considering if he was about to be sick.

"You're right. We have to be more careful and learn from our mistakes. But we cannot turn around now. Bria is out there, and so is your mom. Also, the wind blows east, I don't even know how we'd turn around if we wanted to. Or perhaps you haven't noticed? The wind here is different from the Silent Sea around Fero, here it seems to change all the time. For now, we are heading east though."

Aaron looked around, realizing Tobias was right. The sun wasn't past its highest point, but they were already sailing fast; and according to Tobias, they were going in the right direction. He had many more things he wanted to say, but the nauseating throbbing in his head took precedence, and he sat down with a moan, leaning his back against the main mast in the center of the deck. What had he expected? Of course, a quest like this would be dangerous. He just hadn't expected it so soon, and for such a stupid reason... And he had forgotten how it felt to be helpless. To be the victim of someone so much stronger. He thought back, longingly, to the short moment in the cabin when he had fought two soldiers off, protecting Mom and Bria. Surely, that had been their Giving that saved them that day, not him. How had he been so foolish to think he could save them now?

"You look terrible. Perhaps you should go back to bed?" Tobias called.

"I think I'll be sick if I go back down there. The breeze helps a bit," Aaron replied, his eyes closed. The cool wind really helped, though he still contemplated whether he would throw up. "Thank you for saving me... Did you get hurt?" he asked after a few moments of slow breathing as he tried to keep down last night's dinner.

"Just a sore head and some bruises, so I will survive. And you're welcome. Bria would never forgive me if I didn't keep you more or less intact. She'll probably scold me for weeks for even letting you get hurt."

"Yes, I reckon she will..." Aaron felt a sting of pain at the thought of Bria scolding Tobias. The pain bore deep in his heart, competing with the many aching wounds and bruises across his body.

"Plus, I'm your friend," Tobias continued. "And... Well, for a moment I thought I was too late. I am sorry, Aaron. So, let's be more careful in the future. No more titles, and no more beer!"

The thought of beer almost tipped Aaron's good

health over the edge, and he felt spit building up in his mouth. "Deal," he agreed.

The winds continued to lead them east at a good pace, seagulls playfully riding the winds alongside their boat. Now and then they passed other boats; mostly merchants headed west for trading with Tidun. Other times they passed small islands, some of them big enough for cliffs, forests, and even villages. Aaron felt a pang of homesickness each time he saw smoke rising from chimneys and fishermen casting their nets.

From what they could gather, they followed the southern route, and expected to reach Naia Island within a fortnight, if Aaron's map was to be trusted. From there, it would be another ten days to reach Tally, and finally a short stretch to Roak. Aaron recalled the cartographer's words: 'Avoid Roak', but they had little choice. Somehow they'd have to find their way to the cursed island. It was hard, however, to worry much about all that as the spring sun raised their moods, and even dissipated the worst of Aaron's memories of the events in Burrow's Keep.

The only problem were the thoughts that came at night, when Tobias lay snoring in the bed across the room. Aaron couldn't help but chastise himself for his weakness in Burrow's Keep, and his mind was plagued with images of Luca pleading for mercy, as well as the bard and the woman, launching punch after punch at him as he lay crying against a stone wall. They hadn't even been Givers, just normal people, and he had been so infinitely helpless. But he knew Tobias was right: they had to keep going.

And that meant he somehow had to get stronger and braver.

—✦—

Aaron was woken by aggressive turns and tilts, much wilder than the normally calm bobbing of their vessel. The cabin brimmed with a thick darkness, which seemed to amplify the roaring sound of the ocean and the cracks of thunder from outside the hull. His stomach churned, and he curled up, pulling the blankets close around him as he shivered in fear. *I should wake Tobias. Surely he will know what to do,* he thought, but the fear paralyzed him... *I wish I was back in Great Oaks. Back home—*

"Aaron, the sails!" Tobias called from his bed, jumping to his feet. His voice forced Aaron back to his senses, and he rolled to his feet and joined Tobias, who was already running up the stairs for the door to the deck. The door opened, and a flood of seawater sent him sprawling right back down. Aaron gasped as the icy water soaked his clothing, while lightning illuminated the black sky outside the open door at the top of the stairs. He swallowed his fear and defiantly followed Tobias into the mad storm.

Rain and wind hammered against the ship, and Aaron gripped the doorframe with both hands to avoid being knocked over by the wild gushes and the ship's aggressive rolls.

"Get the main mast!" Tobias yelled through the roaring wind. Then he set running across the deck towards the distant rear mast.

Aaron nodded, his mind half frozen in fear. Somehow,

it was easier when he just had to follow orders. He got down on all fours and crawled the few steps to the mast. The sail hung loose, flapping wildly in the storm. *Perhaps it was already too late to save it.* Wave after wave threatened to wash him overboard, and he clung to the wooden mast with all his strength, while he began to untie the lines that held the sail in place. They immediately tore loose from his grip and snapped angrily in the wind as he pulled down the sail. A lightning strike let him see the shape of Tobias working at the rear mast. The waves looked like looming mountains behind his bent shape.

"Hold on!" Aaron screamed through the night, another fear joining the already growing choir of panic and desperation that filled his gut. A fear of losing Tobias.

"Thanks, I hadn't even thought of that!" Tobias called back as a wave gushed over him.

Aaron clenched his teeth and kept a tight grip on the mast while he finished the job of tying down the mainsail. "Done!" he called. *What was taking Tobias so long?* Another flash of lightning showed Tobias clinging to the mast now, his legs washed away from under him.

"Get up!" Aaron screamed, panic filling his mind. *No, no no!*

"I—" Tobias called back as another wave drowned his words.

The fear of losing Tobias suddenly outweighed all the other fears in Aaron. He gritted his teeth and set into motion: he paused for a gap between two enormous waves, then ran to the rear mast, not wasting his time by crawling anymore. Tobias was still there, holding on with both arms wrapped around the mast.

Aaron sighed in relief. "Can you hold on a minute longer?" he called to Tobias, his voice barely audible through the chaos of wind and waves.

"No problem! Just, my feet keep slipping! I cannot stay standing long enough to fix the sail!"

"I'll take it down, and then we go back," Aaron commanded, surprised by the calm in his voice. Somehow, standing on deck wasn't as hard to him as it had been just moments before, and he had no problem keeping his balance despite the waves trying to wash him overboard. He untied the three lines holding the sails, then pulled them down. Both sails flapped uncontrollably, most likely already torn... But at least they hadn't snapped the mast. Maybe, just maybe, one of the sails remained intact enough for them to reach land once the storm passed, or perhaps they could stitch it up with something from the cargo. He looked away from Tobias just for a second as he tied down the sail. Finally, they were—

"Aaron!"

Aaron spun around, but too slow. Tobias was gone, and a lightning flash illuminated the night that showed him now clinging to the outside of the side railing. Desperate fear filled Aaron, overwhelming even the calm he had felt a moment before. Every part of him wished to save Tobias, no matter the cost. Desperate, he screamed out, his mind consumed by a demand to save and protect him.

Then, as if out of nowhere, a sense of clarity washed over him, returning him to his state of calmness. Only this time, he also felt an incredible rush of strength and balance. The wind and erratic movements of the boat, even the waves, felt like a mere nuisance against the control he possessed. He let go of the mast and slid across the wet deck to Tobias—just in time to see him lose his grip and drift into the black ocean. Raw calculation coursed through his mind as he made a plan: in a single jump, he was back at the mast and tied the longest of the lines around his waist. Then, without hesitation, he ran back to the side of the boat and plunged into the black icy depths.

The water surrounded him, freezing and suffocating. He swam to the surface, strength and speed boiling in his veins. Somehow, he could see as well as if it was the middle of the day. *There!* A hand protruded from the ocean. Only for a moment and already so far away. Aaron swam fast, each stroke of his arms shooting him forward, each kick of his legs adding to the momentum. Almost there... the line stopped him. Resolute, he untied himself and dove into the sea where he had seen the hand, swimming deep into the black depths.

The darkness engulfed him in deadly silence. Even his incredible sight waned in the pitch blackness of the deep sea. Still, he kept going till he finally saw Tobias, hanging lifelessly in the water further below.

Pressure threatened to burst Aaron's ears. His eyes, his skin, everything hurt, but he swam with long strokes, deeper and deeper into the void. Tobias was so close, but he was still sinking, his shape almost vanishing into the darkness.

Aaron's mind was flooded with competing thoughts: *I have to save him*, and *I have to get air and save myself*. Aaron pushed away the second one and kept defying his need to get out of the crushing water until he finally caught

Tobias by the neck of his blue tunic with the last long reach of his arms. Everything in his mind screamed for him to get up. Get air. Remove the pressure. Escape. He held on to Tobias and swam with incredible force and enough speed to shoot up from the water as they emerged. Was Tobias breathing? No time to check now, and nothing to do about it. They had to get to the boat. With cool calculation, Aaron looked in all directions with his enhanced vision, and finally made out the shape of the masts about fifty yards away, where their boat swayed up and down the crashing waves.

Aaron held Tobias with one hand, while he swam as hard as he could. Somehow, he still had strength and breath enough to keep moving. The boat got nearer and nearer, but his power slowly seemed to dull. He felt heavy. Too heavy... He grasped around in the water and there— the line! Aaron caught on to it and used it to pull forward. Yard after yard, they closed in on the boat, wave after wave crashing over them, and Tobias hanging by his side like a rag-doll. Aaron kept telling himself it wasn't too late, refusing to give up. Just two more pulls. One more. He reached out and grabbed the ship's wooden railing, and thrust Tobias up onto the deck with a final display of power. He dragged himself up next to him, and hurriedly dragged his body down the stairs to the room below deck and shut the door.

The boat still tossed and turned, but it seemed like entering a different world here inside the thick wooden hull. A safe world, where the roar of the sea was only a distant nightmare. But the nightmare wasn't over. Tobias lay still, and Aaron cried as he rolled him onto his stomach.

With both arms, he lifted Tobias so his head faced downwards and he could spew out any seawater. Water ran out of Tobias' mouth, but he still wasn't breathing. Aaron flipped him over again and blew air into his mouth. Mom had taught him this, despite his poor ability to focus during her lessons. He continued to breathe air and push against Tobias chest, just like mom had taught them to. Crying, he kept going, but he felt weaker and weaker by the second... The world blackened in front of him, but he still kept going. He had barely the energy to breathe. No thinking. And then, darkness.

Chapter Twelve

Bria shivered as Leonis brushed away a fold in the red robe he had asked her to wear instead of the usual brown ones. She longed to hide from him, to run away, but she knew the punishment for such actions, and so she stood still. Obedient.

His voice was almost fatherly. "We don't want you to stain our excellent reputation with wrinkled clothing."

He continued to inspect Kathrine's robe, and Bria watched as she flinched in pain from even the light brush of his hand. She was pale and barely able to stand after the treatment during the journey. Bria knew her body was covered with deep wounds and scars underneath the red fabric.

"It will be a short walk, just fifteen minutes to the black gate."

Leonis pushed them up the wooden stairs to the ship's deck. The bright sunlight blinded Bria, and she blinked a few times before she could see the outline of the city: Roak. The harbor was busy with people carrying and trading goods. Behind them, rows of tall houses stood side by side, built of black stones and wood. Above it all, a black spire reached far into the sky from somewhere inside the city.

"That's the heart of the island, the city and the school," Leonis whispered, pointing to the tower. He had bent down, like a parent trying to see what his child was seeing. Bria shuttered at the closeness, but forced herself not to move.

"Still nothing to say?" Leonis asked Kathrine. No answer. It had been days since even Bria had heard Kathrine's voice.

Leonis and the two female Givers from the ship led them through the city, along with the group of soldiers from the trip. The air was crisp, and it wouldn't be long before the first snow. Still, the city was bustling with life: traders sold foods Bria had never seen or smelled before, and people wore colorful robes with intricate embroidered patterns. She noticed several children in ragged clothes, scurrying away and hiding in the narrow side streets. Meanwhile, on the broad street they walked on, people respectfully stepped aside for their parade, many even bowing. Whenever people failed to move aside in time, the soldiers pushed them out of the way.

"I'm home," Leonis called loudly as they finally stopped in front of an enormous black gate leading into what looked like a stronghold, the tall spire rising from somewhere within the building. A small door built into the large gate opened, and a bald head peeked out.

"Ah, emissary Leonis. Welcome, sir."

The door opened, and they stepped into a large hall

with several doors on either side and a tall staircase at the far end. A decorative ceiling hung at least twenty yards above, painted with floral patterns in warm, golden hues. Light streamed in through a huge round window at the end of the room, opposite the black gate, and a faint scent of lavender and soap hung in the air. A few soldiers lined the edges of the hall, mixed in with people in white aprons, who Bria assumed to be servants.

Leonis stepped into the middle of the hall, turned to face them, and spread his arms in a welcoming gesture. "Welcome to Roak. Your new home."

Bria felt her gut clench at his words. A small voice in the back of her mind told her to jump at him, bite and claw him to pieces with her nails... But she had learned to drown that voice a long time ago. The cost of such rebellious actions was high, and she would not be the one to pay it. She looked to the side just in time to see Kathrine collapse on the floor. A small pool of blood pooled where she had been standing.

"How rude," Leonis mumbled, and clapped twice.

A group of servants came running and picked up Kathrine, bringing her to her feet although she barely looked conscious. Bria wished she could run to her, but she dared not move; dared not make a sound. She spent all her focus on stopping her own body from shivering. Leonis hated shivering.

"So, we have nice chambers for the good Givers, and less pleasant chambers for the bad Givers." Leonis folded his hands behind his back as if he was lecturing. "So what are you? Good Givers or bad?"

Bria dared a glance at Mom. Hopefully, she knew what to do or say.

"I won't Give for you," Kathrine hissed, using her voice for the first time in days. It was low and unnaturally coarse, and her gaze was fixed on the floor.

"I thought we had been through this," Leonis said. "We have ways to motivate you, but I prefer not to waste talent such as yours."

Kathrine looked up at Bria just for a second, and Bria felt a wave of warmth and comfort. Feelings she hadn't felt for a long time, and she couldn't help but let out a relieved sigh. For a long moment, the feeling filled her to the brim, and through incredibly enhanced hearing, Bria heard Kathrine whisper, "I love you. Live, and do good."

Then, her eyes stopped moving, and she exhaled, collapsing in the arms of the servants that held her on her feet. Bria felt a wave of energy, happiness, strength, and understanding overwhelm her. For a moment, everything was in harmony. Not just in her life, but in the entire world. All was peace and in balance. The feeling was infinitely beautiful, exhilarating, and beyond anything she had ever felt. She sighed as she let go of all fear and momentarily forgot the world around her. Then she realized what had happened.

"She's... She's dead," a servant stuttered, looking from Kathrine's limb body up at Leonis.

"What?" Leonis's voice rang throughout the hall. This was the first time Bria had heard him angry, and it shook her to her core. "Take her to the infirmary. Now!" Leonis yelled.

The two female Givers from the ship pushed the

servants aside, lifted Kathrine, and sprinted through the hall at incredible speed. Leonis spun around and ran along with them, yelling commands in all directions.

Left behind in the hall, Bria stood alone. Empty. All the feelings inside her, all the fear and anger, seemed to collapse on themselves, and they left a hole of... Of nothing. She sank to her knees, tears silently running down her face. She had felt it. Mom's last Giving. Her life leaving her body, and she had felt her love so infinite and warm. Now there was nothing. She barely noticed as a group of servants pulled her to her feet. Her mind was numb, full of profound emptiness, as she put one foot in front of the other without thinking. They led her through long and winding hallways to a small room, where they left her and closed the door behind her. Bria didn't look around, just fell to her knees, then to the floor. She lay on the cold hard stones, crying silently, her hand grasped around the silver bracelet on her wrist.

"Hey, who's blocking the door!" a girl's voice said, cutting through the nothing that clouded Bria's mind, as she felt something hard pushing against her back. She was in pitch darkness, and it took her a moment to remember she was no longer on the boat. And that her mom had died.

"Hey, move! You're blocking the door!" the voice insisted, followed by harder pushes of what Bria assumed was the aforementioned door. Slowly, she rolled to the side, allowing the door to swing open. Candlelight danced through the crack as it grew wider, and a short, red-haired girl peeked through. "What are you doing down there?"

"I... Nothing," Bria responded, looking up from her position on the floor. The girl stepped into the room, and Bria finally looked around in the light from the candle the girl carried. There were two beds, two desks, a beautiful tapestry that decorated one wall, and a red woven carpet covering most of the floor.

"Well, get up then," the girl said, lighting a candle on each table. She was at least a head shorter than Bria, and her red hair flowed over her shoulders with long, unruly curls. "My name is Minerva, but please call me Minny. Everyone does... I am a second-year student. And who are you?"

"Er... Bria." It felt weird to speak.

"Good, well, my bed is on the right. You can take the other one, unless you prefer the floor. At least, sleep on the carpet if you must be down there. The rocks are freezing cold."

"I... the bed is good."

"You are new here, aren't you?" Minny crouched next to her, looking at her as if she was inspecting a curious object she had just found.

"Yes. But I am not—"

"Goodness, where did you get those bruises? Are you —" Minny asked, then gasped and lowered her voice: "Are you a rejecter?"

She reached out and touched Bria's cheekbone. Bria pulled back, shocked by the sensation of the touch.

Minny pulled her hand back. "Oh, sorry."

"It's... It's okay. What's a rejecter?" Bria asked, moving up to sit on the edge of the free bed, and gaining some distance from the strange girl.

"Someone who refuses to use their Giving to work for The Rule, or rejects to use it at all, for that matter," Minny responded, as if it was the most obvious thing in the world. "So, are you a rejecter?"

"I... I am not a Giver. I have no powers."

"A rejecter, it seems. Usually, they'd keep you guys in the catacombs."

"No, really, I have no powers."

"Well, as powerless as you are, you are in the student quarters at Roak School of Giving. So apparently, someone seems to disagree," Minny said, plopping down onto her own bed.

"No, they brought me here and... And my mom. She is a Giver, but... Well, she was..."

The memory of her mom hit her like a fist in the stomach. The pain was physically tangible as tears burst from her eyes, and she bent forward under the weight of the sadness that filled her.

Minny's hand gently touched her shoulder, followed by a stream of feelings that mixed in with the sadness; feelings of comfort, safety, and a confusing mix of other things. She looked up and saw Minny's face strained in concentration.

"My mother died. Just now as we arrived. They killed her, because I am not a Giver, and because she didn't want to serve them." The words streamed from Bria, like water from a broken dam.

Minny gasped and, for a brief second, waves of confusion streamed into Bria, making her nauseous. Then the stream stopped entirely, and Bria felt empty again. The tears had stopped, though.

"I'm sorry," Minny said in a low voice.

Bria woke to the sound of a loud bell and pulled the pillow over her head with a groan. A small hole in the bedroom's rear wall allowed just enough light to enter for her to know the sun was up. She had barely slept that night, although she suspected Minny had been Giving her calmness to help her rest. Minny was already busy making her bed.

Bria felt infinitely lonely and empty, but somehow opened her mouth and said, "What now?"

"Breakfast." Minny shook her pillow and put it back on her bed. "Hurry, you don't want to be late."

"Late for what?"

"Breakfast, you sloth!"

"What's a sloth?"

"It's... Oh never mind. Well, make your bed and come with me."

Bria did as instructed and followed Minny out the door. To her surprise, there were other children, teenagers, and even a few adults in red robes filling up the hallway. For a moment she froze, her heart clenched in an icy fist of fear at the sight of the many robed figures. Then, Minny pulled her forward into the bustling crowd. All around her was chatter and laughter, boys and girls talking and teasing each other as they walked through the hallway. They turned several corners until they finally entered a large dining hall, long tables brimming with foods, and the air rich with a smell of spices foreign to Bria's nose. Sun streamed in from tall windows filled with stained glass panels, sending patterns of colors through the room.

Bria's belly rumbled in salute as Minny sat them down on a wooden bench. Part of her wanted to resist the urge to eat, but her stomach protested, and she hurriedly filled a plate with foods from the various trays across the table: eggs, bacon, porridge, fruits, bread, and cheese. She ate greedily, gulping down big mouthfuls with rich amounts of sweet elderflower lemonade. Although food had always been available aboard the ship, she had never eaten enough to get full, and now she felt like she had been starving and thirsting for weeks. Looking to the side, she noticed Minny staring at her in concentration.

"What?" Bria asked, some egg falling out of her mouth as she spoke.

"You looked like you were starved."

"I was," Bria said, taking another sip of lemonade. Then she realized what Minny was doing: using her Giving to make her eat! "Stop it!"

"I'm sorry! But you looked like you needed to eat, and I know it can be... hard," Minny said, concern in her eyes.

Bria didn't know if she should laugh, cry, or be angry. Finally, Minny's face relaxed, and Bria felt like she would never want another bite of food in her life. The ensemble on the plate in front of her disgusted her, and she pushed it away with a dissatisfied grunt. Then she watched with dismay as Minny filled up her own plate.

"Are these all Givers?" Bria asked, as she tried to distract herself by looking around the room. Her gut clenched as she noticed a tall table at the end of the room with blue robed emissaries, and she forced herself not to look for Leonis. The thought of him sent chills down her spine, and seeing him might just break the protective bubble of nothing that still kept her sane—and kept the memory of Mom out of her mind... She swallowed, trying to unclog the lump in her throat and suppress the impending tears.

"Yes. Some are better at Giving than others, of course, but they all Give to some extent," Minny replied.

"You mean... all Givers don't have the same powers?" Bria said, her voice only quivering slightly.

"No, of course not!" Minny responded with a grin, as if this was a ridiculous thought. "Oh, you don't know?" she continued, apparently noticing the confused look on Bria's face. "Well, most only Give a few senses, or only strength or other physical abilities. Many cannot amplify their Giving, and can only Give to one at a time. That stuff differs a lot."

Bria nodded. "And you?"

"I'm good," Minny replied, raising a clenched fist and smiled, showing her white teeth. "Most probably, I'll go to the Conservatory in The Capital this year and finish my training. At least you know about The Capital, right? King Eldrik's own city, at the heart of Meridian. Biggest city on the biggest island in all the Worldsea."

Talking with Minny served as a great distraction from the suffocating sadness, and Bria was about to ask more questions about the Conservatory, and her training, when a hand landed on her shoulder and interrupted them.

"Bria of Great Oaks?" the owner of the hand asked. He was a tall blond-haired boy, with perfect teeth and long golden hair brushed back and away from his face.

"Yes?"

"I am Lord Vanguard. The board has sent me to aid you in finding your classes and—Goodness, did you bathe, ever?" the boy said, retracting his hand with a grimace.

"Shut up, Marcus. And you're not a lord yet. If anything, it's *you* that stinks with all that arrogance," Minny snapped before Bria could formulate a response.

Bria sniffed her hair and concluded that she probably had to agree with Marcus's assessment, lord or not. She really did need a shower. Not that she cared about it, and she couldn't help but smile at Minny's defense.

"Well, no time now. You will join the first years in the east chapel for logic class," he said while turning to leave. "Come on, stinky."

He strolled away, and Bria looked at Minny for advice on what to do. Suddenly, a sharp sting of pain shot through her, and she grimaced for a moment before she could control herself. She clenched her hands around the edge of the table and stayed seated in defiance. After all, this pain was nothing compared to what Leonis had done to her.

Who does this arrogant boy think he is, to attack me like this? No way I'll let him control me. I am done with this! An ember of anger lit in the pit of emptiness that reigned inside of her as Marcus slowly turned his face and looked at her while the pain intensified. Dark spots danced before her eyes, but she refused to flinch.

"Stop it, Marcus," Minny yelled, jumping to her feet.

"Sure," he said, his lips pressed together in an expression that looked everything but satisfied.

The pain waned, and Bria suppressed a sigh, while a

smile tugged at her lip. *How I love defying these losers*, she thought, as she got to her feet at a ridiculing slow pace. She was taller than Marcus, and she reckoned she could beat him in a fistfight any day—if he'd ever indulge in a fistfight without using his powers to cheat, that was.

"Thank you. I'll see you later," she said to Minny, and turned to Marcus. The tantalizing flame of anger towards him was already proving to be a valuable tool for shutting out the debilitating emptiness from the loss of her mom. She would follow this arrogant lordling, for now, but she swore she would knock him out if he tried any more of his Giving on her. "Let's go."

"I will not have the likes of you humiliate me. When I say walk, you walk, when I say bow, you bow," Marcus whispered, just loud enough for Bria to hear as they headed through a long corridor, past students, servants, and guards in ornate armors and long red capes. They had already turned several corners, and Bria had lost track of the maze-like corridors. "Understood?"

She ignored Marcus's question and was reprimanded by another sting of pain.

"And you'll answer when I speak!" Marcus spun around, raising a fist in a threatening manner. Bria kept her gaze locked on his and didn't flinch. No way that a *boy* like him would scare her. She looked at his raised fist, hoping he would punch. It would be a welcome touch after all that strange and unplaceable pain she had received since the Giver started toying with her, and it might just inspire her to punch him right back—which would be an incredible relief of all that emotional stress. She closed her eyes, awaiting the impact with the hand.

"That's quite enough, Marcus," a voice interrupted. "Is that the new student? Bria, I presume?"

The voice came from the open doors of a large room, and Bria turned to face the man who had been talking: a middle-aged man with a short white beard, short white hair and skin in a warm golden hue that Bria had never seen before. He wore a black robe with silver patterns embroidered along the edges, and he was tall: almost a full head taller than even her.

"Certainly headmaster, I was merely addressing her lack of etiquette, hoping to aid a fellow student in her apprenticeship."

"Certainly. Please follow me, Bria," the headmaster said, and walked back through the big doors, without waiting for a response or sparing Marcus any further attention.

Bria looked Marcus deep in the eyes without a word, then turned and followed the headmaster, a sly smile finding its way to her lips.

"Please call me Karim, no need for all that headmaster nonsense. Only the nobles care so much for their titles, and it does absolutely nothing good for anyone."

Karim walked them through the center of the long room. Rows of tables and chairs stood on either side, most of them occupied by students who stared at them with curiosity. Karim directed Bria to a table at the front of the class, and she sat in silence, wondering what would happen now. She had to admit that she had enjoyed the brief conflict with Marcus; that was a situation she could understand and act on. Now, she was back to uncertainty, and her throat clogged as she remembered sitting at the table in the cabin and listening to mom as she taught her and Aaron about herbs and healing.

"Good morning." Karim sat down behind a big ornate desk in front of the rows of student desks. He folded his hands on the table as he spoke, and Bria let out a sigh: the tall man emanated a sense of tranquility that put her heart at ease.

"Good morning," the class responded collectively. There were around twenty students, from what Bria could count, all wearing red robes similar to hers.

"In my classes, we will still not be using any Giving," Karim said.

Bria heard disappointed sighs from several students around the room.

"Instead, we will continue to train our minds to harness logic. If we do not have logic ourselves, we will have nothing to Give away, and we won't know when and where to best use our powers. But first, we have a new student. From the westernmost islands of the Silent Sea, west of Tidun, if I am not ill-informed? Great Oaks, on Fero Island, it is called?"

Bria nodded.

"Came here with your mother, didn't you?"

Karim's eyes bore deep into hers, and she felt genuine interest and care. He reminded her of her grandfather, and for a moment, she was tempted to trust him, even like him. But then she remembered who he was and where they were. She clenched her teeth and nodded, trying to shut out the tranquil feeling that grew in her, and focus on the flame of anger Marcus had lit.

"You must be happy to hear that your mother has recuperated from the hard journey."

Bria gasped as her heart skipped a beat, if not several. *Was mom alive? Was she—*

"Marcus didn't tell you? Oh... Well, you can see her in the infirmary after class, but first—"

"Where is she?" Bria was already on her feet, the classroom dead quiet around her. She didn't care. Nothing else mattered, she had to see Mom! For years, she had wished and dreamed that someday her first mom, Katja, would return to Great Oaks and tell her it had all just been a long trip at sea. And the thought that her second mom, Kathrine, was doing just that, made her stomach bubble with overwhelming excitement and joy.

"In the infirmary. But, I'm sorry, the class is only just starting and—"

Bria turned and ran out of the classroom, her red robe fluttering around her.

Chapter Thirteen

Aaron woke up soaking wet and shivering from the cold. At least the boat had stopped its wild tossing and returned to its customary peaceful bobbing. Next to him, Tobias was snoring. Snoring! Aaron sat up, blinking in the light that came through the cracks of the door at the top of the short staircase. Tobias was snoring. Meaning he was alive.

"Wake up," Aaron said through chattering teeth, pushing Tobias with a hand that was numb from the cold.

Tobias grunted and opened his eyes. "What? Why? How... How did I get here?" Tobias slowly sat up, his face pale and his teeth chattering in choir with Aaron's.

"I guess you thought it was a good idea to go for a swim in a storm, so I had to fish you back out of the ocean." Aaron grinned. He had done it—Tobias had survived!

"I... I barely remember anything. Thank you."

"I guess we're even then," Aaron said, patting Tobias

on the back with a hand too cold for him to feel the impact.

Quickly, they changed into dry clothes and went to the deck, where the sun's warming rays bathed the boat's battered remains. Both masts had cracked in the heavy winds, and the sails were completely torn. They sat with backs against the mainmast, looking over the vast open ocean surrounding them. For a while, they just sat there, warming in the sun until their teeth chattering relented.

"How could we be so dumb?" Aaron asked. He was still high on the excitement of Tobias surviving, but the realization that they were now lost at sea was slowly hitting him. How long could they drift before they'd run out of water and food? A week? Two?

"Well, I guess when people in the tavern in Burrow's Keep talked about chubby seas, it wasn't an understatement. At least we won't have to worry about pirates because—"

Aaron was interrupted by a loud voice calling across the ocean. "Surrender, or die!"

The two boys looked up. There, a few hundred yards away, a large black ship sailed towards them, pushed forward by a gentle wind. The ship had four masts, each carrying several sails and multiple flags in various colors and patterns. Even at this great distance, it was an awe-inspiring ship, and chills ran down Aaron's spine. This was a blackwood ship, and—from the sound of it—pirates manned it.

"I'll be damned," Tobias said and ran below, returning a moment later with the war hammer in his hands.

"I don't think this is one for fighting," Aaron said,

looking at the approaching ship. Surely they couldn't fight an entire crew of pirates, no matter how majestically strong Tobias was. Tobias hesitated a moment before he nodded and lowered the war hammer with a grunt. Aaron himself was too exhausted from fear and action to get riled up, even if this was probably their impending doom drifting towards them.

The ship had "Blackskull" written in large dark letters on the side of the bow, and at least thirty men and women stood on the deck, blades raised. They looked rowdy, like unwashed drunk adults with swords, supporting the conclusion that these must be pirates. Aaron finally felt a tingle of fear. *Perhaps this will be the end,* he thought. Somehow, the hopelessness of it all made the situation almost comical.

"We surrender, okay?" Aaron called back across the sea.

"Great. Then prepare to be boarded! And don't try fighting, or we will leave you on a raft for the sea to take you," a pirate answered.

The two boys looked at each other and shrugged. What else to do than wait? They sat back down, and after a short while, the pirate ship lay next to theirs. Hooked lines flew over the railing, attaching the two ships. Now they could clearly see and hear the pirates yelling and swinging their weapons.

"Is it just you two on the boat?" a pirate called from the huge, black ship.

"Yes. And our sails and masts are broken, so we're not

going anywhere, if you're worried about us running away," Aaron replied.

"Such easy loot! And dare I say, you were lucky we caught you! Drifting like this, you'd never reach shore!" the pirate replied, then sheathed his scimitar and did an impressive jump, from the pirate ship to their little merchant vessel. His black cloak fluttered around him in the air, looking almost like wings, and his long black hair swung loosely around his head. His nose was pointy, and his eyes were piercingly dark. Aaron felt a distant memory make its way into his consciousness...

"I sure hope there is something valuable in the cargo, 'cause this ship is rubbish," the man commented as he turned to face the two boys and stopped dead in his tracks. His face paled. "Wait, who are you?" He looked at Aaron, concentration painted on his face.

The strange sensation grew in Aaron's stomach. "Aaron. From Great Oaks."

"Aaron?"

Finally, Aaron placed the memory. This was... But it couldn't be! "Dad? But you... died? How are you alive?" Fear and sadness welled inside him in a cocktail that threatened to overwhelm him.

"I am so sorry," Flint said, his voice dripping with bitter misery. "So much time has passed, and I..." He fiddled with the dark cloak, looking down at the wooden deck.

"You never came back?" Aaron stuttered, unsure of what to say.

"I... I have a lot to explain."

A rough male voice cut through the air. "Hey, Flint. What's keeping you?"

"A moment!" Flint yelled back. He shook his head, then put on a forced smile as he continued talking to Aaron in a low voice: "I'm afraid the explanations will have to wait."

"Flint? But you were lost at sea with Bria's parents ten years ago!" Tobias had taken a step forward, the war hammer resting heavy in his hands.

"Yes, yes, it's me. And I will explain. But, for now... I cannot believe you're here, in the middle of the ocean, Aaron! Do you know what could have happened? Please, will you and..."

"Tobias. Ruben's and Sofie's son," Tobias aided, war hammer still at the ready.

"Oh, you look just like your father!" Flint responded, smiling at Tobias, and stepping towards him as if to embrace him. Tobias took a step backward, and Flint awkwardly stopped halfway into the motion, his smile fading. "Oh, well. I guess it's only natural that you don't remember me... Either of you," he mumbled.

Aaron and Tobias exchanged glances, and Aaron felt at a complete loss for how to feel. Anger? Sadness? Really, he just felt confused. After a moment of awkward silence, Flint cleared his throat and continued.

"Please, what are you doing here? I never thought... Well, of all the people one could meet on the Outer Sea, I never thought it'd be you!"

"We are on our way to save Mom and Bria... John's and Katja's daughter," Aaron replied. He still couldn't wrap his head around what was going on.

"Save Mom? And Bria? But they should be in Great Oaks?"

"The Rule took them," Tobias answered.

"The Rule took Kathrine?" Flint burst out, his body tensing. Aaron felt a moment of fear; it was as if Flint grew taller in front of them, a menacing wildfire lit in his eyes. Just for a moment, then he seemed to remember where he was and relaxed. "Well, I suppose it just adds to the mountain of things we need to discuss. Please come aboard the Blackskull. It's not as bad as it sounds; in fact, we don't have any skulls lying around at all, as far as I know at least. There will be plenty of time to explain everything. And, er... Well, your own ship probably wouldn't do you much good anyway."

A wooden plank was placed between the two boats, and the boys traversed onto the Blackskull's deck, while the pirates studied with curiosity, murmuring.

"Take everything valuable," Flint instructed his crew. "But, er, keep it separate from the rest of our storage for now." He looked at Aaron and blushed. The crew promptly followed his command and started emptying the merchant ship, while Flint turned to the boys. "I won't steal your goods. I'll explain it later to the crew."

"Never mind the goods, they came with the boat, which we too have stolen," Aaron replied.

"You stole a boat? That was bad, Aaron. Very bad indeed!"

"Well, you're a pirate. I mean, you literally called our boat 'easy loot', so I don't think you should be the one to judge."

"Very well," Flint answered with a skewed smile. "Now,

tell me again. Why are you at sea, on a broken boat, in the middle of the southern trade route?"

The boys told their story, starting from when The Central Rule emissaries arrived in Great Oaks, and how they had taken both Kathrine and Bria to Roak, to how no one in Great Oaks was willing to bring them back, so the two boys had stolen a boat and headed east until the storm had destroyed their sails.

Flint listened carefully, and Aaron couldn't help but notice how he flinched at every mention of Kathrine's name. "So... Are you saying Kathrine is a Giver?" he asked after the tale was done.

Aaron thought for a moment. "I... I don't know. She told the emissaries that she was, I think. But maybe it was just to protect Bria."

"I see... Well, I guess I should bring you up to speed on other matters."

And so, Flint explained how he, John, and Katja were caught in a storm. How he miraculously survived and found himself beached on a small overhang on the cliffs until pirates had rescued him. The same pirates he now captained.

"But... Why did you never come back?" Aaron asked. Flint looked at him for a while before answering, as if he was weighing his options. "I can't tell you. Not yet."

Aaron's heart sank, but he didn't object. Too many emotions were fighting for space in his mind, and he needed to think about how he felt. Happy that he had found his dad. Sad and angry that his dad had been alive all those years without coming home.

They pushed the merchant vessel loose to drift. Without the sails, they couldn't sail it to land, and it was too large to tie to the side of Blackskull. It had been a great loot, and the pirates were celebrating lively on deck, while Flint promised he would keep a large share for the boys. Then, he finally introduced them to the crew.

"Fortune has it, that the great loot we just gathered was shipped by none other than my own son, Aaron, and his friend, Tobias!"

The crew fell into confused mumbling, but soon they openly discussed the obvious similarities between Flint and Aaron: the dark hair, dark brown eyes, pointy nose and pronounced cheekbones.

Eventually, one pirate approached them. "Flint's son, eh? Incredible! I'm Lulu, the only man on this ship who is both stronger, smarter, and handsomer than your father."

Lulu was middle-aged, if not actually old, and looked incredibly unfit for a pirate, Aaron thought. His beard and hair were long and messy, and he opened his mouth into a wide smile, showing several gaps where teeth were missing. Aaron and Tobias barely had time to shake his hand, as suddenly all the pirates wanted to introduce themselves.

"And I'm Crook," another pirate introduced himself with a toothless grin. He shook the boys' hands so aggressively that Aaron feared he might sprain his wrist.

"Laura. A pleasure to meet you," a young woman with piercings in her lips, nose, eyebrows and ears, added.

And so it continued, pirate after pirate, while Aaron tried to remember them by specific traits. Ricko was missing a hand, El spoke in a coarse, whispering tone, Kian was the chef and smelled of spices; and so forth.

"Very well, very well," Flint said, interrupting the crowd, as most people had gotten the chance to greet the boys at least once. Some of them had greeted them twice, and Lulu at least three times. "Aaron and Tobias will be guests on our ship for as long as they should wish. They already paid the fare with the loot they brought us today."

The pirates cheered loudly, patting the boys on their backs. Their great mood rubbed off on Aaron, and, to his own surprise, he found he was smiling. In the stories, pirates were always gruesome and cause for fear. Flint's crew, however, was more of the merry sort, it seemed.

"Now, let's eat and drink!" Flint announced, to even greater cheers.

The crew led the boys below deck to a spacious room with tables and benches in the same black wood the ship was made of. The sea was calm, and soon beer mugs were filled for all, including Aaron and Tobias. Flint hesitated for a moment, apparently considering his responsibility as a parent and trying to calculate Aaron's age.

Cold cut meat, fresh bread, butter, salt, and various sausages were passed around the table, and Aaron ate while the crew talked loudly and heartily. The whole thing was surreal. Here he was, eating a feast with his dad and his crew of pirates. His heart lifted with every joke, and every pat on his back, and he hadn't the space in his mind and heart to be angry at Flint. Not yet, anyway.

Flint soon excused himself and engaged in a deep conversation with Laura, checking several maps and a compass at the corner of the table.

Meanwhile, Lulu squeezed onto the bench next to Aaron and Tobias. "So, if I may ask, what brings you out here on the open sea? And how did you find Flint? Half The Rule is searching for him without luck, but you found him in a ship with two broken masts!" He laughed and took a big gulp of beer, splashing drops in all directions as he slammed the cup back onto the table.

"Well, actually, we are here to save—" Aaron began, but stopped as Tobias gave him a kick under the table.

Tobias quickly took over. "We left home as crew on the merchant vessel. Last night, the merchant was washed overboard, and we found ourselves adrift. It's fate or chance that you found us when you did."

Aaron looked at Tobias, grateful for the interruption. After all, even pirates had to fear Givers and who knew what they might think of their daring rescue mission.

"Chance or fate indeed!" Lulu repeated loudly, beer mugs raised in cheers around the table. He took a deep swig, burped, and continued. "Just like it was fate or chance that we found your father back then. You see, he was nearly dead when we came across him, lying in some bushes next to one of our storage caves, way out west. First, we thought him dead. Out of curiosity, but Crook climbed up and poked him. It turned out he had just decided to take a nap on that small outcrop at the side of the mountain." Lulu roared with laughter, some nearby pirates joining in, all remembering the story.

Crook took over the storytelling. "We took him along, but it took the bastard several days before he came around. Weeks before he spoke to any of us. Not sure why we brought him actually... Anyway, we did, and look at him now, all smart and captainly," he said with a wide toothless grin. Beer sprayed from his mouth with every word, and Aaron made a mental note to sit at a safe distance from Crook at future meals.

"Your dad is a remarkable man," Ricko added. "Since he joined, fate or chance has brought us more fortune, more beer and food, and, dare I say, fun. To The Raven!"

He raised his mug in a salute. Around the table, the crew responded with lifted mugs. "The Raven!"

"The Raven?" Aaron asked.

"Yeah, it's a stupid name, really. Ravens are birds, not pirates, but—"

"No, I mean, my dad is the pirate they call The Raven?"

"Ah, yes! You see, he has a sense for shiny things, wears black, and has an incredible ability to... Well, how do I put it... Fly. Or, well, not exactly flying, of course, but he can jump and swing on ropes like no one else! He has even made a fool of the Givers from The Rule on several occasions!"

Aaron and Tobias looked at each other. Chance and fate had surely played tricks on them this day.

Aaron and Tobias were given hammocks in a half-empty storage cabin at the end of the ship. They could faintly hear the heavy snoring of the crew through the thick wooden walls, and Aaron praised himself lucky for the private room. Still, he couldn't find peace, as emotions and thoughts finally found the space to flood his mind. Was he happy? Angry? Sad? In truth, he didn't really know. On one hand, he barely remembered his dad. But he remembered how sad Mom had been when he disappeared, and that was Flint's fault for not coming back. On the other hand, he was happy. Flint had saved them and his crew, and somehow, he felt at home with the crew. A feeling he hadn't had for so long; even with Tobias's family, he had felt like a visitor. But here, he felt like he fitted in. Like they were family, not just caretakers or protectors. For now, he decided not to get carried away by any of his feelings. After all, they had to focus on what was important: getting to Roak and saving Mom and Bria.

They met with Flint in the navigation room the next day. They stood around a large table covered in maps, notes, and various instruments that Flint said they used for navigation. The room's thick black walls kept out the sounds of the ocean, and there was a comfortable scent of oiled wood and candle wax. Aaron and Tobias again described what had happened in Great Oaks, and why they had to go to Roak.

"Roak is far too dangerous," Flint immediately said.

"But that's where Mom and Bria are!" Aaron protested.

"You don't understand. Roak is a Central Rule stronghold. No one enters or leaves, unless they work for The Central Rule, or are nobles. We cannot go near those waters without risking a battle. A battle we would lose."

"Lulu said you can make fools of them. The Givers from Central Rule."

"That was once. And we got lucky. It was a Rule Battleship, but with only a single Giver, and not a very good one at that. And there's a lot of difference between escaping a battle, and entering a hornet's nest like Roak."

"Escaping seems to be your thing, yes?" Aaron snapped, feeling his face getting warm. His plan of ignoring his feelings failed faster than he had anticipated.

Flint looked hurt, but said nothing in response to Aaron's comment.

"Well, how close to Roak can we get?" Tobias asked, breaking the tension in the room.

"Nearest island is Tally, but that's still a good hundred miles west of Roak," Flint answered, pointing to a smudge on the map in front of him. The boys had already considered Tally as a stop along the way, but Flint's map indicated it was a fair bit further from Roak than they had thought based on Aaron's little map.

"And even Tally isn't particularly safe for... Well, for anyone." Flint continued.

"Sometimes, one has to take a risk for someone else," Aaron said through a lump in his throat. *Flint had to help them! At least he should care about Mom...* Aaron's thoughts filled him with bitter anger. "If you don't care, just get me and Tobias close enough to Tally, so we can reach land there and figure the rest out without you."

Flint looked at Aaron with worry in his eyes, and a stern face. "I don't want you to risk this, Aaron. Or you, Tobias. Kathrine wouldn't have wanted this. The Central Rule is as cruel as it is powerful, and if they truly believe Kathrine and Bria are Givers, there's nothing we can do to save them from Roak. I am sorry."

"We both set out, willing to risk our lives. We already have," Tobias responded, his voice calm but rising.

"I know."

"Aaron saved my life, that night of the storm before you found us. He pulled me up from the sea when I almost drowned. I don't know how, but somehow, he saved me. Together, we will make it," Tobias straightened his back and placed his hands firmly on the table.

"Then you did what I could not," Flint said, his voice low.

"What do you mean? Of course you couldn't, you weren't there and—"

"The day John and Katja died. Bria's parents. I saved myself. Not them. If anything, I caused their death, and I won't do something like that again. Therefore, I cannot take you where you wish to go. There is no purpose in you dying in a Central Rule prison hole. And that's final."

Aaron felt as if he had just been punched in the stomach. The thought of Flint abandoning Bria's parents to die horrified him and he found that he was clenching his fists as hard as he could.

"Not saving John and Katja is no excuse to also abandon Mom and Bria!" he said through gritted teeth.

Flint looked down at the table and gave no answer. Aaron turned to leave, but Tobias grabbed his wrist, stopping him in his step, then asked, "You have made it here in this world, Flint. Perhaps... Perhaps we could stay aboard your ship for a while, try to change your mind?"

"You and Aaron may stay as long as you like," Flint answered. "But, I cannot keep you out of all dangers. We are pirates, and I cannot deny my crew the trade they live off."

"We will be careful," Tobias replied and let go of Aaron, who stormed out of the room.

Aaron tried to avoid Flint after that. Instead, he and Tobias spent their days with Lulu and the rest of the crew. They learned how to tie proper knots, how and when to use the different sails, how to read the stars, and how to set and keep a course. Still, shame washed over Aaron every time he thought of Mom and Bria, and how they were probably going through torment as he was out here pirating with his father. A father who had left them all behind, and who had somehow been part of causing Bria's parent's deaths.

At night, when the shame weighed the heaviest on his mind, he thought hard about what to do—but in the end, he always concluded that Tobias was right. They wouldn't make it far alone, with no ship and no actual skill for traveling. Here, at least they learned the trade of sailing. Somehow, they had to convince Flint to bring them closer to Roak.

Days turned to weeks, and Blackskull set course towards warmer waters along the Slavers Stretch, which was the route used by The Rule for transporting goods from the Southern Islands to Meridian and The Capital. Now and then, they came across merchant vessels: Flint ordered the crew to ignore the first few—causing great protests—but eventually they started pirating. To Aaron's surprise, it was quite orderly, with most merchants giving up their goods rather than picking a fight. In these cases,

Flint and his crew only took half the loot and did no harm. 'Good and sustainable business' Flint called it. But when the merchants refused, the crew fought—sometimes even to the death.

It felt unreal to Aaron and Tobias, who had never seen a person killed before. Such action was beyond imagining in Great Oaks. Out here at sea, however, it was part of life, and somehow it was easier to accept when the victims had chosen the fight themselves. Still, Aaron never stopped feeling sick from the brutality and blood. Luckily, most ships surrendered at the mere sight of Blackskull, and slowly but steadily, the two boys grew used to life at sea.

Chapter Fourteen

Bria stormed out of the classroom and into the hallway, which was empty of students now. A guard in shiny, ornamented armor, a red cloak hanging lazily from his shoulder, stood leaning against the wall, straightening in surprise as he saw her.

"The infirmary. Where?" Bria inquired.

"Er, that way. The end of the hallway, to the right, and—"

Bria ran in the direction the guard had pointed before she heard the full explanation. At the end of the hallway, she asked another guard, then ran, then another, and so forth. She continued like this until she finally stood at the end of a large room that smelled of lavender mixed with various other herbs. Beds lined the walls on either side, several of them occupied by sleeping or moaning red-robed students. This had to be the infirmary, meaning her mom was in one of these beds. Her heart beat fast as adrenaline rushed through her.

"Excuse me. What do you think you are doing here? In

the middle of school hours as well," a gray-haired lady in a white robe stepped in front of her, blocking her way.

"You have my mom. I mean, Kathrine. I am here to see Kathrine. From Great Oaks," Bria said, catching her breath and stretching her neck to look past the lady. Her mom wasn't in any of the beds she could see from there.

"If I had a coin for every person who said that today, I'd be rich. Tenth bed on the right, just around the corner. And do try to be quiet. She needs rest."

The lady stepped aside, and Bria scurried past as fast as she dared. She continued down through the long hall and around the corner, where she froze dead in her tracks.

Leonis was standing at the end of her mom's bed, conversing with a group of blue-robed emissaries. Instinctively, she turned on her heels to run away. Then she gritted her teeth and turned back towards the small assembly of emissaries. *I cannot let my fear of Leonis stop me now. No more!* She stepped forward, trying her best to cling to that determination.

As she approached, she could see that Kathrine was pale, but had opened her eyes. Bria ignored the emissaries and ran the last few steps, fell to her knees, reached over to Kathrine and hugged her. Tears streamed down her face as she felt the gentle touch of Kathrine's hand brushing over her hair.

Leonis broke the silence. "Touching."

Bria gritted her teeth, doing her best not to either cower or scream at him. Rage and fear fought to gain the power over her mind.

"Is this the daughter?" a man asked.

"*Adoptive*, unfortunately. But she has a strong

motivational effect on the subject's Giving," Leonis answered.

Bria was just about to yell out as she felt a hand on her shoulder. "Go back to class, my child. Your mother will be well soon enough," and an overwhelming feeling of comfort and safety flowed through her, flooding her mind and heart. It felt as if she was nestled under a warm blanket, safe and warm, while hearing the rain against the window outside. Every inch of her longed to follow the man's command. She kissed Kathrine goodbye, and stood up, bowed to the group, turned, and left the infirmary. All she ever wanted was to serve, even though a voice at the back of her mind was screaming for attention, telling her that she was being manipulated. The little voice stood no chance, and she made it halfway back to Karim's classroom before the Giving faded enough for her to stop and consider what had happened, and what she had seen. Most importantly, her mom was alive, and she felt lighter than she had since they left Great Oaks. Perhaps it would all be well after all. As long as Leonis stayed away from them, maybe they could find a way... She promised herself to return and visit Kathrine again later that day, perhaps the emissaries would be gone then.

All the students were occupied with scribbling down notes at their individual desks as she re-entered Karim's classroom. The headmaster looked up from his own notes and waved her up to join him at his ornate desk. He handed her a piece of paper, along with a quill and a glass of tint. "Do you know mathematics?" Karim's voice was low and meant only for her.

"A... A little." Bria looked down at the paper that contained various numbers and letters in a confusing constellation.

"Good. Let me help you."

A strange feeling streamed through Bria, and suddenly she saw logic all over. She instinctively understood little things, such as how the coarse surface of the paper in front of her must have been designed to exactly absorb the viscous tint in the glass next to it. And looking at the text on the page, she saw structures where she had just seen chaos. Karim pointed to the first part of the page, where there was a grid of nine squares, each containing nine smaller boxes. Some boxes had numbers, but most were empty.

"Write numbers into the empty boxes so that each number from one to nine is represented, once in each row, once in each column, and once in each of the nine large squares."

Bria nodded in understanding. She had always loved learning, and logical challenges were among her favorites.

Karim continued to the next part of the page where it said, '$175 + X - 136 = 12 * 9$'

"Find the value of X by adding, subtracting, multiplying, or dividing on both sides of the equal sign," Karim instructed.

The logic was simple, and Bria nodded again, a smile curling her lip. This would be easy. Finally, Karim pointed to the last part of the page that contained a brief bit of text:

'Formulate an argument on why wet clothes dry faster in the sun than in the shade.'

"Are you ready?" Karim looked at her, his dusty-blue eyes calm and patient.

Bria nodded, her mind already busy at solving the many challenges on the paper. Then, as if out of nowhere, the stream of clarity disappeared. Once again, the paper was a confusing chaos, and Bria strained herself to remember the understanding she just had. She looked up at Karim, but he stopped her before she could complain or apologize. *Had it all just been his logic?* She felt stupid as she looked down at the paper full of confusing challenges and tests.

"Take your time; it gets easier with some practice. Once you are done, come to me and I will answer all the questions you may have about Roak and tell you whatever I know about your mother. Is that a deal?"

Bria nodded, pulling her gaze from the paper. *Did he really say he would answer... Anything?* Her hands were shaking slightly as she carefully carried the paper, the quill, and the ink back down to one of the little tables. She hadn't even had the time to realize how badly she wanted answers, and how many questions she had about this new world she had ended up in. So far, it had been nothing more than a torturous playground for people like Leonis to treat her as they so wished. But perhaps there was more to it. Perhaps Karim could somehow help get her and Kathrine out of there.

After logic class, Bria went with the rest of the students to an outdoor courtyard where they'd practice physical performance—whatever that meant. None of the other students talked to her, but she noted that many whispered and pointed at her when they thought she wasn't looking. She suspected their distance was because she was slightly older and taller than most of them, but it could also be because of her rough smell; she still hadn't had the chance to wash. She cared little about it and ignored the looks as she walked along with the group in silence.

The Physique class courtyard was an open space the size of the large dining hall, surrounded by tall white pillars. Along the sides of the open square were stones in different sizes, metal bars, wooden fences, and boxes, as well as various other equipment she didn't recognize. In the middle of the courtyard stood a young, narrow-faced woman in plain black pants and a red vest. The muscles were clearly visible on her crossed arm, and the sun reflected off her ebony skin, which was several hues darker than any Bria had ever seen before. Her brown hair was held back in a thick braid, which was even longer than Bria's.

"Take off your robes, no need for those idiotic dresses out here," the lady commanded in a strange dialect that Bria couldn't recognize.

The students obediently removed their red robes, leaving them standing shivering in thin pants and shirts in the icy winds of the early winter. The professor seemed untouched by the cold, Bria noticed. Hesitantly, she took off her own robe, uncomfortably aware that there would be several lash marks visible on her arms and neck...

"A new student." The professor turned to Bria, who felt an instinctive urge to take a step back. The professor examined her, her expression turning to a smile. "Welcome. You look like you will do just fine here. I am Kindra, and in my classes you will build your physical abilities, so that you have something to Give once you start your training to be a Giver."

Bria was about to object that she wasn't a Giver, but Kindra had already turned to the rest of the class. "Everybody pick up a rock and start running laps around the courtyard, instead of standing there like a group of shivering chickens. Ten rounds. Pick a rock that's not too light and not too heavy either. Know your strength!"

The students went to the side of the courtyard and each picked up a small boulder. Bria watched as even the largest of the boys picked up relatively small rocks. She herself picked up one of the biggest; it was still considerably smaller than the ones they used for building houses and garden walls in Great Oaks. They began running, and soon Bria found she was the fastest in the class, despite the large rock which she balanced on one shoulder. She grinned as she heard the boys behind her swearing and spitting, trying hard to keep up. After the ten rounds of running, Kinda instructed them to do various types of push-ups, pull-ups, and crawling exercises. Bria felt happier than she had since she left Great Oaks. For the duration of the training, she forgot to think about all the troubles they had gone through. For a moment, she even let go of the image of how Mom had fallen dead on the ground in front of her. At the end of the class, she was exhausted but smiling, and she felt triumphant as Kindra patted her on the back, before dismissing the class and sending them all to wash off and get changed.

As much as Bria loved Physique class, she equally hated Diplomacy class, which started after lunch. Professor Raku, a short, plump man in a white tunic, seemed as dry as a biscuit as he introduced the class, but evil as a devil once the teaching began. One by one, he humiliated the students in various ways. He seemed an expert in noticing the weak spot of each of them, and he appeared to find great joy in stabbing at those spots, encouraging the other students to partake in the ridiculing. Sometimes he would ask questions, and if a student failed to answer—to his satisfaction—he would punish the entire class, except for that student. Several students cried during his class, and Bria clenched her teeth to not do the same, as Raku ridiculed her strength, her accent, and her smell in front of the class.

"Control yourselves! You are not animals, even if some of you look and smell like it, in particular our young Bria here," Professor Raku scolded. It was one long class of torture, and as they left the classroom, Bria couldn't help herself from punching her fist hard against the wall in anger.

"Don't blame the walls for your failures, Stinky."

Bria spun around to see Marcus laughing at her. Without a second thought, her fist was in the air, slamming against Marcus's grin. Whining replaced laughter as he collapsed against the wall, his body sliding down towards where Bria was ready to place a knee in his groin. To Bria's frustration, a loud yell stopped the fight before she could complete the marvelous move.

"How dare you!" Professor Raku called, and a flash of pain shot through Bria. The next thing she knew, she was looking up from the floor at the faces of Marcus and Professor Raku.

"Three days in the catacombs," Raku proclaimed.

Bria stayed on the ground for several minutes, fuming with anger. It wasn't fair that some people were born with powers like this... That these damn Givers could just do with her as they wanted! When she finally got up, both Raku and Marcus had left, and only a few curious classmates had stayed behind to see what was happening. Bria clenched her teeth to not yell at them and went directly to the infirmary to see Kathrine. She lay in bed, pale but awake. Luckily, there were no emissaries around her this time, and she smiled as Bria approached and sat down on her bed. Bria did her best to push away the anger and focus on Kathrine. "I thought you died." Bria stroked her mom's hair. It was so much thinner than it had been back home.

"I thought so too. Somehow, they woke me back up. I... Anyway, how are you? You look good in red."

Bria blushed as she looked down at herself. She was still wearing the long, red student robe. "It's just for now. We will leave as soon as you are back to health."

"I... Perhaps... Tell me about your day."

Bria told Kathrine everything about Minny, Marcus, headmaster Karim and the different classes she had had, leaving out the part where she had punched Marcus and earned three days in the catacombs, whatever that meant. Kathrine listened attentively, but said little, and Bria kept talking. Only hours had passed since she thought she had lost her mom again. But now... Somehow, it felt almost like back home. It was the first time in over a month that they could talk without Leonis close by, and the words streamed from Bria like a mountain brook at the first spring sun.

"Catacombs for three days!" Minny dropped the bread roll she was about to put in her mouth. It was dinner, and students were talking and laughing all around the large dining hall. The sun had gone down, and the light from the tall windows was replaced by large candles and chandeliers, illuminating the room in warm hues and spreading a scent of beeswax. Bria had already told Minny about her mother and the different classes, and had finally come to the part where she had punched Marcus in the face.

"Yes. What does that mean?"

"First off, good job on punching that jerk. But catacombs, that is way too hard a punishment! It's where they put the rejecters! I never heard about them putting normal students there..."

"Is that bad? I mean, I never want to work for The Rule anyway, and I am not even a Giver, so I guess it's where I should be."

"The catacombs are bad, Bria! They torture people there. Usually people break after just a day or two, the worst cases lasting perhaps a week. Three days for a fistfight is absurd!"

Minny looked as if she was caught between anger and disbelief, her face turning red and her mouth hanging open. Bria was about to object that it wasn't really a fight, since she was the clear victor from the first punch, but figured it wasn't relevant for the present discussion.

"I bet it's because you are from a non-rule family. Some people look down on that," Minny continued.

"Non-rule?"

"Your family doesn't work for The Rule, right? Most Givers are from families that have fostered several generations of Givers, so everyone works for The Rule. Marcus's dad is Lord Vanguard, fleet commander, and left hand to King Eldrik, only ranked below Lord Silverhand. And my dad is a general in the Central Army."

"Oh... Well, I am not a Giver. And no one in my family ever was, I think," Bria said again. She had a strange and frustrating feeling that Minny simply didn't believe her.

It wasn't until late in the evening, as Bria changed out of her red student robes, that she found the folded paper with logic challenges from Karim's class. She had completely forgotten about it, as well as his offer to answer all her questions if she could solve the questions—an offer she could not let slip. "Minny. Can you Give me some logic? Or, smartness, or whatever you people call it when you make people know stuff?"

"Logic? Why? I'm kind of using it right now, actually." Minny looked up from a letter she was working on.

"Karim said he would tell me more about Roak if I finished all these questions, but I can't figure it out without help." Bria held the paper in front of Minny, who grabbed it from her hand and looked at it.

"You shouldn't need help for this. Karim would be upset."

"Well, how would he know?"

"I... I suppose. It's just..."

"What?" Bria took the paper back from Minny's hand.

"I... Er... I'm not very good at Giving knowledge and logic." Minny said, looking away from Bria.

"But you Gave me all those feelings last night?"

"I can Give feelings. And strength. Most of the time, at least. But not knowledge and stuff like that."

"Oh..."

"But I can still help you with those questions if you like!"

Minny pulled the chair from the other desk over next to hers and gestured for Bria to sit. With great patience, she went through the exercises one by one, and it was late in the night when Bria finally put down the feather with a long yawn. It had taken half the night, but they had finished the assignment; and she couldn't wait to finally get some answers from Karim.

"Well done," Karim said, raising his eyebrows as he looked down over the paper. "Minny helped you, I would guess? Not to worry, you did as I asked, I suppose. Skip

Diplomacy class and meet me in the central courtyard after lunch."

Bria's heart grew considerably lighter with Karim's offer, allowing her to miss Raku's horrific Diplomacy class, and she went to Kindra's Physique class full of energy. Today they were wrestling. Some of the students had apparently decided to go hard on her and use dirty tricks when Kindra wasn't looking. Unfortunately for them, Bria was more than accustomed to such tricks, and she promptly rewarded Erik's—a boy from a noble house in the Inner Sea—attempt at throwing sand in her eyes by kicking him in the groin. Elisa—a white-haired girl from a noble house on the far north island of Orgrim—tried to tear at her long blonde braid just to find that she completely ignored the pain. In fact, getting the opponent to pull her hair was an old trick, to lure the attacker close enough for her to get in a proper punch. Bria growled in satisfaction every time another opponent surrendered, and at the end of the class, she was bruised and tired, but happy.

Bria wolfed down lunch and finally had the guards direct her to the central courtyard. Here, Karim stood waiting in his familiar black robe, lined with silver patterns matching his white beard and hair. "You are making good friends in class, I see."

"What? Oh..." Bria became embarrassingly aware of the cuts and bruises she had on her face. At least the similar wounds on her arms and legs were covered by the long red robe.

"I heard about your little fight with Marcus, and I managed to talk Professor Raku into postponing your punishment until you have been here for a week."

Bria didn't know if she should thank him, or take this chance to ask what the catacombs were. She stayed silent for now, remembering once again how unsure she was of how she should feel about the headmaster. He seemed like a kind, grandfatherly person. But first and foremost, he was the leader of the school that kidnapped her and her mother. And, he was able to manipulate her with his Giving.

"Is your mother back to health?" Karim gestured for them to walk, and Bria took her place next to him. The courtyard was almost as big as the one for Physique class, but this one was richly decorated with small sculptures, several trees and bushes, and even had a stream running through. Some trees still had leaves despite the wintry winds.

"I think so. She was better today than yesterday. And the day before that she was... Well, I thought she was dead, actually."

"The masters of Roak have strong powers, and the doctors have great medicine. Rarely have so many Givers been summoned to aid a single person. She was on the brink of dying, but on Leonis's command, we brought her back. She must be very special, your mother."

Bria felt an icy sting in her stomach at the mention of Leonis's name, and her body shivered for just a second.

Apparently, Karim noticed her reaction as he continued. "As you have seen now, The Rule can torment but also heal. In the case of Leonis, he works directly for

King Eldrik, and even I cannot stop or command him... But the world isn't simply divided into good and bad, as I hope you will come to see here. I agree Leonis can be quite a handful and—"

Heat rushed to Bria's face. "A *handful*! He kidnapped and tortured us! We just want to go home. I am not even a Giver! There is absolutely no goodness in what you did to us!" Bria yelled out before she could compose herself. *How dare he neglect the torture they had gone through? If The Rule and Leonis had saved Mom's life, it was only for their own selfish reasons!*

"I am sorry," Karim sighed and turned and looked at Bria, who did her best not to storm off right then and there. His eyelids hung heavy over his dusty-blue eyes, and he genuinely looked sorry. Bria tried to feel if he was Giving her any feelings or manipulating her, but she couldn't feel anything out of the ordinary. Still, her anger relented slightly.

"Home is far away. You and your mother's best chance of going home is to serve. There is freedom in serving, kindness is given in exchange of obedience."

So that is his deal; trying to get to Mom through me, Bria thought. But she refused to let Karim manipulate her like that, no matter how badly she wanted his answers and to learn about Roak.

"We will never serve The Rule. Not me, and not my mom," she said in a voice as icy as the wind that flew between, carrying flakes of snow. Then she spun around and rushed back through the courtyard with long steps, her face warm with anger and her heart racing as if she had been in a fight.

Chapter Fifteen

"What's that?" Laura asked Crook, who was holding a monocular, looking at a dot on the horizon.

"I think it's a Rule ship, but I cannot be sure. Been out there for a while now," Crook responded, handing her the monocular.

Aaron was coiling ropes nearby but looked up at the mention of The Rule. "A Rule ship? Is it after us?"

"Probably not... We are too far from the Slavers Stretch to be any threat to them."

"I could have sworn they've gotten bigger, though," Crook argued.

"Not bigger, just closer," Laura corrected without lowering the monocular.

"I know that, you—" Crook began, but Laura cut him off.

"Indeed, they are sailing this way. Strange."

"Can we out-sail them?" Aaron asked.

"Possibly," Laura said, and turned towards him. "Any experience with The Rule, boy?"

"Not really," Aaron said, trying to sound unworried.

"Well, better keep it that way. They are damn efficient at what they do," she replied. "I'll alert the captain, just in case."

Laura handed Aaron the monocular, and he looked through it until Flint arrived. He was still doing his best to avoid his dad, and he handed Flint the monocular without a word. Flint received the monocular in similar silence and put it in front of one eye.

For a moment, Aaron felt as if the sun was blinding him, and he rubbed his eyes. When he looked again, Flint was already folding the monocular and turning to them. Most of the crew—or at least those awake who hadn't been up and steering the ship all night—had already gathered around.

"Rule battleship," Flint said. "Around a hundred men, most likely two or three Givers, I reckon. It is headed in our direction, at a slightly higher speed than us, so I suggest we change our course."

Immediately, the crew set to work, each person knowing his or her exact role and tasks. Aaron couldn't help but wonder how Flint could learn all that from a quick glance at such a distance. To him, the ship had been nothing but a distant smudge on the horizon, even with the monocular.

"Always had a strong eye, your father," Lulu said as he walked by Aaron. "Now, help me pull some lines. We gotta angle the sails."

Aaron set to work, and soon their ship steered starboard, changing their course.

"Let's see if these bastards are following us, or if they were just going in the same direction," Lulu said.

Hours passed, but the battleship still grew on the horizon, and a dark mood grew among the crew, with murmurs of a possible fight. Aaron had somehow never considered the obvious risks involved with being aboard a pirate ship. Everything had felt safe, at least for him and Tobias, since they arrived. But the thought of ending up on the bottom of the cold ocean, or as a prisoner on a Rule ship, was terrifying. He envied Tobias, who had spent the whole day sleeping after his night duty, unaware of the imminent danger.

"Can we fight them?" Aaron asked Lulu in a low voice as the sun was setting.

"We can try," Lulu answered. "But they outnumber us, at least three to one, and they have Givers."

"But you said Flint fought such a ship before?"

"Escaped it, not fought it," Lulu answered. "And that was mere luck. It was the middle of the night when their ship approached us, and Flint himself, that sly bastard, took a rowboat and went to their ship completely unnoticed. Somehow, he destroyed their rudder without them finding out. After that, we just sailed off, leaving the battleship behind, drifting and yelling at us, but with no steer." Lulu chuckled. "But I don't reckon he will take such a risk again. He has responsibility now, you see, that changes a man. He's the captain, and he has you to protect."

"Well, he left me before, you know," Aaron responded, bitterness coating his tone.

Lulu took a long moment before responding. "I know. And I cannot begin to understand why he did it. But, I know that when we found him... he was broken, somehow. He wasn't like he is today. For several months, he barely spoke to us, he just worked hard, almost didn't eat or sleep. We kept him around, thinking him to be strange but useful. It all changed that day, when he sailed off and saved us from The Rule battleship. Something must have changed in him 'cause suddenly he talked, and ate and slept again, like the rest of us."

Aaron pondered Lulu's words. Perhaps he was right, and perhaps, something had happened to Flint that they couldn't understand. But that explanation just wasn't enough to forgive him for leaving them all those years ago. Not even close. Not to mention that he hadn't saved Bria's parents; what was it he had said? If anything, he had caused their death? Aaron shook his head, dismissing the trail of thoughts he had already followed so many times before. It wouldn't lead him anywhere, so he went to the small storage room below deck to find Tobias. The Rule ship was closing in, and they had to make a plan.

"So, if they get close enough, we are done for?" Tobias asked.

"That's how I understand it."

Aaron had woken Tobias and explained everything

about the battleship and what Lulu had said regarding their chances in a battle.

"So, what can we do? Just wait for the fight?" Tobias answered, his hand resting on the war hammer.

"I don't know. But we cannot die here and fail Mom and Bria."

"So, better to surrender then?" It didn't sound like Tobias preferred that.

"Honestly, I think it might be," Aaron said. "I mean, I hate to leave… the crew behind, but we could claim to have been hostages. Who knows, maybe that battleship is our ticket to Roak?" Aaron had almost said 'to leave Flint behind', but stopped himself. He refused to stay behind for his dad. He didn't deserve that.

"I agree," Tobias said in a reluctant voice. "But, the crew will… will they lose the battle?"

"We cannot change that by staying." Aaron's gut ached with the words. He knew Lulu, Laura, and Crook: all of them would fight to protect them, likely to the bitter end. But it wouldn't be enough; Lulu had said that himself. Aaron hoped they would understand. He hated it, but somehow they had to continue their quest to save Mom and Bria.

As quietly as possible, they packed their few belongings into oilskin satchels. They didn't want to draw any attention, so they couldn't ask Flint for their share of the gold hidden in a chest in the navigation room. Then they waited, watching the battleship closing in as the night grew darker. The plan was to launch Blackskull's rowboat when the battleship was within rowing distance when nobody was looking. Sure, the crew would notice something eventually, but Blackskull only had one rowboat, so they would have no way of stopping them.

The boys waited another half hour until the sky was at its darkest, and the battleship lay only about a mile away. Aaron couldn't help but walk up to Lulu and give him a hug. *What a miserable and dishonest goodbye,* he thought, fighting to swallow the lump in his throat. He sent a nod in Flint's direction—he was his dad, after all—then they headed to the stern where the rowboat was tied to the side of the ship. It felt terrible to leave like this. Wrong, in so many ways. Aaron clenched his fists and reminded himself of how Flint had left him behind all those years ago, and that Mom and Bria needed them. They had no choice.

"We will take the watch for the next hour," Aaron offered Laura, who had been manning the rear deck. She nodded and went down for a bite of food. "Might as well die on a full stomach, I guess."

"Let's go," Aaron whispered as soon as she was out of sight. The war hammer was strapped to Tobias's back, and they both took out the satchels they had hidden under their coats and threw them into the little rowboat. They started turning the lever that would lower the boat, a job which usually took several people to do. Luckily, Tobias was strong as a bull, so they got the boat down to sea level without attracting attention. They climbed down the rope and landed in the little boat, detached the lines and grabbed the oars. Aaron let out a deep sigh; no one had stopped them—though he couldn't help but wonder if this was luck or misfortune, as they started rowing towards the approaching battleship.

Thick clouds hid the moon, and the night was infinitely dark once they made some distance from Blackskull's lanterns. The wind sprayed drops of salt water in their faces, and Aaron felt incredibly small in the tiny rowboat in the middle of the vast, black ocean; and for the first time in weeks, fear crept up on him. His mind and heart yearned for them to turn around and return to the warmth and safety among the Blackskull crew. But he knew they couldn't. They had to press on. Looking at the black nothingness below and around him, he couldn't understand how he had found the courage to jump in and save Tobias before. The mere thought of diving into the void below sent shivers down his spine.

A man yelled from the battleship, "Who's there? State your intentions, or we will fire on you!"

Aaron exhaled and looked at Tobias. "Here we go."

"We are here to surrender," he called back to the gigantic ship rising from the black sea in front of them. "May we board?"

After a moment, a rope ladder lumped down the side of the ship, and the two boys climbed it. Aaron's heart beat fast as they made it up the steps and crossed the railing to the deck—where they found themselves surrounded by crossbows, all loaded and aimed at them. A blue-robed emissary stood among the soldiers, and a burst of intense pain rolled through Aaron, sending him to his knees. Tobias did the same next to him, and they both screamed and squirmed in white hot agony, while soldiers tied up their hands and feet with a rough rope that cut into their skin. Aaron almost passed out before the pain finally relented, and they were dragged to the middle of the ship and tied to the mast where the emissary squatted down in front of them. Aaron felt the all too familiar sensation of fear filling him up; almost as dizzying as the pain had been. *This was a big mistake!* He pressed backwards, turned his face away. Anything to get away from the Giver, whose face was getting closer and closer. The fear was revolting.

"So, you come from The Raven," the emissary said, jolts of fiery pain and mind numbing fear shooting through the boys, one at a time.

"No," Aaron stuttered between two jolts, using the last sliver of self control he had left. "We were... captured by him! We... escaped!"

"Liar!" the emissary spat. Every fiber of Aaron's being longed to hide, look away, anything. "Now tell the truth."

"I'm his son! Please, stop!" Aaron whimpered, tears streaming down his face. The pain and the fear relented for a moment.

"His son?" the emissary said with a raised eyebrow. "Well, this sure is convenient."

Aaron could do nothing but cry and try to catch his breath and gather his thoughts. He could barely remember what had just happened, but Tobias was looking at him, horror in his eyes. Then Aaron realized what he had done, and his heart sank heavy. He looked back at Tobias, his eyes open wide. He wanted to ask what they should do, hoped maybe Tobias had an idea, but the emissary dazed him with a punch in the face before he could say anything.

"We have your son. Surrender your lives to the ocean, or we will torture your son to death," the emissaries voice rang from the battleship, amplified by the power of Giving. Another two blue-robed emissaries had joined the first.

No answer came back.

"What does he mean?" Aaron whispered to Tobias.

"I think they want the crew to... jump overboard without a battle, to save us," Tobias said slowly.

Chills ran down Aaron's spine and thoughts rushed through his mind. *I have cursed us all! The crew, Tobias, myself. All for being such a coward. For surrendering instead of fighting. How could I have been so stupid?* His throat tightened and his stomach churned with remorse and shame.

Minutes went by, and the emissary repeated the order.

Still no response.

The voice rang a third time, but this time added the message, "If you have not thrown at least ten people overboard within the next ten minutes, we will begin torturing your son, and attacking your ship. Either way, you will die. Surrender now, and we will treat your son with *some* kindness."

He spoke the last words with a ring that had no kindness to it at all. *Would Flint and the crew fight an impossible battle to try to save them?* Aaron wondered. *Surely not... More likely, Flint would try to sail off and leave them behind instead. Maybe he was already busy destroying the rudder of the battleship at this very moment, so that Blackskull could make the escape...*

Aaron and Tobias sat there, hopeless, when suddenly a sharp sound cut through the air like a whiplash. A steel dart had shot down from the night sky, piercing straight through the chest of a soldier near the two boys. The soldier was dead before he could scream, but the thumping sound of a dagger piercing into the wood was unmistakable. Aaron gasped and looked up as several more darts shot down, each shooting through a soldier with enough force to continue its path down into the wooden deck. Then, out of the darkness, shot a creature. A person, clad in a black coat, floating down from the night sky, and slamming onto the battleship's wooden deck with wood-splintering force.

Soldiers yelled out commands, screaming as more darts flew in all directions and found their targets. Aaron caught a fleeting glimpse and recognized the face—of his dad! The cloaked figure shot up from the deck again and disappeared into the black night above. Aaron gasped and watched in awe—his dad had come to save him! But, how was he doing this? He moved like... Like he wasn't human.

More darts rained down from the sky, and screams and chaos erupted as soldiers fled for cover, leaving their bleeding comrades to die on the deck. Finally, the emissaries seemed to regain some composure, and focused their powers: a group of soldiers gathered around them with shields and crossbows. One soldier leaped from the deck of the ship, shooting straight up into the night with incredible force. Meanwhile, two soldiers fired bolt after bolt into the darkness.

A moment later, Flint emerged from the sky again, this time landing atop the soldier who had jumped up to attack him in the air. Another soldier leaped at him, attacking with speed far beyond human. Flint brushed off the attacker, graceful as a dancer, untouchable like a shadow. Aaron gawked as Flint dodged bolts and swords, all the while throwing darts at opponent after opponent. He wanted to call his father's name, let him know where they were, but was surprised to find he had no voice. Actually, he had no strength to do anything, his arms as heavy as lead.

One emissary was down now with a spear driven through her chest, but the other two still stood. A group of soldiers —enhanced with the power of the Givers—protected them from the whirling darts. Several minutes went by, and Flint kept fighting. Apparently, he had finally run out of darts, and now he simply used fists and whatever weapon he picked up from the deck. Each punch sent a soldier flying over the side of the ship, each kick resulted in a scream. Again and again, Flint shot up into the darkness, and each time, it left another splintered hole in the wood from where he kicked off. Finally, he landed right between the two emissaries and their soldiers. Blades spun faster than Aaron could follow with his eyes, and Flint looked like a cloud of smoke, untouchable by any weapon. He danced around the hundreds of stabs and slashes. Aaron couldn't make out the details, but chills ran down his spine as he heard the crack of bones when Flint snapped the emissary's neck, instantly slowing down half of the soldiers. Flint easily sent them flying away across the deck, as he continued fighting, aiming to kill the last emissary.

Suddenly, a bolt shot through the night from behind Aaron and Tobias. It hurtled towards Flint, who had his back turned—he screamed as the unexpected bolt buried itself deep into his side. Aaron yelled out, seeing his dad stagger in pain. Another bolt flew and hit Flint in the arm, and another in the back. Flint still fought, but he was slower now, as if his immense power and speed were fading. Meanwhile, Aaron felt his own power returning. He screamed for his dad to get back up. Screamed for him to fight. To survive. Another bolt, another hit.

Blood dripped down Flint's arms as he collapsed to his knees on the deck in front of the emissary, screaming as the emissary did his evil work on him. Aaron felt rage bubbling inside him, filling him up like boiling water under pressure. This had to stop! It had to! As if out of nowhere, he felt it: an intense wave of power surged through him, with a force that washed away all thoughts and fears. Instinctively, he tore the ropes holding his arms and legs, and grabbed the heavy war hammer that stood leaning against the mast. He hurled it at the surprised emissary and watched as it crashed into him, sending him flying backwards. Instantly, Aaron jumped, following the path of the hammer and catching it, before it followed the shattered body of the emissary across the battleship's railing. Without thinking, he swung the hammer at every soldier that approached him, while instinctively dodging crossbow bolts and arrows from all directions. Somehow, his body knew what to do. Each movement led to the next until there were no enemies left. Then his rage finally waned, and his thoughts returned. In front of him, Flint lay bleeding on the deck, his eyes glassy.

"I'm sorry," was all Flint said before his eyes closed.

Tobias said nothing as he emerged from a hiding spot behind the mast they had been tied to. He glanced around at the many dead and wounded soldiers, then helped Aaron carry Flint to the rowboat. Aaron felt like he was going to be sick, but forced himself to keep it down. Forced himself to not look around at all the dead, and not look down at the blood covering his own clothing. Not to think of what he had just done—or how he had done it. *So much death...* He pushed all thoughts out of his mind, just focused on getting Flint to safety.

They rowed as fast as they could back to the Blackskull. Flint still breathed, but he was bleeding badly. Aaron wished he had listened more carefully when mom taught him how to treat such injuries. The only thing he remembered was to press against the wound, but that was easier said than done with so many cuts.

Several crew members immediately set to cleaning and patching Flint up as they reached Blackskull. No one mentioned the fight, and no one celebrated. Silently, they watched the battleship glide away like a ghost ship through the dark ocean, its lights finally swallowed by the horizon. It seemed like something terrible had happened, and everyone wished it not to be true by simply never mentioning it again. Only Lulu came by and patted Aaron on the back, though he offered no words of consolation. Even Tobias was quiet and kept his distance.

Finally, Aaron couldn't keep the thoughts out anymore. He pulled himself away from the rest of the crew, to the bow of the ship where he threw up into the black ocean. Then, he cried, images of bloodied bodies and broken limbs flashing before his eyes. Of his own bloodthirsty rage, sending people to their death, plummeting them into the ocean. He was disgusted and confused. How had he even done that? It felt like that time in the cabin, as he had fought the two soldiers during the purge, but back then Mom and Bria had been there to Give to him... But what about the night he saved Tobias from drowning in the ocean? He had felt strangely powerful then too. Still, it was nothing compared to what had just happened. He had never felt such raw, raging power, and such relentless anger. It had helped him to kill dozens of men, while Flint, his father, had killed many, many more. They had defeated three emissaries, and he had acted out of instinct—killed out of instinct. And he had done it well... He barely dared to finish his own thoughts: was he a Taker? One of those monsters The Rule had defeated to keep the world safe?

He had saved them all, but there was nothing to celebrate as the dark night finally passed and gave way to a gray morning. Aaron sat shivering from the cold at the bow, watching as the sun rose. He was beyond tired and beyond miserable.

Chapter Sixteen

Bria sat in the back of the room in Logic class. After she had run away from Karim in the courtyard the day before, she wanted to sit as far away as possible from him. Even the thought of Physique class couldn't cheer her up, and it only got worse as she saw Marcus waiting in front of the training courtyard as they arrived. To her surprise, he didn't approach her, but just talked with other students.

Soon she found out why, as one girl raised her hand at the beginning of the class. "Why are we being set to train with a non-Giver?"

Kindra eyed the students. "Giving isn't important until you have passed your first semester and tests here. But I am sure you can all—"

"She's not a Giver!" Erik pointed at Bria, and the rest of the class started murmuring.

Bria turned to face Erik, her face warm and her fists closed and ready for a fight. "I am still stronger than you and your pathetic friends!"

Kindra stepped forward between them. "All students at Roak were brought here for a reason, and I don't want you to question that. Now, Givers or no Givers, physical training is important."

Kindra turned to the rest of the class and listed the exercises of the day. Bria was so angry that she could barely muster the attention to hear the instructions. Sadly, there was no fighting that day, so she had to save her vengeful mood for another time.

Professor Raku began Diplomacy class, gesturing towards Bria. "Apparently, a violent, uneducated, non-Giver has joined us. An animal among us, hoping to pick up scraps of learning. Or, more likely, enjoy the free food and shelter till it decides on a better refuge."

The rest of the class continued like that, Raku scolding and ridiculing everyone, but Bria by far the most. When class was finally over, Bria felt more feelings than she ever thought a person could. She wanted to scream, punch, run, and cry, but forced herself to walk out of the room without a sound, her steps fast and her gaze firmly focused on the floor. All she wanted was to—

"Bria."

She looked up and saw Karim. Before she could turn away, one emotion won against all the others: an overwhelming desire to serve. Her mind fought against it, but she couldn't stop herself from joining Karim, obediently waiting for his words. His orders. *Damn those Givers!*

"Walk with me." Karim turned and began walking, ignoring the looks of the many students gazing and whispering.

They are probably wondering why the headmaster would want to talk to a non-Giver, Bria thought. To be honest, she wondered the same herself.

"I am sorry to manipulate you like this, but I need to talk to you. First off, rumor has it that you are not a Giver."

"The rumors are true," Bria answered, obediently.

"So says Leonis. I have arranged for a quick trial next week to make sure. It will be directly after your time in the catacombs. It is the board's opinion that the catacombs should cleanse you of any rejective thoughts."

Bria nodded, clenching her teeth. Half her mind still demanded she run, or at least scream at Karim.

"But actually, I am here for other news. I am happy to let you know that your mother will be let out from the infirmary today."

Bria spun around and looked up at Karim. "Really? Can I stay with her? We could live in one of the student chambers!"

"Yes. If she agrees to serve The Rule, she will be left to stay in the rooms, and you could share one with her if you so wish. Although I fear Minny would miss her new roommate."

"That's fantastic! We can... wait, what if she doesn't accept serving The Rule?"

"Then she will stay in the catacombs until she changes her mind, I'm afraid."

"But, why? What are these catacombs, anyway? My mom and I will never serve The Rule, so you might as well give up now."

"They are prison cells designed to punish and discourage. Bria, I beg you to reconsider your opinions. People die in the catacombs if they continue to reject long enough. I implore you to save yourself and help me save your mother. You must convince her to serve." Karim had stopped walking and faced her. His face was serious but kind, and Bria again sensed sincere worry in his droopy, dusty-blue eyes. And to her surprise, she no longer sensed the intense longing to serve. She didn't feel any strange feelings meddling about her mind. Or perhaps he was just more subtle in his manipulations?

Either way, the warm feeling of anger took power, and Bria broke free from his gaze. "You won't turn us. We will *never* serve The Rule! So, I suppose I will see my mom in the catacombs, then."

Minny spent days trying to convince Bria to beg Raku for a different punishment. Anything to avoid the catacombs; but in reality Bria looked forward to it. It meant she would finally see her mom again, and she assumed the catacombs —whatever they were—couldn't be all that bad. Finally, an early morning before breakfast, a servant picked her up to lead her to her punishment. Minny looked like she was about to cry, but Bria just followed in silence as the servant guided her through the long hallways. Nothing in the school could be as bad as Leonis's ship, and she had survived that. She would also get through the catacombs, she told herself, ignoring the nervous tingling in her fingers.

They walked through the main entrance hall, passing the black gate, which was locked as always, and down a staircase to a lower part of the stronghold. Bria hadn't been in this part before, and she wrinkled her nose as she was met by the smell of rot and moldy food. She pulled her robe tight around her and buried her hands in the deep pockets to keep them warm. Finally, the servant stopped in front of a narrow staircase, protected by two guards. Behind them stood two emissaries in their blue robes, apparently waiting for her. To Bria's surprise, Professor Raku was one of them, and he smiled as he grabbed Bria's wrist. For a moment, she could smell and hear everything much stronger: it smelled of old blood, and she could hear the slow breathing of people suffering. The breath of someone who had suffered so long that they no longer whimpered, just heaved air in through painful contortions of their lungs. Fear clenched her heart like an icy fist, and for a brief moment, she felt paralyzing panic fill her veins. She whimpered involuntarily, and Raku honored the noise with a slap across her cheek.

"The animal must learn to be silent, or it will be punished."

Bria took a deep breath to control herself from making any sounds as they pulled her down the staircase and into a long room lit only by the torch in the other emissary's hand. Cage-like cells filled either side of the passage going through the room, each cell separated from the others and from the passage by thick metal bars. The smells and sounds were stronger here, and Bria looked around for any way of escape. Her heart was beating fast, and she felt her legs giving way beneath her. *I have to get out! This is a tomb!* Cold air filled her lungs as she heaved in shallow, quick breaths.

Raku opened the door to one of the cells, and Bria fought against them with all her strength as they pushed her into the cage-like confinement. She stood no chance against their enhanced power, and Raku grinned as he pulled the red robe off her, leaving her in her thin, white undergown, then forced her arms against the wall above her head. Here they clasped heavy cuffs and chains onto her wrists, so that she could not lower her hands below her shoulders, or squat far enough down to sit. The cold air prickled her skin, and she blanked it out in panic. She couldn't hold back the sounds anymore, and she screamed, barely feeling Raku punching her repeatedly in the face to make her stop. The punches must have knocked her unconscious, because everything went black.

When she opened her eyes again, she was alone in the darkness. She blinked her eyes a few times to make sure she had actually opened them.

"Bria?" The weak voice came from somewhere across the hallway. Somewhere in the darkness.

"Mom... Mom!" Bria straightened her legs to ease the tight pull from where the chains and cuffs held her entire weight by her wrists. Her whole body shivered from the cold and the pain. This was much worse than she could possibly have imagined. She took deep breaths, trying to calm her pounding heart.

"Bria, my dear. What are you doing here? You shouldn't be here."

"I punched a boy in the mouth. He deserved it." Bria felt a sliver of pride thinking back to the situation. The memory helped her steady her heart just a bit.

"But... You are no Giver. I asked that they send you back home. The headmaster, Karim, promised me he would help you..."

Karim had promised Mom to help her? Well, he wasn't doing the best job at that. But, it also wouldn't be enough: she had to get away from Roak, but she had to get Mom with her as well. She wasn't going to leave alone. "Karim said they will test me in a few days when I am out of here, and then I suppose they will realize their mistake. But, Mom. I will not leave without you!"

"There is no way, Bria. They know what I am. They will never let me go."

Bria thought hard for a moment. Her heart was beginning to calm, and now she felt how her arms hurt terribly, not to mention her face from the punches. She tasted fresh blood in her mouth.

"How long have you been here?" Bria asked.

"I don't know. I think they give us food twice a day, so I would guess I have been here for three and a half days."

Bria did her best to keep down a gasp. Three and a half days like this? "How are you doing?" she asked, trying her best to stop her voice from trembling.

There was a long moment of silence, then Bria's vision

increased dramatically, and she could see through the thick darkness. A few of the other cells had prisoners hanging, and Kathrine hung clung to the wall in the cell directly opposite hers. Her face and body were covered in whip marks and dried blood, and she was skinny. Far too skinny.

"Mom! You'll die like that! You... You have to change! You have to serve them!" Bria blinked as the world went dark around her again. Her heart sank heavy in her chest, and she felt stupid for how she had just felt pride for something as stupid as punching a boy. Tears rolled down her cheeks as the misery of seeing her mom like this hit her like a sledgehammer. This was all wrong!

"No, Bria. I will stay this way. They saved me from death the other day. I cannot imagine they did that just to let me die down here. I will find my own way to fight them."

Hours passed, and Bria felt her arms grow more and more sore until she couldn't feel them anymore. This was a great, but disturbing, relief. Meanwhile, the cold crept into her bones, and her body entered a state of constant shivering. Eventually, an emissary brought a torch and trays of food. All the prisoners had their arms released while eating, and Bria got a closer look at the others. They were children or young adults, and the emissary asked each of them if they still refused to serve. Each prisoner said they would do anything for The Rule, but they were still put back in their cells. Only a single girl, who begged to serve while crying at the feet of the emissary, was taken when the emissary left. Kathrine, in contrast, didn't even answer the emissary's question. She simply sat in silence, barely touching the food. Bria desperately tried to feed her, but Kathrine argued it would only prolong the process. Then, they were all hung back on their respective walls in their own cages; left to wait what felt like an eternity in the cold darkness, until another torch and another emissary came to repeat the process.

"Please, Mom, give up!" Bria begged again and again during those days. Kathrine sternly rejected every time, and eventually, Bria started drifting in and out of consciousness herself. Still, she sometimes came to her senses and felt how Kathrine sent her warmth and strength.

"Stop Giving to me mom! You need it yourself!"

"I love you, Bria. But I will not serve The Rule. You must be free and forget about me."

"I can never forget you!"

No matter how hard Bria tried, how much she begged and cried, Kathrine's answer remained the same.

Finally, after what seemed like an eternity, Karim himself came to Bria's cell with a torch. "It is time for your trial, child."

"No! No! Free my mom! She will serve! She will!" Bria felt a sickening desperation rising in her, her heart, her cold body shivering with a misery so deep that it seemed to have no ending. It felt as if she was suffocating, and every inch of her longed to embrace and save her mom, who hung limp on the wall across the room.

Karim turned and looked at Kathrine. "Will you serve?"

"Let my daughter go. She is not a Giver." Kathrine barely moved as she spoke.

Karim turned to Bria and moved towards her chains. Bria pulled away from him. She couldn't leave! Not without Mom! Not without saving her!

"There will be other ways to save your mother. But if you wish to stay on Roak, close to her, you have to convince the board today that you can Give," Karim whispered, barely loud enough for Bria to hear.

"But I can't!"

"I will help you. If you let me."

A calming feeling flowed through her body, like the gentle touch of a warm breeze on a summer day, and she relaxed her muscles, allowing Karim to loosen her chains. He didn't hold her or command her, just walked back out of the cell.

"I will save you, Mom," Bria whispered as she followed him. "Somehow, I will."

Bria's eyes hurt in the light at the top of the stairs, and she blinked away tears as she got painfully adjusted to the bright hallway. Karim waited patiently, then sent her with a servant who took her to the baths.

Her mind was full of thoughts as she walked: *should I trust Karim? If I want to save Mom, then it might be the best—and only—way. But how could I possibly pretend to be a Giver? I already tried everything.* Meanwhile, a voice in the back of her head called for her attention, no matter how much she tried to ignore it: *this could be a chance for escape; give up on Mom, and let them throw me out of the school—out where I can run far away from Leonis, Raku, the catacombs, and perhaps even The Rule. Somehow get back to Great Oaks, Tobias and Aaron...*

The thoughts filled her mind as she washed in silence, feeling the lukewarm water sting against her bruised and torn skin. She needed help to pull on the heavy red robe, as her wrists were too sore and weak for the movement. Finally, the servant led her to the large room they usually used for Diplomacy classes. She flinched and instinctively felt an urge to run away, as she saw Leonis and Raku sitting next to each other at a long table in the middle of the room next to a group of seven other blue-robed emissaries. It calmed her slightly to see that Kindra and Karim were among the emissaries as well, Karim at the center of the table in his distinctive black robe with silver embroidering. Kindra smiled and waved as Bria entered, and Karim gestured for her to sit on a small chair directly in front of the table, which she did while trying her best not to look at Raku or Leonis.

"Leonis tells us he has seen no trace of power in you. And you have, on several occasions, admitted to not being a Giver." Karim spoke as calmly as if he was discussing the weather, and Bria felt some tension leave her body. She looked down at her swollen wrists. They were every possible shade of blue, and the throbbing pain was hard to ignore.

"Please let me and my mom go home. We won't do anything against The Rule." Bria's voice was weak, barely more than a whisper.

"We shall see. Leonis has assured me that he has thoroughly tested your ability to Give physical power aboard his ship, so we will skip those tests and go directly to the giving of emotions. Professor Raku, if you will?" Karim gestured for Raku to step forward.

He stood up, his face contorted in a satisfied smile. Bria's heart sank; what kind of evils did he have in store for her now? "May I suggest something to guarantee she does not conceal her skills? After all, we cannot know that she has been properly tamed in the catacombs, and she has already proven to be quite the unreliable beast. She might still be lying about her lack of powers," Raku said to Karim directly, not sparing Bria a look.

Karim furrowed his brow. "What do you have in mind?"

"A simple consequence, nothing more. It won't hurt her."

Karim nodded slowly, and Raku clapped his hands. A door opened behind Bria.

"You wished to see me, professor?" The voice came from behind Bria, but she dared not turn to look. Still, there was no doubt in her mind that it was Minny who had entered the room.

"Thank you, Minerva. Bria here needs to include you in her trial for her talent as a Giver."

Bria was about to protest, but a look from Karim caused her to stay silent. Instead, she tried to make eye contact with Minny, as she stepped up to the long table next to Raku. They hadn't seen each other for several days, and she only just now realized how much she had missed her new friend. Hopefully, all would go well, though a dizzying tingle in her stomach made it hard for her to keep such hope.

"I am sorry, Minerva. You know I value your skill

highly. Unfortunately, Bria needs some inspiration before she will show her powers. And she seems to care little for anyone else than, perhaps, you. Leonis, will you begin the process?" Raku put a hand on Minny's shoulder, as if he tried to comfort her, while Leonis stood up and adjusted what looked like a leather strap around his wrist.

"Minerva will undergo increasing levels of pain until I feel you Give me any emotion. Any at all." Raku looked at Bria, a twisted smile on his face.

"No! Don't hurt her!" Bria's heart beat fast, and she jumped to her feet. "She has nothing to do with all this!"

Should she give up and tell them again that she couldn't Give? Surely that was exactly what Raku was waiting for: a clear excuse to throw her out of the school. Evidence that she couldn't Give, even after days in the catacombs. The words were at the tip of her tongue, but she had to... She had to save Mom. Even if it cost pain—and even if it caused Minny to suffer. She sank back into her chair.

"Begin," Raku commanded. Bria looked at Minny. At first, she just stood still. Slowly, her face twitched, and she began to moan. Quietly, then louder and louder.

"Stop it!" Bria yelled out, as Minny's voice rose to screams of agony.

"Then do as you are told!" Raku's voice thundered through the room, as he kept looking at her with a perverted grimace of satisfaction. Desperate, Bria looked inwards again. Was there anything? Any way she could Give? There was nothing, just like all the other times... She focused on the deep sadness she felt when she heard Minny crying from pain. She imagined passing that sadness into

Raku. Still, Minny's screaming grew ever more intense, till it finally stopped. Bria opened her eyes just in time to see Minny collapse on the floor. She twitched a few times, then lay still.

"Nothing. She Gave me nothing." Raku stepped over Minny's body and returned to his seat, with arms crossed and a triumphant smile on his face.

Karim looked up from the table, and for a moment, Bria could have sworn she saw a tear trickling down his cheek. Kindra was already on the floor, helping Minny sit back up. Bria felt empty and sad, tears streaming down her cheeks. How could they be such monsters, even against their own people?

"Now, for the test of logic." Karim stood and walked around the large table so he stood directly in front of Bria. "Sit." He gestured onto the floor, and he himself sat down in a cross-legged position. Confused, Bria slid down from her chair and positioned herself on the floor across from him.

"Hold." He reached out his hands, and Bria took them in her own.

"What do you know the most about in this world? Something you learned as a child, perhaps?"

"I... I know a lot about... A lot about the herbs and plants on the side of the mountains back home." Bria's voice shivered involuntarily, and she couldn't help but send glances at Minny who lay in Kindra's arms.

"Focus, and share that knowledge with me, please." Karim closed his eyes, and after a moment, Bria copied him, trying her best to ignore the sound of Minny whimpering. Instead, she thought back in time, imagining all the days she had been gathering herbs with Kathrine. The memories hurt, but they were beautiful. There was an incredible calm to them, and she felt like she had taken a dive into a different world. Her world.

She remembered the names of the plants, where they would grow, and at what time of year. Knew the texture, the smell, and the taste, and how they could clean wounds, calm upset stomachs, relieve pain. She wished so badly to share her knowledge, her world, with Karim, and she imagined him walking next to her on the mountain. Imagined telling and showing him everything she knew. Imagined that her own mind and his shared the same memory, the same brain. She felt the gentle summer breeze playfully tugging at her hair, and the familiar scent of pine filled her nose. The grass was soft under her feet, and her red student robe had been substituted for her red dress with embroidered birds and fish. Then, she heard Karim's voice, as clear as if she was standing on the mountainside next to him.

"Bria. You are not a Giver. You do not have the power. But if you wish, I can lie and tell the others you do, and you can stay here, as long as this secret stays between you and me. I will do this in return for you helping me save your mother. She is the strongest Giver any of us have ever seen, and they will never let her go. It is of the utmost importance that she chooses to serve while she is still at Roak."

Bria felt a tear running down her cheek as she looked down from the mountain, over the village of Great Oaks.

Her life. Somehow, they had ended up on the little patch of grass where Tobias had given her the silver bracelet. But she knew it was fake; in reality, it was so incredibly far away. Slowly, reluctantly, she nodded.

"Let me stay, and I shall help you convince my mom. I promise."

Chapter Seventeen

The cool wind and the ocean mist tingled against Aaron's skin as the first radiating beams of sun made their way over the horizon, coloring the sky in red and orange. He had been up early and had wrapped himself in thick layers of clothing so he could sit comfortably at the bow of the ship. His nights had been restless ever since the fight on the battleship, and it had become a habit to get up early and watch the sunrise.

He watched the fish swimming playfully alongside the boat as the light turned the ocean from black to azure. Sea birds that flew far overhead occasionally plummeted straight into the ocean in a daring dive for breakfast. It was beautiful, but none of it could keep the dark images out of his mind for long: images of men falling before him, horror in their eyes. Of his father, moving like a cloud of smoke, killing and flying, more beast than man. And of himself, raging and killing in a similar manner. At least he had fought to save Flint, himself and Tobias, and the men he had killed were soldiers from The Rule. They deserved nothing better. Still, he did not know how he had done it. Didn't dare think about it; the word Taker kept coming to his mind, but he dared not linger at that thought. Surely, someone must have Given him and Flint power. Perhaps one of the crew members secretly had such powers? Or perhaps... He simply didn't know.

The crew had returned to their normal routines, while Flint lay healing in his chambers. Aaron, however, was left to his own. He appreciated the solitude to gather his thoughts, but he felt lonely. No one talked to him, not even Tobias, and no one asked him to help around the ship. It seemed almost as if the crew were afraid of him, and they looked at him as if he was some wild animal prowling around the ship, waiting for a chance to attack. And perhaps he was? He hadn't been able to control himself that day on the battleship.

Crook's voice disturbed Aaron's somber thoughts. "Flint's wanting to see you."

These were the most words anyone had said to him for days, and Aaron stiffened at the sound. Crook left before he could answer, so he slowly got up and walked to Flint's chamber, the captain's quarters at the stern of the boat, hoping not to pass too many crew members on the way.

The air in the faintly lit room was thick with herbal scents, and dust hung still in the few streams of morning light that made their way through the small, round windows that lined the rear wall. It felt like he was disturbing the stillness of the room by simply being there, and Aaron closed the door as quietly as he could.

Flint lay on a mattress at the end of the room, sickly pale, but with his eyes open. His arms were covered in bandages, and he looked old and weak. And sick. Somehow, Aaron had never thought of his age or health; Flint had seemed infinitely strong and youthful ever since they came to Blackskull.

Aaron uncomfortably shifted his weight from one foot to the other, and finally, Flint spoke in a faint voice. "Do you feel bad about what happened on the battleship?"

Aaron hesitated for a moment before he found the courage to speak. It had been so long since he had used his voice. "I know I shouldn't have left you all like that. I am sorry, I hadn't thought it through properly."

"I forgive you for sailing off. I understand you have your own path that you must follow. But I am talking about the soldiers and emissaries we killed. The fight."

Aaron looked at Flint in surprise, and hesitated a moment before answering. "I don't feel bad for anyone working for The Rule." Pictures of his mom and Bria sprung to his mind. The Rule deserved what it got, and worse. "Why are you asking about that?"

"I see... I know that we did what we had to do, but we must be better. Else we become the monsters they say we are."

"What are you talking about? I don't know what happened on that battleship, but they attacked us and would have killed us," Aaron protested in confusion. The images of the battle haunted him, but that didn't mean he felt bad about it.

"Aaron, you and I... we have the power to Take."

Aaron felt a chill run down his spine as his legs grew

wobbly. That was a terrible thing to say. Even to think it was terrifying... To be a Taker was even worse than being a Giver. Much worse.

"I have known it for years, and I suspected it might have passed to you. In the fight on the battleship, you proved it to be true."

"But—"

"There is no doubt, Aaron. I felt your power on the ship. You are a Taker, just like me."

"But... No! I'm not evil! I just want to save Mom and Bria and go home! I don't want anything to do with this!" Aaron protested. He wanted to turn around and walk out of the room, but his wobbling legs seemed to have a different idea, and he sank into a chair.

"I know you are not evil... but you are a Taker. And because of this, people will fear and despise you."

Aaron's throat clogged. Did the crew know? Did Tobias? "But they shouldn't fear me? I'm not going to hurt anyone," he replied quietly, unsure if he should feel ashamed or scared.

"I know you didn't ask for this power, and I know you don't want to hurt anyone, Aaron... but things will be different from now on. A Taker spreads fear, both among enemies and allies. Your powers will make you do things that will even make you fear yourself; do things that you'll regret for the rest of your life. Even kill your friends."

"I would never do that!" Aaron objected. What was Flint even suggesting?

"Aaron, that night at sea when Bria's parents died, I used the power of Taking to take their lives and save my own." A tear rolled down his cheek, but his body remained motionless. Aaron stared at him, waves of feelings tumbling around inside him. It was too much. Finally, his legs answered, and he got up and stormed out of the room.

He hid in his bed most of the day, then moved back to the bow where he sat, staring at the horizon as the sky slowly darkened. Sprays of cold salt water kept him pinned to reality, as the ship pierced wave after wave, while feelings threatened to drag him into a pit of misery. Shame, anger, fear, sadness, a longing to care for his wounded dad, and hatred towards the man who had killed Bria's parents. Flint disgusted him, but he was also disgusted with himself, knowing that he too had the power of Taking. And he had no idea what to do.

I can't be a Taker, he kept repeating in his mind. *It can't be true. There has to be another way.* But deep down, he knew the truth. He had Taken, and he had used his powers to hurt and kill.

Finally, a voice broke the constant sounds of the ocean, and Lulu slumped down into the net next to him. Aaron said nothing. The idea of talking made his throat tighten up.

"So, er... Nice water," Lulu began.

Aaron nodded.

"Did you know I have lived my entire life aboard Blackskull?"

Aaron looked up at Lulu in surprise. The large man looked thoughtfully towards the horizon.

"I mean, I've been to land of course. But, I was born

aboard this ship. Grew up here, and I expect to die here too. When I was a kid, we called her Lu'Tau."

"Her?" Aaron's voice came out like a hoarse whisper.

"The ship. Blackskull. My family sailed and traded in the south back then, and no one bothered us. That was before the Southern Rebellion and the War of the Child. We had to escape when Lord Silverhand and his army came south. We were honest people, but some people remembered that the blackwood ships, such as Lu'Tau, had come from the Tiranin people. Old enemies of The Rule, that disappeared generations ago. But it was enough that we had to either leave the ship—or escape."

Aaron thought back to the bard at Tides Turn in Great Oaks and his story of how Prince Tua and his wife Luana had fought against The Rule, and lost.

"So, your family was Tiranin?"

"No, no, of course not. The Tiranin disappeared hundreds of years ago, headed into the Eastern Void to drift till a storm took them, I suppose. But my family always told me we descended from a group of children saved by the Tiranin, and that we were given blackwood ships when the Tiranin left."

Aaron nodded, remembering the old story of the Tiranin. It seemed like Lulu had shared a deep and important story with him. But why? His heart sank, realizing that this might be a goodbye—the last time they spoke, before the crew would force him and his dad overboard. It would only be fair…

"I am telling you this," Lulu continued. "To let you know that you are not the only one outcast from The

Rule. In fact, the ship itself is outcast... And, if a Taker should be home anywhere, I think it should be here."

Aaron stiffened at the word 'Taker', and it took him a moment to realize what Lulu was saying. *Home.* His heart lifted slightly, and the lump in his throat relented, giving him space to breathe properly.

"I have talked to the crew and we have decided we will accept you and Flint."

Aaron turned his head and looked at Lulu in surprise. The pirate was smiling, and he reached out and patted Aaron on the shoulder. Aaron shivered at the touch, and at the strange feeling of hope that took root in him.

"They don't all like it, but that'll be their problem."

Aaron looked back at the black ocean beneath the bowsprit. It felt as if a heavy weight had lifted from his shoulders. "Thank you," he said with a deep and relieving sigh.

Aaron returned to Flint's chamber the next day. He had been up all night thinking, and he had decided what to do; they had to move forward. No matter the past and his strange powers, they had to save Mom and Bria. Even if it meant he had to forgive—or at least accept—Flint for what he had done. He entered the dimly lit Captain's Quarter, where Flint lay in the same position as yesterday. The heavy silence still filled the room; this time, it was Aaron who broke it first.

"You killed Bria's parents."

Flint didn't answer, but a slight tilt of his head let Aaron know he was listening.

"You killed them, but I know you wish you hadn't. That's why you never came back home. You are a Taker, and you fear the harm you can cause."

Flint nodded, slowly.

"Very well. Apparently, I am a Taker too. So, now what do we do?"

Flint slowly pushed himself up in the bed. "Thank you... I know that all this doesn't excuse my actions, but thank you for not running away yet. You're already better than me in so many ways." He winked, then his teeth clenched in strenuous effort as he tried to sit, a painful grimace painted across his face.

"Are you okay?" Aaron reached out a hand to support him.

"Yes, I'll be fine. I had forgotten how hard it is to live without Taking."

"You... What?" Aaron asked.

"I had grown used to Taking, to regulate my strength."

"Like, all the time? But isn't that dangerous?"

"Not dangerous, no." Flint let out a moan as he lifted a cup of water from the table and drank. "You see... I have learned that our powers are much more perilous when we don't know how to use them. Now that I have learned to understand them better, I can use them to protect rather than harm. And I remain in control." Flint cleared his throat. "And this is the answer to your question, about what to do now: you must learn to control your powers. And, if you agree, I would like to teach you."

Aaron contemplated the offer, but he knew what he

had to do. What choice did he have? Perhaps his powers could even be used for the better, if only he learned to use them right... And to his own surprise, he felt a tingling sensation of excitement growing in his stomach as he nodded.

"Then teach me."

The following day, Flint called the entire crew for a meeting. Here he explained everything to them, even telling them about Bria's parents, and how he had slowly learned to control and use his powers. He admitted to having used it aboard the ship many times to increase his vision, technique, and strength, and agreed to ask beforehand when doing so in the future. As Lulu had said, the crew had already realized Aaron and Flint's powers since the fight on the battleship, and accepted them aboard the ship. Nevertheless, several crew members gasped during Flint's tale, and Tobias stepped back as Flint told about Bria's parents.

Finally, as everything was said, Lulu got up and spoke on behalf of the crew. "As long as you keep saving us from those damn battleships." He hugged Flint and Aaron, while a large part of the crew cheered and laughed. Aaron noticed Laura and several other crew members did not cheer or look happy at all, though. In fact, they sat angry and silent, leaving as soon as Flint stopped speaking. Even worse, Tobias was looking at the floorboards, staying outside the group. He walked away in silence before Aaron could catch up and talk with him.

Chapter Eighteen

Bria heard Karim's voice, this time from the real world, rather than the mountainside she imagined them standing on.

"She Gives. Her power is weak, but it is there. It can be cultured, I am sure, though I fear she will never have any meaningful amount of skill. Still, she has earned her right to study here at Roak."

Karim had stood and released Bria's hands without her noticing. It felt as if she'd woken from a long and resting slumber as she finally blinked her eyes open.

Leonis and Raku both protested loudly, but Bria ignored them. Instead, she glanced over to the floor where Minny lay, supported by Kindra. Slowly, she crawled over and sat next to them, stroking her hand over Minny's curly red hair. "I am sorry."

Minny didn't answer, just sobbed.

"Get her back to your room," Kindra instructed, helping Bria to get Minny standing. Leonis and Raku had already stormed out as the two girls began the long, stumbling walk back to their bedroom. Bria got lost several times, and her whole body ached with pain. Still, she kept going, ignoring the looks from the passing students, servants and guards until they finally made it to the little chamber where she let out an exhausted sigh as she carefully laid Minny on her bed.

"Why didn't you stop him?"

Minny's voice was barely a whisper, she still shivered and tears rolled down her cheeks. Bria wished she could tell the truth, but she remembered her promise to Karim. "I... I can only Give weakly, and only knowledge it seems."

Bria kneeled next to her friend, but Minny turned her head and looked away.

The next morning, Minny still didn't talk to her, and Bria felt almost as isolated as she had in the catacombs. She sat alone at breakfast, trying her best to cover her bruised wrists with the sleeves of the red robe while she ate. It was harder than ever to focus in Karim's Logic class, let alone stay awake. Unsurprisingly, she had developed a cold in the catacombs, and the other students kept an even bigger distance to her now.

Physique class at least offered some distraction from the haunting images of Mom, pale and starved, clinging to the wall in the catacombs. Finally, Diplomacy class was as terrible as always: Raku clearly wasn't convinced of her right to be at the school, and he continued his favorite hobby of humiliating her in front of the class.

As she lay in bed at night, she realized she hadn't talked to a single person all day other than the professors. Her heart sank even deeper, as she thought of her mom, in pain in the catacombs, all alone. She had to find a way to visit her, and to save her... Silently, she cried until sleep overwhelmed her and offered her some much-needed rest.

Bria rose early the next morning and went to the catacombs before breakfast. To her frustration, two guards stopped her before she could go down the narrow staircase that led to the cells.

"No access for students."

"But—"

"No access."

Disappointed, Bria turned on her heel and went for breakfast. In Logic class, she went up to Karim and asked if he could give her access to visit her mom. To her great relief, he simply wrote her a note allowing her free access to the catacombs. Slightly uplifted, she went through Physique class, and lunch. Even Diplomacy was sufferable with the thought of visiting her mom. As the class ended, she ran straight to the catacombs, the two guards letting her pass after a thorough inspection of Karim's note.

She shivered as she walked down the stairs, and a part of her wanted to turn around and run back up, but she clenched her fists and continued down into the darkness, reminding herself to bring a torch next time.

"Bria?" Kathrine's voice was gentle, like a breeze pushing a leaf. And weak, Bria thought to herself. Nothing like the voice that once scolded her for staying out too late with Tobias back home.

"Mom."

"You should not waste your time here in this darkness."

"I am not. I miss you. If you would only—"

"I will not serve The Rule. Please, be still my child. Be still, and move as close to the bars as you can."

Bria did as instructed, although confused by the purpose.

"I am here." Katrine's voice rang powerful in her mind, like Karim's voice during the trial.

"Mom! How—"

"Karim has taught me. Not on purpose, of course. He used it to speak to me when he was here last time, and I figured out how to copy his technique. Except he needs physical touch to do it. I have found that I have a slightly longer reach…"

Suddenly, Bria was back in the cabin in Great Oaks, sitting on the bench beside the fireplace, across from Kathrine, who combed her hair while a pot of tea heated over the fire. Bria looked around in amazement—it all looked so real! Felt real.

"This way I can endure for much longer. I don't even feel my body. I live in my mind, and in the mind of anyone close and willing to let me in. Fear not for me, my daughter. I will be fine, and I will find a way to fight them. Each day I practice, and I can reach further and further with my Giving. Eventually, I might even break the defenses of the emissaries."

"Defenses?" Bria asked, half focused as she reached her hand towards the fireplace. It burned with real, fiery flames. Warm enough to hurt her if she kept closing in, she felt.

"The mental barrier the emissaries use to protect themselves from other Givers. Even the weakest of them have almost impenetrable defenses, but I will find a way through it. If I can do that, I can overpower them. All of them!"

The fire in the fireplace grew to a blaze, and Bria pulled back. It was just a blink of an eye, then it returned to its peaceful flickering.

That evening, Bria confronted Minny; she couldn't live like this anymore. She needed a friend, or at least someone else than Mom and the professors, to talk to before she lost her mind.

"I am so sorry Leonis hurt you. I never wanted you to get mixed up in all this, and I would have done anything to stop it if I could. So, could you please just use your Giving and somehow prove to yourself that I am not lying?"

Minny stiffened, her feather pausing in the middle of the page she was writing on. Then Bria felt the familiar sensation of wanting to serve. Far weaker than when Karim did it, but strong enough for her to recognize the effect, although she was certain she could outmatch it with her own willpower.

"Can you say that again?"

Bria repeated her words the best she could. Then Minny spun around and hugged her. "I am sorry. I... I knew. I think I knew all along that it wasn't your fault."

Bria returned the hug, unsure of what to say, but sighing in relief; a heavy weight lifted from her shoulders.

"It was so scary. I have never experienced anything like that before," Minny said, still embracing Bria. "Is that what they did to you on the trip to come here?"

"Yes. That and many other things. That guy, Leonis, seems to solve most problems by dishing out pain," Bria responded.

"I am sorry... I never realized what they did to... you know, people like you. I guess that's why people reject serving at first. I am glad you have changed your mind though."

Minny eased the hug and looked at Bria, who felt a tingle of shame. There was so much she wished she could tell Minny, but she just had to nod and smile. She had never imagined how good it would feel to repair a friendship. And she had never imagined she could be friends with a Giver. *What a strange life,* Bria thought, as she fell asleep that night.

Weeks passed and Bria grew accustomed to life at Roak, learning that the large complex of buildings held much more than classes for aspiring Givers. In the east wing was a large library that had her wishing she was better at reading, and an entire quadrant was devoted to research and experiments. This area was prohibited for anyone not wearing the blue emissary robe, and even Minny had no idea what was going on in there. Bria couldn't help her curiosity, but any attempt to even go near the few doors into the Experiment Quarters had the guards politely, but firmly, sending her back towards the Student Quarters.

The classes also got better; they still didn't rely on Giving, and she generally did well. Even Diplomacy class was becoming sufferable, as weeks passed and she grew increasingly resilient to Raku's humiliations. Unintentionally, he was making her his top student by treating her so poorly. This had the added benefit that whatever comments the other students might have, in or outside class, grew entirely powerless against her. Even Marcus's frequent attempts to upset her failed, and his mockery grew increasingly desperate. At one point, he had to run a hundred laps around the courtyard as Kindra caught him enhancing the strength of a girl wrestling against Bria.

Bria and Minny celebrated half the night after that, with stolen cake and apple wine from the kitchen. When they were caught the next day—the evidence of the stolen goods scattered all over their floor—they were given a similar punishment of running a hundred laps, which they agreed had been well worth it. Bria smiled the entire run, enjoying the cool air and running slowly so that Minny could keep up with her.

Outside of class, Bria visited Kathrine every day. Despite the horrifying state of her body, her mind truly seemed as strong and healthy as ever. She practiced increasing the reach of her Giving, and eventually she could even reach the students in the hallway above the catacombs. Bria tried to walk up there, and she could indeed feel streams of Kathrine's Giving despite the thick rock barrier and long distance between them.

"Eventually, I will be able to reach you all over the school, and help you!" Kathrine said as they sat in her mind-world, next to the fireplace, in the cabin back in Great Oaks. They were drinking a dark spicy tea, and Bria could barely believe it wasn't reality.

"You think so? That would be amazing!"

"I can always tell you apart from everyone else, just from your energy. The signal is so incredibly weak when you are so far away, but I am sure I will learn!" Kathrine replied eagerly. She looked younger, and somehow wilder, than Bria remembered her from back home before they had been abducted.

Every week, Karim invited Bria for a walk. He no longer used his Giving to persuade her, and she even looked forward to the regular walks, although she would never admit this to him.

"How is your mother?"

"She is okay. Her body is sick and weak, but her mind is strong."

"Good. Unlike Leonis, I would not wish her to turn into a useful tool. I would prefer she served willingly."

"She won't. I don't think she will ever change her mind."

"Do you tell her of your life?"

"I do."

"And does she understand it is not all bad?"

"I... I think she does."

"Eventually, she will want that as well. The freedom to be with you, and have a normal life. She will understand that this is the only way, and she will understand that The Rule is more than cruelty. It is—"

"But it is cruel. The Rule took everything from us," Bria protested, and stopped dead in her tracks. A cold wind blew some snow down from the roofs, whirling it around in the air between her and Karim. Usually, this subject meant the end of their conversation.

"Yes... The Rule is cruel. It is designed to use cruelty to hide its weakness, and especially the Givers have become quite a weak spot." Karim was talking slowly now, and Bria felt a gravity to his words that she had not sensed in their earlier talks.

She decided to continue the conversation today, as she paced onward next to him. "But, the Givers aren't weak? The emissaries are the most powerful people in the world, aren't they?"

"Yes, a single emissary can turn a conflict to the king's favor. But the kingdom is big, and there are only a few hundred Givers. King Eldrik needs more, always more, and stronger."

"A few hundred?" Bria asked, a chill running down her spine. She had never imagined there would be so many.

"Yes. Our best estimate is that one out of ten thousands are born a Giver. At that rate, the Worldsea would harbor a thousand Givers. Since many Givers will hide or be killed because of their powers, The Rule only knows about two to three hundred Givers currently. And mind you, many of these are too weak to have any significance. An outstandingly strong Taker could likely challenge the entire Rule as it is now."

"A Taker? I mean, they don't really exist, do they?"

"They are much rarer than Givers, perhaps one for every hundred to a thousand Givers. But they exist. Of course, most will be killed by The Rule, or even by their own communities or families, and so there hasn't been a Taker uprising for over a hundred years. But it could happen, and King Eldrik knows and fears this."

Bria took some time to consider Karim's words before she continued.

"So, King Eldrik needs Givers to protect The Rule from the attack from any Taker that might arise?"

"Yes. But also to ensure an unchallenged and relatively peaceful dominance, all the way from Meridian to the Silent Sea where you come from, as well as the Southern and Northern Islands."

"I guess this is why my mom is so important to him... But, why must Leonis torture her like this? I mean, The Rule doesn't have to be so cruel, does it?"

"Leonis is cruel because he has never learned any other way. He was raised and trained to break Givers, rebellions and whole cities if need be. And your mother has become his most prized project, I fear. Her power is admirable, to say the least, and Leonis will not stop until he controls her. She must serve, or she exposes the weakness of The Rule. And The Rule handles its weakness through cruelty and death. Just like Leonis, King Eldrik knows no other way."

Chapter Nineteen

Aaron stood on the main deck, blinking in the sharp sunlight. The wind was quiet, and the boat barely moved on the waveless sea, so the crew had plenty of time to stand around and watch him; which he was only too awkwardly aware of. It was his first class in Taking, and he feared he would make a fool of himself in front of everyone —or even worse: lose control. He noted Tobias wasn't there, along with Laura and the other crew members, who opposed accepting him and Flint due to their powers.

"So, all of what I can teach you is based on my own discoveries," Flint said. He had bound his dark hair into a ponytail, and wore his usual black outfit, although several bandages were visible across his chest and wrists. "First off, Taking is like Giving, except you draw from what others have instead of Giving them something you possess. When fighting, I tend to Take strength, speed and technique. Other situations may require more subtle combinations of skills or senses. May I Take from you, to show this?" Flint asked Aaron.

Aaron nodded and felt his strength drain from him, like water spilling out of a bucket. He almost stumbled forward, as he was too heavy and weak to stand upright.

"I've Taken a lot of strength from you now," Flint stated, and demonstrated by jumping ten feet straight up, landing with a hard thump in front of Aaron. The crew gasped, and Lulu even clapped. "Now you try jumping."

Aaron tried, but he could barely rise to a full standing position. It was nauseating and strange to feel so weak, and he found himself longing to get his strength back. He sighed as a warm sensation rolled over him and his power returned.

"Are you okay?"

Aaron nodded, straightening his back. Everything felt normal, as if nothing had happened.

"I will now take a series of other things from you," Flint said.

Wave after wave of strange sensations roared through Aaron. Each of them seemed to have its own effect: first, he lost most of his sight, then he went partially deaf, then he got awfully tired, and finally he lost all ability to think at all. The experience was dizzying, and he drew a deep breath when Flint finally stopped. On the outside, nothing had happened, and the crew stood waiting, as if they expected some brilliant display of power.

"Good. Did you feel the difference depending on what I was Taking?" Flint asked.

"Yes. It felt... strange. I can't put my finger on it though."

"Other people just feel the effect of our powers, but Givers and Takers can sense the actual stream of abilities.

And, importantly, when fighting against Givers: we can block it."

"Block it?"

"Yes. That is why Givers are relatively powerless against each other. Even a weak Giver can protect themselves from Taking and Giving. In a fist fight between two Givers, two Takers, or even a Giver and a Taker, both parties would be left only with their own natural strength, assuming the other knows how to block. In time, you will learn this too."

Aaron nodded, and Flint continued.

"Next lesson. You can either Take from a specific person, or you can Take from groups. Of course, it is much more challenging to draw powers from several people, and there is a limit on how much you can channel. But it is still enormously powerful! For example, during the fight on the battleship, we both took from several soldiers at once. This made us much stronger and faster, but it also made them weaker and slower. Here, let me show you the difference."

Flint turned to the group of pirates and asked if they would allow him to Take strength from them for a moment. Some nodded, while others stepped back.

"I will Take only from those who nodded. Then, I will jump. Before, I Took all that I could from Aaron and jumped as high as I could. Now, I will draw a little from each of you instead. Don't worry, you should barely feel it."

Flint stepped onto a metal plate lying on the ship's deck. Then, he crouched down and kicked off. Aaron gasped as Flint shot into the sky, while the metal plate drilled itself slightly down into the blackwood deck from the force of his jump. Flint roared through the air, up and beyond the tip of the highest mast. On his way down, he unfolded his cape to slow down the fall, landing in front of the crew, who marveled and applauded.

"Amazing," Aaron whispered. He couldn't wait to fly like that. Have such power.

Flint laughed at the expression on Aaron's face. "Not so bad to be a Taker after all?" He winked. "As you can see, Taking from several people is superior. Also, if you do it right, you can amplify the power you Take severalfold. That's how you get power far beyond the individual abilities you Take. It's hard to explain, but the stronger you connect with someone, the more you can Take, and the more you can amplify or minimize the powers."

"Why would you ever minimize?" Aaron asked. His whole body was tingling at the chance of flying like Flint, and he saw absolutely no reason to limit his powers.

"For example, I might aim to calm a crowd by Taking anger from several people. In this case, I would minimize the anger as much as possible. The feelings I Take would likely consume me if I didn't."

Aaron hadn't thought about such unwanted consequences. Certainly a good reason to practice restraint. But... "Er... Just to know. Is it dangerous to Take?"

Flint took a moment before answering. "Yes, and no. You cannot Take someone's injury, so you cannot accidentally walk around picking up broken legs and what not. You can, however, take the sensation of disease, pain, even madness, I believe. Such things may drive you to dangerous actions. On the battleship, you took everything; including anger and the will to fight. Those feelings can take control of you and cause you to... Well, to do things you might regret. And, it could have left you too careless to protect yourself."

Aaron shivered, recognizing himself in Flint's words. He barely remembered what he had done on the battleship, but he remembered he had been in a wild rage beyond his own control. Now he understood better why that was.

"So, yes, and no. With proper training and control, you will learn to be safe. But, no reason to worry about everything now. First things first: try Taking strength from me."

Flint stepped next to Aaron, so he stood only an arm's reach away. Aaron was uncomfortably aware that the crew was looking at him with curiosity and excitement.

"Er... I don't know how."

"Oh, of course," Flint answered with a laugh, scratching his head. He reached out with his left arm and lifted the sleeve to his elbow, where there were no bandages. "Here, hold my arm. It is easier when we touch. Then, try to imagine being surrounded by water, like diving into a vast and lifeless ocean. Then, imagine me as another person in the weightless nothingness, and reach out towards me in your mind. Imagine streams of energy flowing from me and into you."

Aaron closed his eyes and tried to do as instructed, ignoring his surroundings. He imagined streams of energy flowing from Flint and into him, but he was pretty sure it was just imagination. Until suddenly, he felt it: a surge of energy surged into him like a wild river through Flint's arm. It was overwhelming, but it felt good! The force grew, pulling him now, tearing at his inner self. It raged with thunderous force, and he felt consumed by the power, longing for more! *More!* Then, suddenly, it stopped.

He shivered in the sudden emptiness and reached out to resume the stream, but it was as if a barrier had come between him and Flint. He opened his eyes, and to his surprise, found Flint lying on the ground in front of him, gasping for air. Around him, the crew was mumbling. They had taken several steps back. Some had even raised weapons. Terrified, he glanced down at his hand that had touched Flint's arm. It looked normal, and he felt normal, but he had felt so... so full of power. He shivered at how fast he had lost control.

"You are strong," Flint said as he slowly got up.

"What happened? I am sorry, I didn't mean to—"

"It's okay. I blocked you. You... You seem able to Take a lot by nature. So, we need to teach you control," Flint stated, shaking his arms and legs as he stood up, seemingly unharmed.

Aaron sighed in relief; he had Taken. But he now knew that Flint was correct when he said he had to learn to control it.

Over the next few weeks, Flint and Aaron practiced Taking every day. First, they practiced Taking just one power at a time. It took several days before Aaron finally succeeded in isolating and Taking a single sense—first, hearing: Flint kept bringing up suggestions such as 'Imagine your hearing becoming stronger and stronger, and how that power flows from me,' or 'Imagine your ears growing to enormous sizes.'

Aaron tried again and again, imagining all kinds of flows with no effect. Sometimes, he would accidentally Take other things, or everything, from Flint, who instantly blocked the flow when this happened.

Finally, on a gray afternoon, as Aaron was about to give up for the day, he finally succeeded. They had been at it for hours, trying again and again without success, but suddenly, his world became full of sounds. The ocean, the birds, crew members talking and working across the ship, and even the sounds of what he guessed were animals in the dark ocean below came into clear focus. It didn't hurt; it wasn't too loud. It was all just there somehow. He gasped, and it was gone.

"Good job!" Flint patted him on the shoulder and embraced him.

Aaron wondered if this was what it felt like to have a dad? If it was, he definitely liked it. After another week, he could Take a handful of different abilities with reasonable control, even over short distances. Then he learned to Take with moderation, and to maximize and minimize what he Took. One time, he put most of the crew to sleep, when he accidentally targeted everyone around him and Took too greedily. This left him jumping up and down with uncontrollable energy until Flint rushed in and took his consciousness, forcing Aaron's Taking to end.

That day, even Flint asked for a break, seemingly frightened by what Aaron thought was a peaceful accident. According to Flint, he had never heard of a Giver, or Taker, that could target so many people, and channel so much power simultaneously.

Except for that minor accident, most of the crew found the training and experiments as grand entertainment. Some, however—in particular Laura and Tobias—avoided Aaron at all times, leaving him with a confusing mess of feelings. Happy for the time he spent with Flint, and excited that he was learning skills needed to save Mom and Bria. Sad that he had lost a friend. He wished that he could just talk to Tobias, but somehow, he always kept his distance despite the confined space on the ship. In fact, they hadn't exchanged more than a few words, since it was revealed he was a Taker, and eventually Aaron decided Tobias would have to come to him if he wanted to talk. At least his training was progressing nicely, and Aaron spent most days jumping to the tips of the masts or swimming at full speed next to the ship. Anything was possible, it seemed, and his biggest challenge was restricting himself from letting go and Taking either too much, or the wrong powers.

Finally, after a month, Flint introduced the hardest exercise of them all. "You have to learn how to shield yourself from Givers. We start tomorrow."

Apparently, defending oneself required one to block out thoughts, and Flint ordered Aaron to practice this by meditating at the ship's stern from early morning to late afternoon. The first day passed with hour after hour of boredom, Aaron's legs stiff and aching from sitting still on the hard wooden deck. *This is ridiculous,* he thought, after sitting the first half day, and he had to restrain himself from Taking strength and punching something. When he complained, Flint just insisted he had to be patient and trust the process, as if that was any kind of useful advice.

Another day passed like that, equally frustrating and unsuccessful. Aaron just couldn't keep his thoughts out, and most of all, he thought of Tobias: *Why is he skulking like someone hurt him? After all, he isn't the one who has to deal with being a Taker.*

Another day of meditation passed, and Aaron brimmed with frustration. The sun had long set, and a rare cool wind on the warm southern sea had gotten him too cold to stay seated. Annoyed, he stood up and headed towards the cabin for a blanket, so deep into his angry thoughts that he didn't notice Laura before he walked straight into her. She snarled as he looked up—they were the only ones in the stern of the ship, and he took a few steps back from her.

Her face was bent in a menacing grimace of anger, visible even in the faint light of the moon and the stars. "You should know, a Taker destroyed my village: killed everyone," she hissed.

Aaron tried to clear his head from the many hours of meditation and come up with an answer, but Laura continued before he could make one.

She took a step towards him. "He thought he did the right thing, I suppose. Thought he was fighting against The Central Rule. Our village made the sails for their ships, and so he killed them."

"I... I am sorry."

"You are a monster. Eventually, you will kill, just

because you can. You already did. A predator is a predator," Laura said.

She moved closer and closer to him, and he took another step backwards. Her hand was drawing dangerously near the scimitar in her belt, and Aaron readied himself in case he had to fight her, feeling the tingling sensation of power that radiated from Laura. Power that he could Take if he needed to... *This is what my dad said. They will fear me.* For a moment, he considered calling for help—but then what? He had seen Laura with her sword, and she would cut his throat before anyone could get there. He had to Take. Had to—

Tobias appeared, as if out of nowhere, and stepped between them. "Leave Aaron alone. He didn't choose to be a Taker, and he is not going to slaughter villagers. He's a good guy."

For a moment, it looked as if Laura might jump at Tobias, her eyes tingling with anger. "Just wait and see." She spat on the ground, spun around and walked off. Aaron realized he had been holding his breath, and he exhaled with a deep sigh. Tobias still didn't look at him, just walked forwards, towards the rest of the ship.

Aaron made a quick decision and ran in front of him, blocking his way. "Hey! I know you don't like that I am a Taker, but I can't do anything about it! As you said, I didn't choose this." Blood rushed to his head as he finally let out the words he had been waiting so long to say.

"I should go home," Tobias answered quietly, looking down at the wooden deck.

"I... What?" Aaron looked at his friend in confusion. This wasn't what he had expected.

"You don't need me. You are a Taker. You almost lost your life saving me from the ocean, and you will only grow stronger, so I should go home."

"No! No, Tobias. I... I need you. I mean, I understand if you don't want to stay now that you know about my... Taking," Aaron's throat tied up as he spoke.

"I'm okay with you being a Taker."

Aaron could have cried out right there and then. "Well, why didn't you tell me? I thought you hated me now, because of this weird power, gift, curse, whatever you want to call it."

"I don't love it. But as long as you use your power for good, I don't think being a Taker makes you a bad person... But you don't need me. You can keep yourself safe without me, and if anyone can save Bria, it's you." Tobias still didn't look up, but Aaron heard the bitterness in his voice. "If anything, I will slow you down."

"Tobias, you are my friend. And Bria's boyfriend, I guess. We both need you, not just for your strength. I need you much more now than ever! I mean, who... Who would be my friend now? Look at what just happened with Laura! Probably even Bria won't want to see me!"

Tobias looked up. "I hadn't really thought about that. But I promised Bria and my dad to look after you and keep you safe. And now I don't think I can do that anymore. What if I am the one that brings us into danger? I have no special powers."

"Please, Tobias. Don't go. We will save Bria together. We have come so far, and... I've missed you. And you just saved me now! I need you here."

"I... I don't know."

A smile tugged at Tobias' lips, and Aaron's heart lifted a bit. "Well, can we please be friends again while you think about it?"

Tobias nodded and they went down for dinner. And just like that, they were back to talking.

After that day, meditation became easier; and finally, as Aaron sat in a deep state of relaxation, he felt a tingle. Like a thought trying to slither its way into his mind. A foreign influence, forcing itself on him. He ignored it, but it became stronger. More forceful. Confused, he tried to shut it out, but now it pounded against his bubble of peace.

Finally, it made its way in, and everything went dark around him. Just for a moment, then it stopped and Flint stood in front of him. "Good job. You have learned the basics."

Finally, Aaron understood what the meditation was for. He kept up the tedious training for weeks, sitting on the deck in the heat of the late summer sun. Somehow, Flint could Take as easily as breathing, and defend himself with similar ease. It seemed that it came to him as the most natural thing in the world, and any attempt to Take from him felt like punching against a mountain. As impenetrable as Flint's defense was, Aaron's was equally weak. He felt the assault of Flint's powers, but it instantly overwhelmed him every time he tried to guard against it.

So the summer came and went, and it was fall when Flint came to Tobias and Aaron and sat them down for a talk. "I have been thinking. All of this cannot be a coincidence. I mean, finding you two drifting on the ocean, and you being a Taker, Aaron. So, I have agreed with the crew that we will take you to Kings Harbor on Tally before winter sets in. From there, we will try to find you a way to Roak."

"Really?" Aaron said, his heart lifting.

"Yes. It will take some weeks to get to Tally, and I don't know what you should do once at Roak. But, if Bria and Kathrine really aren't Givers, they might just have been left to live their lives as servants. In that case, you might smuggle them off the island and go home."

As always, the thought of Mom and Bria spiked a sense of shame in Aaron's chest. He had spent too much time enjoying life with his dad. Hopefully, his newfound powers would be worth it, and... Well, he refused to think they might be too late.

"But if they are in the school, I urge you to give up the fight and get out of there as fast as possible. Remember, once a Giver has been turned to The Rule, they can never be brought back."

The boys nodded, although Aaron wasn't convinced he would give up—even if Mom and Bria were at this school, whatever it was. With his powers, he was sure he could get them out, no matter what. And there was no way they would turn to the side of The Rule. Finally, they were heading to Roak, and finally they would save Mom and Bria, no matter what it would take.

Chapter Twenty

Bria had been in Roak for almost three months, and winter held a firm grip on the school. The walls were freezing cold, and students wore gloves and heavy boots around the hallways. The only exception was Physique class, where Kindra still insisted students remove their robes, leaving them shivering in their thin undergarments. Bria looked with dismay at the white coat of snow that covered the training courtyard as she pulled the thick red robe over her head and shuddered as an icy breeze caressed her skin. *The first minutes are the worst,* she told herself, as she stepped out into the courtyard along with her quivering classmates. The distinctive sound of teeth chattering filled the air, and Bria clenched her jaw to avoid joining the choir.

Kindra wore her usual vest and pants, and seemed unbothered by the temperature. "Today we will be training the art of jumping. Explosive leg movements. Why is jumping important for a Giver?" she asked, patiently walking back and forth in front of the class.

"To dodge attacks?" Sandra suggested, a slim girl who stood next to Bria offered. Sandra had used to bully Bria, but now they were almost friends. Only *almost*, of course, since Marcus had managed to ensure no one befriended her too much, except Minny who had stuck by her side through thick and thin.

"Wrong," Kindra replied. "Dodging an attack by jumping is almost always a bad idea. Any other suggestions?"

"To jump over buildings?" Erik suggested.

Bria had come to hate Erik Weatherhorn, who was from a lesser noble house and did everything Marcus suggested. Luckily, he was useless at all disciplines, and—at times—Bria found she almost pitied him as much as she disliked him.

"Better suggestion. But no." Kindra looked across the group of freezing students and seemed to decide this was enough academia for one day as she answered her own question. "Jumping is important, because it is the most visible evidence of a strong Giver. If you can Give a handful of soldiers the power to jump twenty feet in the air, the enemy will know they have no chance, without a single drop of blood being spilled. Understand?"

Nods of agreement caused a momentary break in the teeth chattering.

"So, are there any of you first years who know how to Give strength and speed?"

Sandra and several others raised their hands. To Bria's surprise, at least half the class kept their hands down. *Damn hypocrites,* she thought, *bullying me for not Giving, when they can barely Give anything themselves. My mom could best all of them...*

"Good. Today will be your first chance to use your powers in my classes. Pair up two and two, or three and three, so each group has one student who can Give speed and strength!"

A hum of excitement spread through the group of students, and even Bria felt her heart lifted slightly. They were normally never allowed to Give in class. She turned to Sandra, who nodded in an agreement to team up.

"Erik needs a group!" Kindra called. *Of course, no-one wanted to team up with the weak little weasel,* Bria thought, smirking while squatting up and down to gain some heat.

"Sandra, Bria. Take Erik, he needs a group."

Bria's smirk faded as Erik joined them. *How could he look so nonchalant even when he had just been humiliated in front of the class like that? Such a weirdo...* She readied her muscles, in case he decided on a dirty attack once Kindra looked away.

"So, you cannot Give strength and speed?" Sandra asked him.

At least this seemed to bring down his mood, though only for a second. "Nah, I don't want to waste my powers here in Physique. But let us see what you can do," he replied, dodging her question, obviously pretending not to care.

"Now, see how high you can get your partner to jump," Kindra called across the class of students excitedly warming up like Bria. Several students were already jumping several yards into the air.

"Want to try?" Sandra offered.

Bria readied herself for a jump when Erik interrupted. "Let me go first. If you mess up with the Giving, I can block you. Stinky here probably can't even do that."

Finally, Bria felt some warmth return to her, and she was just about to launch at Erik when Kindra stepped in. "Very well, Weatherhorn. Let's see a jump."

Bria growled and lowered her fist, while Sandra turned her attention to Erik. He looked more nervous now that Kindra was watching.

"Let her in," Kindra ordered.

Erik and Sandra both stood locked in concentration.

"I..." Erik replied, looking strained.

"Just remove your shielding," Sandra said, stepping close to him, reaching out a hand and touching his arm. He shuddered, sweat appearing on his forehead.

"I... I can't," Erik stuttered through clenched teeth.

"Let me," Kindra said, rolling her eyes as she stepped forward and put a hand on Erik's arm too. He screamed out for a second, then sunk down onto the snow where he sat, gasping for air. "I've shattered your shielding," Kindra explained. "I'll do that at the start of every class from now on, until you learn how to release it yourself. Agreed?"

It didn't look like Erik agreed at all, but Kindra had already turned her attention to Bria. "Now, Sandra and Bria, let's see what you can do."

Bria forced her eyes from Erik, that still heaved for air on the snow covered ground. Giving really was a mystery to her. Hopefully, she wouldn't have any such problems. At least she had never had any problems with Mom's Giving. She made eye contact with Sandra and nodded. Sandra's face returned to a state of focus, and Bria stood waiting for the familiar wave of strength to roll over her. Nothing happened. Was she supposed to do something? Kindra just looked at them, did she expect some kind of—

"Jump," Sandra whispered, interrupting Bria's line of thoughts. Was she already Giving? Bria felt nothing... Still, she kicked off, and to her own surprise, she flew almost a yard into the air.

"Good job!" Kindra patted both of them on the back, and a wide smile spread across Bria's face. All she had done was a small jump, but it had been together with Sandra. With another Giver that wasn't her mom. Her heart lifted in a feel of... belonging?

"Thank you," she whispered to Sandra, who, to Bria's surprise, reached out and embraced her in a hug.

"That's the first time I've made someone jump so high!" she said, triumph in her voice.

Next to them, Erik still sat on the ground, breathing as if he had just run a sprint.

The class continued, and Bria jumped higher and higher, to both her own and Sandra's excitement. It was an exhilarating feeling, and Bria didn't feel the cold at all anymore. Sandra said she could feel the stream growing every time they tried.

The class was almost over, when Kindra announced a small competition of who could jump the highest. Bria and Sandra had made great progress, but some other students were jumping more than twice person's height now, so Bria didn't have great hopes for victory. Still, she wanted to do her best and hopefully impress Kindra.

"Luke and Bast," Kindra called.

The two boys stepped forward, and Bast made an impressive jump, almost reaching the height of the white pillars surrounding the courtyard. Several students gasped and clapped.

"Uma and Mirrel."

The two girls stepped out, and Uma prepared for a jump: she was almost as tall as Bria, and Bria respected her a lot for her physical strength; she wished they could have been friends. If only Marcus hadn't decided to hate her and pitch everyone against her... Uma set off and launched even higher than Bast. If she had angled it correctly, she could have landed on the roof of the passage that ran parallel to the open courtyard. Bria clapped in enthusiastic applause along with most of the other students, while Bast spat on the ground, realizing his loss.

"Sandra and Bria."

Bria felt flutters in her stomach as she did some quick squats and small jumps to warm up. She locked eyes with Sandra, and prepared. Apparently, the other students could feel it clearly when they were Given powers, but Sandra was kind enough to mimic her when it was time. *Now!*

An unmistakable rush of powers raged through her as she kicked off from the ground with all her force. The snow under her boots crackled, and she shot straight up, the icy air whistling past her. The sensation was incredible! Such power! Such... Such height! At the top of the jump, Bria gazed down and around, and felt her stomach clench. She was so high up that she could see the inner sides of the enormous outer walls of the school, and the courtyard had shrunk to a white patch far below her. For the blink of an eye, she hung still in perfect balance between the opposite forces of updrift and gravity. The world was calm and beautiful. And then, the ground started to get closer. Her momentum had turned, and she accelerated towards the frozen ground with terrifying speed. Surely this would break all her bones. She closed her eyes and landed with a heavy thump. To her surprise, her legs caught her without breaking. She sighed in relief and blinked her eyes open.

All the students looked at her in disbelief, and even Kindra let out a gasp. "Who did... How did you Give that much power?" Kindra asked Sandra, who looked as confused as everyone else.

"I don't know! I just did as I did during the training..."

Bria didn't hear the rest of the conversation, as she tried her best to hide the wave of excitement that filled her. She knew what had happened—this must have been her mom's doing!

She visited Kathrine in the catacombs instead of having lunch. As she reached the end of the narrow staircase, she was immediately enveloped into Kathrine's mind world. Only a month ago, it had taken several minutes to get into the feeling of being in the cabin. Now she was aggressively pulled in, whether she wanted it or not. Kathrine was standing by the fireplace, her long, brown hair hanging in loose curls down her back. Her face looked younger than Bria had ever seen it, and behind her, the fire in the fireplace was roaring. For a moment, Bria felt fear.

Kathrine gestured for Bria to sit down. "Good jump."

"Thanks, Mom. How did you do that?"

"I told you, I can sense you. Today I felt extra energized, and I figured it was time to Give you a little help."

"It was great! You should have seen the other students, it was magnificent!"

"That's good, my dear. So now, do you see what I mean? I have grown stronger. So. Much. Stronger."

Bria nodded, feeling the sliver of fear growing in her heart. The fire in the fireplace blazed stronger with every word Kathrine spoke, and Bria wondered what would happen if she got burned in a mind world like this.

"Today we will escape," Kathrine said, interrupting her thoughts.

"Today?"

"Yes! It's a matter of time before the emissaries understand my powers. And I am ready to leave now!"

In the back of her mind, Bria had a hard time ignoring the vision of her mom's actual form—her physical body—starved and bruised, hanging from the wall like a rag doll.

"I am strong enough to break through the emissaries' defenses, and I will get the next one that comes down here to carry me out. I am afraid my body is too weak to walk, but I will make the emissary Give me what strength I need."

Bria nodded, half in disbelief, half in fear. A thousand thoughts ran through her head. What about her life at the school? What about Minny? Her promise to Karim? And... What would they even do once outside the school, trapped on a prison island in the middle of the winter? Would Mom survive the escape?

"Are you... Are you certain?"

"Dead certain. Are you ready?"

"I... Yes. Can I... Can I pick up some things?" Bria fumbled with her words. To her own surprise, she didn't feel the happiness and excitement she had expected. She had dreamed of escaping Roak with Kathrine, but... But now it felt wrong, somehow.

"Go. And bring me some clothing too. But be back soon, they will feed me at nightfall."

Bria nodded, and the mental image of the little cabin faded around her. Back in the icy catacombs, she spun around and ran back up the stairs, past the two guards, and straight to her room. Quickly, she packed her normal clothing and a half-eaten sandwich from the day before. Then she put on her thick boots and, with a sting of guilt, packed Minny's boots, as well as some of her friend's clothing. When all was bundled together, she ran out the door, praying no-one would stop her on the way and ask about the big satchel of stuff she carried on her back.

"Hide." Kathrine ordered.

Bria squeezed herself into the dark corner of an empty cell. Actually, all the cells were empty now, and Kathrine was the only prisoner left; the other rejecters must have succumbed fast under the cold conditions. Minutes went by, and Bria felt the cold penetrate through her red wool robe. How could Kathrine possibly be alive under these circumstances? It was pitch dark, and the only sound she could hear was Kathrine's slow breathing. Eventually, the smell of rot faded as she grew used to it. Still, the cold gnawed at her, as half an hour passed. An hour perhaps? Finally, the faint glow of a torch approached, rising to a blinding light.

"Still not talking?" The emissary had stopped in front of Kathrine's cage and unlocked the gate. "Well, you have to eat, crazy witch woman. Even you have to eat and—"

There was no physical motion from Kathrine or the emissary, but Bria sensed how something had changed. The blue-robed emissary continued to unlock Kathrine's chains, and for the first time in weeks, Bria saw Kathrine move her physical body.

"Come, my child," she whispered.

Her voice—her real voice—was a coarse whisper. Bria stepped out from hiding, and towards Kathrine. In the torchlight, she watched her mom stretch her arms and legs, as if she had just woken up from a long sleep. Bria gasped at the view of her starved body: her limbs seemed so infinitely weak and her cheeks hollow. Her eyes were like dark pools, sunken deep in their sockets. Bria shivered. How would they possibly make it out, let alone survive outside in the cold outside of the school? How could Kathrine even stand in this state?

"Did you bring me something to wear?"

"I... Yes."

Bria pulled out a set of trousers, a thick wool shirt, wool socks and Minny's boots, and handed them to Kathrine. Her hand shivered as she almost touched her mother's pale, emaciated hand. For a moment, she feared Kathrine wouldn't be strong enough to hold the clothes. Then she noticed the emissary had slunk down into a sitting position against the cage bars. Somehow, Kathrine must be using his powers.

"He will walk us out of here. Do you have something more anonymous than the red robe you are wearing?"

Bria nodded and quickly changed into normal clothing.

"Good. Let's go."

Kathrine sunk down a little as the emissary rose, but she was still standing. Everything about her looked weak, her skin so pale, and half her hair had fallen out—nothing like the mother she remembered—and Bria had to remind herself of how strong she was in her mind-created cabin. The emissary began walking, and they followed.

"These are going straight to the headmaster," the emissary instructed the two guards atop the staircase.

The guards pulled blades from their scabbards and blocked the exit. "I am sorry. She is not allowed to leave under any circumstances."

"Bria, take them out," Kathrine whispered.

Bria felt an overwhelming sensation of energy as power roared through her body like wildfire. She didn't hesitate, but moved directly into one of the fighting positions Kindra had taught them. With incredible speed, she launched forward, moving past the motionless emissary with unnatural dexterity. She slammed her fist into the face of the first guard before he could raise his weapon in defense. Then she spun in mid-air and kicked the other guard on the side of the head. Both of them sank to the floor with a crash.

"Let's go," Kathrine instructed, and they continued walking.

The emissary walked in front, like some kind of mindless servant. Bria's senses were sharpened, and she noticed every motion, every sound, as they walked through the hallways. Servants and guards kept their distance. *They must be frightened by the vision of Kathrine's corpse-like figure,* Bria thought. Finally, they made it to the large entrance chamber with the black gate, flanked by four guards.

"Stop them fast, before they call for help," Kathrine whispered.

Bria burst into action again, sprinting up to the four guards that stood by the gate. With incredible ease, she danced between their blades, launching punches and kicks in perfect coordination with her dodging maneuvers. The guards fell to the ground in seconds, and Kathrine stepped up next to her.

The emissary was already busy, unhinging several locking mechanisms. Some of them appeared too heavy for the visibly weakened man, and Bria assisted, all the time looking over her shoulder, hoping no more guards would appear. That no one would stop them. They were so close. The gate squeaked and opened ever so slightly, and Bria felt the cold air against her face.

"Mom, it's—"

Bria stopped dead in her tracks as she looked back and saw Kathrine standing face to face with Karim, the two of them holding onto each other's arms. Neither of them made a sound, but Bria felt how the strength that had passed into her faded. Next to her, the emissary came to his senses and wits again, looking around in confusion. Bria's heart sank as more guards and emissaries came running, gathering around Kathrine and Karim, who stood like statues in an intense but silent battle in the middle of the room.

Karim sweated, his body shaking, while Kathrine stood firm. Several emissaries put their hands on Karim, closing their eyes in focus. Still, Kathrine didn't move. Bria looked at the open gate behind her. Would they even notice if she ran? But she couldn't leave Mom.

Another moment passed, and Kathrine was quivering slightly now. Five emissaries supported Karim, who was sweating and shaking uncontrollably. Determined, Bria clenched her teeth. She had to do something! Enhanced strength or not, she could still fight. She bent down into a tackle stance, ran past the guards that surrounded Karim and Kathrine, and threw herself against the tall man. To her surprise, Karim's shaking body was like an immovable boulder, and the collision almost knocked her out. She stumbled backwards, dizzy from the impact. Meanwhile, more emissaries had joined, and two guards grabbed her and pinned her to the floor.

Kathrine finally fell, first to her knees, then straight on her face. Bria screamed for it to stop. For Karim to stop. It was all too similar to the day they arrived at the school, and Bria's gut wrenched in desperate panic. She wriggled with all her strength, but she stood no chance against the grip of the two guards.

"Don't let her die. Take her to the hospital, eight emissaries at all times, no matter what you do, keep her alive. And feed her, for heaven's sake," Karim ordered, wiping the sheen of sweat from his brow, leaning against a guard that supported him. A group of emissaries picked up Kathrine's body and carried her away.

"I thought we had a shared understanding of things," Karim said, turning towards Bria, his voice bitter and cold.

Bria tried to kick herself away from him, but the guards kept her in a firm grip. Waves of disappointment, self-loathing, and incredible sadness rolled through her. She had never felt anguish like this before. It hurt much more than any physical pain ever could.

"There is no way that I can protect you from this," Karim said as he turned and left.

The feelings faded and gave way to another emotion: fear.

Leonis stepped forward. Of course, it had to be him. "To the Central Courtyard, please," he instructed the guards with a smile.

"But she's—"

"No. She's not. She has no power of Giving. This one is, in every practical way, just an ordinary girl. Isn't that right?" Leonis said, his pale smile widening.

The guards hesitated for a moment, then lifted Bria to her feet and dragged her through the school's tunneled hallways. A large group of students had already gathered to observe the spectacle. What did they think of her now? And what would happen to Mom? Perhaps Leonis would finally be allowed to kill her. For the first time in weeks, she thought of Tobias. Surely, this would be the end. She wished dearly that he would find someone else, and live a good life. And that he would take care of Aaron. Poor little Aaron.

The guards tied her to a leafless tree in the corner of the courtyard, where the snow lay deep and untouched by footprints. Bria had walked the paths of the courtyard with Karim so many times, but usually students weren't allowed here. Today seemed an exception as students gathered around, as if it was some kind of show. It felt like one of Raku's classes, with the crowd of students mumbling, whispering her name. She tried her best to ignore them, to breathe and stay calm. She wished the icy knot of fear in her stomach would turn to the burning feeling of anger. It would be much easier to scream than cry. Better to rage than to hide. She looked around, all too aware there was nowhere to hide.

She spotted Minny standing in the first row, confusion painted in her face. "I'm sorry," Bria whispered, hoping she would read her lips.

Marcus's voice rang through the crowd. "I told you she didn't belong here."

Bria didn't object. Not in words, and not in her head. She didn't belong, and she never had.

Leonis cleared his throat and said, "Bria from the village of Great Oaks has slithered her way into our midst, a stranger among us. But now, she has shown her true colors. She was caught trying to free one of our most dangerous enemies from the catacombs. An enemy of us all, who has the power to control and use the power of other Givers."

Gasps ran through the crowd.

"And for her crime, Bria should be punished with death."

Silence fell over the students, and Leonis looked across

the crowd like an actor savoring his audience. "But we are in no hurry." He faced Bria with his perverted smile. "And you may yet serve The Rule in your own way," he finished in a lower voice, his words meant just for her.

He turned to face the students again. "I want each of you to help Give Bria the punishment she deserves. Give her the pain she would have caused upon you if not stopped in time. I want everyone to Give as much as they can, so you can remember the cost of betraying your allies. Betraying your friends. Who will begin?"

"I will!"

Marcus stepped forward, with a pretentious strut to his steps. His golden hair combed back and his face contorted in a courtly smile that barely hid his excitement.

So this will be the game for now, Bria thought as she clenched her teeth and prepared for the pain. At least it might prove a distraction from the turmoil of thoughts and fear that raged through her mind: pictures of Mom, Aaron, and Tobias. Faces that she would never see again.

Leonis released the rope, keeping her tied to the tree, while Marcus dramatically cracked his knuckles. Then it began: powerful waves of pain rolled through her, like metal spikes piercing her skin. She flinched, but stayed on her feet. In front of her, Marcus looked strained as he tightened a studded leather band around his arm so that a trickle of blood rolled down, reaching his hand. Bria felt nausea from the pain, but she refused to bow down. Not to Marcus.

Defiantly, she kept eye contact with him for what seemed like an eternity, before Leonis interrupted and asked the next student to take their turn. Bria enjoyed a brief moment of satisfaction as Marcus tore off the studded leather band and threw it on the ground, marching away while cursing.

Then the next student began: this time, Bria could barely feel the pain, and Leonis only gave her a few moments. Then another student, a girl who brought her to her knees with a strange sizzling pain she hadn't experienced before. Then another, another, and another. They kept coming, and Bria lost count. She felt how Leonis regulated her dizziness, forcing her to stay aware of the pain. Again and again, she fell to her knees, just to be pulled back up, until they had finally reached the end.

The last student, Minny, stared at her with tears in her eyes. "I am sorry."

Then, a spike of pain forced Bria to the ground where she stayed, sobbing. She felt as if every feeling had been burned out of her, wrenched from her soul like one would squeeze water from a cloth. There was nothing left but the deep emptiness she had forgotten. A hole of all-consuming nothing, with no space for thoughts, feelings, or life.

"Mercifully, I will let her live. But I will grant her a signet, so the world knows she has betrayed The Rule."

Leonis gazed around, as the crowd of students turned silent again. He pulled out a knife, and a wave of willingness to serve overwhelmed Bria, filling the pit of nothingness. She had no willpower to fight back with, no awareness that she even had to fight. So, she stood up in front of him, and watched as he brought the knife closer and closer to her face. A light flared in the depths of her heart: a distant longing to scream, bite, claw, and hide like an animal trapped in a corner. But the will to serve overwhelmed the feelings, even as the blade cut deep into her skin.

Slowly, painfully slowly, Leonis carved patterns across her face. Cut after cut, the blood blinded her, painting the snow around her feet. She barely felt the pain in the pit of nothingness that consumed her. The students gasped, but she stayed still. Her arms hung limp, there was no will to fight left in her. Nothing but emptiness.

"This is the face of a betrayer. Throw her out of the school, to the streets where she belongs."

Two guards pulled Bria forward through the crowd of students. Warm blood dripped down her body, her hair sticking to her neck and face. She could barely blink her eyes open, and when they finally hurled her into the snow in front of the gate, she didn't have the energy to get up. Perhaps this was the end.

She hoped so.

CHAPTER TWENTY-ONE

Aaron's heart bubbled with excitement as they pivoted the sails and set Blackskull's course north: away from the Slavers Stretch and towards King's Harbor on Tally—the closest island to Roak. Apparently, the city was named 'King's Harbor' in the hope that King Eldrik might someday visit. To the best of the crew's knowledge, this had never happened, and they assured Aaron and Tobias that the city was far from worthy of a king's visit.

After months on the Slavers Stretch, intercepting Rule ships bringing spice, minerals, ores and fabrics from the far Southern Islands, their cargo was brimming with valuables. Now, they headed for the Western Sea, where such goods were more easily distributed without The Rule's attention. Meanwhile, Aaron's Taking had gotten better and better, and he could even make weak attempts at shielding. His biggest challenge, other than shielding, was to keep powers separate once he took larger amounts. In particular, it was hard to not Take the feelings of people, he found. But, as long as he didn't Take too greedily, he could control it, and Flint promised it would get easier with practice.

It would take a month to get all the way to Tally, but there were high spirits aboard the Blackskull, as the crew looked forward to trading their loot for coin and alcohol. They made stops in several harbors along the way, all hidden in minor coves and well off from the larger official harbors and towns. Still, these small harbors had their own life with taverns, guards, and pier masters—though neither guards nor anyone else bore the sigil of The Central Rule, Aaron noticed.

Flint implored Aaron and Tobias to stay away from the taverns. Of course, Lulu, Crook and the others ignored this and brought the boys everywhere, insisting on teaching them everything 'about life', from gambling to tavern brawling and flirting with the bar staff, although Aaron concluded the crew had little success with the latter.

Tobias proved to be a natural talent in this environment. He easily beat two or three adult men in a bar fight, and his curly blonde hair seemed to attract every second woman and a fair few of the men, in the room. In contrast, Aaron drew little attention, and stayed out of the brawling as much as possible. His fingers tingled with the urge to Take, but he had sincerely promised not to flaunt his powers. It didn't matter if they were surrounded by criminals or The Rule—anyone would kill a Taker on the spot if they found out. Finally, after weeks of merriment and sailing, Flint let the crew know the next stop would be King's Harbor. It was the largest city on Tally and an official trade port of The Rule, so they had to be extra careful there. But, in return, the people were easier to beat in cards and brawls, Lulu assured them.

Aaron couldn't ignore the bittersweet sting in his heart as they finally spotted the island on the horizon. He had grown accustomed to the crew, his dad, and life at sea, and he had learned more aboard Blackskull than he believed he had learned the rest of his life combined. Everything from card games to reading the stars and navigating a ship. Not to mention, how to use his powers as a Taker.

The crew hoisted a stolen sail from The Central Rule, hoping their ship would be assumed to be that of a wealthy noble family—blackwood ships, after all, were far too rare and expensive for anyone but the richest of houses. Then, they used tar to cover the big white letters writing 'Blackskull' on the side of the ship. Aaron felt bad for this. Blackskull was a proud ship that deserved its name, whether or not they had any skulls on board. Flint assured him they would wash the tar right off once they got further away from the Inner Sea, and that they would desecrate and burn The Rule flag—just for good measures.

It was with a heavy heart that Aaron helped furl the sails as they docked Blackskull, after having bribed every pier master who seemed to have any opinion about the non-nobleness of the crew. Finally, it was time: the two boys greeted the crew members' goodbyes with tears in their eyes. In fact, Lulu was outright crying, using his beard to dab away the tears as he hugged them, promising them repeatedly to keep Flint safe. Then Flint put on his familiar black cape and hood, and led Aaron and Tobias off the ship and towards the narrow city streets. Aaron looked longingly after Lulu and the rest of the crew as they headed straight to the nearest tavern, his heart dropping as he forced himself to look away from them. They had to focus now and find a way to Roak.

King's Harbor was, by far, the dirtiest, ugliest, and biggest city Aaron had ever seen. The houses were two or three stories tall, built in brown timber, and—what looked like—chalked stones that had aged into an unsavory green-brown surface of dirt. Most of the buildings leaned dangerously over the docks and the road, and Aaron wondered how they were still standing. Between the houses were busy, narrow alleys where the fresh ocean breeze refused to enter. Here, the air was thick with a sour smell of old, wet grass and mud, and Aaron and Tobias covered their noses with their shirts, as they walked through the passages accompanied by Flint. The locals, however, didn't seem to mind, and even the tiniest alley was crowded with people in lumped rags as well as guards leaning lazily against the walls, too busy with games and conversations to pay any attention to the three of them as they passed. Aaron tried to hide a blush as they passed young women decorating the alley corners, close to naked despite the cool fall air.

"The smell is from the peat they burn to heat their houses," Flint clarified, pushing forward through the crowded alleys without slowing. "They get it from the bogs that surround the city. Cheap and efficient, but dirty."

He continued to lead them through an intricate labyrinth of streets and passages, ignoring the many people who approached them to beg, sell, or talk. Aaron did his best to avoid the many hands and voices that tried to lure him into houses that might be stores or perhaps something worse.

"Now, getting to Roak is only possible on ships from The Central Rule. After all, Givers are the greatest commodity of The Rule, and you are entering their biggest treasury, except perhaps The Capital itself. Luckily, getting stuff to Roak has always been dangerous and thus lucrative. For the way back off the island, you might have to be... creative," Flint said as they reached a slightly less crowded alley.

"How long is the trip?" Tobias asked, walking and crouching under strings of laundry that hung at head height.

"A day and a half of sailing."

"Do you know someone we can go with?" Aaron asked, hoping they wouldn't have to stay too long in King's Harbor. He couldn't understand why the crew were so excited to go there. The city was even shadier, and much dirtier, than most of the improvised harbors where they had traded their stolen goods.

"I have no contacts for that, but I know a place that might just have the people we are looking for. But remember, you can't trust anyone here, and especially not anyone affiliated with The Central Rule. Oh, and smugglers even less so. If they can, they will sell you to the emissaries, or at least to a slave trader," Flint answered.

Aaron gratefully remembered he was a Taker; not to

mention he was traveling with Tobias, who had somehow grown even taller and stronger over the last few months. They would be all right.

Flint led the boys further and further into the city while he was talking. Beggars, rather than half-naked women, filled the corners now, and rats scurried away as they walked. Here and there, they heard yells and crying babies, but the city was quieter as they moved away from the harbor.

"Here," Flint said, stopping them in front of a wooden door, flanked by a sign that said 'Eldrik's Honor'. Had he not halted them, they would have never noticed the discreet door. "It's one of the places where The Rule's people drink, if they want to avoid the rowdier company, and the company of those that might bear grudges against them."

Flint pushed open the door and let Tobias and Aaron enter, before following them. Inside was a calm atmosphere, scarcely populated tables and low-voiced conversations. The air even seemed fresher here, and on a small stage at the end of the room, a young woman played a lute. Something about her caught Aaron's eyes, and he couldn't stop looking at her while Flint led them to a table near the bar.

Her eyes, he thought, *they look different. Blue or green? Perhaps even Brown.* He couldn't tell across the distance, and he longed to Take just so that he could see them clearly. *Or is it her face? No, it looks ordinary, I suppose. Her flat brown hair, black shirt vest and gray pants don't stand out either. But she is... Something different.* A strange but comfortable tingling sensation spread through his stomach just from looking at her.

Flint gestured for the barkeep to bring them beers, and Aaron forced himself to look away from the lute player.

"How is drinking beer going to help us find a boat going to Roak?" Tobias asked in a low voice.

Flint looked at them with raised eyebrows, smiled, and blinked. Then said loudly, so all the people sitting at the nearby tables would hear, "To Roak? I'm not going anywhere near that place! Although the price you offer would be tempting enough for me to do the detour. Fifty gold coins? What a bargain. But no, I am headed south, I'm afraid."

"Shh, what are you doing?"

Flint's outburst had snapped Aaron back to reality, and he looked around to see if anybody had heard them. Sure enough, several people were looking at them from around the room...

"Just relax. Now, we wait and see what happens." Flint sounded as careless as if they were playing cards back on Blackskull, and not at all like they were sitting in a Rule establishment, surrounded by potential enemies in a city full of gods-knew what kind of dangers.

A moment later, the burly barkeep placed three beers on the table in front of them. He looked at the two boys for a moment. "Roak, you say? Those women go back and forth to Roak now and then." He nodded to a nearby table where two young women sat with goblets of wine, one with brown hair in long curls, the other blonde with straight hair.

"Now don't you go telling stories about us, Rufus," the brown-haired woman said as she rose from her chair.

The barkeep raised his eyebrows in a warning gesture and returned to the bar, while the woman walked over to their table, a careless swing to her step. She wore a red dress with decorative brown embroidered patterns along all the edges, and a slim belt in brown leather hung around the waist. The belt held a sheathe, which revealed the hilt of a bejeweled dagger, as well as a heavy coin pouch hanging in plain sight, suggesting she came with means. Her confident walk, and her expensive clothing, sent Aaron wondering about her age and trade: at least ten years older. Perhaps even from a noble house? She was beautiful, clearly, although Aaron found he would much rather spend his time looking at the lute player.

"He is right, though. We are going to Roak. Tomorrow, in fact. So, why do you want to go there?"

Aaron realized he had been staring and quickly drew a large gulp of beer while looking away. He accidentally inhaled half of the drink and sputtered all over the table to save himself from the imminent drowning. He was becoming almost as bad at being around women as Crook. Coughing heavily, he was all too aware that Flint and Tobias were staring at him, along with the beautiful woman, and probably every other person in the tavern, of course—including the lute player.

Desperate, he Took a stream of intelligence and confidence from a nearby patron and cleared his throat. "Our uncle," he coughed. "He's a farmer there." He waited another moment while holding down a cough before he continued. "But that's not the real reason. We want to work for The Central Rule. For years, our life on the outer islands has been tough, from the purges, hard winters, and failing harvests. We decided to seek a better fate."

The woman measured Aaron with her eyes. "Pragmatic. I like it. And perhaps even handsome when not showered in beer. Too bad there's only two of you while we are three sisters. That might just lead to drama."

Aaron blushed and looked away, hoping she wouldn't notice his burning cheeks. Tobias looked almost as helpless, although he had strategically avoided pouring beer all over himself.

"Would you allow us passage with you to Roak then?" Aaron asked after composing himself with some more confidence from the nearby gentleman—who now looked pale and worried, like he was ready to get up and run away from the women that sat across from him, trying to have a conversation.

"We would." She carried a scent of spice and soap, Aaron noticed. "But we can't."

"Why not?" Aaron protested.

"Pragmatic but naive," the lady stated. "A pity."

"What?" Was she mocking him? Aaron breathed deep and asked again in a calmer tone, "Why not, if I may ask?"

"You may, and I will even answer, simply because one cannot smuggle people into Roak. And that's it."

The last words she said louder, and looked Aaron deep in the eyes for just a second. Then she got up and returned to her table.

For a moment, Aaron was about to protest, but then he noticed the slip of paper she had left on the table. It read: "Red dock, Maiden's Breeze, hide under deck before sunrise, fifty gold coins."

He sighed and felt dumber than he had in a long time. They had definitely spent too long with Crook and Lulu.

Flint paid for the beers, and the three left the tavern. Aaron sent a last look at the lute player, which sent his stomach turning over with the same strange tingling feeling. Flint seemed in a good mood, lively with stories of old times and adventures. Only when they were several hundred yards away, he stopped his stories and turned to the boys with a serious face.

"At least one of those sisters is a Giver. The fact the girl could overhear the barkeep, and the way you two acted... And I sensed some Giving too, though it was hard to discern. It was subtle, not like when they fight. I might be too superstitious, but beware. Whatever you say close to these sisters, they might hear you."

Chills ran down Aaron's spine. A Giver. Right there in the tavern? He hadn't felt anything.

"And, perhaps just as importantly, they might suspect that one of you is also a Giver," Flint continued.

"Why would they suspect that?" Tobias asked.

"Because some Givers can sense when we channel, and Aaron was Taking during the conversation."

"You were?" Tobias asked, looking at Aaron with surprised painted on his face.

Aaron nodded. "Just a little."

"Also, two young boys traveling together with so much gold to pay? It is too good to be true, and the most likely explanation would be that you have more up your sleeve than the eye can tell. So, I still think they are your best chance to get to Roak, but just be careful. And definitely don't show your powers in front of them again. You are both strong enough to make it, even without Taking... Perhaps also dumb down a bit. Stuff like that."

They all stood in silence for a moment, before Flint continued. "I am so worried for you two. But, you will do okay, I am sure. I wish I could go with you, but I am afraid I'd be little help, since I am technically speaking 'wanted' by The Central Rule across the entire Worldsea. But, if you ever need me, I will do anything I can to help you. *Anything*. Now, let's pack your bags and settle for the night. You have new adventures ahead of you."

They returned to Blackskull and packed their belongings. Dried meats, water pouches, hundreds of gold coins, fake documents stating fealty and employment to The Central Rule—just in case—and an extra set of clothes. Then they slept a few hours before getting up in the middle of the night. Flint led them to the red dock, as the brown-haired lady's note indicated.

"Goodbye, for now," he said, embracing each of the boys. "I will see you again, I am sure. And, please. Save Kathrine and Bria. But even more importantly, be safe."

With these words, he turned on his heels and left them. Aaron noticed he Took away all their worries, their tiredness, and even some of their sadness. As Flint got further away, the effect faded, leaving an emptiness inside Aaron. *At least this time, I got to say goodbye,* he thought. A part of him wanted to chase after him, stay with him on Blackskull, and be a pirate. He felt Tobias's hand on his back.

"It's going to be okay. We will come back, remember?"

Aaron didn't know if he believed any of that anymore. It had been so long since they had left Great Oaks, saying those very words. He clenched his fists as they turned and walked down the red painted dock to search for their ship. They were so close to Bria and Mom now: too close to turn around.

"Maiden's Breeze," Tobias read from the side of a two-masted boat. Far smaller than Blackskull, but bigger than the old merchant's vessel they had stolen in Great Oaks. They looked around, surprised to see that no one kept watch over the vessels. Then they stepped aboard and opened the hatch to the ship's hold. They exchanged a few glances, then jumped down into the dark storage room. The hold was empty, except for a few bags and boxes, and no comfortable place to lie down. Not that Aaron could have slept even if they had a bed: his heart was beating fast and his palms getting sweaty, as silence fell over them like a suffocating blanket. He listened carefully for any sound of guards or the three sisters. Could it all have been a trap? Long minutes passed, and he heard nothing except his own breathing, eventually joined by Tobias's quiet snoring. How could he possibly sleep in this situation? Then, his own eyelids started to feel heavier, and finally the ship's gentle rocking lulled him to sleep.

Chapter Twenty-Two

Aaron woke to the familiar bobbing of a ship in motion, and it took him a moment to realize they weren't on the Blackskull anymore. They must have already left the harbor. He took a bit of Tobias's hearing to be certain. Indeed, they were at open sea.

"Morning, sleepyheads."

Aaron spun around and looked up at the face of the blonde-haired woman sitting at the table with the brown-haired woman from last night. Tobias woke as well, the war hammer already in his hand.

The blonde woman seemed amused and not at all intimidated. "I've allowed myself to take the fifty gold coins, thank you very much," she stated with a smile.

Tobias and Aaron grabbed their purses, both considerably lighter.

"Per person."

Aaron was about to protest, but Tobias put a hand on his shoulder.

"My name is Miandra. You can call me Mia. And what are your names, mysterious boys from the outer islands?"

They introduced themselves while they stepped up on deck. It was a beautiful day, a fresh breeze carrying them eastwards. Aaron noted the sails were perfectly set on the two masts, and the wooden deck was well-treated and cared for.

"About time," a voice called from the stern, and Aaron's heart did a somersault as he looked up and saw the lute player from last night sitting cross-legged, tuning her lute and looking down at him from the elevated deck with a smile.

"This is Eleanor," Mia said.

"Call me Ellie," Ellie added.

"I'm Tobias," Tobias called.

"And I am Aaron. You're the lute player from last night," Aaron declared, his face widening into a smile. Something about her was definitely special.

"Aye,"

Aaron's mind was racing, equal parts trying to make up something clever to say, equal parts trying to decipher that strange feeling in his gut. It wasn't as strong as yesterday when he had first seen her, but still...

"And my name is Patricia—I don't think I presented myself properly yesterday," the brown-haired woman in the red dress from the night before called from the ship's wheel. Her hair was tied back today, and she looked more serious than she had the day before.

"But we all call her Petra," Mia added in a low voice.

"So you are sisters?" Tobias asked as they joined Ellie and Petra on the main deck.

"Indeed," Ellie answered. "Petra is in charge, most of the time anyway, while Mia is the nice one of us. And I just play the lute."

Mia took the word. "But please, tell us more about you two. Why do such promising young men want to serve The Rule?"

Aaron shrugged. "Who else is there to serve?"

"Well, as Ellie said, we usually just do as Petra says," Mia answered.

"Indeed. Actually, could you two boys help coil those lines?" Petra asked in a tone that didn't invite rejection. She pointed to a row of loose lines, and Aaron and Tobias set to work.

"And who do you serve then?" Tobias asked Petra, his hands busy coiling the thick rope around the pen. The woodwork was smooth, and the lines of the highest quality.

"The Rule, of course," Petra answered. "But mostly we just serve ourselves. The Rule just happens to pay well."

"I guess we are not that different then," Aaron said.

"Well, the difference is that you guys are smuggling yourself into an epicenter of soldiers and emissaries, most likely to end up dead or imprisoned. In contrast, we are certified traders of The Rule, and worst case, we will sell you as slaves," Ellie said.

"So what is it, are you traders or smugglers?" Aaron asked in a brisk tone, too fast to stop himself. He looked at Ellie, and suddenly it was clear to him: she sat, a calm smile on her face, but when he concentrated—and searched his mind for just the right signal—there wasn't a doubt: she was Giving emotions to him. Thin, sensitive streams of energies flowed from her in patterns so subtle that they were almost impossible for him to sense, and nothing like the charging waves of Flint's power.

"Bold words for a boy at our mercy," Petra said, a teasing tone to her voice. Aaron was too perplexed by his discovery of Ellie's power to answer. "Pragmatic but naive, handsome but somewhat dumb."

The three sisters laughed, and Aaron felt as Ellie's influence faded out. *Is this why I feel so strange about her?* he wondered.

"So... What, do you actually trade? It seems your cargo hold is pretty empty?" Tobias asked.

"Information," Mia answered. "And news. Sometimes, rare scrolls."

"Information about what?" Tobias pressed on.

"Curiosity can get you far, though often in the direction of trouble," Petra said. "But it is no big secret. We sell the information we pick up while traveling the outer islands, such as news of aggressive storms, ruined villages, pirates, and where they might be found... Oh, did you know that man you spoke to last night?"

"No, we saw him arrive on a large ship and hoped he might be going to Roak," Aaron replied. He forced himself to focus on the conversation, while he tried his best to keep an inner shield up, in case Ellie tried to Give to him again.

"That man was The Raven. The famous pirate. You have, unbeknownst to yourself, conversed with one of the most dangerous men outside the grasp of The Rule. That's why we are heading to Roak today, to let them know he is on Tally. Too dangerous for us to catch him ourselves, but The Rule will take care of it," Ellie said, casual as ever.

Aaron stiffened. They would send out emissaries to catch his dad and the crew? He hadn't even considered the risk they were taking to get them this close to Roak... Surely they would kill his dad, Lulu, and the rest of them the first chance they got. Should he try to stop the sisters from telling about Flint and the crew? If there was any way possible—

"Why so quiet?" Mia asked.

"I... Er, I was just shocked to hear that we had been talking to The Raven without knowing it. So... How much does The Rule pay for such information?" Aaron fumbled. He had to find a way to help his dad before he said too much.

"Well, if you think you can sell it to them first, you can forget about it. The emissaries wouldn't trust two boys like you. But the pay is good, especially if it should lead to successfully bringing down such an infamous band of pirates."

Aaron wished he could discuss the situation with Tobias, but as Flint had told them, there was no way they could talk. Someone could hear even the slightest whispers, with their hearing enhanced by a Giver. Instead, they just kept coiling the lines while Aaron thought hard about what to do. Next to him, Tobias looked equally distressed, as he kept looping the rope in inconsistent sizes, as if he had never done it before. Finally, Aaron took a chance and channeled a stream of intelligence from Tobias.

This dramatically decreased the already low quality of Tobias' work, and Aaron hoped the sisters didn't notice how Tobias was basically just moving rope from one hand to the other now. *Better to spread it out a bit,* he thought.

Carefully, he reached out, and took intelligence from Mia and Petra. He dared not touch Ellie in case she sensed it. This was a challenging level of precision, taking a bit from each, while aiming away from Ellie.

When he finally managed it, he could comprehend the scenario in much greater depth, though he no longer felt the emotional gravity of the situation. He also realized he had to pretend to be less intelligent than he actually was, but still persuade the sisters to not reveal Flint's location to The Rule.

"We wouldn't dare try to sell such secrets. I fear our work will be by the blade, or more likely by the plow. But you mentioned the price is higher if they catch the pirate. What if The Raven is already gone when they arrive at Tally? What if they think that you... That you lied?"

Carefully, Aaron Took bravery from both Mia and Petra.

"They would get angry. It would be terrible for our business," Mia burst out.

Petra nodded in agreement, while Ellie glared at her two sisters. "Since when have we feared the emissaries like that? They know they can trust us, we've never misled them. At least not a lot."

Aaron slowly let go of his channeling, hoping that the seed of fear had been planted. This would have to do for now. "We went out drinking with him all night," he said in a casual tone. "Didn't seem like a pirate captain to us, did he?"

Tobias shook his head.

"Anyway, he was carried back to his ship, too drunk to

walk, his crew insisting they would leave first thing in the morning. Heading north, I believe."

Would the bluff work? Aaron felt sweat dripping from his brow. It had been exhausting to perform such precise Taking, but he hoped it would be enough to sway their minds.

A long moment of silence drew out before Ellie smiled and said, "We will see. Thank you for your honesty."

The rest of the day, they chatted about more relaxing matters while maneuvering the ship in the gentle wind. They passed several ships from The Rule, but none of them made any effort to intercept them. Evidently, the Maiden's Breeze was a well recognized ship on these waters.

The sisters seemed delighted with the company, and the boys happily shared stories from their home. Tobias looked proud as ever when the sisters said they had heard of Fero Island and the famously high-quality iron from the Iron Peaks. Ellie even had a blade in a peculiarly dark metal, which she claimed was made from an iron alloy transported all the way to Roak from Great Oaks. She let each of them hold the dagger, and Aaron was surprised by how cool and heavy it felt in his hand. Ruben would have been thrilled to see such a piece.

Finally, as the last red rays of sun disappeared behind the horizon, they had dinner in the big room below deck. The sisters served sweet wine, fresh bread and cheese, and various fruits that Aaron and Tobias had never seen before. Then the three sisters agreed on watch duties, and dismissed Aaron and Tobias to the storage hold they had been hiding in earlier, but—to their great joy—offered them a rich stash of blankets to make simple mattresses and covers, turning the small storage room into a pleasant bedroom.

Aaron lay down, enjoying the familiar rocking of the boat and the sounds of waves outside the protective wooden hull of the ship. He could barely believe it. They were going to Roak! He had almost forgotten that Ellie was a Giver: after all, it had been a lovely day, and his heart bubbled with joy. Hopefully, he would see her again—and Petra and Mia too, of course. Still, there was something special about Ellie... He had almost dozed off when Tobias interrupted him.

"Aaron?"

"Yes?"

"What if... What if we are too late?"

A chill ran down Aaron's spine. He had pushed away that thought for so long. It was fall now, and almost a full year since Mom and Bria were kidnapped.

"We won't be," he replied, ignoring the lump in his throat.

"But what if we are?" Tobias insisted.

Aaron thought for a moment. *If someone has hurt my mom and Bria. Or killed them...* A bitter anger ignited in him.

"If anyone has hurt Mom or Bria, I will make them regret it. I fought all those soldiers on the battleship, remember? And I am much stronger now."

"I'm not sure if that's the right thing to do..."

"They deserve it, and worse!"

"I guess... But, what would it help us? Or anyone?"

"So they cannot do the same to anyone else!" Aaron felt the spark of anger growing in his heart. "Just think of what they did back in Great Oaks. How many people died when the reapers came for Bria?" *Not to mention they killed Luna*, he thought.

"Perhaps the emissaries deserve it, yes... But I don't think the soldiers know what they are doing. Or have any choice in the matter."

"They choose to work for The Rule."

"But, so do the sisters. And they seem like nice people."

"They are going to tell The Rule where they can find my dad!" Aaron burst out. "And then The Rule will come and kill him, and Lulu, and all the others."

"Perhaps... Perhaps you are right..." Tobias replied, and Aaron calmed a bit.

"How about this: if it comes to a fight, I'll try my best to hold back a little? And, hopefully, we won't even have to fight at all," Aaron offered.

Perhaps Tobias was right, at least to some degree. Still, he couldn't make any promises if Mom and Bria had been hurt or killed—and as much as he appreciated Flint's teaching about controlling his power, he still couldn't find pity in his heart for anyone working for The Rule.

"And what if Bria and Kathrine have been turned to work for The Rule as Givers?" Tobias pressed on.

"They would never do that," Aaron replied, surprised by the certainty in his heart.

"Just... If they have, promise me we won't fight against them. I... I don't think I could do that."

"Of course not, that would be ridiculous. But they won't be. They'd never do that..."

Tobias nodded, his face painted with worry. It took a long time before either of them fell asleep that night.

Aaron kept his eyes closed a while after he woke up. The hull was thin enough that he could hear the waves gently pushing against the side of the boat, and seagulls calling somewhere in the sky above. He would miss the sound of the ocean; hopefully, it wouldn't take them long before they could leave Roak again, with Mom and Bria. He yawned as he stretched, careful not to wake Tobias as he went up on deck.

A cool fall breeze filled the two sails, and the sun shone from a cloudless blue sky. And there, on the horizon, was Roak Island. Finally, he understood why the place was so hard to get into: it stood as a dark mountain, fifty yards of black, vertical rock piercing straight from the sea. Spiky rocks protruded from the ocean around it, as if nature had felt the need to add further defenses, in case a boat should get too close.

"Looks like a welcoming place, doesn't it?" Ellie called from the wheel, a grin on her face.

Aaron caught eye contact with her for a moment, feeling his stomach drop in a warming flutter of nervous happiness. She looked beautiful, and her eyes were... Once again, he noticed the strange tingling: she was Giving him something, though he couldn't tell what it was. Was this fluttering feeling from her Giving, or was it his own feelings? He couldn't tell, and he wished he could focus enough to block her out. For now, he just had to tread carefully.

"Looks like a good place to live with our uncle," he said, walking up towards her, with a smile he hoped looked casual and relaxed.

"Certainly. He's a farmer, you say?"

"Yes."

"Interesting. He must live outside the city, then?"

"I... Yes, by his fields and sheep," Aaron replied.

Hopefully she wouldn't ask too many questions, but at least he had a fair idea of what to answer, as long as it revolved around the life of a farmer, assuming that farmers in Roak weren't too different from those around Great Oaks.

"Must be a wonderful life, growing crops and herding sheep," Ellie answered with a yawn. "Can you take over here? Just lead us south around the island."

She let go of the wheel and stepped away from the helm so Aaron could take her place.

"Really?" Aaron asked in surprise at her trust in him.

"Sure, just don't get too close to the rocks. I can tell you and your friend know your way around a ship, and I could use a nap." She sent him a smile that made his knees go soft and headed to the door leading into the body of the vessel.

Aaron took the wheel and did as instructed. Soon, Tobias joined him and helped with the sails. The Maiden's Breeze was much more responsive to any changes in the rigging than Blackskull had been, and it was a joy to test their skills on the fast ship.

They spent the morning sailing around to the southern end of the island, and in the afternoon they reached a wide opening in the black mountains where a fjord pierced into the otherwise impenetrable landmass. The sisters explained this was the only way into Roak, and that the fjord led all the way to the heart of the island, which itself was shaped like a bowl with the center much closer to sea level than the outer mountain edge. Aaron marveled at the sister's skill with the sails as they rigged them to steer directly into the crack between the mountains, the black rocks towering towards the sky on either side of them. Here and there, shelves were cut into the raw mountain, and catapults and guards stood watch as they made their way up the fjord. After half an hour, Petra ordered the boys to go below deck and stay hidden while they made their way past some closer inspections.

From the hull, they could hear guards board the vessel, and the sisters talking with them, giggling and flirting. Most guards let them pass just like that. Others needed a bribe. Tobias held his hammer ready, just in case someone insisted on checking the cargo, but the sisters did their job to perfection.

Finally, after several hours, Petra knocked on the deck and called the two boys out—they have arrived at the city. The sun had set, and there was a looming darkness which put Aaron's senses on alert. Lanterns and the night sky illuminated the docks enough for him to see the front row of buildings were built in the same black stone as the island itself. Looking around, he noted that the whole city seemed to be built in an enormous valley. Far into the distance, the island grew steep, and the black stone stood like walls towards the world, shining silver in the moonlight. He shivered involuntarily. This whole island was a fortress.

"Welcome to Roak."

"Wow", Tobias said in a low voice next to him. Aaron had to agree; this place was daunting, to put it mildly.

"Now that you're on the island, you can go around pretty much as you like, as long as you stay away from the school," Petra said.

Ellie added, "The official name of the city is Rules Reap, named after the prison in the center. But, over the last few hundred years, it changed to simply being called Roak, since it's the only thing here on the island. And the prison turned into the infamous school, which is there by the spire." She pointed to an enormous spire that pierced into the dark sky from the heart of the city.

Aaron pulled his long sheepskin coat tight around him as they disembarked. An icy wind had picked up, and the air had a smell of frost now the sun had gone down. Despite the cool, the docks were still lively—though in a manner far more orderly than Aaron and Tobias had grown accustomed to from the harbors that Blackskull frequented. Workers carried goods to and from the ships, some beggars sat huddled against the walls, and *many* guards patrolled the area. In fact, a large group was marching towards them right now, led by three emissaries.

"Should we worry?" Aaron whispered, his heart picking up pace. The sight of the emissaries woke both fear and adrenaline in him.

"Not at all," Ellie answered. "Just shake hands and act natural. They greet all who land here."

Aaron tried to relax, but it was hard to ignore that gnawing fear. Next to him, he sensed Tobias stepping out into a wide position, as if preparing for a fight. The war hammer stood between them, leaning against his leg.

The group of guards stopped in front of Tobias, Aaron, and the three sisters. One emissary nodded in greeting to Ellie, who nodded back. Then he reached out his hand to Aaron, who shook it as Ellie had instructed.

All went dark around Aaron as waves of confusion crashed into him. Fear, starvation, fatigue, sadness, all so profound and strong that it nearly made him faint.

Instinctively, he started Taking from all directions. Strength, senses, and bravery from everyone, and a bunch of other things too—anything to help him survive. He barely stayed conscious, let alone in control, from the combination of the violent waves of pain and dizziness that emanated from the emissary and his own aggressive Taking. His weak shielding was useless against the emissary's violating attacks, so he drew in as much power as he could, from anyone close enough for him to reach. A flame of rage kindled in him, along with a nauseating power. He grabbed the war hammer and jumped as high as he could.

With unnatural strength, more strength than he had ever used before, he soared to at least thirty yards in a second. Finally, the pain and confusion faded from the sheer distance, just like his Taking, giving him a moment to overview the situation, his senses and intelligence still sharpened. Thirty-five guards and three emissaries. Plus

Ellie and the two other sisters. He drew the war hammer and launched it while still airborne, sending it hurtling towards the emissary that had just been shaking his hand.

The hammer hit home, and the emissary was slammed to the ground with a moan. Aaron took all the courage he could from the surrounding guards as he fell back towards the ground, and they started to panic and scatter. Some simply collapsed and sobbed. *So far, so good*, he thought. However, as he came closer to the ground, pain and confusion rose in him again. There were still too many Givers left.

He landed beside the war hammer. Almost blinded by his powers and the onslaught of the Givers, he swung it straight through two guards. They flew away screaming. Ready for another—

"Stop!" a sharp voice cut through the chaos in his mind. He spun, ready to attack, but then halted. Mia held a knife pressed firm against Tobias's throat. "You can take his pain, but not his wound. If you move, he dies."

Aaron tried hard to focus for a second, although his nature screamed for him to attack, destroy her, destroy all of them. But slowly, Ellie's Giving and the three remaining emissaries gained power over his mind and his senses. He couldn't shield from it, and slowly but certainly he lost grip of his Taking, as pain, feelings, and all kinds of confusing impressions overwhelmed his ability to keep focus.

"Why?" Was all he could say before he crumbled to the ground. A strike to the back of his head, and he passed out on the cobblestones.

Part 3

The Streets of Roak

Chapter Twenty-Three

Bria woke, her back aching from sleeping on the thin rug hidden under the old abandoned house's floorboards. At least it wasn't freezing anymore. It had been a hard winter since they threw her out from the school and she still woke up at night, shivering in cold and fear, thinking back on how weak she had been that day. She had been lying in a pile of snow for hours, bleeding from the deep cuts across her face, ready to die. Expecting to die. But somehow she survived.

As a reflex, she grabbed her wrist and felt the reassuring patterns of the silver bracelet Tobias had given her. It was her last link to the life she once had, and her greatest treasure. She had been tempted to trade it for food many times when she was starving, but had defiantly kept it.

Carefully, she listened for any intruders before rolling up her rug and a few blankets, leaving the silver bracelet with the bedding. If the guards saw her with it, they would surely assume she had stolen it and take it from her. Then, she pushed away the floorboards, and stuck her head up into the living room of what had once been a family home. Now, the house was full of shattered furniture and glass. A thick coat of dust hovered in the beams of sunlight that entered between the boards sealing off the broken windows. People said a Taker had lived here and avoided the house, thinking it cursed. She dared not sleep in the actual house in case someone broke in, but she had deemed the tight spot under the floorboards safe enough.

Bria quickly reset the floorboards and then went to listen by the door: no sounds. She opened it, scurried out, and shut it behind her. From the outside, it looked like it was nailed shut, with boards crisscrossing the frame; one of her prouder tricks. The street was empty, as usual. Most people avoided this neighborhood, especially in the early morning and at night. After all, most people in Roak were well-off, many holding titles and prominent positions in The Central Rule. They cared little for the homeless, who lived in the intricate web of passages that spread through the city, like a chaotic spiderweb surrounding the school. The school sat in the middle of the web like a fat spider. From everywhere in the city, one could look up and see the black central spire, like a monument to cruelty and control. Bria despised having to look at it every day, although a small part of her missed it too. The school had been a place of fear and torture, but also of friendship. And it was where her mom was, still now.

"Still thinking of going back there?" Tails's voice came from behind her, and Bria swung around while pulling her knife. She instinctively squatted into a defensive position. "You daydream again. Forget to listen."

Tails pushed aside Bria's knife with a sly smile. His curly, black hair was uncombed as always, and almost covered his green eyes. He was shorter than Bria, although he was a few years older. Weaker too, Bria liked to think. But Tails had been in Roak for much longer, and knew his way around. He had earned his name from always running when dangers reared and had taught Bria to do the same since the first time they met. Tails was Bria's only friend in Roak, and—although Bria would never admit this to him—he had been the sole reason she had made it through the winter. He had given her blankets and food, and his cheerfulness, even on the coldest and darkest of days, had helped her believe things would get better.

"What's up?" Bria asked, lowering her weapon and ignoring his question.

"Not much," Tails answered.

"No fresh stories of running from the guards, stealing from the rich, sleeping with beautiful women?"

"Not since yesterday, no," Tails responded with a grin. "But perhaps today we can amend that," he said with a wink.

"Don't even try." Bria laughed and raised the knife again. She liked how he flirted with her, despite her scars. He had never even commented on them, and she almost forgot about them whenever it was just the two of them.

"Not that, the stealing, dummy. Unless you'd be interest—"

Bria cut him off, rolling her eyes and turning to walk down the street. Tails followed next to her.

"Anything in mind?" she asked. "For the stealing, that is."

"For once I have something in this mind of mine, yes. Heard about the ball at the school? Nobility and even royals are attending. Should take up the guards attention. I think it would be an opportune moment to look more at the treasuries of these aforementioned nobles."

"Stealing from the nobles?" Bria asked, slowing her pace. They had never dared such an act before. Surely the punishment would be death.

"Breaking into a noble house, yes. We've done it before. Before your time."

"Yes, and what happened? You ran away, the rest got caught and hanged, I suppose?"

"One time, yes. The other times, no," Tails answered, his voice lowering.

Bria reminded herself again of how little she knew about Tails's past. She had heard he had once had a family, but now he was alone... She shook her head and let it go. There was little room for sadness and consideration on the streets of Roak. Instead, she chewed on the idea a bit. Robbing a house could give them the money to survive for weeks or even months. Perhaps buy clothes. Some nights in a real bed. All tempting ideas, but the risk...

"I was hoping you'd join me," Tails continued. "Because you're great. But also, for reasons I cannot fathom, the sisters seem to trust more in you than me. And for this job, we need a few extra hands."

"You asked the sisters?"

To her own surprise, she felt just a tiny pinch of

jealousy. She knew Tails often met with the three sisters, and they had worked together before. Still, she knew even less about the three girls than she did about Tails, other than that they were surprisingly well-dressed and well-mannered for street people. She assumed they made their money providing a different type of services.

"I talked to them, and they said no," Tails shrugged. "Unless you are part of the mission."

"Me? But... Why?"

"I agree, they don't know what's good for them and—"

Bria interrupted Tails, with a playful push. "Well, I suppose they just want at least one person that won't run away at the first sight of a chicken."

"A rooster, and they had obviously trained it to stand guard! It looked armed! Some people tie knives to their little feet and use them for fighting!" Tails protested.

"Of course," Bria cut in, hoping to change the subject before they reignited what had been their biggest fight to date.

"So, will you come along?"

Bria's stomach decided to join the discussion with a deep rumble. "I'll consider it. When is the ball?"

"Three days from now," Tails answered, and sat down. They had made it to the central market square. It was still early, and merchants were rolling in their wares on big carts. Like every morning, Bria and Tails sat in line with other homeless, offering their help with setting up the stalls. And, as usual, Bria was picked out among the first. She was taller and stronger than any of the others, although

Tails often complained the merchants simply liked her for her long golden hair and her silly western accent.

"See you later then," Bria whispered to Tails, as she got up and followed the merchant to his stall.

It was a beautiful sunny morning, and Bria felt light and happy as she assembled the wooden stall. She had worked for Kirk, the ceramics merchant, several times before, and she knew him to be both kind and well-paying.

"I tell you, if it wasn't for those damn scars, I'd hire you for my stall, even as an apprentice!" Kirk said, as he had so often before, applauding the speed and ease with which Bria finished her work.

"Well, I'll let you know when they go away," Bria replied with a laugh, feeling a sting of pain as she always did when reminded of the scars across her face. They would never go away. Still, she'd learned that humor was the least painful way forward, as most people seemed determined to mention them in every second sentence.

"The pots go in the bottom today, and plates and tiles on the table," Kirk instructed as Bria carefully unloaded the heavy clay pots from Kirk's horse-wagon.

When she was done, Kirk paid her the handsome sum of three copper coins. Enough for both bread and a slice of meat. Bria thanked the plump merchant heartily and returned to the line of homeless waiting for tasks. If she was fast, she could work for several merchants in a single morning. Moments later, she was hired to help a man setup a temporary fence for his horses. Then, a woman wanted her to unload a carriage full of wool. Finally, a noble wanted her to carry his wares while he traversed the market with a business associate. When the afternoon came, Bria sat next to Tails with her little pouch full of coins.

"How much today, Goldilocks?" Tails asked.

"Fourteen copper. And you?" Bria responded with a smile. He always seemed to have a new name for her, but Goldilocks was among her favorites.

"Fourteen! Good gods, you could buy half a mansion for that! You could even... I don't even know what to do with that much money," Tails replied. "I got a good four. A humble and appropriate amount."

Bria looked at it for a moment, then poured her own coins into his hand. "Well, then we have eighteen copper all together."

Tails stared at her. Once again, Bria had to remind herself how uncommon friendliness was among the homeless.

"But we don't spend it on beer this time," Bria stated with a stern look, and held out her purse.

Tails poured the coins into Bria's little leather pouch and quickly kissed her on the cheek. "You're the best," he said, and Bria felt heat filling her cheeks. She quickly turned her face in the opposite direction.

They waited a few more moments, just in case other jobs turned up. Then they got up to leave, Bria walking a few steps behind Tails. On a good day like today, she simply had to do it... As always, there was a small line of the young and crippled who hadn't made any money. Bria gave each of them a copper coin before Tails could object. To her surprise, Tails didn't even complain today, instead he just put his arm around her shoulder and smiled at her. It really was a beautiful spring day, Bria thought. They headed away from the market and towards the cheaper neighborhoods where the coins would get them further.

They walked through the streets arm in arm, excited to have their daily meal.

"A big loaf of bread, sausage, and beer!" Tails said.

"No beer, water is free," Bria replied, poking him in the side.

"A small beer, at least," Tails responded, turning to Bria with innocent eyes.

"To share then."

"A big one to share and—"

"Stop there!" a man's voice rang out from a side street.

Bria glanced over her shoulder just in time to see two guards. She felt Tails's arm pulling her as he was already half-running, but she stood still. They had done nothing wrong, and there was no reason to run. Instead, she turned towards the two guards.

"How may we help you, good sirs?" she asked in the most polite tone she could muster.

The two guards stepped closer, close enough that Bria could smell beer on their breath.

"Just a routine check, Scarface," the first guard stated, as the other patted down Tails for any weapon. They found nothing and continued with Bria. She praised herself lucky that the bracelet lay hidden in her secret hiding spot, and her little knife was too well hidden for the drunk guard to find it. The man was rough, touching her more than he needed to, but he found no weapons and no—

"Aha!" he said in triumph and pulled the leather pouch of coins from its hiding place under her shirt. "Hiding stolen goods, are we?" The guard emptied the coins into his hand.

"We made that money working on the market!" Tails protested.

"Shut up!" The first guard slapped Tails in the face, sending him falling backwards.

To Bria's great surprise, Tails still wasn't running. She herself stood still, although her clenched fists were shaking now. "Sir, we have been working hard at the market today. I am sure the merchants we have assisted will account for this if we go a—"

The guard slapped her in the face too, and she felt tears coming to her eyes as blood streamed from her nose. Warm anger rose in her, and with a scream, she leaped forwards, kicking, punching, and biting at the guards. She had no plan, just anger and rage. It only lasted a moment, then she was lying on the ground, a knee pressed heavy into her chest.

The beer-breath of the soldier was close to her face, his spit hitting her as he spoke. "Take it easy, Scarface." The soldier got up, kicked her in the side, and then they left with her purse.

Bria just lay on the ground, eyes closed, silently taking in the bitter mixture of pain, sadness, anger. And hunger. A hand lifted her head just a little, while another hand brushed her hair back and wiped the blood away from her nose. She opened her eyes and looked up at Tails.

Somehow, he had a smile on his face. Not a happy one, but a smile.

"It's all right, goldilocks," was all he said, and Bria let him hold her for just another moment. Then, the anger returned, and she sat up.

"I'm in. Let's rob a house!" she said, fists clenched and mind determined.

Chapter Twenty-Four

Bria and Tails spent the next two days planning the heist with the sisters. The sisters' better clothing and manners gave them access to the expensive neighborhoods of Roak, and they decided on the best target for the burglary: Lord Willow's mansion. He was supposedly some lesser advisor to King Eldrik, who spent most of his time in The Capital. Usually, his mansion stood well-guarded on all sides, but the sisters agreed that most of the guards would be busy guarding the harbor and the school during the ball.

The plan was for Bria and Tails to break into the mansion together with Ellie, the youngest of the sisters, despite Bria's objections. Meanwhile, the other two sisters, Petra and Mia, would keep watch and provide distraction. This should give them enough time to escape if anything should happen. After all, Tails was a master of escape, and Bria was an even faster runner than him. Ellie argued she would easily hide, run, or simply talk her way out of any situation. Looking at the innocent face of the sixteen-year-old girl, Bria couldn't help but agree on the latter.

Finally, the day came. As expected, most of the guards left and headed towards the school, and as darkness fell over Roak, there were only two guards left. They circled around the house drinking from heavy wineskins, while talking loudly. Bria's heart was beating with adrenaline. She had stolen before to make it through the winter, but this was a whole different level of crime, and images of dangling corpses at the market square galleys flashed before her eyes.

She insisted they stayed hidden, till it was the middle of the night, despite Tails's complaints about the crisp evening air. "At this rate, my fingers will freeze off before I pick any locks!"

Bria finally obliged, as no sounds could be heard from the street, other than the scurrying of rats and pursuing cats, and the two guards who were now drunk, and singing unsavory songs as they walked their repetitive round. Crouched, they snuck their way up to the garden fence that surrounded the mansion. The guards had just left around the corner, and their rowdy song, something about a man and a donkey, grew distant. That would leave them out of sight for at least a few minutes.

"Go!" Bria whispered.

Tails climbed the fence with ease. Silent as a cat, he landed on the other side, swiftly followed by Ellie. Finally, Bria climbed over, just in time, to avoid being seen by the guards as they came back around the corner. Outside the fence, the two sisters had already walked up to the guards and started talking with them. *They do their job well*, Bria thought, as she glanced around.

Surely, they would know it already, if there had been any guards or dogs in the garden. Not to mention roosters, she thought, stopping herself from imitating a rooster's sound behind Tails. To her great relief, all was quiet except for the loud conversation of the two guards now trying to impress the sisters with stories of their victorious bar brawls. The girls giggled and laughed in the flirtatious manner Bria had never understood, but some mastered so easily.

Bria led the group up to the mansion, where Tails pointed to a balcony on the second floor. Without a word, they climbed onto the rough wall. The coarse rocks had plenty of tempting edges to grip, but most were either too sharp and cut their hands, or slippery from mold and moisture. It was a daring climb, and Bria sighed in relief as they finally made it to the small balcony. Up there, they were visible to anyone looking from the street, so they had to hurry: Tails pulled out his lock-picking tools and got to work. Bria felt cold sweat on her brow as his work dragged on. Now and then, the lock made a clicking noise, but it was always followed by Tails swearing.

Finally, after what seemed like ages, they heard a louder click and a triumphant sigh from Tails. "Let's go," he whispered and opened the door.

The room they entered was too dark for Bria to see anything at first, but after a moment, she could make out some details. It was a bedroom, big and luxurious, the bed bigger than any she had seen before. The bedposts reached all the way to the ceiling and reflected the scarce moonlight. Perhaps they were even coated in gold, Bria thought, though she couldn't tell in the dim light. But there were no treasure chests, or other obvious valuables, from what she could see.

"Where do we search for the money, then?" she whispered to Tails.

"We look for valuables, not money. Money is too obvious, so people hide them. Valuables, on the other hand, are displayed openly to brag to guests," Tails whispered back.

"So where do we find the valuables?" Bria hissed.

"I have no idea."

"But you said you've done this before!"

"Not in a house like this! Well, I'll check the bed." Tails jumped into the bed, bouncing on the soft mattress and blankets.

"Tails!" she hissed. The bed looked so soft and warm, and for a moment she was tempted to join him, but they had no time for such shenanigans. Her heart was beating fast, and every sound sent her flinching in alert.

"Oh, sorry. Er, maybe look for drawers or, I don't know, chests."

Tails lazily got up, while Bria and Ellie started rummaging through shelves and drawers. They found various pens and papers, and a map of the Eastern Sea in a little cupboard, but nothing shiny or obviously valuable, although Ellie insisted on bringing the map and a bunch of other documents. Good quality clothes lay stacked on shelves, but were too heavy to carry and too bothersome to sell. The only thing that ended up in Bria's satchel was a small silver comb that lay on the bedside table.

They continued into a living room beautifully furnished with mahogany furniture and a glass chandelier, which must be worth a fortune. A single chair could probably feed them for a month, but how would they possibly carry any of that stuff out of there? Again, they searched cupboards, tabletops, anything, but found no treasure worth mentioning. They were just about to head downstairs when something sparkled and caught Bria's attention.

"Wait!"

Tails and Ellie froze. There, at the top of the stairs, was a chest. *An actual chest*, open, and filled with gold coins. Tails saw it too, and eagerly reached out for it. Bria was too slow to stop him as he lifted the chest, and they heard the distinctive sound of rope being pulled through a pulley system, followed by a thundering "GONG".

"You idiot!" Bria yelled, her ears hurting from the loud noise.

"Well, how was I supposed to know?" Tails asked, perplexed, still holding the chest.

"Just RUN!"

They raced back to the bedroom and the balcony door they had entered through. Guards yelled somewhere in the distance, and they heard the distinctive sound of a metal gate swinging open. Tails was quickest and reached the balcony door first. He threw the chest onto the bed, gold coins raining down on the floor, then he swung the door open and began climbing down towards the garden. Bria followed right after him. Luckily, the two guards were rushing to the front door, not noticing them climbing down from the second-floor balcony. Adrenaline had taken over, and Bria barely thought, just followed behind Tails as fast as she could while the stones cut and tore at her hands. *If only we make it to the grass,* she thought. *I hope Ellie can run!*

At that thought, Bria looked up and realized Ellie hadn't followed them. *Should I climb back up and find her?* She only had a second to consider before a scream interrupted her thoughts. Tails had slid and fallen the last ten feet down the wall. She looked down just in time to see him sprint away, and to see the two guards now looking right at her. Panic grabbed her. Should she climb back up? Jump down and run? She would never make it. And what about Ellie?

Gravity helped make her decision, as she slipped and fell like Tails, praying she would land well and could sprint off after him.

Damn that boy, she thought as she hit the ground, instantly skidding and slamming her head against the wall.

When Bria blinked her eyes open, she was hanging over the shoulder of one of the guards. He reeked of sweat and beer, and could barely walk straight. His buddy who followed behind seemed equally drunk as he swung a lantern back and forth in step with his staggering walk. But where were they? No longer outside. Somewhere inside... Her head hurt, and she had a strange iron-like taste in her mouth.

"Awake yet, princess?" the guard behind her grunted.

"Let me go!" Her head pounded from the sound of her own voice.

"Shut up, Scarface," the guard carrying her answered.

"Let's just throw her in there," the guard with the lantern said, and pointed to a cell.

"No, another floor down. Wouldn't want her to scream and disturb the party upstairs."

Bria thought for a moment... The party? That meant... They were in the dungeon under the school. She had heard of this place: a small maze-like prison. The Rule didn't need it to be big—they always got rid of their prisoners fast.

"You'll be hanged tomorrow at midday. Perhaps a whipping first," the guard carrying her said as they trudged on. "I'm sorry, but that's just how it is."

"Just let me go! I didn't steal anything!" Bria tried to twist free of the burly guard's grip, to no avail. Her heart was beating faster with the realization of what was going to happen.

"You broke into Lord Willow's house. That is an offense punishable by death. If we let you go, it would be us hanging in your place."

They continued down the stairs, the guard with the lantern stepping ahead to light the way. Every heavy step of the guard sent shivers of pain through Bria, and she felt like she was going to be sick. What now? Surviving a whole winter, just to be whipped and hanged at the marketplace... Would Kirk be sad when he saw it? Would the sisters and Tails be there? Confusing thoughts streamed through her head, none of them helpful. But then she noticed a ring of keys in the guard's belt. She had no idea what they were for, but they were keys, and she could reach them from her dangling position. Carefully, she reached down, grabbed the ring, and pushed it up her sleeve.

"Your own private room, princess."

The guard lifted her off his shoulder and thrust her into a cell. Her feet and legs tingled as they had fallen asleep from the long time over the guard's shoulder, and she almost stumbled and fell. They slammed the gate behind her, and she heard it lock with a click.

"See you tomorrow at the gallows."

Bria sank to the floor. Her legs shivered, and she wasn't sure if it was from being carried so long, or from the growing fear in her chest. The moist walls, the unmoving air, and the penetrating cold all brought back memories. Memories of a world she had fought hard to forget; of Mom, shackled to a wall in the catacombs. Fear slowly turned to panic, and she focused on her breathing. In, out. Calm, long breaths. It would be okay, she told herself again and again. The guards were gone, and so was the comforting torchlight. The darkness was suffocating, and the place was dead silent, except weak, rhythmic drips somewhere far away.

Deep breaths. Finally, she mustered the strength to stand. With shaking hands, she pulled out the keys and found the lock in the darkness. One after another, she tried them. Her hands were shaking as the lock rejected the keys, one by one. All the while she listened for footsteps, but there were none. Images flashed before her eyes. Pictures of chains, icy darkness, whips and cuts and... 'Click'.

The door unlocked, and Bria let out a sigh as the images faded. Quickly, she pushed through the door and reached for the opposite wall to guide her in the impenetrable darkness. The stones were rough, moist, with sharp edges that cut her hands now and then, but she dared not let go. Dared not get lost in the darkness. So, she followed the wall in the direction she thought she had come from. The dungeon was like a maze, and the corridors went on and on, while Bria wondered if she would ever find the exit. More likely, someone would notice she had escaped... or find her at the end of some endless tunnel and whip her harder for her failed escape attempt.

Finally, her darkening thoughts were interrupted as she turned a corner and saw light from a side tunnel spilling into the passage. The air was fresher here, and the light flickered, like a flame rustled by the wind. Quietly, she snuck closer, and carefully peeked down the side tunnel.

Indeed, a torch hung on the wall next to a heavy wooden door. The way out, Bria presumed. But next to it stood the two guards. Should she somehow distract the two men? Wait for them to leave? Her palms were sweaty and her heart pounding. Behind her was only darkness. Perhaps she should hide and hope they left?

The voice of one guard interrupted her thoughts. "... She is from the far west. A monster."

Bria pulled back from the corner and held her breath to better hear the words.

"They say even the emissaries cannot keep her down.

Tied her up in some special cell in the catacombs, they did," the other guard replied, his voice slurred from the alcohol.

"Aye... Evil matters, such powers."

"Better if they killed her, I say."

Bria felt a strange rush of pride. For months, she had pushed away the images of her mom's weak body, chained to the catacomb walls. But this must be her they were talking about. So, she was still fighting, somehow.

"Dammit! My keys are gone!"

A loud noise filled the hallway as a chair was knocked over and fell to the ground. The sound of heavy boots shuffling back and forth.

"The thief must have taken them!"

The footsteps grew louder, and Bria's stomach coiled up in ice cold fear as she pressed against the wall. The torchlight was getting close to the corner! She couldn't hide... not here. They were too close! She decided in the flash of the moment and ran back into the darkness from where she came.

The thin leather soles of her worn-out shoes allowed her to move almost silently as she turned another corner and was engulfed in darkness again. Still, she could hear the men's heavy boots approaching, and she tried her best to control her breath. Surely they would hear her heavy panting; if not her heart, which felt like it was about to beat right out of her chest. She ran her hand against the walls, leading her through the blinding darkness. Perhaps there would be a side passage. *Anywhere* to hide?

There! About hip-height was a hole into the wall. Without hesitation, she crouched and pushed into what seemed like a small tunnel of sorts, and she moved several feet in before a damp wall blocked her from moving further. The smell of rot was strong in there, and something crunched under her feet as she positioned herself in the tight space. She dared not think of what she was stepping on, just prayed the guards would pass her without noticing. The light of the torch was closing on the opening to the tiny tunnel.

Footsteps so close. Closer... Bria held her breath as they passed. They hadn't seen her! She waited another long moment before she let out a sigh and squeezed back out from hiding. This would be her only chance for escape.

She ran back towards the side tunnel where she had seen the two guards. She almost missed it in the pitch darkness, but the draft guided her to the heavy wooden door. This had to be the exit! She fetched the keys from her pocket and almost dropped them as a yell pierced the silence from somewhere far below. The guards must have found her empty cell. Adrenaline forced her frozen fingers to work faster. One after another, she tried the keys on the big lock, as thundering footsteps filled the hallway. Key after key failed, some even getting stuck in the lock, so she had to wrench them out. The running came closer, but she forced herself to stay focused.

One more key!

And this time, a distinct 'click'.

Bria pushed the door open, letting in a cool gush of wind. *Fresh air!* Outside, the starry sky gazed down at her and—a guard. He sat, leaned against the wall, and he was...

Snoring? She could hardly believe her luck, as she sprinted across the large open space surrounding the school and into the maze of alleys where she finally stopped and sank down against a wall. She had made it out!

She headed to the market square the next day, like always. It was a normal day, except Tails hadn't been there in the morning, and that the two guards from Lord Willow's mansion were hanged at midday. Bria felt a sting of pain as she watched the ropes tighten around their necks. That would have been her hanging there if she hadn't made it out. And despite how they had treated her, she still couldn't help but feel sorry—even guilty—for their death. If she hadn't broken into the mansion, they would still be alive. She looked away from the dangling corpses; there was no room for sadness or remorse on the streets of Roak.

She stiffened in surprise as she heard Tail's whispered voice close to her ear. "Bria! You're alive!"

She spun around and punched him right in the face. "That's for running away, and being bad at it too, drawing those guards to me!" she said as Tails fell over backwards. The three sisters stared at Tails, then at Bria, then giggled.

"What?" Bria shrugged while Tails got back up.

"Damn, what a blow! I guess I deserved that. But, you're alive!"

"Yes, I noticed. No thanks to you!" Bria felt a tingle of remorse as she turned and saw blood trickling down from Tails' eyebrow.

"Well, I... I am sorry," Tails said, wiping the blood with

his sleeve. "But, since you're alive. I actually have something you've got to see!"

He grabbed her hand and pulled her through the crowd and down a narrow side street. The sisters followed, and the small group continued around corners, through narrow passages, and down a residential street, not fancy, but nicer than the streets they usually frequented. Finally, they stopped in front of an abandoned house.

"What's this?" Bria asked, impatiently.

"My new house!" Tails answered proudly. "Er, I mean, our new house," he quickly corrected. "If you like, at least. It's bought and paid for."

He produced a paper from his inner pocket. It looked like some official document, The Rule signet stamped at the bottom next to several signatures curled in black ink.

"What's that supposed to mean?"

Confused, Bria looked around. Was it some kind of joke? Or a trap?

"Ellie never escaped from the manor," Tails said, pointing to the youngest sister. "She just waited for the guards to run off after us. So, she came to me this morning with a bag full of the coins we left behind!"

Bria's jaw dropped.

"Don't worry about it. We took our share too," Petra, the oldest sister, assured her.

"And we figured you two did most of the work so..." Mia added, the middle sister.

Bria looked from the sisters, to Tails, to the house, and back. It took her at least a minute before she could talk. "But... Why? I thought..." Bria couldn't gather her thoughts around any meaningful question.

"Bria, I honestly thought you were... Well, dead. And I guess I blamed myself. For running, for attracting the guards, for not sticking up for you," Tails said, looking down at the ground. "So when the sisters brought the money, I thought about it a bit. After all, it's not awfully safe to run around with a bag of gold, so an investment seemed smart. And I figured this would have been what you would have wanted. A home, and a place big enough to help other homeless as well. The sisters asked around a bit, and this morning we bought the best house we could afford. And, here it is."

Tails waved his hands at the partly destroyed building. The roof was missing some tiles, and planks covered the windows, but it looked like a robust two-story house. Bria just stood, her eyes wide. This was... Incredible!

"You dumb idiot!" she said, and hugged Tails so hard that he had to remind her he actually needed air to survive. Bria's heart was jumping with joy. They owned a house!

Chapter Twenty-Five

Aaron blinked his eyes open to find the world spinning hazily around him. A strange white light hurt his eyes, and he felt dizzy. The back of his head ached with an intense throbbing from where he was hit, back on the dock.

"He is awake," a voice said. Aaron could vaguely make out the shape of a person.

"Run the test," another voice said.

Streams of extreme sensations rushed through Aaron, and he bent and arched his body, squirming to get away, until darkness engulfed him again.

He opened his eyes again. This place had a different type of bright. *Sunlight.* His hands felt the surface of a smooth stone floor under him, and nausea threatened to overpower him as his memory slowly returned. The sisters had sold them, and they had... He had lost the fight.

"Finally."

Aaron tilted his head to look where the voice had come from. A blue-robed emissary stood just a few steps away. Instinctively, Aaron reached out with his Taking, but was blocked by the emissaries shield.

"The sisters didn't lie about your skill. Untrained and delicate. Such a strange abnormality," the emissary mumbled, as if he was talking to himself rather than to Aaron. "But here there is no one to Take from. No one, but your friend."

He stepped to the side, and Aaron gasped as he saw what was behind him. Tobias hung elevated three feet over the ground, a rope around each arm, pulling them to either side. The ropes reached all the way to the walls, where they went through metal loops and continued down to large hooks. Each hook connected to a large sack that hung dangling over the ground. Tobias was sweating, his face bent in focus and his muscles tightened.

"Tobias!"

"Don't listen to anything he says!" Tobias replied in a strained voice.

"You can Take from him whenever you like," the emissary said, his voice calm. "I won't stop you. Take his strength and fight me."

Aaron carefully reached out with his Taking and concluded that the emissary told the truth. There was nothing stopping him from Taking from Tobias. What was this game?

"Take," the emissary lured him.

"Why? What is this?"

"Don't be stupid. This is your one and only chance. Just Take, and surprise me with your power."

A chill ran down Aaron's spine as he realized the ploy. If he Took from Tobias, the chains would tear his body apart. He felt a tingling sensation of the emissaries Giving; his dazed mind stood no chance of shielding against it, and feelings started to grow in him.

"I won't Take from him," Aaron said, as much to himself as to the emissary. He longed to serve the emissary, and he fought hard to ignore the deep wish to do as ordered. Once again, he reached out towards the emissary, aggressively and with all his Taking. Again, his attack bounced right off the shielding.

"Don't be stupid! The other emissaries would have killed you both by now. You're lucky the sisters came to me, I just wish to study you. Show me your powers, and I will do what I can to let you live. Both of you." The emissary's eyes glowed with eager greed, his voice shrill. "Just Take!"

A wave of pain rolled through Aaron, and he whimpered involuntarily. He looked around for *any* chance of escape. A weapon. *Anything*. They were in a large hall, floor and pillars made of polished black stone. Tall windows let in the yellow light of the sun, but they were too high for him to reach without Taking... And there was nothing else. No furniture, no torches, only a large door at the far end. The emissary replaced pain with fear, and Aaron curled up trying to make himself as small as possible. His heart was pounding as cold sweat dripped from him.

"Take!" the emissary commanded again, his voice rising.

Aaron couldn't stop it. It was too much. His whole body shivered. *Perhaps I could Take... Just a little. Just a—*

"Aaron!" Tobias's voice cut through the maddening fear, and pulled him to his senses. No! He had to stop! He clenched his teeth and retracted his strands of Taking.

"*Aaron...*" another, much milder voice sounded in his head. A voice he hadn't heard in so long. His mother's voice.

"Mom?" Aaron whispered.

The emissary took a step towards him, wonder painted across his face. "What? Mom?" he asked.

Aaron ignored him. He was sure he had heard her.

"*I am here, my child. You must escape. Escape Roak with Bria!*"

"Mom! We are here to save you!" Aaron yelled through the room, unsure if she would hear him. He couldn't see her anywhere, but he felt a warm feeling of safety spread through him. A feeling of home.

"Shut up! What are you talking about?" the emissary commanded, while frantically looking around for whoever Aaron might be yelling to.

"*I can Give you a little strength. Not much, at this distance. Use it well.*" Kathrine's voice told him.

Aaron felt a surge of power rage through him and looked up just in time to see the worried face of the emissary. *Thank you mom.* Aaron smiled and launched past the emissary, aiming for one of the heavy bags that kept Tobias' arms stretched out.

"Stop!" the emissary screamed, and set into motion with incredible speed.

There had to be another Giver somewhere, Aaron concluded. But, Aaron was faster as he unhinged the first weighted bag from its hook, releasing the pull in Tobias's arms.

Tobias let out a sigh as he fell to the ground and released the ropes from his wrists. Aaron was already fighting the emissary, who was stabbing a dagger at him with incredible speed. The attacks were remarkably fast, and time after time, Aaron found himself unable to dodge fast enough. Cut after cut pierced his skin, and he felt dizzy as blood drained from him, mixed with the onslaught of fear and pain that emanated from the emissary.

"Take from me!" Tobias called from somewhere.

Aaron reached out, but he couldn't focus. Feelings overwhelmed him, and he could barely keep his attention from moving away from the stabbing blade anymore.

"I can't! You have to knock out the—" Aaron said, as the emissary punched him on the side of his head, quieting his words and sending him sprawling on the ground.

Out of the corner of his eye, he saw Tobias leap at the blue-robed figure with a roar, his hands raised and ready to punch.

When he opened his eyes again, Aaron was immediately struck by nauseating pain. Not pain like that from a Giver. No, this was good old-fashioned pain from real injury. It felt like his whole body had been torn and shattered. Still, the first thought in his mind was that he had heard Mom's voice. She had spoken to him, Given to him.

A voice tore him back to reality. "This should show us just the creature you are."

The same emissary as before stood looking down at him in dim light, and Aaron looked around to conclude they were no longer in the big hall, but rather in a sort of prison cell, and everything hurt. Everywhere. He heard a moan and looked to the side. There lay Tobias, in a pool of blood. Cuts and wounds all over. Cold fear rushed through him.

"Go on, take his life. Take his strength if you really are a Taker. You can use it to fight me. Take everything and kill your friend. Then I'll let you live. It's your only way to survive. Your wounds will kill you if you don't."

Aaron reached out, using his Taking to claw against the emissary. Of course, he was shielding himself, and it felt like he was clawing against ice. He could see through, but had no chance of entering. He sent out streams of Taking in all directions, but there was no-one to draw from. No one but Tobias, and he had almost nothing left to offer. So little power left...

"Stubborn. Take your time, if you must. But soon it will be too late, so I suggest you get a move on," the emissary said, his voice dripping with suppressed eagerness. He stood, watching intently, with a notebook and a quill, ready for taking notes.

Aaron's head swirled with pain as he tried to focus. He was dizzy from blood loss. How long had passed like this? *Are you there, Mom?* He tried calling for Kathrine in his head. But there was no reply. *Please, Mom. I need you.*

Nothing. He had to do something before it was too late. Or at least, say goodbye.

"Tobias," he stuttered. His voice came out as a coarse whisper; he looked at his friend, and to his surprise, he saw Tobias's lips moving ever so slightly.

"He is right. Take from me, or we both die. Tell my parents that... I wish... I had said goodbye when I left them." Tobias coughed, twitching in pain from the motion.

Aaron felt an icy fist catch hold of his heart, threatening to burst it. He couldn't do it. Wouldn't do it. It would kill Tobias if he did! And even with Tobias's last sliver of power, would he even be able to stand up? He had never imagined he could feel so broken... Still, perhaps it was the only way? Perhaps it was mercy to end Tobias's pains now. A minute passed, then another. He knew what he had to do, and that it would soon be too late.

"Please," Tobias whispered. "Save Bria for me."

A flame lit inside of Aaron at his sister's name. Tobias was right. It was the only way. His mom had said Bria was out there, somewhere... He waited another minute while gathering his thoughts and energy to Take. This couldn't be the end. At least not without a fight.

"Goodbye, my friend," Aaron whispered.

He wished he could reach out a hand and at least touch Tobias. But he couldn't. He was too injured to move a muscle. Instead, he reached out with his inner streams and sent them deep into Tobias, connected to his very life-force. To his health, his strength. And he felt how Tobias was ready to let it all go.

"Goodbye."

Chapter Twenty-Six

Bria shuttered in the chilly fall breeze and pulled up the collar of her long coat. It had been a long day running errands for the guards, and—once again—she hadn't made it home before nightfall. Up ahead, she could see light streaming from the windows of the house. Her home. Her nostrils filled with a rich smell of roast and rosemary, and she could almost taste the food before even entering the house. She reached the door and stepped in, hanging her jacket, leaving her boots just inside the door, and settling into her wool slippers. The fire burned merrily in the fireplace, and the big living room was warm and illuminated in a welcoming hue of red and orange. Her stomach growled in anticipation as the magnificent smell of food intensified from the kitchen.

"Perfect timing!" Tails called from the kitchen, followed by a ruckus of pots and pans.

Bria's heart melted as she looked at the dark wooden table set for two. Tails had even lit candles and served two goblets of beer. He stepped out from the kitchen, a brown apron around his waist and the large cooking pot full of whatever it was, that gave such an amazing smell.

"Welcome home, Goldilocks."

She rushed up and kissed him on the cheek, before sitting on one chair. He placed the pot on the table, sat down, and served a large portion of stew for each of them.

"This is delicious!" Bria burst out as he took the first bite.

She hadn't tasted food this good since Great Oaks! Or perhaps at the great dining hall at the school, but that was part of her memory she refused to let in. The meat was tender, and the herbs and spices were perfectly balanced. To Bria's great joy, Tails had shown interest in cooking and had become better and better at it during the six months they had lived in the house.

Tails blushed and took a bite. "Well, perhaps short on salt," he argued, while Bria ate with the speed and rigor of a person who had starved for days. "Easy dear, we have plenty!"

"Too good! Can't talk!" Bria answered as she pushed some bread into her already full mouth.

Since getting the job running with messages for The Rule soldiers, she was always hungry. It took a good half hour before she finally leaned back in the chair, too full to even think of another bite. She noted Tails had only eaten two full plates, whereas she had eaten three and a half, and she burped proudly. What a life they had made for themselves.

"I don't know how you do it, my dear Tails."

"Easy. Fry the onions and the meat first, while you chop—"

"Not the cooking, silly, the whole thing. You make me happy," Bria interrupted, and reached out her hand. Tails too reached out and took hers.

"Well, this time I had help," Tails answered. "I met the sisters, and they practically paid for the meal as if... Wait, that reminds me. I almost forgot."

"Forgot what?" Bria asked, curious to hear what the three girls were up to now. Any story with the sisters was usually an interesting one.

"The sisters had made a whole bag full of coins from bringing in a Taker last night. Can you believe it? An actual Taker! I didn't even think such creatures existed," Tails said, gesturing with his free hand for dramatic effect.

"Oh, really? Well, I knew they existed, but I thought they'd be too rare and dangerous to catch one. Can't be as bad as the stories they tell, if the sisters could bring one in."

"Apparently they tricked him into going with them willingly," Tails said. "The poor boy was going to Roak, for whatever unfathomable reason, and they simply brought him along. Ellie said he went wild once he realized they were trading him in, and that he beat up a bunch of guards and even an emissary down at the harbor before they could stop him. But they got him chained up in the end."

Bria raised an eyebrow. She'd heard about a fight at the harbor last night, though she assumed it was nothing more than a drunken brawl. She fiddled with her silver bracelet, as always, when she thought. Karim had mentioned Takers, and how they could threaten The Rule. Even a single Taker...

"Well, the real reason I wanted to tell you was that the

Taker apparently traveled with a friend, and the two of them came from out west. Like you. What was the name of your old place again?"

Bria glanced up at Tails. A frightening thought struck her, but she dismissed it immediately. *It couldn't possibly be...* "Great Oaks. Fero Island. Where were they from?"

"Something like that, but I don't remember—"

Bria's heart skipped a beat. "Damn it, Tails. I... They could be... Could be coming for me!"

She felt dizzy. Just a moment ago, she had been too full of food to move, and too in love to worry about anything. Now she leaped to her feet, adrenaline pumping through her veins. She knew she was probably fooling herself, but... What if she wasn't? What if Tobias had come to save her, and dragged Aaron along on the trip? Something she had both dreamed of and feared. "We have to go find the sisters," she said and got up. "Now!"

Tails stumbled to his feet. "Now? Why?"

"I had a family in Great Oaks, remember? A life!"

"But no one in Great Oak was A Taker. Right?"

"Of course not. But I'm also not a Giver, and that didn't stop The Rule from kidnapping me," Bria answered and pointed to the scars on her face. She was already pulling on her boots and grabbing her pouch. In it, she had a small knife and the keys for the Roak dungeon. A secret reminder of her escape, that even Tails didn't know about.

They stumbled out the door, locked it, and headed down the street.

"But, Bria, no one knows where the sisters live!" Tails argued, trying to keep up with her pace.

It was true that the sisters had always made a big effort to keep their home private. No one questioned this, as it was an unfortunate habit for the homeless to steal from each other. Actually, the only well-known home of any so-called street people (who Bria insisted they were part of, despite being home owners) was Bria and Tails's house. And Tails had strongly opposed this for several weeks before he finally accepted.

Usually, the sisters would head towards the eastern part of the city when they went home, and that was all Bria really knew. So that was the direction she went, maneuvering through the dark, labyrinthine streets she knew like home. She wasn't worried about the darkness. She knew the city, and she and Tails could outsmart any guard and outrun any street gang, if they couldn't downright defeat them in a fight.

"Bria, wait! Where are we going?"

"To a bar. I bet Ellie goes to bars close to her home," Bria answered. This was the best clue she could come up with, as she knew Ellie worked as a bard whenever she had the chance.

"Good point."

Finally, they made it to the rich neighborhood east of the marketplace. Here, the streets were wider, and horse-drawn carriages drove or parked along the road. Bria had always wondered why the sisters went this way home at night, but they must have found themselves some lucrative hideout here.

She ignored the suspicious looks from the many guards

they passed, and pulled her hood deep over her face to cover her scars as they went into the first tavern that sounded like it had a musician playing. Bria went straight to the bar. There stood a fat barkeeper with a well-trimmed mustache and an apron that had probably been white once. Now, both the mustache and the apron carried the stains of what Bria hoped was tomato soup.

"Do you know of Ellie, a lute player and singer?"

"Who's asking?"

"This one."

Bria slid a silver coin over the table, ignoring Tails's objections.

The barkeeper's eyes lit up, and he quickly swiped the coin into his fat hand. "Sure, I know her. But she's not here today."

"And where might she be? Any other places with musicians such as her?"

The barkeeper held out his hand, and Bria put another silver coin in his palm with a dissatisfied grunt.

"Two streets up, at The Cauldron. She plays there most nights."

Bria turned and headed off without sparing a moment for a thanks. *Two silvers! This better be worth it.* She walked fast, dragging Tails after her till they reached 'The Cauldron', a well kept building with a bard on an elevated stage, but it wasn't Ellie. Once again, Bria slid a coin across the bar and asked for Ellie.

"Sure, she plays here now and then. She's a nice girl."

"Indeed. Any idea where she lives? Or where she might be tonight?"

"None. And don't you go looking for trouble with her, she's a nice girl, as I said, and well-connected."

"We don't want any trouble. We just have an important message for her."

"Very well, very well. The gentleman there might know where she is."

The lady pointed to a young man sitting at a table with a group of friends. He looked like the kind of man Ellie might fancy, but far too much like Marcus, and clearly like a son of a noble house for Bria to ever like him. His blonde hair was combed back, and his skin clean and velvety, giving Bria the thought that he had never worked a single day in the sun. She nodded and went straight to the table, ignoring her instinctive dislike of the young man. The conversation quieted as she neared.

"What do you want, Scarface? And what's up with your skulking friend back there?" another clean-skinned young man at the table said.

Bria looked back at Tails, who did in fact look like he was skulking. Other than that, she ignored the rude comment and turned to the young man the bartender pointed out.

"Sorry, I am in a bit of a hurry. I am looking for Ellie, and I believe you know her. I have an important message for her, and I need to find her. Now."

Bria disregarded the stares and whispers of the group of friends. They looked at her in the way drunken young men often did, and any other day it would have earned them a slap across their face. Instead, she grabbed another coin and handed it to the young man. To her surprise, he simply looked at her hand with the coin, then pushed it back.

"Sorry, this knowledge is not for sale. If you are truly a friend of Ellie, tell me something about her that only a friend would know, and I shall help you. If not, get lost."

Bria raised an eyebrow. This man sounded almost honorable. Could she trust him? She had a feeling that she knew what he was fishing for: Ellie's most careful secret. One she had only shared reluctantly after months of friendship and collaboration. The secret that Ellie was a Giver. Perhaps she could let him know without saying too much? She considered it for a moment before Tails intervened.

"Ellie has *given* us much. We just need her address." He emphasized the word 'given' in a way that left no doubt if the listener knew what to listen for.

The young man nodded slowly, and Bria sighed in relief. Tails always had her back, even when he didn't understand her mission.

"Come with me," the young man answered, and got up, to great protests from his friends. He ignored them and led Bria and Tails out of the tavern. A few streets further, they entered an even fancier street, with large houses and gardens populating both sides of the road. Here there were guards every ten yards, and it was not an area Tails or Bria would ever frequent. Likely they'd be thrown straight off the street, if not for the young man who walked with them. Finally, they stopped in front of what appeared to be a small mansion. The young man pointed at the front door.

"Here. The Riverwatch Mansion."

Bria's jar dropped and Tails let out a whistle.

"You shouldn't be here!" Petra hissed. She glanced out from the wide blackwood door, holding it only slightly open. Bria jammed her foot in and pushed. Finally, the door opened and Bria and Tails entered.

"You are nobles!" Tails burst out.

"Yes," Petra answered, rolling her eyes. "How else do you think Ellie, a Giver, could roam around the way she does?"

"And how else do you think you could buy a house without explanation for how you got the money? And why no guards have ever come to harass you at home? We have been holding our noble hands over your place," Mia added.

"But... How can we trust you?" Bria asked, her mind a mess from this new information. She had her hand inside the pouch, holding the small knife in her hand. After all the other things, this really was the drop that tipped the cup.

"You've trusted us for a year already. Just keep doing it, and we are fine," Petra argued. "Now, why are you here?"

Bria hesitated for a moment, then let go of the knife with a sigh. "We will discuss this later. That's not why we are here. Last night, you caught a Taker and his friend. I need to know who they were."

"Oh, sure. Two boys, our age I suppose. But don't worry, the guards will take care of the Taker," Petra answered.

"I'm not worried about that, I just need to know who they are. Names, origin, stuff like that."

"Why do—" Petra began, but Ellie interrupted her.

"They were charming young men, from a place called

Great Oaks. Aaron and Tobias. Aaron was the Taker, Tobias was the handsome sidekick with a rather large—"

Bria gasped. She suddenly felt dizzy and sat down. It really was them, coming here and getting themselves caught after mere seconds on the island!

"Hammer," Ellie said, finishing her sentence. "What's in it for you?"

"Aaron is... my brother. And Tobias was my.... Er..." Bria answered, looking at her bracelet and glancing up at Tails. "He was a dear friend."

Her mind was full of confusing thoughts. *Those idiots!* For so long, she had hoped someone would come and take her back home, but now she wished deeply that they hadn't. They would die because of her! She had to do something... Fear and adrenaline whirled through her, forcing her to her feet, and without a second thought, she stormed out the door. Tails and the sisters called after her, but she was fast. Soon, the concerned calls faded in the distance. The only chance she had—the only hope—was that they would be in the dungeon. And that she wasn't too late.

She gasped for air as she reached the center of Roak. A place she had avoided for so long... In front of her stood the school's black walls, towering above her like a mountain. The place where they had cut her face. Where they had tortured her and still tortured her mom, according to the rumors among the soldiers she helped deliver for. Bria had tried so hard not to think back, and she took a deep breath to keep calm. She didn't have a choice.

A single guard stood carelessly by the rather

anonymous entrance to the dungeon. Few people knew what the door led to, and even fewer would be dumb enough to care about the dungeon. It was a temporary place to keep people before hanging them, nothing more. Silently, Bria unpacked the little knife from her pouch. It wouldn't help much against an armed guard, but it was the only weapon she had. Hopefully, she wouldn't have to use it.

She raised the hood of her cloak, unbuttoned a few buttons in her dress, and walked up to the guard, swinging her hips in a way that she hoped might intrigue him. It felt dumb, but it always seemed to work for the sisters. "Cold evening, isn't it?" she asked as she got close. Hopefully, her scars wouldn't be visible in the faint moonlight.

"Sure is, ma'am," the guard answered. He was young. Good.

"Lonely too." Bria put a hand on the young guard's arm.

"Er… yes. You shouldn't be here, though."

"Really? Then, where should I be?" Bria asked. "Perhaps there's a more private space. What about in there?" She pointed at the door to the dungeon.

"Sorry, no. No one can enter." His voice was shaking slightly.

Is it really that easy? She stood very close now, and she could feel the breath of the young guard against her skin. She couldn't help but quiver at the feeling. "Sounds very private to me, if no one is allowed to enter." She moved her hand on the guard's chest. His heart was beating fast, perhaps even faster than her own. Adrenaline rushed through her, and it was hard keeping her hand from shaking.

"Er... Yes, I guess... What... What should I pay?" the guard finally asked, looking frantic from side to side.

"For you? It's free. I am not really that kind of girl. I just got so lonely tonight," Bria answered.

The guard hesitated, and Bria's heart skipped a bit. *Dammit, I should have said a price...* She started to doubt herself, the knife firmly gripped in the hand that wasn't resting on his chest. She almost had it pulled out, when he finally gave in.

"There's a small chamber for the guards just inside, but we have to be quiet, okay?" he whispered. His voice was shaking, and so was his hand as he unlocked the door and pushed her inside, following behind her.

Bria recognized the hallway from her escape half a year earlier. There was a single torch on the walls, and she blinked as she adjusted to the warm light. Behind her, the guard was about to open another side door, when his gaze fell upon her and he stopped.

"Wait. Those scars. Are you—"

Bria felt panic rise. She had barely dared to think this far ahead in her plan.

"I am sorry," she whispered

Bria put one hand behind his head, leaned in and pressed her lips against his; the kiss deep and long enough for her to pull her knife, and slide it into his throat, sending warm blood gushing over both of them. He squeaked, but the blood in his throat drowned any scream in a gurgling cough. She held on to him as he heaved for air, felt his weight in her arms, and his warm blood washing over her hands. Time felt frozen, and the moment dragged out in painful length until the guard silently sank to the ground.

Tears streamed down Bria's face as she tried to shake his blood from her hand, wipe it off her dress, and wrench it from her hair. She had killed him. He had been almost as young as her, and she had killed him! She tried to remind herself that she had to save Aaron and Tobias, no matter the price. That the young guard would have done the same to her, or worse. But it didn't help. Her legs were shaking, and she felt sick, unable to look down at the body. The tears kept coming as she forced herself to move. One step after another. She reached out to take the torch off the wall, her mind half dazed, when she felt something. A hand. Almost a year on the street had polished her instincts, and they took over; she spun around, her knife raised and ready to attack. Then a wave of calm washed over her. In front of her stood Ellie.

"I ran after you the best I could. After all, we are the one who got your brother into all this trouble," Ellie said.

Bria fell into Ellie's arms, letting her tears run loose.

"Quite a bloodbath you have taken," Ellie commented. "Really would have preferred another day for a hug, but well."

"I... He... I killed him and..." The words got stuck on the lump in her throat. How could she possibly explain or justify this to herself or anyone else?

"You did what you had to do," Ellie said, helping her. "Just don't make it a habit. Now, let's move before we have to kill even more guards to get through this."

CHAPTER TWENTY-SEVEN

Aaron was just about to Take Tobias's life when a crash broke the silence and disrupted his channeling.

"Aaron!"

A voice rang, as from a thousand miles away. Something in Aaron clicked. *Bria. Am I dead?* Suddenly she was there, bent over him, crying, stroking his hair.

"I need you," Aaron could barely whisper. He broke the bond with Tobias and channeled straight through Bria's gentle touch, drawing eagerly, like drinking water after thirsting for days. He took her strength, clarity of mind, her health and tolerance of pain, and multiplied it all manyfold, many more than ever before. His muscles bulged with power, his skin tightened around the open cuts, and his entire body started the fight to survive.

"I'll explain later," Aaron said, as Bria grew pale in front of him. "I can't believe we found you! I missed you so much and—"

Aaron stopped as he took a closer look at Bria. He only

now noticed she was covered in blood, and that long white scars criss-crossed her face. She looked like herself, but so different at the same time. Older, and more serious, and somehow so infinitely hurt... But she was really there. He had found his sister, or rather, she had found him.

"I'll also explain later, little brother. We have to get out of here. Fast," Bria said, her breath fast as if she had been running. Aaron eased his Taking, and her breathing calmed.

"Wait. Tobias. We need to carry him. I... I cannot help him." Aaron looked at Tobias, who stared straight up in the ceiling, his eyes glassy. Bria grew even paler as she looked over at the bloodied shape.

"Is that... Tobias? Quick! Ellie! Help him."

Aaron watched as a girl stepped out from behind Bria. *Ellie!* He jumped to his feet, ignoring the cracks from his broken bones, instinctively drawing even more strength from Bria, preparing to attack. Behind him, Bria sank to the ground next to Tobias.

"She's with The Rule," Aaron growled, ready to leap at Ellie.

"Stop, no! She's with us! She's the one who told me where you were!" Bria hissed through staggered heaves for air. "Please, stop, Aaron. I can't breathe!"

Aaron stared down at her and realized what he was doing. He eased his aggressive Taking, giving her back some strength. The rush of power waned, and he sank back down to the floor as the nauseating pain flooded his senses. He couldn't possibly trust Ellie, but fighting her—a Giver—would be impossible in this state without draining Bria entirely.

"Let me," Ellie rushed past Aaron and bent over Tobias. She tore her dress and wrapped the fabric tight around Tobias's open wounds. Here and there she realigned a snapped bone, keeping them in place with thick wraps of cloth. Bria turned to Aaron and did the same to him. He clenched his teeth, determined not to scream out in pain.

"Ready?" Ellie asked.

"Ready," Bria replied.

Aaron sensed how streams of Giving flowed from Ellie into Tobias's lifeless body. After a moment, Tobias gasped as if breathing for the first time in his life, and he blinked.

"What is..." he asked with a cough, his body shaking in visible pain.

"Can you walk?" Ellie asked.

"I don't know," Tobias answered in a coarse voice. His face contorted as he slowly got to his feet. He spat a mouthful of blood onto the floor.

Aaron felt riddled with misery to see his friend in such a condition. He had failed them both. He could keep his own body going by Taking from Bria, but he could do nothing to help Tobias, and he had to admit he was happy Ellie was there. *Finally, a good use for Giving.*

"Bria?" Tobias asked in disbelief, finally on his feet and standing in front of her. A wide smile spread across his face, even outperforming his grimace of pain, as he fell into her arms, hugging her tightly against him. For a moment Aaron feared Tobias would knock her over with his enormous bulk, and he relented his Taking to help Bria stay on her feet.

"Tobias, you stupid giant!" Bria said from the embrace, her voice shaky.

Ellie broke the moment. "There's no time for this! Let's get out of here!"

And they set into painstaking motion.

The emissary lay motionless, but breathing, on the ground outside. Next to him was his open notebook.

"You defeated an emissary to get to us?" Aaron said, stepping over the body.

"Yes... There was this ridiculously heavy war hammer here by the side of the wall, so I hit him in the head with the handle while Ellie distracted him," Bria replied, as if it was no big deal.

"Great!" Aaron grabbed the war hammer, channeling a little extra strength from Bria so he could hold it. The hammer felt light as a stick to him.

"You've gotten stronger, I see," Bria remarked as they made it to the stairs.

She had an arm around Tobias, supporting him in his slow walk. He made no complaints, but the way he hunched over and left a trail of blood made it clear that he was in no fit state. Ellie walked next to them, equally hunched over, drained from the intensive Giving to keep Tobias standing.

Aaron feared he looked just as bad himself, but his Taking allowed him to walk relatively well. Never had he maximized so much power from such a small input.

Bria led them through a maze of intricate passages and stairs, now and then stopping to listen for footsteps. One time, they had to stand still for a while, while two guards passed by in a crossing tunnel, and they all held their breaths to not be heard. It was a slow and painful walk, but finally they reached a large wooden door where a guard lay in a pool of blood. Aaron looked at Bria, wondering if she had done this too. They had seen the pirates kill, but somehow it felt different when it was his sister.

"Please, don't ask," she said, and unpacked a set of keys and tried them in the door, one after another. The sound of the keys cut through the silence in the hallway. Aaron looked over his shoulder and took some of Bria's hearing to enhance his own. There were definitely footsteps, but he couldn't make out how far away. Key after key failed, and Aaron stepped from one foot to the other in frustration. This would take too long.

"Step back, and try to relax," he ordered. Without waiting for an answer, he stepped up to the door. For a brief moment, he channeled almost all her strength, and she fell to one knee as he slammed the hammer into the lock, blowing open the door with incredible force. "Let's go."

An icy wind hit them as soon as the door burst open, and Aaron took a moment to get used to the dark night.

"Hey, who's there?" a voice called. Aaron spun around without thinking and slammed his fist into the guard's face. The punch sent him flying, skidding over the ground before he rolled to a halt. More voices could be heard further away from guards running towards them. He reached out and channeled from them, returning Bria's power.

"Run!" He put an arm around Tobias, and they set into motion.

Bria went in front, leading them across the open square around the enormous building they had just left, and in between the houses through narrow alleyways and side streets. Ellie followed behind them, panting as she still Gave to Tobias to keep him upright. Aaron did his best to Take from the nearest guards, and any other people he could sense inside the houses. It was dizzying and by far the most complicated Taking he had ever done, not even able to see his targets, and his power varied from moment to moment. Soon they heard horns blowing and alarm bells ringing.

"They're assembling the guards!" Bria called.

They kept running, as fast as they could, until Bria pushed them around a corner and down a dark alley, squeezed between two large houses. Aaron would never have noticed this spot by himself.

"Break! I need a break!" Ellie gasped, heaving for air. Tobias seemed close to passing out, and Aaron carefully laid him down on the ground, while doing his best to ignore the throbbing pain that roared through every inch of his own body.

"I can't believe it really is you two!" Bria panted.

"We are here to save you," Tobias replied from his position on the ground. He was pale but conscious. Aaron sensed how Ellie was Giving frantically to keep the giant man awake.

"Heroic, but rather useless, to go looking for me in the

dungeons, wouldn't you say?" Bria replied, forced laughter masking the worry in her face.

"We were just about to handle it," Aaron protested. *Was she really mocking them after all they had done? Surely they would have...* Then he remembered just how close he had been to Taking Tobias's life in there.

"I'm so sorry, Tobias. I... You know I didn't want to..."

"It's okay. Let's just get somewhere safe," Tobias whispered. He didn't look like he could keep going much longer.

"Home is this way," Bria said, heading down the narrow alley. Aaron increased his Taking so he could lift Tobias.

Finally, they entered a wider street, where Bria stopped in front of a worn-down house, warm light emanating from the windows. In the faint moonlight, Aaron noticed someone kept a small garden in front of the house, which now stood rather bare and waiting for winter. *Had she called this place... Home?* Bria unlocked the door, stepped into the house, and gestured for the boys to follow.

They stepped into a warm, bright room, and a young black-haired man rushed over and helped Aaron lower Tobias to the floor, while Ellie sighed and sank into a chair by the fireplace. Finally, Aaron looked around the room and saw... the other two sisters from the boat.

"Bria, they are with The Rule!"

He aggressively drew strength and speed from the two sisters. Finally, he could let his powers loose, and he felt energy rush through him like a raging river. He readied the war hammer and planted his legs firmly on the wooden boards, ready for a jump or a sprint. Blood seeped from his many wounds, and he felt broken bones burning with every movement, but he tolerated it easily now he could Take freely.

"Stop it, Aaron!" Bria commanded. "They told me where to find you. They're on our side!"

Meanwhile, Mia and Petra had forced themselves up, knives and a small crossbow in hand, although they both panted for air, barely able to stand under his relentless Taking.

"We told you, Bria. He's a Taker. A dangerous man," Ellie stated from her chair.

Aaron's Taking bounced right off her inner shield, and he growled at her, but could sense how she still Gave to Tobias for whatever reason.

"He's my brother," Bria interrupted. "And he has come all the way across the world to save me. However, clumsily that turned out."

"How well do you know these sisters?" Aaron asked. "Ellie is a Giver. She might be manipulating you," he said without taking his eyes from Ellie's. *Why did she, even now, make him feel so strange?* Her eyes were definitely green, he concluded, and her gaze met his in a way that made him nervous, almost causing him to mess up his Taking.

"Yes, of course I know Ellie is a Giver. I've known them for the better part of a year. Almost since I came here!"

"As we told you on the boat, we work for The Rule only because it serves our own purposes. And one of our purposes is to help Bria aid the homeless of Roak. We only do what we must," Mia stated between two strained breaths.

"Such as selling out friends?" Aaron continued,

forcing his eyes from Ellie's. He longed to attack, knowing he could easily defeat them.

"When such a friend turns out to be a Taker, yes!" Petra yelled, desperation in her voice. She had sunk into her chair again, and heaved for air.

Ellie finished on behalf of her sisters, "That made us more money than we could spend in a year! Enough to feed half the homeless of Roak for months. And how were we to know that you were Bria's brother? Honestly, you're damn lucky to have such a sister. No one else would have dared to sneak into Roak dungeons like that!"

She still sat down, her stare intense, and confusing. Aaron hadn't the energy to sense or even consider blocking her if she was manipulating him with Giving; but he couldn't ignore her logic. He sighed and released Mia and Petra from his Taking's iron grip. The hammer fell from his hand, and he sank to the ground, pain and dizzying tiredness finally overwhelming him. He had never maximized so much and for so long before, and finally realized how drained he was, as the world blurred before his eyes.

Aaron and Tobias spent long days in bed in painful misery, waiting for the slow process of healing. Mia and Petra helped clean their wounds, correct their broken bones, and stitch what could be stitched. Ellie came by daily and Gave healing and strength to Tobias. Bria allowed Aaron to Take her strength and healing, but even with the additional regenerative power, the injuries took ages to grow back together.

Aaron still had a hard time trusting the sisters, but with their gentle care he grew to accept them. They were equally reluctant to trust him, but Bria was adamant in her protection of him, and somehow, she accepted his powers without hesitation. It warmed his heart, as he unloaded a worry he hadn't even realized he had: that Bria and his mom would despise him when they found out what he was.

Clumsily, Aaron and Tobias tried to tell Bria the story of their trip, Aaron's dad, and all the things they had gone through. Aaron couldn't help but feel Bria dismissed at least half the stories as fever dreams or exaggerations, and he was too tired to contest it. To his surprise, however, Bria nodded in understanding when he mentioned he had heard Mom's voice.

"She has changed... Grown incredibly strong. The soldiers and guards talk of her. Even the emissaries fear her," she explained.

Bria told them about her and Kathrine's trip across the western sea, her time at Roak, about Karim and the other professors, and how she had finally been evicted from the school as she tried to save Kathrine. When she told of how they had scarred her face, and how she had somehow survived the winter, Aaron felt painfully aware of how late they had been with their rescue, how much she had needed them to come earlier. It was shameful to think of how much he had enjoyed his life on Blackskull with Flint.

CHAPTER TWENTY-EIGHT

Bria smiled as she watched Aaron and Tobias sleeping. Their cuts and bruises were slowly healing, and they looked so peaceful, just older versions of the boys she remembered from Great Oaks. Her tiny little brother had grown as tall as her now, and her... Her Tobias had come with him halfway across the Worldsea to find her. She reached out and stroked his blonde curly hair. Back home, it had always been dark from soot, but now it was soft and clean. She felt a lump in her throat as she looked down at the silver bracelet on her wrist. Downstairs, Tails was in the kitchen, and a strange mix of guilt and shame grew in her chest. She had loved. No, she still loved Tobias. And she loved Tails. Now she didn't know where to place her emotions, so she sighed and tried to push them away. It was bittersweet and terrifying to have both Tobias and Tails in the same house. So far, she had managed to keep them apart—or at least to not act in any loving manner towards Tails when in the room with Tobias. But the conversations were getting more and more awkward, as she tried to wriggle around the truth. She had to tell them. Both of them.

"Tails, I need to... I need to tell you something," Bria said, stepping into the kitchen. A delightful scent of broth filled the air and Tails was stirring a large pot of stew.

"What, my dear?"

"Tobias, he... He was my boyfriend back home."

Bria felt so ashamed as she said those words out loud. Surely Tails would be sad. And angry. He was always so nice to her and—

"Oh, that explains why you haven't properly introduced me yet. And why you act so awkward around him, I suppose," Tails said, interrupting her line of thought. He turned from the big pot and looked at her.

"I understand that you must be angry with me."

"Angry? I'm not sure, but I don't feel angry right now at least... I mean, he seems like a nice guy. I wish I had his curls, not to mention his height and muscles. I guess I see why you like him."

Bria tried her best to sound reassuringly. "But, just to be clear, that was a long time ago."

"Well, he left his family and traveled halfway across the world to save you, so I don't think he's quite over you."

Tails' voice was calm, and Bria couldn't sense any of the resentment she had expected. She glanced down at her wrist. She should probably just be honest then.

"I... I don't know. I love you Tails, I really do. But Tobias gave me this. And I've really missed him. A lot. I guess a part of me loves him, too."

The lump in her throat was growing, threatening to drown her voice. She took a few deep breaths to calm down after that big confession.

A moment passed. Then, she felt Tails's arms wrap around her. "That's okay.".

"But aren't you angry? Don't you love me too?" Bria asked, feeling even a bit upset over his lack of response.

"I do. But I don't think you are going to leave me because of Tobias, are you? I don't know a lot about these things, but I am pretty sure that a human can love more than one person at a time and—"

"But it's not the same!" Bria protested, pushing Tails away from her. Her mind really was a mess now. This was nothing like what she had expected! Why couldn't he just be angry?

"Well, call it what you want. I'm not leaving, and I'm pretty sure he is too weak to go anywhere right now," Tails said. "So, I guess you are stuck with two men that you love and who love you. To be honest, that is quite a privilege. Remember when we didn't even have money for food?"

Tails resumed stirring the pot, while Bria tried her best to formulate something she could yell back at him. The sound of hard knocks on the front door interrupted her.

"Are we expecting anyone?" Tails asked.

Bria swallowed her words and marched over to the window. A whole troop of soldiers stood lined up in front of the house.

"Soldiers!" she gasped. Adrenaline kicked in, pushing aside her troubles with Tobias and Tails.

"Open up, or we will knock down the door!" a voice called, followed by more hard knocks.

Tails tore off his apron as he ran towards the door. "Hide Aaron and Tobias. I will keep the soldiers distracted for as long as I can."

Bria stood, frozen to the ground. She had no idea what to do and—

"Go!"

She shook her head, regaining her focus, then ran up the stairs while Tails opened the front door. Heavy footsteps filled the living room, followed by a strange scream. Tails had apparently decided that screaming like a maniac would be the best distraction. Bria had to admit that even she felt rather distracted, as she almost burst out laughing. Quickly, she opened the door to the two sleeping boys and shook them roughly.

"What, ouch!" Aaron complained.

Tobias didn't complain, but flinched in agony.

"Soldiers! A lot of them. Downstairs."

"What's that weird screaming? Anyway, I'll take care of them," Aaron said, rubbing the sleep from his eyes. "May I Take from you Bria?"

Bria felt how her strength was starting to wane before she had even answered. Meanwhile, Aaron rolled over, reaching for the war hammer which lay under the bed.

"You... What? You want to go down there and fight them?" Bria could barely believe what was going on.

"Yeah, they're soldiers. From The Rule. I guess we will have to hide the corpses, which will be a bother, but I—"

"They are people, Aaron!" Bria protested. "I deliver their messages every day, and they are just as human as you and me. They have children and homes and..." Bria ran out of words. *How could he talk about killing so easily?*

"But Bria, just... Have you seen what they did to us and to you? To Mom? They deserve nothing less!"

Bria felt her face getting warm. "No killing! Take Tobias and hide on the roof, okay? Take my strength, but no killing!"

Aaron looked like he was about to object, but a hard knock on the bedroom door sent him to his feet.

"I'm naked. Give me a second," Bria yelled, just as most of her strength and speed left her. She almost lost her balance, but Tobias caught her and stabilized her before Aaron picked him up like a rag doll and slung him over his shoulder. Quickly, he climbed out the window, Tobias on his back. It was a wicked sight, the gigantic man being carried like a sack of potatoes by Aaron, who was much smaller. Bria waited a second for some of her strength to return, then opened the door to the hallway.

The soldier in front pushed the door open as soon as she unhinged the lock and marched straight into the room. It took a moment before he looked at her and stopped dead in his tracks. "Oh, Scarface, I... Er, I apologize. I didn't know you lived here and..."

Bria looked up and realized it was one of the officers she frequently delivered messages for. He had two kids and a wife who worked making ropes for the school. His name was Birkan, and he always treated her kindly; although she was sad he still used her nickname 'Scarface'. But then again, so did all the guards and soldiers.

"It's okay, I was just sleeping. How can I help you?"

"Well, er... We've been looking for a dangerous criminal

for some time, and now we are doing home inspections. I'm not supposed to tell anyone, but I guess you would know anyway, the rumor is out all over town. It's a Taker!"

Bria gasped and pretended to be shocked by the news.

"He has black hair and a slim figure. Hawkish nose. Have you seen him?"

"Actually, that does sound familiar. Downstairs, did you see the—"

"The guy downstairs? Oh yeah, he has an interesting... character," Birkan said. "A relative of yours? Anyway, it is not him, obviously. We are looking for someone very dangerous, mind you."

"Oh well, then no, that's not him." Bria had to fight hard not to giggle. Tails had played his part well. Birkan reached into his pouch and pulled out a silver coin and pressed it in her hand.

"We might have accidentally knocked over a chair or two downstairs. I hope this can compensate."

Bria gasped at the sight of the coin and curtsied. What a strange day! She thanked Birkan for his kindness, while doing her best to keep her face steady. She was sure she could hear footsteps from the roof.

She continued to make small-talk as they walked through the rest of the house. The soldiers casually looked under tables and in cupboards, but seemed to make no genuine effort now that their leading officer was at ease. In fact, it felt nice to show Birkan her little world, and she proudly showed the nice teapot they had found just a week before behind one of the taverns. As they left, Birkan assured her they would find and slay the Taker before he could bother her or anyone else.

Bria sank into a chair with a deep sigh as soon as the door closed behind the last soldier. She waited another few minutes to gather her thoughts before she brought Aaron and Tobias down from the roof. Her issue with Tails and Tobias was one thing, but Aaron's blood-thirst towards anyone from The Rule was disturbing, if not outright terrifying. She had to talk to him.

"People aren't just automatically evil because they work for The Rule. I even had friends at the school, and these soldiers have families at home. They are just working to make a living!"

Bria had raised her voice without noticing. She didn't remember them ever having such a fight, and she was sorry Tobias was there in the next bed to witness it.

"How can you be so naive? If we want to free Mom, we should at least take a chunk out of The Rule as we do it. The fewer soldiers and guards left on Roak, the fewer people there'll be to stop us. We cannot go around being nice to everybody! I mean, they would kill us, or at least me, in the blink of an eye," Aaron yelled back.

"Well, can you blame them? Takers are—" Bria gasped and stopped herself when she realized what she was saying. "I am sorry, I didn't mean to say that..."

"But you are right." Aaron looked down at the bedcovers. He was still covered in bandages from the last time someone found out that he was a Taker. She knew he had been hurt more than just physically when the sisters had sold him and Tobias to The Rule.

"Look, Aaron, we need to make the world realize you are not a bad person," she said in a low voice, putting her hand on his arm.

"No. I don't care what they think. I am just going to get Mom, and then we get out of here, okay?" Aaron snapped back.

"I..." Bria's anger had made room for sadness. Aaron had become so hard. And part of her understood why he had to be that way. But he had to understand that killing would only worsen things.

"We'll save Mom as soon as Tobias and I are back to health."

"But we don't even have a way to get into the school," Bria protested. "And Mom is... She is different. She is—"

Ellie's voice sounded from the door. "And you absolutely have to improve your miserable shielding before you enter the school."

Bria turned around to see the three sisters entering.

"We couldn't help but overhear your discreet conversation," Petra said. "And, well. We have concluded we owe you an apology for how we treated you. When we suspected you were a Taker, we just assumed you were dangerous... And well, evil."

"And, to be fair, you wanting to kill everyone who has ever touched a Rule sigil does make you sound a bit evil and dangerous," Mia added.

"Yes. So, in short, we agree with Bria. You can't just kill everyone from The Rule. Actually, maybe *you* can. I feel like we still haven't seen the full extent of your powers. But you shouldn't. Believe me, it won't fix everything, and it won't save your mother. The Rule will not run out of soldiers, so you'll need a better plan than just killing," Ellie finished.

Bria looked at the three sisters, grateful for their intervention. Somehow Aaron seemed to listen more when it came from them, and Ellie especially seemed to have a good influence on him.

"Okay. So what do you suggest then?" Aaron asked.

His teeth were clenched, but at least he seemed to be listening.

"If we help you, will you promise not to kill any more soldiers from The Rule?" Ellie asked.

"But what if it's in self defense?"

"Well, try to maybe just knock them unconscious instead, will you? And all that is actually considered in our plan to help you. So, do you promise?"

"I promise to do my best, but if I have to kill someone to survive or to save Mom, I will do it."

"Well, I guess that's good enough for now," Petra concluded.

"So, before we can save your mom, you need to work on your shielding. I will begin training you for that during the day. At night, you will practice sneaking. With power like yours, you should be able to sly your way through even a city like Roak, and that should teach you how to deal with guards in a less violent, and attention demanding manner," Ellie explained.

"But learning to shield myself could take a long time. We can't wait for that," Aaron objected.

"You don't really have a choice. Inside the school, even the students can Give. And you'll be stuck in narrow hallways, so you cannot just jump or run to gain distance.

Believe me, you have no chance without it. So, you'll have to be patient," Ellie answered.

Aaron didn't look happy about it, but he nodded.

Ellie's training began even before Aaron had fully recovered. She gave him simple challenges, such as balancing a spoon on his nose or holding a full cup of water without spilling. Even the slightest error sent her mocking him for his weakness and lack of progress, and most classes ended with Aaron and Ellie screaming at each other.

"Do you really have to be so hard on him? He hates it when you make fun of him," Bria said, pulling Ellie to the side after the first day.

"That's the entire idea," Ellie grinned. "Remember Diplomacy classes with Professor Raku? Shielding is about not letting other people in. Kind of like ignoring what other people say to you. I couldn't care less if he can balance a spoon on his nose or not."

"Oh."

Bria thought back, surprised she hadn't figured this out herself.

"But he is not a good student. Maybe it's different for Takers, I don't know. But he takes everything in... He must have been easy to tease as a kid?"

"So easy!" Bria laughed, thinking back to all the times she had made fun of him just to see him get angry or to get him to compete with her.

"And did you talk to Tobias and Tails yet?"

Bria's mouth fell open. "How do you know?"

"It's obvious. Also, as a Giver, I can sense emotions. And I know you like them both, so..."

"I talked to Tails, and somehow he seems okay. But I don't know what to say to Tobias. It's been so long."

"The truth is a good start. Then it's up to him what to do with it, I guess."

Ellie shrugged and Bria sighed, somehow, it sounded so simple when Ellie said it.

Bria waited another week until Tobias had healed enough to get out of bed. In fact, he was the one who suggested they went for an early morning walk. The sun was rising, painting the town in yellow and red, and they could hear the sounds of families waking up in the houses. Children crying, parents cooking, and dogs barking. They could see their own breath like little clouds forming in front of their mouths, and Bria tightened her scarf.

"Damn, I've missed being outside," Tobias said, and took a deep breath, apparently unbothered by the cold.

"You could have just said so, and Aaron could have carried you to the roof every day." Bria grinned.

"That was the most painful thing I've ever experienced!"

"Well, you made a graceful potato sack."

It felt good to be teasing each other and talking about unimportant things. She felt the chilly touch of frost a little less when walking close to him. He didn't smell of fire and coal anymore, but he still emanated heat. Radiated strength and warmth, and he was close enough for her to bask in it, even if they didn't touch each other.

"How things have changed... Remember when I was the one saving Aaron, when he would fall from the oak trees back home?" Tobias said.

"He used to be absolutely useless. I bet he could even beat me up now, with those tricks of his," Bria replied.

"It's... It's good to see you again," Tobias said, changing the subject and stopped as he put a hand on her shoulder. She stiffened from his touch and fought the longing to pull him into a hug. It was a bittersweet longing. *I have to tell him.*

"Tobias, it's truly good to see you too. I've missed you so much. I... I have thought about you a lot. But I need to tell you something."

Her scars prickled, as always when she went out in the frost. Even the warm rays of the sun suddenly seemed gray. "Tails and me... We are together. We have lived together for some time now."

Tobias's face turned into a subtle grimace. It was barely noticeable, but his smile faded ever so slightly. His hand quietly slid down from her shoulder, and he turned back to stare forward. Slowly they walked onward, Bria pulling her cloak tighter around her.

"I guess I suspected something was wrong. So... It's best that I leave," he mumbled.

"No! No. I... I told him about you. About us. You don't have to leave. I totally understand if you hate me for this, but I didn't know you'd come and—"

"No, I get it. And I guess I am happy there was

someone there for you when I couldn't be. I... I want you to be happy and safe."

"It's not just about being there for me. Or about keeping me safe. I guess I needed help now and then, but that's not why I am with him. Or why I missed you, for that matter. It's just what happens when people spend time together, I guess. But please don't leave, Tobias. You will always be welcome in my life."

"I don't just want to be welcome in your life, Bria. I want us to spend our life together."

"But Tails is part of my life too now. I cannot just ignore that."

"I guess I understand... So, you'll bring him home with us to Great Oaks, I guess?"

He looked at her, his jaw muscles tight.

Home to Great Oaks? She would be an outcast with these scars. And with her history, everyone knew who she was, and who The Rule thought she was. A Giver.

"I don't know... I'm not sure that I'll come home with you."

For a moment, Tobias looked like he might yell. His eyes narrowed and his brows closed in over his nose. "You're not coming home?"

"I don't know! I just... Look at these scars on my face, Tobias! I will never be who I used to be."

"I'd be with you, nonetheless." Tobias said, and his face softened.

"I... Thank you. But, I have a life here now. I know it sounds stupid, but Tails and I, we make a difference here. We help the homeless kids out, and we... We have our life."

"So, that is the life you are choosing? A life with him instead of me."

"No! I don't know. I... I want you both in my life!"

Bria felt her heart beating fast. How could she possibly explain how she felt? Tobias looked at her for a long moment, while an icy breeze found its way past her scarf and made her shiver.

"I will stay until we have saved your mom. Then I'll leave you two to live your life. Here, there, or wherever you want."

He turned and marched back to the house, leaving her alone. Tiny snowflakes whirled around her, and the red sunrise had given way to a dull gray sky. Cold tears rolled down her cheeks, and she felt the all too familiar hole in her heart grow just a little larger. She said nothing, just embraced the cold, like a bittersweet compliment to her self pity. This was not what she had wanted. Not at all. Was she greedy for wanting him to understand? But he said he wanted to be with her... The thoughts grew louder and louder, till the empty hole in her heart filled with bitter anger. She clenched her fists and continued down the road to work at the marketplace. At least she could make some money helping the merchants or delivering messages for the guards.

Anything to distract her mind.

Chapter Twenty-Nine

Aaron clenched his teeth, trying his best to balance a spoon on his nose, while ignoring Ellie's mocking commentary and her continuous assault of Giving that slammed against his shielding. His forehead was dripping with sweat from the immense concentration.

"Perhaps Takers are just weaker than Givers. This is like fighting against a child!" she said, laughing at him as she broke through his defense again.

He winced at the sudden stabbing pain. It wasn't much, just enough to signify his failure. "Just shut up! I need a break!" he gasped.

"So handsome and so spoiled," she replied with a crooked smile.

Another stream of Giving followed with no break. Aaron instinctively pushed against it, but his defense shattered immediately and another stab of pain rolled through him.

The training continued for hours every day, and Aaron found himself fuming with anger after each lesson. He even missed Flint's boring hours of silent meditation. Still, he had to admit he was slowly getting better. He grew used to ignoring being mocked, and now was shielding without even thinking about it. It seemed like his mind entered a certain state of distance from the world every time Ellie sent her Giving towards him. But it still wasn't enough to stop her from breaking through.

It didn't help his mood that Tobias walked around with a permanent angry frown stuck to his face. He had been silent and distant for several days, before finally telling Aaron about his breakup with Bria. Now the two of them couldn't even be in the same room without ruining the mood for everyone else around.

"Are you coming for dinner?" Bria asked through the open door to their room. A heavenly scent of spices trailed up from the kitchen, and Aaron's stomach growled in response.

"I take that as a yes. And you?" She gestured at Tobias.

"I'm not hungry. I'll eat some bread later, and let you have your meal together," he replied without looking at her.

"Suit yourself," Bria replied, her lips pressed together in a thin white line. She turned and went back down the stairs.

"If you like, I can bring you a plate of—"

"I'm not hungry, I said!" Tobias replied angrily. "Not for anything *he* has been making, anyway."

Aaron let out a sigh. Unfortunately, Tails was a nice guy, and he found it almost impossible to share his best friend's dislike of him. "Okay. Well, we will go out with Ellie later, right?"

"Yes," Tobias replied, and rolled over in bed, turning his back and dismissing any further conversation.

That was how they got through the days: by looking forward to going out at night, practicing their skills. Ellie used her Giving to enhance Tobias's strength and speed, while Aaron practiced Taking from the people sleeping in their houses, giving him the ability to roam all over the city without running out of power. In contrast, Tobias had to stay close to Ellie, who—despite their best attempts to persuade her—refused to let him carry her around on his back. Apparently, that was considered demeaning among Givers.

Aaron loved the freedom, the cold air fluttering his coat around him as he shot through the night, the feeling of being weightless at the top of a jump, and the mind blowing speed when he sprinted through the streets, never losing his breath. And to share it with Tobias made it all better, even if he often had to slow down for the others to keep up.

To Ellie's great annoyance, the two boys challenged each other to increasingly daring maneuvers in the air. She claimed they were being 'easy targets' as they jumped high above the streets and house, and she insisted they spend their time practicing techniques for sneaking around instead. For that, they would usually sneak around the city until they found a guard who stood alone. Then, Aaron practiced Taking the guard's awareness to send them to sleep, or intelligence to make them too confused to realize what was going on around them. With similar results, Ellie could Give tiredness to knock the guards out.

Unfortunately for Aaron, Taking that much awareness and intelligence both gave him a headache and confused him, as if his mind was somehow too full. So, after some thinking, he changed strategy to Taking senses from the guards instead. This was much easier, but left the guards suspicious the moment they realized they had suddenly gone deaf and blind. If the guards ever spotted them, Aaron simply Took the speed and voice of the pursuers, and watched as they moved in silent slow-motion towards them.

The three of them became like ghosts in the night, and Bria frequently returned from her job as a messenger, with stories of people claiming to have seen their shadows moving through the night sky. The stories got mixed up with those of the mysterious Giver—Mom—who even the emissaries feared. This gave birth to all kinds of theories about what was going on, ranging from: 'students breaking out of school at night to play around' to 'an uncontrolled Giver who had broken free from the school and formed a band of wild outlaws'.

Luckily, The Rule had already given up hunting for the supposed Taker. After all, rumors of a wild and powerful Giver haunting the streets at night were much more comforting than the thought of an actual Taker. Not to mention, less of a loss-of-face for The Rule.

Aaron had not gone close to the school in the two months since the escape from the dungeon, and, to his great frustration, the sisters had still not found a way to sneak into the fortress-like building. The density of guards and emissaries increased as one got closer to the black buildings, and Ellie insisted they kept their distance at all times during their nightly training. Apparently, the guards had been severely punished after their escape from the dungeon, and defenses had gone up. The Rule might not admit it openly, but they seemed to recognize *something* was afoot in Roak.

It was the middle of winter when Aaron's chance to take action on his own finally came. Ellie and the sisters were on a mission to collect information for The Rule, and for once, Aaron could go out and explore the city on his own. Tobias complained as darkness fell over Roak and Aaron left him behind in the house, but they both knew it was too dangerous for him to go near the school without Ellie's powers.

So, Aaron snuck alone through the night, entirely dressed in black with no metal to reflect the moonlight. Only a Giver would notice him as he jumped from roof to roof until he reached the row of houses closest to the school. He pulled his long coat tight around his body and wrapped his scarf to cover most of his face against the freezing air. If it wasn't for his enhanced powers, he would surely have slid on the icy roof he crouched on.

From where he sat, it was an open area of fifty yards to the school's outer walls. Fifty yards patrolled by scores of guards marching back and forth throughout the night. It was strange to think how the sight of guards—any number of them—used to strike fear in his heart. Now they looked like nothing more than an interesting, perhaps even entertaining, challenge to overcome. They would be no match for his powers if he got into a fight. Still, he remembered his promise not to kill, and he knew Ellie and Bria would scold him for days if he got caught, so he decided to stay hidden. Carefully, he sent out streams for Taking in all directions. Any Giver could sense if he took aggressively, so he tried to limit himself.

One of his streams reached what seemed like a young, sleeping woman. *Perfect.* Slowly, he took her senses, allowing him to investigate the front of the school: the walls were around sixty feet tall, fashioned from rough, black rock. They looked as if they had been carved out of the island itself, just like the tall spire behind them. This type of rock was close to unbreakable, even with his strength.

The huge school gate comprised two heavy wooden doors without doorknobs. Ellie had told him these doors only opened once a day, for one hour, to let in products and let out waste. Even the people working at Roak were prisoners there, and only the most trusted servants were responsible for trading goods that were brought to the gate and dragged into the school under the watchful gaze of both guards and emissaries. No one entered the school. No one left.

On top of the walls, guards patrolled day and night. Aaron longed to just run and jump past them. He knew he could do it, but not without being seen, and he had no idea what would meet him inside of the fortress-like school. Ellie and Bria had described it as a maze of corridors, filled with guards, emissaries and student Givers. He forced himself to remain patient, and to search for a better option. There had to be a way in without getting seen...

Slowly, he climbed from roof to roof around the enormous building to search for any weak spots. Even a fortress like this, had to have some way in, he told himself, hoping the notion to be true. Perhaps a backdoor or a sewage entry? He didn't quite know what he was looking for, but he kept going, ignoring the biting frost that sent his fingers numb.

Half the night passed before he found what looked to be the best possibility yet: on a tower at the side of the school, there was a small window only thirty yards up. The angle was just right, so guards manning the wall could not easily see it, and there were fewer guards on the ground on this side of the school compared to the front. Unfortunately, it looked like it was shut with heavy metal bars from the inside. Still, he took note of the location and decided he would return to examine it further the following night. For now, his teeth chattered from the cold, and he was longing for his warm bed.

—✦—

Aaron returned to the tower window the next night. He didn't know exactly what he hoped for, but perhaps something would show up. Some idea. So, he sat perched on a roof in the pitch darkness of night, freezing to his bones, when finally something happened.

Using his enhanced vision, he noted the steel bars were unlocked and unhinged from the inside of the window. A moment later, the window opened, and a woman looked out in all directions. She quickly pulled her head back as a patrol of guards marched by on the ground. The guards, however, were too busy looking towards the city and noticed nothing. As soon as they passed the next corner, the woman peeked out again.

A girl rather than a woman, Aaron concluded at a closer look. To his surprise, she threw a black rope out the window and climbed out and down. His heart skipped a beat. From where he was sitting, he could clearly see a patrol of soldiers less than a hundred yards from passing the corner to the tower. In just a few moments, they would see her. He wanted to call for her to go back. But what would it help? She didn't have the time to go back up, and nowhere to hide. Surely they would catch her. Surely she would be... He hadn't felt fear since they had escaped the dungeon with Bria and Ellie, but now it hit him, that uncomfortable, gut wrenching feeling. It wasn't fear for himself, but for the girl, and that made it much harder to push aside.

Instinctively, he intensified his Taking from an unknowing old man who lay sleeping in the house he was sitting on. With enhanced strength and agility, he jumped off the roof, landing on the cold ground with a light bump, then went straight into a sprint, wondering how long he could keep the connection to the sleeping man. He found out just a moment later, as the exhilarating wave of power waned.

The girl hung on the side of the tower now, holding on to the rope, just around the corner from where he knew that a patrol of soldiers would appear any moment. He had lost his superior vision, but even without it, he could see the girl desperately making her way down the wall. And just as clearly, he could see the first soldiers passing the corner.

"Hey, who's there?"

Aaron wasn't sure if the guard was yelling at him or the girl on the wall. Quickly, he turned and ran towards her. To have any chance of saving her, he would have to get her down. *Fast*. Soldiers were already running, coming in from the side. He couldn't make out their words, but they yelled louder, making enough noise to attract half the city's soldiers.

"Quick, jump down," Aaron called to the girl. She was still hanging fifteen yards over the ground, frozen dead in her track at the appearance of the guards. "I will catch you!"

The girl looked down at him and the approaching soldiers in horror, and finally turned as if to climb back up. *Dammit*! Aaron reached out with his inner powers. For just a moment, he channeled all the girl's strength. She lost her grip on the rope and fell to his arms. He caught her easily and sat her down.

"I will distract them while you run," Aaron instructed the girl, hoping she would understand. She looked at him, confusion and fear in her eyes, but she nodded. "Go!"

The girl ran as the first crossbow bolts pierced through the night towards them. The soldiers were close enough for Aaron's Taking, and he began with strength, speed, vision, and endurance. A good brew for fighting. Hopefully, he had spread out the Taking enough that they wouldn't notice, and realize they were fighting a Taker. Still, the little he Took from each was enough to fill him with incredible power. Like a raging bonfire, it threatened to get out of control, and he minimized the Taking a bit. He felt fear, anger and other feelings gnawing at him, and he did his best to pinpoint the streams of emotions that snuck their way into his mixture of Taking. It was still incredibly hard for him to keep things separate when Taking so much and from several people.

The power was exhilarating, and he picked the crossbow bolts out of the air to ensure none would hit the girl. She was running fast towards the line of houses. *Good.* Aaron ducked under a spear thrust and spun sideways to avoid another. *Should I kill them? No. I promised not to kill.* Instead, he turned to the nearest soldier and caught hold of his belt. Like a rag doll, he picked him off the ground and threw him at three of his comrades, all yelling out in surprise. Aaron took as much bravery as he could, and the attacks paused for a moment.

"A Taker! A Taker!"

Yells came from all directions now. *Damn, I went too far. The girls will be angry about this...* More guards came from around the corner and bolt after bolt shot towards him. Half the city guards would be after him soon. He instinctively dodged bolts, blades, and spears while trying to make a plan. He couldn't get too far away from the guards without losing their powers... So, he would have to lead them all closer to the houses in the city, where he could channel from the sleeping citizens instead.

He stopped taking bravery and turned toward the

front line of houses. Hopefully, he gave the impression of trying to escape, still dodging attacks and flying bolts. It felt silly running so slowly, but he couldn't let the soldiers fall behind. Every yard, he felt his powers dwindling, and he still needed to dodge the bolts, after all. They could reach much further than his Taking. A bolt shot past, cutting his left cheek as a reminder of this. Just another twenty yards and the houses would be there. Ten yards. Finally, he sensed people in their homes, ready for him to Take from. Sleeping people were much harder subjects, but Aaron focused and shifted his Taking from the soldiers. His powers dwindled from the arousing fire to the familiar stream.

He dared a glance over his shoulder: at least fifty guards chased after him now, but fortunately no emissaries had joined them. He set into a sprint and—as he connected to a strong man sleeping in one house—finally found the power he needed to rise to the roofs. In a single leap, he made it to the top of a two-story house, and for a brief moment, savored the calm safety of the elevated position. It would take the soldiers a while to reach him here.

Aaron peeked over the roof's edge down at the street. The soldiers were already kicking down the door to the house, and bolts shot towards his face, but weren't even close to hitting the target. He grinned as the adrenaline slowly released from his body. *If only my dad could see me now, trailing dozens of guards around the streets of Roak.* Then, his grin froze. There, among the soldiers, was the young girl, her arms firmly locked in the grip of two soldiers.

Aaron acted before thinking. Like an arrow, he shot down from the roof and into the middle of the group of guards. With a hard crash, he landed directly next to the two guards that held the girl. He gave them no time to react, as he aggressively channeled strength from both of them. They collapsed while he picked up the girl and kicked off from the ground with brutal force, shattering the pavement under his feet as he took off. The girl screamed as they soared through the night air at an angle that sent them both forwards and upwards. He had simply aimed to get away from the guards, fast and far, but it seemed they had enough momentum to shoot over an entire row of houses and land on the other side. *Perfect.*

"Prepare for landing," he whispered to the girl, then channeled her strength to brace for the impact. He ran another hundred yards with her in his arms, before he dared to stop in a small side street. Finally, he looked down at her; she had passed out. He eased his stream of Taking and carefully put her down on the ground. For a moment, he feared he had Taken too much. Killed her by the sheer brutality of his channeling. Was such a thing even possible? But no, she breathed... She looked like she was around ten years old. Maybe twelve? Her brown eyes were full of terror as they blinked open.

"Are you okay?" he asked.

'Taker! Taker!" the girl screamed.

"No, wait, I saved you, I—"

"Taker! Stay away from me!" the girl continued to scream. She crawled away from him, got to her feet and ran.

"Wait!" Aaron called, but now he heard approaching

guards. The girl made it around a corner, and Aaron looked down at his hand. They were bloody. When had he drawn blood? He didn't remember... He had been careful, hadn't he? The guards were coming around the corner now, and he forced himself to focus. He Took strength from the first guards and shot up into the night sky, leaving them all behind on the street below. He had blown his cover, but at least he might have found a way to enter the school.

Chapter Thirty

The official story was that it was a band of Givers, but the rumors were all over the city: a Taker had attacked the school. Aaron tried his best to explain to Bria that he hadn't had a choice. It was either exposing himself, or they would have caught the young girl... Although, they most likely ended up catching the girl anyway, he concluded bitterly. Still, he felt sorry for his actions, as soldiers and emissaries walked from house to house the next days, searching for the mysterious attacker. He and Tobias patiently hid on the roof again, while guards searched and destroyed half of Bria's and Tails's home. Luckily, they refrained from using Giving to torture any information from them. Apparently, the sisters had put the house under official association with their noble bloodline: the Riverwatch house. Still, the guards had been far from gentle, and Bria fumed for days as she cleaned and repaired around the house.

"We have plenty of coins, we can buy a new teapot," Aaron said.

Bria was sitting at the dining table, trying to glue it together piece by piece. "This is MY teapot!"

"The glue won't work, it will never hold any water," Tobias said.

"And now you are an expert on glue? Perhaps the glue here is better than back in Great Oaks!" Bria snapped.

"Sure," Tobias replied coldly.

"He is right though, the glue won't hold water, my dear," Tails added, sitting down next to her and putting his arm around her shoulders. "But perhaps we can use it as a flower pot. The plants won't mind a few cracks here and there…"

Aaron felt a sting of pain looking around the living room. All the plants from the window sills had been knocked over, and the dried herbs had been torn from their drying strings by the chimney and ground into the floorboards. Two of the chairs were broken, and the ashes from the fireplace had been carelessly thrown through half the room. Upstairs, the beds had been torn and knocked over, and the soldiers had even poked a hole in the roof at one place, so that snow now made its way into his and Tobias's room.

A knock interrupted the bleak atmosphere, and Aaron's heart instantly lifted as he opened the door.

"We are back!" Ellie said. The sight of her sent the same tingling sensation through Aaron's stomach as the first time he had seen her. Perhaps he should tell her that—

"What happened here?" Mia asked, pushing past him and into the living room.

"Guards searching for Aaron," Bria said from her chair.

"In the teapot?" Petra added.

"What did you do now to cause all this ruckus?" Ellie turned to face him, a smile pulling on her lip, which he couldn't help but reciprocate.

"Well, I might have made a bit of an appearance... But hey, I found a way into the school!" Aaron replied with a blush.

"The door?" Ellie asked, raising an eyebrow. "We talked about this, you cannot just—"

"No, a window! And I saw someone escape from it, so I know it's at least somewhat unguarded."

"Really? Which window?"

"On the east wing. A tower, around thirty yards up. It was barred from the inside, but I saw a girl escape from there," Aaron replied.

"Oh. That must be the laundry tower! They have that window for getting air through. After all, laundry needs that... But you'd never get through those steel bars, Karim enforced them with Fero iron."

"Fero iron?" Tobias asked.

"Well, not exactly. But, an alloy that includes iron from Fero. It appears to be quite efficient at limiting the powers of Givers. And, I'd guess, Takers as well."

Aaron was too busy defending his plan to discuss the qualities of metal anymore. "But that's no problem! A girl escaped, and they haven't setup the bars again. I might, er... Have distracted them a bit, so that they forgot about the bars."

"I guess that's why they invited all the emissaries to gather. A Taker roaming free in Roak looks bad for The Rule," Mia said, exchanging glances with Petra and Ellie.

"They are assembling all the emissaries?" Aaron asked.

"Yes. Two nights from now in the tower. That's why we came back so fast, to deliver juicy news for their gathering," Ellie said.

"And we were actually going to suggest we save your mom that night," Mia continued.

"Really?" Aaron said, unable to hide his surprise and excitement.

"Your shielding isn't ready. But this way, all the emissaries will be out of the way at least, and the students will hopefully be in their beds," Ellie answered. "It will be a dangerous mission, but, no fear, no fun, as they say."

"Who in the world says that?" Tails asked, lifting an eyebrow.

"I'll come with you," Tobias said as he stepped forward.

"Obviously, I'll come as well," Ellie replied with a smile. "After all, I know the school like the back of my hand. And worst case, I'll just pretend you took me hostage."

"Charming," Aaron replied, unable to stop from smiling.

"Not to mention beautiful and clever," Ellie added, sending Aaron's heart racing.

"I will come too. After all, the second half of this is an escape mission, isn't it? That's my specialty," Tails said. Tobias's face tightened, and Aaron feared he would object or say something.

"Well, such bravery I have to see to believe. And, she is my mom too, so I will come as well, if we really have a way in we can use. Aaron, you will at the very least be able to use me and Tails for your Taking," Bria added and stepped forward.

"Another dangerous mission for us, it seems." Tails laughed and put his arm around Bria's shoulder. He seemed as unworried as if they were planning a trip to the marketplace.

Aaron nodded in agreement, although he would have preferred for Bria to stay out of this. The thought of losing her was still too present.

"I will come with you to the school to keep a lookout and help distract any curious guards while you get in," Mia offered.

"And I will have the Maiden's Breeze, rigged and ready to get your mother off the island. Just get her to the docks before sunrise," Petra said.

Aaron's heart jolted with gratitude and excitement. Finally, they would save his mom.

The next two days were the longest and slowest of Aaron's life. Time just couldn't go fast enough as he spent hours sitting on the roof and looking up at the school's black spire. He feared what he would see in there. *Bria said Mom had changed... But surely that was just a facade against her captors.* He couldn't believe they had turned her to work for The Rule. Wouldn't believe it. He tried to push away his dark thoughts, but they kept coming back to him.

Finally, the night came, and they all dressed in their darkest clothing. Aaron packed a rope, Tails brought his finest set of lock picks, Tobias the war hammer, and Ellie her knife. Other than that, they were unarmed. The only way to succeed would be through sneaking.

"What is... that?" Aaron asked, as Ellie unwrapped a leather tie with what looked like tiny metal shards embedded in the material.

"Oh... Givers can only Give what they have, right? So, we often have to inspire certain feelings in ourselves for more effect. This belt inspires pain."

She pulled down her pants, sending heat rushing to Aaron's face, as she tied the band around her right thigh. A drop of blood trickled down the leg.

"You get used to it," Ellie stated, as she noticed Aaron's blushed and worried face. "In fact, Givers are trained to always be in pain, but to always spread it out among whoever is near, so we don't feel it so much."

"That sounds terrible!"

"Oh, that's nothing! If you really need to hurt someone, be ready to hurt yourself first. Teeth and a knife can be a great—"

"Please, Ellie, now is not the time for such inspiring tales," Bria interrupted, to Aaron's relief. Ellie shrugged and grinned, and they all headed out the door and into the dark night.

The air was freezing; the wind blowing snow through the empty streets. Hopefully, it was early enough for them to carry out the entire mission, while the emissaries still had their meeting in the tower. Perhaps they could even leave the island before anyone noticed Mom was gone.

Here and there, voices and music issued from taverns, but the streets were lifeless, except for the occasional homeless taking shelter under roof overhangs, huddled in thick layers of blankets, or scurrying off as soon as they saw the group. Usually, Bria would hand out some coins, or even invite them to spend the night in front of the fireplace in their house, but not tonight.

Tonight, the six of them wandered silently through the labyrinthine alleys that connected the bigger streets in the spiderweb of Roak. The anticipation was palpable, and Aaron felt his heart beating fast, his fingertips tingling with the craving to Take. He resisted the urge, more or less, Taking only a bit of senses from sleeping people here and there, so he could hear and see if any guards caught sight of them. The loudest sound in the night came from the snow that crunched under their feet as they walked.

Finally, they stopped in the opening of an alley, a clear view of the school's eastern wing before them. His stomach churned with excitement and nervous fear. The enormous building seemed colder and darker than ever and there were dozens of guards between them and the laundry tower.

"I suppose I should get to work then," Mia whispered. "Be careful, right? Ellie, don't let the boys kill themselves, and more importantly, keep yourself safe."

"As always, sister."

"Now, if you will?" Mia said directed at Ellie.

Aaron felt the strange sensation of someone Giving close to him. It felt like he could almost grasp the stream of power going from Ellie to Mia, if he wanted to. Months of training with Ellie had really taught him a lot...

He had wondered for the last three days if Ellie would come along on the Maiden's Breeze when they escaped, but not dared to ask. *If not, this would be their last night together...*

"I will draw their attention. Get in there as fast as possible," Mia whispered and ran off. A moment later, Mia's scream, amplified by Ellie's Giving, rang through the night as clear as shattering glass.

"The Taker! He is here!"

All hell broke loose, shouts and horns, countless guards storming towards the side street just some twenty yards away, where Mia had called from.

"He was right here! He ran that way! Thank Eldrik you saved me in time! Come, we must catch him..." They heard Mia shouting as her voice slowly grew to a normal pitch, and increasingly distant. More and more guards came running, but no-one cared to look into the small dark corner where they were hiding.

A few moments later, there were only two guards left between them and the window. Now was the time. The guards were shivering, obvious even without Aaron's enhanced vision. They looked from side to side, clearly afraid. It was strange to think of just how much fear his very being instilled in these people. "I'll take them," he whispered.

"Don't kill them," Ellie replied.

Aaron nodded, drew strength, and kicked off from the wall behind them, setting into a sprint towards the guards. He reached them with dizzying speed, leaving them no time to sound any alarm. As soon as he was within reach, he took as aggressively as he could, and both guards dropped to the ground, senseless and powerless, but alive. He gestured back to the group, and they followed.

Aaron felt the arousing swirls of power from the two soldiers he Took from, as he grabbed the war hammer from the sling on Tobias back. "Ready?"

They all nodded.

Then he jumped, straight from the ground to the window, thirty yards above the ground. Upon hitting the wall, he hammered the war hammer's pick between two stones, holding the handle so he hung just in front of the closed window. He pushed it open and threw down the end of the rope. Ellie could help them jump high, but not all the way up.

Tobias came first, jumping the first thirty feet, and climbing the rest using the rope. Aaron simply hung by one arm from the war hammer, holding the rope with the other, while Tobias squeezed his large body in through the window. Bria followed, then Tails. Only Ellie left. How long before the guards would return? She took hold of the rope and began to pull herself up. It was incredibly slow; but without another Giver, there was no way to speed her up. Aaron cursed and let go of the war hammer, letting himself drop the thirty yards to the ground. Ellie looked at him in confusion.

"I know you won't like this, but I need you to get on my back."

"Well, I wo—"

"Now!" Aaron commanded as a patrol of soldiers reappeared between the houses in the distance. He knew the guards' normal eyes still couldn't see them, but it would only be a matter of seconds. Apparently, Ellie finally understood and jumped on his back. Her body against his sent a wave of confusing emotions through him, which he tried his best to ignore as he set off, jumping from the ground with all his force. Hopefully no-one would notice the shattered hole in the cobblestones under the window, but he could do nothing about that now.

Ellie gasped as they shot through the darkness with incredible speed, all the way up to the war hammer, where Aaron regained his grip and let Ellie climb into the tower. He followed and closed the window behind them. They heard yelling as the soldiers found their two passed-out comrades, but they had made it inside without being seen.

Aaron sighed as he released the stream of Taking from the two soldiers outside, his body feeling weak and tired as always after Taking and maximizing such amounts of power.

The room was dark and moist, and full of clothes hanging from lines. Aaron felt Ellie Give to him, and he accepted it without resisting. For a moment, he could see and hear clearly in the little room. Then Ellie's Giving shifted to Bria, then Tails, and finally Tobias. It had been enough for each of them to gain an impression of the room. Along the walls, deep shelves held various robes and uniforms. Across the room was a hatch in the floor, presumably leading down toward the school complex.

"Luck seems to follow the bold," Tails remarked as he unfolded a bundle of blue fabric, in the faint light coming in from the window. It was an emissary uniform, in heavy blue wool, with The Central Rule sigil on the left side of the chest.

"You mean for us to wear... those?" Bria asked.

"Absolutely. That way no one will question us!" Tails replied with a grin, already pulling the robe over his head.

Aaron nodded in agreement, and they all changed into the blue robes. No robe was big enough to cover both Tobias and the war hammer, so they agreed Ellie would Give some strength to Aaron and let him carry the hammer under his robe. Hopefully, it would also calm any true emissaries, when they sensed Giving. After all, five emissaries walking in a group in the middle of the night was an unusual sight, even at Roak.

Aaron opened the hatch in the floor and led them down a long, spiraling staircase. They reached its end around ground level, where a door led into the wider school complex. Aaron carefully listened as he opened the door, fighting his instinctive urge to Take to keep himself safe. Luckily, the corridor was empty, but he could hear the snores of many people on either side of the passage.

"These are the servants' quarters. Your mother won't be here," Ellie whispered and pushed them onward down the long, dark corridor.

They walked through several similar passages, and passed by several guards in shining armor. The plan seemed to work as the guards stepped out of the way and bowed in respect. They continued around corners, up and down stairs, down hallways. This place really was like a maze, and eventually, Aaron gave up trying to remember their way back.

"These are the student quarters," Ellie whispered as

they walked through a well-lit hallway with red woven carpets on the floor. Beautiful paintings hung on the walls between wooden doors on either side. Behind the doors, Aaron could hear snoring, as well as some chatting, and he noticed Bria had stopped in front of a door halfway through the corridor.

"This is... This was my old room," she whispered.

Tails put a comforting hand on her shoulder, and they moved forward. Tobias stood next to them, misery painted on his face, but his jaw clenched tight.

"Your mother should be in the catacombs. We have to keep going," Ellie instructed.

They proceeded another ten minutes to a staircase, blocked by two guards. Aaron tightened his grip around the war hammer under the blue robe.

"We are here on behalf of the board," Ellie said in a casual tone, and the two guards stepped aside. Aaron sighed and relaxed as they walked past the guards and down the stairs. He had to admit that Ellie's idea of sneaking rather than fighting really did work rather well.

Ellie took a torch from the wall, and the warm light filled the darkness as they continued down the stairs. This place had a different feel. Not luxurious, like the rest of the school, in contrast, it smelled of mold and... blood? And it was cold enough that Aaron could see his own breath in the torch's light. They stepped into a wide crypt with row after row of cell-like rooms barred by steel pillars. He could hear whining, even without enhanced hearing. He could also sense that Bria was shaking behind him. "Are those... prisoners?" he whispered to Ellie.

"Givers that resist, waiting to be broken," she

explained, and put her hand on Aaron's shoulder. A stream of sight and hearing flowed into him, and he could see faces and bodies in the cells. Children. The nearest one looked like a young teenager. He was chained to the back wall of the cell, his body bruised, half-naked and starved. The chains were too short for him to lie down and rest, and he dangled from the wall, almost like a corpse. Ellie Gave Aaron smell and the rancid odor of old blood, rot, infected wounds, and rusted iron threatened to overwhelm him. He gasped, dizzy from the horror. Ellie Gave him some courage, but he still felt sick. This was beyond anything he could have imagined.

"I'm sorry, Aaron," Ellie said. "I'm so sorry for what they have done to Bria and your mother. Please, no matter what we find today, your mother will not be the same as what you remembered. But we will save her."

Aaron just stood in silence for a moment. None of them spoke, and he prayed the others couldn't see what he could. This was a place of evil, much more than he had thought. Behind him, he faintly heard Bria whimpering.

"We have to find Kathrine and get out of here," Tobias whispered, pulling Aaron back to his senses.

"Yes... Yes, you're right," Aaron replied.

They continued down the row of cells, Aaron leading the way with his enhanced vision. They were so close to her now. They had to be.

"Water," a weak voice begged from a cell.

Aaron turned and his heart dropped as he saw the dirty face of a little boy clung to the wall. Anger and sadness fought for control in his mind at the thought of the emissaries who did this to little children. His grip tightened around the war hammer, and he took a step towards the cage. Just a tiny bit of Taking, and surely he could wrench open that lock and—

"That's not what we are here for," Ellie hissed.

"We can't... We can't just leave them like this."

Aaron felt his heart beating fast. He had to do something. To stop this evil.

"If you save them from here, they will just be hunted down in the streets. There is no escape from Roak. Even my sisters and I wouldn't be able to get them all off the island, and their punishment would be even worse once they were caught. The Rule prefers dead Givers to unruly Givers," Ellie whispered, pulling Aaron back towards the middle of the passage.

"Dammit," Tobias hissed and pulled Aaron's arm. "I agree with you. We cannot leave them."

The group stood still, as if waiting for someone to decide what to do. For Aaron to decide. He stood for a moment, unsure. *How long would it take to tear open the cages and free the prisoners? Would they make it in time? And then what?*

"How far is the main door?" Aaron finally asked Ellie.

"Aaron, what do you intend to do?"

"How far? A five-minute walk? Ten? Can you open it from the inside?"

"I... Yes, it opens from the inside. It's five minutes from here, just a few stairs and a corridor. But—"

Aaron made up his mind. "Then we will free them. All of them. We will take them with us through the main door and be gone before anyone notices. No one will question us in these robes, and we will be gone before they can stop us... As you said, we cannot hide such a large group, so we won't. Once in the streets, they will simply have to hide and scatter with the homeless. Or perhaps we steal a big ship and sail out of here with all of them... Some way we will manage. We cannot leave them like this, Ellie," he pleaded. "And, after all, these are Givers, and we cannot have them turned to help The Central Rule."

"Aaron, no, that's insane! I hate this as much as you, but—"

Ellie protested, but Aaron had already made up his mind. He handed the war hammer to Tobias, and they set to work. He Took strength from Bria and Tails, amplifying it as much as he could, to save as much as possible for them to keep for themselves. They both slouched as if they had suddenly grown much heavier, but neither protested. Then Aaron tore a rock out of the nearby wall and hammered it against the first cage's lock. Behind him, Tobias did the same using the war hammer. Loud clangs and bangs rang through the hallway.

The rescue mission had begun.

The boy in the first cell pushed away from him, as far into the corner of the cell as his chains allowed him. It took Aaron a second before he remembered he was wearing the emissary robe.

"We are here to free you!" Aaron tore the ring that held the boy's chains attached out of the wall. "We aren't emissaries. Wait in the hallway, and we will all escape together."

The boy was too scared to move, but Aaron couldn't wait, so he moved on to the next occupied cell. Each lock came off with a mighty crash, and his improved hearing let him know that the school was slowly waking up from the noise. People were running in the hallways above them. Hopefully, the confusion would keep them safe for a while.

Another cell door swung open—a young woman. Another door—a young girl. Still no sign of Mom. Aaron ran down the side corridors, looking for more occupied cells. Where was she? Had he missed a cell?

"Guards!" Ellie screamed, and Aaron looked over his shoulder. *Dammit.* He hadn't expected them to show up so soon. A group of guards charged against the freed prisoners, who stood with Tails and Bria in the middle of the large room.

"I'll take them!" Aaron called back.

Anger bubbled in him, and guards were exactly what he needed. He stopped Taking from Bria and Tails, and sent out several streams towards the entrance. It was hard to target correctly in the growing crowd of people, but he tried his best to only hit the guards. Once connected, he drew all their vision, hearing, strength, speed, and probably a few more things. His Taking was ruthless, and he couldn't control exactly what he took. Surely, some feelings spilled into him, but he couldn't be picky right now. Flint would have been disappointed, but this was a desperate moment. He felt explosive, bursting with power, and the first several guards fell to the ground. He minimized the stream a bit, afraid he could burst from all the force in him.

"Tobias and Ellie, protect the group! I'll double check the hallways here on the sides."

Tobias set off running towards the few guards who still stood, swinging the mighty war hammer and letting out a terrifying roar. Without Ellie, he was magnificently strong. With her, he was an unstoppable giant.

Aaron turned back to the task at hand, sprinting down side corridors looking for any cells that weren't empty. At the end of a side passage, he found a young man who stuttered his thanks as Aaron tore his cell apart in the blink of an eye. Finally, at the end of another corridor was a heavy, iron door. The distance to the guards was almost too far for his Taking, but Aaron still had the power. He took a run up and slammed against the door. It stood unmoving. He growled and tore a large rock from the wall, and slammed it against the lock. With a loud crash, the door flew open to reveal... Nothing.

The room behind the door was a small, square cell, completely empty. Emotions raged through him like a wild sea, threatening to drown him. *Now what?* He didn't even try to hold back his Taking anymore, and waves of smell, vision and sound clashed against his sharpened mind, together with waves of rage. Bursts of incredible force shook every muscle in his body as he ran back to the rest of the group. It felt like he was drowning in an ocean, except he was drinking it at the same time, inhaling it and somehow living. Everything hurt everywhere, but his mind blocked the pain as a mere signal of mortality. Not something to be considered. He had to find his mother! But the rest? They would just get in his way...

"Take the prisoners out the main gate!" he roared through the catacombs in an unnatural voice, his voice like an earthquake.

"But where is Mom? She should be here! She was always here!" Bria yelled back, her voice trembling.

"Just do it! Go!" Aaron commanded.

All the guards had passed out, either from his channeling or from Tobias's war hammer, and Aaron hurried the prisoners towards the empty staircase. Except —it wasn't empty now. Two emissaries with shields and swords stepped down, moving with unnatural grace and speed. Several prisoners screamed and sank to the ground, apparently unable to guard themselves from the Giving, just like Tobias, Bria, and Tails. Only Ellie still stood upright.

Aaron grinned; the emissaries were mere disturbances on the road to where he needed to be. What he needed to do. He took two long steps, and jumped through the room, bolting like lightning over the heads of the prisoners. Tobias raised the hammer just in time for him to grab it from his hand mid-air.

The emissaries were Giving him waves of pain and all sorts of other sensations as he shot towards them. He couldn't focus on shielding against the attacks, but the pain was nothing compared to the power filling every inch of his body. None of it could stop him. He crashed into the first emissary, war hammer first, crushing his head. Aaron touched the ground and spun, slamming the iron-buckled handle of the hammer against the head of the other. A gasp of relief came from the crowd behind him as the Giving ended, but Aaron had no time to enjoy the small victory. "Where else can my mom be?" Aaron growled at Ellie, while smearing blood from his face.

'The... the meeting! She must be in the tower!"

"Where?" Aaron roared.

Without thinking, he was Taking Ellie's courage and strength, his very nature wishing to bend her to his will. He felt her defensive shielding for just a second, before it crashed under his thundering Taking.

"Aaron, stop! You're hurting me!" Ellie cried, crouched in fear.

"Talk!"

"Please... Take my knife at least, use it," with shivering hands, Ellie handed her knife to Aaron. Instinctively he grabbed it, and suddenly the storm in him calmed. It wasn't gone, just infinitely weaker.

"Please, come with us Aaron. We need to get out!"

Ellie sobbed, looking up at him from the floor. Aaron's heart sank as he looked around. Corpses, prisoners. And his friends. He had to choose now, or it would be too late... He had to save his Mom. "I am sorry."

He dropped the knife, and the storm resumed instantly, enveloping him in explosive waves of power. He was the storm, the raging thunder and the sundering tide. "Where is she?" His coarse whisper shook the ground.

"Up! Up three floors! Then the end of the hallway to the left," Ellie cried.

"Lead them to escape," Aaron ordered, and turned away from her.

Chapter Thirty-One

Bria watched in horror as Aaron roared for them to leave. His eyes were wild, nothing like her little brother. *We need to stop him. We need to get him out of here and—*

"Bria, we have to escape!" Tobias shook her back to reality.

"But, Aaron—"

"He's going to find your mom. Let's go!"

Tobias turned and charged up the stairs, Ellie a few steps behind him. Sounds of fighting ensued, followed by Tobias's voice calling from somewhere at the top of the stairs. "It's clear. Bring them up."

Tails was already bringing the huddled prisoners to their feet, and Bria forced herself to look away from Aaron and followed his example. *They are all so weak. If only I could Give...* Finally, the little parade made it up the stairs, and they all set into motion, left towards the main gate. The corridors were empty, and Ellie and Tobias went in front, scouting down side passages as they moved forward, one corridor after the other.

"Bria, behind you!" Tobias called and stormed past her to block the way.

She looked over her shoulder just in time to see an emissary leading a group of guards.

"Kill them! Their robes are fake!" the emissary yelled, and the guards moved towards her with incredible speed. Tobias intercepted them before they reached her, Tails, and the prisoners.

"Get out! I will hold them back!" Tobias yelled, as he knocked out the first soldier and took his sword, using it to block the swipe from another guard.

His bulky body filled half the hallway, and it was clear that the only way past him was through him. He moved with incredible speed, dodging attack after attack, but Bria saw stains of blood from where the guards' blades had sliced his skin open.

"No, Tobias!" Bria screamed.

There was no way even Tobias could block a whole group of guards alone when they had a Giver as well!

"Tails, get them out of here!" Tobias yelled without looking back.

Tails grabbed her hand and pulled her towards the large entrance hall.

"I'll keep him alive," Ellie assured Bria as they passed. She was sweating and her face pale, her whole body shaking in exhaustion.

"Please..." Bria said, unsure how to continue her sentence, and feeling Tails tug her hand to keep moving.

"Ellie, go with them!" Tobias roared through the battle noise from behind them.

"No chance, big boy, we are doing this together now," Ellie replied in a faint voice, and walked towards the battle.

"Let's go! The prisoners need us—we are not out yet!" Tails yelled in Bria's ear. She nodded reluctantly, forcing herself to look away from the ongoing battle. To look away from Tobias, who stood like a single man against a tidal wave of attacks. Protecting them. She turned and ran together with Tails and the prisoners. The passage was clear, and slowly the sound of battle faded behind them.

They slammed open the last door and rushed into the enormous entrance hall, running towards the huge door at the opposite end. So close to freedom! So close—

Bria stopped, frozen in her tracks. On the floor in front of the exit sat Karim, cross-legged and calm. "Good to see you, Bria."

No, no, no! Not him!

"Get out of the way! Please," she yelled, desperation rising in her. They had no Givers with them now. Tobias and Ellie were still fighting somewhere in the hallway behind them—if they were still alive. And even with Ellie and Tobias, they could never have defeated Karim. Behind her, the huddled prisoners had stopped, but Tails stood beside her, dagger in his hand looking like he was ready to fight.

"Where is your brother?" Karim asked calmly, rising to his feet.

Bria had forgotten how tall he was. "Upstairs, taking care of your friends!"

"Really?"

A ruckus made Bria look to the sides of the room. Soldiers flooded into the great hall from the side doors now. They were trapped!

"Yes! And he will defeat you all!" Bria replied, her heart sinking, but a flame of defiance lighting in her. How many soldiers were there? Thirty? Fifty? They didn't stand a chance, but she wouldn't go down without a fight.

Karim raised an eyebrow and looked like he contemplated for a moment. Then he reached out his hand and made a gesture, asking her to step closer.

"Stand with me," he commanded, and Bria felt an overwhelming urge to serve. She clenched her teeth to try to stop herself, but she couldn't. Slowly, she, Tails, and the prisoners walked up to Karim.

"It's about time you came back," Karim whispered as she stood next to him.

"What?" Bria looked at him. Was this some new kind of torture? A game?

"I have looked forward to this day for a long time. I suppose sometimes it takes the bravery of the young to awaken the heart of the old."

"What are you talking about?"

Karim didn't answer, just winked at her, and turned to the gathered soldiers ready for attack. "Stand down!"

The soldiers stared at each other, confusion painted on their faces.

"I said, stand down! These people are with me," Karim

repeated. The soldiers slowly lowered their spears and swords.

"Keep your blades ready men!" a familiar voice rang from the crowd. "Your treachery runs deeper than I thought, Lost Child."

Professor Raku stepped forward from between two soldiers, a wicked smile on his face that made Bria's heart freeze. *Professor Raku!*

"Raku, this is not—"

"We've suspected your failed allegiance for a long time, Karim. The king himself has ordered me to overlook your doings, and his wisdom was right, I see. So, you've joined forces with that primitive girl? Disgusting! Good thing we already moved her mother to The Capital... And where is your precious Taker? Dead I presume."

Bria's heart dropped. *So Mom was already gone. It had all been for nothing.*

"Stop, Raku! Order the soldiers to drop their weapon, or I shall enforce it myself!" Karim said, his voice loud and strong.

"It is you who must surrender, Karim!" Raku growled, an expression of disbelief on his face. Or was it worry?

Karim didn't answer him, just sighed and looked down at Bria. "Be nice to the soldiers, will you? They do not know what they are doing."

Then, Bria felt an extreme rush of power fill every inch of her body. She let out a gasp as the power roared through her like nothing she had ever felt! Next to her, Tails looked equally confused.

"Kill them!" Raku ordered, and the crowd of soldiers launched towards them.

Bria felt stronger than ever, as she awaited their attacks with no other weapons than her feet and hands. She stepped into one of Kindra's defensive stances and waited for the first attacker. She easily dodged his wild flinging blade, and a punch to his wrist forced him to drop the sword. A kick in the stomach sent him flying backwards with a moan. Another attacker came from behind, and she kicked him in the chest without even looking. Through the corner of her eye, she saw Tails move like a shadow from one enemy to the next. *This would be easy.*

Soon, the attacks came slower, as the soldiers had learned they were not so easily defeated. Bria followed Tails's example and started charging from soldier to soldier instead of waiting for their attacks. She carefully knocked out each, doing her best not to break more than a rib or two. She had just picked up a fully armored soldier, and was about to throw him at one of his comrades, when a voice froze her mid-movement.

"Stop!"

Raku's voice pierced through the battle noise, and Bria looked just in time to see Tails, firmly caught by two guards, and Raku holding a knife pressed against his throat.

"Surrender, or he dies!" Raku sneered. All the fighting had stopped, and Bria felt panic fill her heart. The air brimmed with tension.

"Let the boy go," Karim's voice was clear and thick with authority.

"Your life for the boys then," Raku replied.

Bria made eye contact with Karim for just a moment.

A long moment passed...

"What would you have me do?" Karim asked.

"Come closer and drop your shielding."

Karim took a slow step towards Raku. "We both know that I am much more valuable to you than any of these people," he said.

"So? How many must I kill before you surrender? A Giver without allies is a useless weapon against another Giver. Even you would be useless, Lost Child."

"Will you promise to let them all go? All of them, on a boat, with a document clearing them of all prosecution?" Karim asked, taking another step forward.

"You really do care for these creatures? Sure, I will let them go. You have my word."

"And can I trust it?" Karim stood almost close enough for Raku to reach out and touch him now.

"Certainly."

"Do your best, Bria," Karim said, looking back at her, as Raku reached out his free hand and touched him; Bria gasped as Karim sank to the ground. The overwhelming strength left her body, leaving her with a feeling of profound weakness. She hadn't even noticed all the cuts and bruises she had gathered across her body. In front of her, Raku's knife still pressed against Tails's throat.

"It's all right, Goldilocks," Tails mouthed from his captive position, a sad smile on his face.

Then, the blade cut into his throat, blood spraying onto the floor.

"No!" Bria screamed, her heart and mind exploding in desperate fury. She launched forward, only to be stopped by the iron grip of the surrounding soldiers. "Tails!" she screamed as she clawed at the hands holding her. She was forced backwards by a strong pull in her braid, but she ignored the pain and kept pushing forward.

"Still the same animal I see," Raku said, stepping toward her. Tails lay still on the floor in a spreading pool of blood next to Karim. It blackened Bria's eyes as she fought to break loose from the soldiers while waves of nauseating pain rolled through her as Raku put his hand on her shoulder. She squirmed to break free, but to no avail.

"I should have done this a long time ago."

Raku's voice sounded like it came from miles away. Bria distantly realized he had drawn his knife and the cold steel pressed against her neck. It cut into her skin...

"Bria!"

Tobias's voice was like a distant echo. For a moment, it cleared her mind, like a flash of light in the dark madness surrounding her on all sides. And one moment was enough. She ignored the pain of the blade as she pulled her head back and bit deep into Raku's hand, tasting his blood in her mouth as he let out a scream. His Giving relented, and another feeling replaced Bria's pain. A feeling of power. Blinded by rage, she pulled one hand free and grabbed the knife from Raku's hand, planting it deep in his chest in the same motion. He let out a gasp, and sank to the ground, staring at her in disbelief.

Around her, soldiers pulled back in surprise, and no one stopped her as she threw herself forward towards Tails, ignoring the blood as she put his head in her lap. Tears streamed down her face, dripping onto his. "Tails?"

No answer.

"Tails!"

He didn't move. Didn't speak. Didn't breathe.

"Do something!" she screamed at Karim, who was slowly getting back to his feet. The soldiers around them fell to the ground, apparently targeted by his Giving.

"I am sorry, Bria. It is too late for him," his voice was soft as thunder, rolling through her mind causing destruction and pain.

"No!" Bria rejected it. Fought against the idea, the thought of Tails being dead. For the third time, she found herself on the floor of this entrance hall, but this time she didn't feel empty. This time, the pain was too intense. Too present. She cried, brushing Tails's dark hair away from his forehead. He still had that damn smile, and his green eyes looked up at her. It wasn't fair! It wasn't 'all right'. She looked up and saw Tobias standing, motionless and still, his blue robe torn and cut and blood dripping from his fingertips, and an expression of profound horror.

Ellie limped down next to her, putting an arm around her. Bria shivered at the touch, and a part of her longed to push her away. Ellie didn't say anything, just sat with her, sharing her pain in silent tears.

Chapter Thirty-Two

Aaron collected a handful of broken chains from the cells and bent them around the wrists of five passed out guards, while Bria, Tails, Ellie and Tobias disappeared up the stairs along with the huddled prisoners. The limp bodies of the guards felt weightless as he dragged them up the stairs. He channeled everything they had in them, and power streamed through him like a raging ocean, enough to consume him. He didn't care. He would take down every last person between him and his mother.

Blood dripped from the war hammer in his left hand as two guards came charging down the stairs toward him. He Took all courage from them before they could attack him, and watched them sag together, crying for mercy and pressing themselves against the wall to hide. He killed them in the flash of an eye and continued, dragging his gruesome collection of guards behind him. At the top of the stairs, he continued across the room to the next set of stairs, where an emissary stumbled into him. Aaron crushed the emissary's head against the wall with his free hand, before he even realized what was going on.

Another floor up, then down a hallway. He still dragged the pile of guards, but sensed at least one of them had died. His incredible strength dwindled just a little. *Not enough to be a problem.* He continued to the end of the hallway, then turned left as Ellie had instructed. A heavy blackwood gate blocked his way. Behind it, the scuffling of feet reached his heightened senses. Many feet. *This must be it.*

He released the chain holding the guards and pushed the gate open with both arms. For a second, it resisted his incredible strength, then the double doors exploded open, crashing into the room. Instantly, a volley of arrows shot toward him, and he threw himself sideways behind the door for cover. His enhanced reflexes and speed allowed him to dodge easily, but at least one of the guards behind him was hit. Again, a fraction of his power disappeared, and he growled in anger.

He managed a quick glimpse round the room, where four emissaries carried crossbows. They stood surrounded by a circle of at least ten emissaries with various swords, spears, and halberds. He reached out to Take from the crossbowmen, but they all blocked his Taking. These people were trained for such attacks, it seemed, and his raw force wasn't enough to break through, as he had done with Ellie.

"Dammit," he whispered. Waves of pain, fear, and confusion from the emissaries clouded his senses, but he still had incredible speed, strength, and even the technical skills of several trained warriors, and knew he had to act fast. He took his knife from his belt, looked out from his hiding spot outside the doors, and threw it. A volley of bolts responded immediately, but they were too slow. The knife hit its target, and one crossbowman sank down.

"Surrender!" a voice called from the room.

Aaron ignored it. He drew the war hammer, peeked out again, and flung it at full force. Another crossbowman cried out as the hammer struck him, and he fell dead on the ground. They fired the two last crossbows to no avail, but Aaron was out of things to throw. It would only be a matter of time before the emissaries realized they simply had to shoot the pile of guards to take away his power. He had to act now...

With a roar, Aaron leaped up and sprinted into the room, leaving the pile of guards outside the double doors. In the blink of an eye, he crossed the distance to the two remaining crossbowmen, jumped and grabbed each by the throat. Both had unnaturally enhanced strength and resisted his grip. Still, they stood no chance against his power, and he kept pushing until he felt their necks snap.

His daring move had cost him two bolts to the gut. He barely felt it with the swirling power of his Taking raging through him, mixed in with the constant pain and nausea from the remaining Givers. He looked around and noticed he stood in the middle of the large, round chamber. Around him, the emissaries all kept their distance, apparently awaiting instructions on what to do. Aaron reached out, whipping his inner streams of Taking against their shields, but they were impenetrable.

Then he heard a creaking sound.

The door behind him closed with the pile of guards

left outside. Slowly, his power diminished and finally disappeared. A wave of desperate weakness fell over him, like a heavy blanket pushing him down. He sank to his knees, as his superior pain tolerance, strength and bravery could no longer keep him standing.

Finally, he realized what he had done and where he was: alone and helpless, bleeding from two crossbow bolts, surrounded by emissaries. Waves of pain shot through him, and he was on the verge of passing out. There was nothing he could do but accept the onslaught of pain, sickness and desperation that flowed from the emissaries. He could feel their streams reaching into him. Tormenting him. He lost all control as rivers of Giving tore at his very being. He had to break free! Had to do something! He had to focus...

He tried to think of his breath. At least he could breathe. He pushed out everything else, just breathing... The waves kept coming, but they seemed more distant now. He tried to relax his muscles, empty his mind. This was the only way. The only chance left.

And slowly, painfully slowly, his shielding came up. His eyes closed as he felt how the Giving faded, and only the physical pain from the crossbow bolts remained. He slowly stood and opened his eyes again, trying to maintain the shield as well as he could. It felt like he was hovering outside his body, looking down on himself.

He sensed how the emissaries still attacked him from all sides and angles. On the surface, they all stood still, but between them raged an intense battle of trying to penetrate his shielding. His bubble of nothingness, his inner ward, being torn and slashed by a hundred whips. Each whiplash was fiercer and harder than anything he had ever experienced, except perhaps from Flint. He could barely stay upright, let alone stay aware of the world around him, but the shielding held. A sense of triumph built in his heart, but was quickly dismissed as a voice broke through the silence of his mind.

"Stop," the voice commanded, and the attacks ceased.

He knew that voice. He took a deep breath and tried to gather his thoughts as he turned and faced Leonis.

"Please enlighten me, boy. Who are you?" Leonis' voice was calm, almost kind.

"Where is my mother?" Aaron stuttered.

"Who is your mother, child?"

A string of Leonis's Giving gently caressed the surface of Aaron's shielding. Not violently as if to penetrate it, just showing its presence. Almost friendly. It was sickening to feel the threat so imminent, like a dagger to the throat and Aaron wanted to scream, hide, and run. Anything to get away. He swallowed his fear and focused on his breath.

He stared defiantly at Leonis. "Kathrine. Her name is Kathrine."

Leonis's eyes widened. "Your mother is a very special woman, then."

"Don't you dare talk about her!"

"But we all talk about her now," Leonis continued. "In great awe. She has gone to serve High King Eldrik Evermore. Your mother is one of the greatest Givers alive."

"She would never serve The Central Rule," Aaron hissed back through gritted teeth.

"But, she would, and she does. We have ways of persuading," Leonis said, his pale face contorted into a wide smile.

Aaron noticed a thin strand of Leonis's Giving had somehow made it past his shielding without him noticing; it was now filling him with doubt, sadness, pain, fear, and a strange willingness to serve. *Have I been too late? Did Mom surrender to spare herself the pain?*

"But you are different," Leonis stated, interrupting Aaron's line of thoughts. "You are a Taker. A creature of selfish potential. A danger to even the ones you love. We could use you for grand purposes. Would you let us? Would you join your mother in fighting for a greater cause?"

Aaron couldn't stop himself from looking up into Leonis's blue eyes. Everything in him longed to say yes, to serve and please the young emissary in front of him. But a small voice inside him called for him to fight. To scream and claw like a wounded animal, even if it meant death. That voice grew, and Aaron tried to spit at Leonis, only he found he couldn't. He was too weak to spit.

Leonis seemed to have read Aaron's mind as he continued. "Sadly, the risk is too high. Therefore, you must die," Leonis said, as casually as if he was declaring what he had for dinner yesterday. Then, he signaled at the emissaries and took a step back. The emissaries drew their weapons and stepped towards him, while Leonis filled him with fear.

Aaron lay cowering on the floor. He felt like he had back on the harbor in Great Oaks. If only there was somewhere he could hide. Some way that he could disappear. His legs were shaking, his whole body shivered in fear as he pushed backwards. He had to get away, had to... His hand touched upon something. Something firm and familiar. The handle of the war hammer. He tried to lift it, but it was too heavy. He could barely move it. Then, an idea struck him.

Desperate, he found the stream of Giving that ran from Leonis and into him. It was a faint hope, but maybe, just maybe, it would work. He focused every last inch of strength and focus in him, and held onto Leonis's stream of Giving. Then, he followed it backwards, through Leonis's shield and into him. Once there, he grew the stream and Took, greedily and aggressively, forcing the gap in Leonis's and his own shield to grow. First slowly, then faster as he felt his power and courage returning.

Leonis fell to the ground with a scream as he was tapped for strength, speed and senses. Alarmed, the emissaries jumped towards Aaron with surreal speed, blades first—but Aaron was even faster as he countered them. He took a long step towards the nearest emissary and slammed the hammer into his chest. In a continuous motion, he moved on, hitting the next in the back, another in the head, hacking at every person in the room until he felt nothing. Nothing but the power he still sucked from Leonis.

The onslaught of the emissaries' whips of Giving ceased, and he sighed. He sensed Leonis desperately trying to Give and hurt him, but his stream of power faded compared to the river Aaron was Taking from him. Hate consumed him, as he bent over the pale-faced Leonis.

Slowly, Aaron allowed him some of his senses so he could see and hear. Then, he leaned the heavy war hammer on his chest and said, "Where is my mother?"

"She's with the king. King Eldrik, in The Capital!" Leonis stuttered, shaking with fear.

Aaron knew he spoke the truth, because he had Taken all courage out of him. "What is she doing there?" he continued.

"She serves as his protector."

"Why?"

"She can Give life. She is incredibly powerful, and she can Give him the youth he needs to live forever," Leonis answered, crying and shaking.

"Why would she do this?" Aaron continued, pressing down on the hammer until he felt Leonis's sternum cracking in his chest.

The man let out a moan. "Please, stop. Please, I beg!"

He was spitting blood as he spoke, and Aaron eased the pressure a little. "Why would she do that?" Aaron repeated.

"We found a way to crack her. To control her. Your mother is gone," Leonis answered, no malice in his voice, just sheer honesty. "It is how most of us came to be what we are," he continued, but Aaron didn't listen.

He had heard enough. He raised the heavy hammer and slammed it down onto Leonis's head, instantly crushing it and ending the channel of strength flowing into Aaron. The second it stopped, he stumbled and almost collapsed. Only the war hammer held him up, supporting him like an oversized cane. He looked down at where the two bolts had pierced his stomach and where blood dripped rapidly into a growing pool on the floor. *I need someone to take from. Anyone...* Before he could finish his thoughts, he passed out and fell to the ground, next to Leonis's corpse.

To his surprise, he woke looking straight into the face of a middle-aged man with a white beard and white hair. Aaron launched his Taking instinctively, but was blocked by a shield as solid as a mountainside.

"You have done well," the man said, looking around the room.

Aaron followed his gaze, looking at the corpses scattered across the room. "What? Who are you?" He was too weak to move, and even talking hurt.

"Karim, I am the headmaster here. I must say you delivered quite a show today."

Icy chills ran down Aaron's spine. Bria had told him about Karim, but he had never imagined him radiating such power. And furthermore, something seemed oddly familiar and even comforting about his face, as if he had seen it before in a long distant memory.

"For a moment, I worried the task was too great, with so many Givers here," Karim said, sitting down beside Aaron.

Aaron noticed a stream of healing and clarity streaming from the white-haired man into him. "You mean... You mean you planned for all this to happen?" Aaron's mind was tumbling with the confusion of it all.

"Yes, and no. You might not believe an old servant of The Rule like me, but I like to think I was Bria's friend when she was here, and I wish The Central Rule to fall. Their cruelty has gone too far. Luckily, you have just single-handedly slain almost every emissary in Roak who was truly loyal to King Eldrik." Karim laughed a warm and dry laughter as he spoke, contrasting the grueling vision of corpses and blood spread over the room. "But I must apologize. I could not keep your mother here long enough for you to save her. Heaven knows I tried, but she was sent to King Eldrik just a week ago. Perhaps you will follow her there?"

"I will follow her anywhere, as long as I live," Aaron replied, looking up into the ceiling. He felt dizzy, and a tear rolled down his cheek. He had been too late.

"Good. Here, let me take you to the infirmary. Fear not, you are under my protection as headmaster of Roak."

Karim called out a command, and a group of guards entered. Aaron instinctively began Taking from them, but Karim put a calming hand on his shoulder. "Relax. And don't let them know your powers," he whispered, and Aaron relented his Taking, letting the guards carry him. He passed out again as soon as they left Karim's side.

Chapter Thirty-Three

Bria sat on the small step in front of the door to her house. Hers and Tails's house. Brown sludge on the ground carried the signs of feet and carriages, the fresh snow falling too slowly to cover the tracks from the days that had passed. Days she had survived in a blurry haze. Tails was gone... An icy wind pierced through the holes between the buttons of her coat, and she suppressed a shiver.

Up the road, she spotted Tobias returning from the school. He had visited Aaron at the infirmary again, she presumed.

"He is still asleep. I left Ellie with him," Tobias said as he stopped.

Bria nodded in response, keeping her gaze just low enough not to make eye contact with him. It ached every time she looked him, or anyone, in the eyes these days.

"Karim instructed to finish the burial as soon as possible," Tobias said. "He displayed the... Displayed Tails yesterday, and everyone believes he was the Taker. Officially, he was burned in the courtyard last night."

Bria nodded again. Karim had asked her permission, but what could she have said? It only made sense. Everybody had been searching for a black-haired Taker with mystical powers. Tails's black hair had been enough to convince the soldiers of their successful kill, and they had celebrated their victory as Karim announced the Taker was dead. He had promised to keep Tails's body safe, however, so he could receive a proper burial at home.

"Is the grave ready?" Bria asked, her voice frail.

Tobias had spent days hammering through the frozen ground behind the house under one of the birch trees. Karim had offered to send one of his few loyal emissaries, or even show up himself to help with the work, but the mere thought of seeing a blue-robed emissary still made Bria feel sick. Fortunately, Tobias had declined the offer before she had to say anything and set about the work himself.

"It is ready... Bria I—"

"Thank you," Bria said, interrupting him, hoping to dismiss any words he might have. She hadn't the room for them in her mind or her heart. "We should do it tonight then. I hate that he lies in the catacombs with all the other dead... Can you let the sisters know?"

"Yes. Did he know anyone else here? Friends or family?"

"I don't think so," Bria replied. She had never asked him about his family, his history, or where he came from. It had never seemed important, but now it pained her that she would never find out. Tobias lingered for a moment, as if he waited for her to say something else, before he turned and walked off, back towards the school.

The sisters had spent most of their time at Karim's office making plans with him for how to move forward from the current situation. Most emissaries had died in the fight, and Karim personally questioned all remaining emissaries, guards and staff, to ensure that only those loyal to him stayed. Those more loyal to The Rule than to him —which was the majority of people and students—had been placed on large ships that departed the island the first day after the battle. A week had passed now, and things seemed quiet, though Bria made no attempts to learn much about the current events. It was bad enough to hear the occurrent celebratory yells in the streets, celebrating the defeat of the Taker. Karim's misinformation had spread like wildfire, and very few people knew what had actually come to pass on that night.

It was dark outside as the ritual began, and Bria's breath gathered like clouds in the light from the lantern she held. Next to her stood the sisters and Tobias, each with their own lantern, illuminating the street in front of the house like a little cluster of stars.

"Are you ready?" Mia asked, her hand in Bria's.

Bria clenched her teeth, holding back tears. A lump in her throat threatened to suffocate her and drown her words, so she simply nodded. Up the road, the night was pierced by the light from six guards who carried torches in one hand, Tails's casket in their other. *Did they know the boy they carried had been part of the group that had attacked and even killed several of their comrades?*

Citizens watched from their windows, the most curious from the side of the road, as the parade made it to their little house. To Bria's surprise, Karim followed behind the guards together with Kindra, his tall frame standing out from the group, and the silver embroidering of his rope reflecting in the moonlight.

"It is good to see you again, Bria, although on such a sad occasion," Kindra whispered, as she pulled her into an embrace.

Bria felt her strong arms around her, and couldn't hold back the tears any longer. They rolled down her cheeks as she held on to Kindra. "Thank you for coming," she stuttered.

Karim placed a warm hand around her shoulders as she slowly released herself from Kindra's comforting hug.

"Condolences. I did not know Tails until the end, but those few moments were enough for me to know he was something special. We found this ring hidden in a secret pocket inside his shirt, and I think you should have it. Guard it well, for just like Tails, I believe it might be much more than what meets the eye."

He pressed a ring into Bria's hand, and she lifted it up to examine it in the lantern's light. It was made of two metal threads spun around each other. One was bright steel, the other dark, almost black. She inspected the intricate ring, running it between her fingers. It was smooth and had a feeling of age to it. She had never known Tails had any such treasure. It must have been valuable to him to not have traded it for beer long ago, and to not even have shown her. She couldn't help but feel a pang of pain from that...

Meanwhile, Tobias directed the parade past the house and towards the grave. They all followed behind, till the guards stopped. They held the coffin directly over the hole, their grip so they held it by a set of ropes. Slowly, the process began as they lowered the wooden casket into the empty space. The silence was palpable, as the coffin sank into the darkness, where the torchlight and lanterns didn't reach. For an instant, Bria wanted to leap forward and stop them. To open the coffin and see Tails's face again, but she stopped herself. She had seen him as they put him in the casket a few days earlier, and it had hurt more than she had thought possible. She couldn't do it again.

Petra cleared her voice and stepped forward. "Goodbye Tails. You have been like a brother to me and my sisters... A friend and an unlikely ally. Your humor and your ability to escape has saved you from many troubles, but your *true* strength has always been your heart and your care for others, even if you often did a lot to hide it. May the peace from before your birth be the peace of your eternal rest."

Bria looked up in surprise as Karim, Kindra and the sisters repeated the last words: "May the peace from before your birth be the peace of your eternal rest" in a low voiced chant. She had never heard that phrase before... She shook her head, clearing her mind, and clenched her fists. She should also say something. Tails deserved that. He deserved so much more.

"Tails... You saved me that day, when you found me in the snow outside Roak. And you saved me just a little every day since then. You taught me to find safety and happiness when surrounded by danger and hardship. You always had a smile, and you made me believe that things could be better. And things got so much better. We got a house, and you cooked, and..." Bria's voice broke, and she took a deep breath before she could continue. "And you fixed things. And I... You fixed me, and..." She stepped back, fearing she might collapse from the weight of the sorrow. "Goodbye," the word pressed past her lips with heart tearing bluntness. She wanted to run as far and fast as she could. But she forced herself to stand and watch as the soldiers shoveled earth down the tomb, covering the coffin, and him. This was the end.

$$\dagger$$

Bria couldn't sleep at night, and she didn't feel like eating or talking to anyone. How long would it feel like this? Her first slight ease in the pain was when Tobias let her know Aaron had finally woken up three days later. She had feared he might never wake up. Or that he would be somehow... different. Karim had told her he might have changed from the intense forces of Giving and Taking that had influenced him, but she needed only moments with him to be reassured he was his old self. Almost too much. It was as if he didn't remember that night. Or didn't realize what had happened.

"Oh, finally a visit, Bria. I thought you'd forgotten about me!" he called from his bed as she entered the school infirmary.

It felt strange walking the hallways, and she had to keep her face hidden so no one would notice her scars. Karim had persuaded her to wear a blue emissary robe with a deep hood, which covered her face almost entirely.

"Shh! Don't call my name in here!" she hissed and rushed to the bed, looking around for any students in the other beds that might have heard him.

"I'm an outcast from this school, remember?" she whispered as she got up next to Aaron's bed. Several of her old classmates were still in the school and might recognize her. She felt a sting in her heart every time she thought of them, but she knew she could never see them again. They might be loyal to Karim, but how would she possibly explain that she was back? Her voice softened as she saw Aaron. He was pale and more covered in bandages than not, but he smiled.

"Sorry, so what can I call you then? Blondie? Goldie? What is it Tails always say?"

Bria pressed her lips together at Tails's name, a ripple of pain rushing through her heart.

"What? I can call you something else if you prefer that to be an exclusive arrangement?" he continued.

"No, Aaron, it's—"

"Maybe just hairy? Like, because of the long hair and—"

"Tails is dead, Aaron."

The words rang in the deafening silence of the infirmary.

"...What?"

"He died..." Bria said in a lower voice, sinking down on the chair next to Aaron's bed.

She hid her face in her hands, tears wetting her palms.

She was surprised as she felt Aaron's hand stroking her hair, and she looked up at his face.

"I am sorry," he whispered.

Words failed her, and she just sat there, Aaron stroking her hair. "Should I take some of your pain?" he whispered.

Bria considered the offer for a moment before she declined. The pain was excruciating, but somehow it felt wrong to not feel it. She shook her head and wiped the tears from her face. "We buried him behind the house three days ago."

"Three days? How long have I been out for? The nurse said it had just been a few days."

"It's been more than a week, Aaron. Ten days today," Bria said, her voice shaking, but she slowly regained control of it.

Another week passed before Aaron finally left his bed. He and Tobias stayed most of their time at the school, planning and scheming with the sisters and Karim. Bria, however, couldn't stand the sight of those black buildings, and she kept to herself in the house.

Today was a particularly cold morning, and Bria sat with her blanket around her eating porridge before going to work, delivering messages for the guards and setting up stalls at the market as usual. The sun was rising, and red light poured in through the dirty windows, illuminating the dust and dirt covering the floor as well as any other surface. It had always been Tails who cleaned around the house... The others had told her to relax instead of going to work, but she found it helped to stay active. And hopefully it would eventually make her tired enough that she could sleep at night. She growled as porridge spilled from her spoon onto the table; she was too tired for this. A knock on the door interrupted her grim mood.

"Enter," she called, sighing.

The front door opened, revealing Tobias, and letting in an icy breeze from outside. He kicked muddy snow off his boots before stepping in and hung his thick brown sheepskin coat next to the door. "May I sit?" he asked, pointing toward the chair opposite from hers.

Bria caught herself wanting to dismiss him, but forced herself to nod. He sat down and started talking. *Of course, he wanted to talk.*

"I have thought a lot about it, and I should have been there... To protect you. And him as well." Tobias let out a sigh. "I am sorry."

"You were there, protecting us from another group of soldiers, giving us a chance to escape," Bria replied, her voice coarse.

"I should have been stronger! I should have—"

"No, you protected us as well as you could. And you sacrificed yourself. You are quite the hero. Happy?"

"But it wasn't enough..." Tobias said.

Bria felt frustration rising in her chest. *Why was this all about him? About how strong he could be?*

"Actually, Tobias, you're right. You should have been there," she snapped at him, surprising herself with the harsh tone in her voice.

His posture stiffened visibly in front of her.

"Not during the battle, there you did all you could. No, you should have been there before. For months, you've stayed away from me and from the life we could have shared. And I wished you had been there!"

"I... Bria, I am sorry. I just missed you so much and... I love you, and I didn't know how to—"

"So now you say you love me?" Bria hissed. "You just needed Tails out of the way? Is that how love works?"

Her cheeks were warm, and she was surprised to find that she was on her feet, looking down at Tobias's face, which was painted with sadness. She sighed and relaxed a bit.

"I don't know how love works, Bria," he replied.

She sat back down, wrapping the blanket around her again. Outside the house rang the playful voices of children, contrasting the raging emotions in her heart.

"I came all the way to Roak, thinking I'd save you and take you back home to the life we had." Tobias's voice was weak. "But I guess that's not how love works. Or life. Things change, and so do people and circumstances. I am truly sorry about Tails. He... He was a good guy, and he deserved your love. And a life with you."

"He did."

A long silence ensued, and Bria was just about to get up when Tobias cleared his throat. "I... I actually came to tell you something. Some months ago, Tails asked me to make him a promise."

Bria looked up in surprise. "I didn't think you two spoke at all?"

"Well, we didn't. Not much at least. But he wanted me to promise that if we got the chance, I would make sure you came with us back to Great Oaks. I guess he knew you would object to leaving and—"

"So now you are going to drag me back to Great Oaks, is that why you are here?" Bria said, her voice rising again. *I really need to sleep, my temper is all over the place*, she thought.

Tobias looked at her, his face stern and his eyes wet. "No. I came because I will not be returning to Great Oaks. Not yet at least... In the end, I only promised Tails to do what I could to keep you safe if he could not, nothing more."

"So you're not going home?"

He shook his head. "I don't think so at least. Kathrine is still held captive and the fleet from the Vanguards is approaching Roak. We should either be gone before the water fills with enemy ships, or prepare to fight and defend this place."

"Vanguard?" Bria asked.

That was Marcus's family. She had been so caught up in her sorrow that she hadn't even thought about the obvious repercussions of a direct attack on Roak. And she hadn't thought of Marcus since she left the school. Somehow his bullying seemed less considerable compared to the rough life on the street. Still, her fists clenched as she thought of him now.

"Yes. That is what we have been planning with Karim. Roak's defense."

"I see... I should help."

"You could also come with Aaron and me instead? We haven't decided yet, but I think we will leave the island before the battle, and somehow try to find your mom in The Capital. I'd love you to come with us."

"Tobias, you're going to The Capital. Someone with

my scarred face would never be safe anywhere where The Central Rule is, and The Capital least of all. For now, I fear Roak is the best place for me, and I don't think anyone could ever conquer it. This place is a natural stronghold. I am sure we will be safe here."

"I hope so. Karim says the same, though he worries, I know. The loyalty of his men is still weak since the battle at the school, and most troops have left."

"All the more reason for me to stay and help."

"Just... If you stay, promise me to be careful."

"Of course, I am the most careful person around, as you know," Bria replied, a smile tugging on her lips, the first for weeks.

He replied with a warm smile that reminded Bria of summer and the smell of iron, bonfires and grass.

"And you remember to stay safe as well. Thank you for helping Aaron, and for helping search for Mom," she added. After all, it was amazing what he did for them. For her.

"We will find her and save her," he replied stoically. "I am glad you kept the bracelet."

She followed his gaze to the silver band on her wrist. She had worn it, even when they hadn't been friends, and she didn't think about it anymore, it was just there. Her heart lifted at the thought of that day on the mountain when he had given it to her. Life had been so simple, and she had been so certain and happy. "It has been my greatest treasure. And, thank you for coming to save me. I guess I never got to say that properly," she whispered, and reached over the table, grabbing Tobias's hand. It was big, warm, and rough, like it had always been. The warm touch sent shivers through her, and for a moment it looked like Tobias might cry.

"You're welcome."

"I know I haven't made it easy for you... I'm sorry it had to be so hard."

"I get it," Tobias said as his voice cracked a little.

"Could we perhaps start over and be friends?" she asked, her hand still holding his.

"Friends," he nodded in agreement.

"And someday we will go home to Great Oaks. But for now, I need you to look after Aaron, not me. At least until Mom is safe."

"I know. He is so strong now, but... He is also weak, if you know what I mean."

"That goes for all of us, I think," Bria replied, the iron grip on her heart loosening just a little.

Chapter Thirty-Four

Aaron's body ached in humming numbness as he woke. Above him was a white-chalked ceiling, and a scent of lavender filled the air. Carefully, he lifted a finger, then a hand. He felt so heavy...

"Easy, easy, don't move," a white-robed woman said as she rushed to his side.

"Who are you?" he asked.

His mouth was dry, and his jaw rigid, aching with the movement.

"Here, drink this," she said, holding a cup to his mouth, and something lukewarm made its way into his mouth. He immediately had to suppress a gag.

"Swallow."

He forced himself to oblige, only succeeding due to years of practice from Mom's medicines.

"So, who are you?" he asked, repeating his question while trying to ignore the bitter taste that lingered in his mouth.

"Millian. I'm a healer. And you? I have never seen you?

They say you helped fight against the Taker in the battle? The only emissary who survived from the gathering in the tower."

She looked at him with a smile that confused Aaron. *Defeated the Taker?*

"What are you talking about?" He turned his head to look around: the room was full of empty beds. Was she... Then he understood: she thought he was one of the emissaries who had fought against the Taker and survived. He looked up at her face, noticing the sparkle in her brown eyes. She was beautiful, almost as beautiful as Ellie, he decided. *Probably best to leave her believing me a hero then...*

"How long have I been here?"

"Don't worry about that, it's been a short stay. There is no hurry for you, I will take good care of you," Millian said, a hand brushing over his forehead and hair.

Aaron grunted and accepted his fate for now. He needed to clear his mind and remember... The battle felt like a distant dream. Had she mentioned a gathering in a tower?

Within hours, Tobias visited him, then Bria, both wearing blue emissary robes. They brought him up to date with all that had happened. They had been too late to save Mom, Karim had thrown out all those disloyal to him, the guards had celebrated the death of the supposed Taker, and... And Tails had died.

Intense and bitter sadness filled him with a drowning sensation. He had a faint memory of splitting up from the others, and that lay heavy on his heart. He had never got to know Tails well, but he had always been kind to him, and

Bria had loved him. He could barely hold back his own tears as she cried next to his hospital bed, and it gnawed at him that it might not have happened if he had been there to lead them out of the school. If only he hadn't left them to search for Mom in the tower... Another failed part of the mission.

Aaron waited several days before he left the infirmary, at Millian's loud protests. He had to admit that her comment about him not being ready might not be entirely untrue, as his legs threatened to give way under him with every step. Still, he had to get out, look at something other than the white ceiling and Millian's kind but entirely not Ellie face. Not to mention the thoughts of his failure to save Mom, prevent Tails's death, and help Bria in her pain. He dared to Take just a little of Millian's strength to stabilize himself as he staggered out of the infirmary and into a hallway. Two guards stood ready, and Aaron's muscles instinctively tightened, preparing for an attack. Then he realized they weren't enemies anymore. He was at Roak, and they thought of him as an emissary, perhaps even a hero.

"Can we help you, honorable sir?" the nearest guard inquired.

"Could you, er... point me in the direction of..." he hesitated. He hadn't really thought of where he wanted to go. Tobias and Bria had brought him up to date on most things, and he wanted to visit Tails's grave. But maybe he shouldn't press his luck with an excursion all the way to Bria's house just yet.

"Oh, you're up," a voice interrupted his thoughts, and Ellie appeared from around the corner.

"Ellie," Aaron said, his stomach fluttering in the familiar but confusing sensation he had every time he saw her. "I was going to—"

"Never mind where you were going, come with me instead," she said, and walked on without stopping, giving Aaron no time to protest.

Aaron felt a stream of strength and speed flow into him, and quickly caught up with her. For once, she was quiet. Usually she always spoke so much...

"Where are we going?" he asked, trying to break the silence in a casual manner.

"The catacombs. I've been meaning to take you there for days, but Millian said you weren't ready to get up."

"She did?"

"Yes, in fact she insisted I didn't disturb you."

"But, why the catacombs? Aren't they empty now? I mean, we got everyone out... Right? Bria said all the prisoners have been given rooms and—"

"There's something you have to see, and it's better you see it now," Ellie said, still walking. Still not looking at him.

She wore a blue emissary robe, and the guards in front of the catacombs let them pass without a question. She picked up a torch from the wall, and they went down the set of stairs. Aaron could smell blood and death long before they reached the large open chamber at the end. The air hung still down there, moist and heavy. A deep silence accompanied the darkness that lazily crept aside for the warm light of the torch. The floor was... White?

"You killed forty-seven people that day," Ellie said coldly.

She held forth her torch, illuminating the floor. It wasn't white. It was covered with row after row of corpses, wrapped in linen and lined up next to each other. The shapes of humans were unmistakable. Aaron gasped. His heart sank like a rock in a dark ocean, and he felt as if someone had just poured a bucket of cold water over his head. Dizzy, he sat down on the last step of the stairs. Row after row, so many dead. He hadn't even... Didn't even remember.

"The ground is too frozen to bury them, and burning them would be too public, so they will be kept here until we can do something else."

"But... Did I really do all this?"

"I guess Karim was right about your memory then... Yes, you did Aaron, even when I tried to stop you. These people had lives. Wives and husbands, children and homes. Dreams," Ellie said, still not sitting next to him.

"I... I am so sorry," Aaron stuttered, his throat dry. "I lost control. I..."

"That is why you need to see this. This is what Bria, Tobias, and the rest of us saw. And if it wasn't for Karim's swift hand, it is what the world would have seen."

Ellie's Giving had stopped, and he felt painfully weak. The cold air prickled his skin, and visions of mangled corpses filled his mind. Visions of him, burning with power and bloodlust, tearing through soldiers. She hung the torch on a wall mount.

"You used your powers against me that night... I am sorry Aaron, but I cannot trust you. Not like this. The other's have accepted you, but they don't see, don't feel, the streams of your Taking. It is too much. Please, stay as long as you like. But when you come back up, don't talk to me again."

Aaron remained in the catacombs until the cold seeped into his bones, and he was beyond shivering. Ellie had asked, he didn't speak to her again. Said he had used his powers against her... He had no memory of it, but then again, he barely remembered the fight. All these people, dead by his hand. He had lost control, done exactly what his father had told him to avoid, and... *I am the monster they think I am.* The thought haunted him, and together with the profound misery over Ellie's word, it left him hating himself more than ever.

So long he had feared what people thought of him, because of his powers. Now he finally understood they were correct. The little girl, who screamed and ran away from him when he tried to save her. Laura on Blackskull, who said he would become a murderer. All the stories. He was a Taker, and everyone would be better off staying away from him, especially Ellie, for he could not bear the thought of hurting her more than he already had.

Finally, he stood and pulled the cloth from the face of each of the dead. The least he could do was look at the faces of his victims. In at least half the cases, the faces and heads were so mutilated there was little left to look at, and he fought hard not to be sick.

I did this. I am a monster. I don't even remember what I did.

For each corpse, he mumbled an apology. Even to the emissaries. He couldn't tell which one had been Leonis, so even Leonis got an apology. Then he took the torch and headed back up from the catacombs and returned to the infirmary. He felt beyond worthless, and his heart ached as Millian wrapped thick blankets around his shivering body. He could just Take her heat, he knew, but the thought of Taking made him feel sick with disgust, and the fear of what he might do, and of what he had already done. He drank her bitter medicine without complaining; he deserved every ounce of the bitter taste. Then he drifted into a restless sleep, haunted by images of men and women falling before him and of dragging a pile of corpses behind him. He had ended so many lives, but he barely remembered it.

✛

Days passed, and Aaron forced himself to function. He wasn't sure if he should somehow explain himself to the others. Apologize? None of them ever mentioned what he had done at the battle. In addition, his heart constricted in pain every time he saw Ellie, who sternly ignored his presence. He honored her wish and never spoke to her. *If only she would yell at me, tell me I had done wrong. Scold me forever, anything but this.*

But she didn't scold him or yell at him, just kept her painful distance and stayed silent whenever they were forced to be in the same room. Tobias was also silent, although he always seemed close by, and offered to talk numerous times. Something Aaron just couldn't do. In contrast, Bria was never around. She spent her days working and staying away from them all. Aaron couldn't possibly expect any of them to understand or forgive, so he carried the image of the dead deep in his heart, only to come out at night in his sleep.

Meanwhile, Karim had begun inviting them all to regular meetings in his office. Apparently, and unsurprisingly, The Rule had decided to send the Vanguard fleet to Roak with an army, and the recent decrease in soldiers and emissaries meant Karim needed to re-plan how to defend the city once they arrived. Aaron didn't like the idea of fighting. More killing. More death. But on the other hand, running away might mean the death of so many others in Roak... He didn't know what to do or feel anymore, he only knew that the thought of Taking revolted him, and made him feel sick.

"If you stay, you will be cherished in our defense," Kindra said. She was responsible for planning the positions of the remaining soldiers, with assistance from Bria, who knew the streets and passages of the city better than anyone else, even the sisters.

"But if you leave, you might still help us by drawing attention elsewhere," Karim said, reiterating some strategic options they had already gone through a thousand times.

Aaron couldn't help but feel like a chess piece rather than a person when they talked about him like that; and he could not understand how Karim could seem so unconcerned about what he had done during the battle... In reality, he just wanted to leave it all behind. Perhaps it wasn't too late to go home? Perhaps they had been too late to save Mom, and maybe he should give up before he hurt more people. Finally, the sisters made his decision on what to do easy.

"We will leave before the battle. We have business in the east, and as much as we would love the glory of war, I fear our prowess is better applied elsewhere," Petra said.

Aaron's heart sank. That meant Ellie would leave, hating him forever, just like he deserved. Still, somehow he wished he had had the chance to change it.

"You can come along if you like," Mia added. "We will drop you off on the north coast of Meridian on our way, and you can do what you must to find your mother."

Aaron's heart lifted, as he looked up. Ellie was looking away, but she was there, so she must have accepted this plan. Going with the sisters meant... It meant so many things. A chance to save Mom. Maybe a chance to apologize to Ellie, and a chance to get off the island without having to fight anyone else. With the sisters, they could probably sail anywhere without him having to kill anyone. He exchanged glances with Tobias, who nodded in agreement.

Chapter Thirty-Five

"I've gathered you all here today to say goodbye," Karim said.

Sunlight streamed in through the red painted windows, coloring his office in a warm shimmer. Aaron had come to familiarize himself with the room during the regular meetings, since he had left the infirmary. Flames crackled lazily in the fireplace, and mild incense filled the room with herbal scents that reminded him of the old cabin in Great Oaks. They all stood on the red, intricately woven carpet that covered most of the dark wood floor, while Karim stood behind his wooden desk in his familiar black robe with silver stitches. He no longer wore the silver sigil of a star representing The Central Rule, Aaron noted.

Bria stood next to him, her head bobbing and her eyes circled by gray. But her face was stern and her arms folded in a determined pose. She radiated power in a way that he had never noticed before. Furious, like an animal caught in a corner and ready to fight whatever it takes, but in control, like a wolf, waiting for the right time to charge.

"Patricia, Miandra and Eleanor, I know you have decided to go east tomorrow, and that you will travel with Tobias and Aaron. I wish you the best of luck on this journey, and that you might reach your destinations and goals with success."

As several times before, Aaron wondered what the sisters' destination was. They had kept this information to themselves so far, only letting him know they would transport them east to Meridian. Ellie still wouldn't talk to him, and he felt bad asking too many questions to Mia and Petra. They probably hated or feared him almost as much as Ellie did, even if they hadn't been there at the battle to see what he had done.

"Bria, you have decided to stay and help me and Kindra defend the city in the coming battle. Your knowledge of the streets of Roak will prove invaluable in this matter."

Aaron pressed his lips together. He knew Bria meant to stay, but he still didn't feel good about it. They had come all this way, and there was no way she'd be safe here during a battle. But, they had already argued the matter twice, and he knew she had made up her mind.

"Tails has taught me most of what he knew about the streets and passages of the city," Bria added.

Karim nodded. "But before we part, I would like to disclose my own plans with all of you. As some of you already know, I was the child taken from the south during what you know as The Southern Rebellion or The War of the Lost Child."

Aaron gasped. Karim was The Lost Child? The one who had caused the whole Southern Rebellion? He looked around and noticed Tobias appeared just as surprised, while Bria and the sisters seemed to already know about this.

"Back then, King Eldrik brought me to Roak to be taught, just like other Givers. He soon realized, however, that I was not as easily bent, and that I was strong. Not as strong as your mother," he said, looking at Aaron then Bria, "but strong enough to be a danger if I should get too close to him or find the right allies. So, he kept me here. The school, the whole island has, in its own way, been a prison for me ever since, surrounded by emissaries to keep me in check. Sure enough, I've had the freedom to travel, but he always kept his loyal emissaries close to keep an eye on me. Until now, when you defeated all of them in a single blow."

Aaron tried to block out the mental image of corpses lined up in the catacombs.

"I plan to defend Roak the best I can. Hopefully, we will succeed."

"Hopefully?" Tobias asked.

"If we fail, we will escape. I swear I will protect Bria with every bit of my power," Karim continued.

Bria rolled her eyes, but said nothing.

"But after the battle, whether we win or lose, I will go south to fight Lord Silverhand. I will finally free my people from their slavery. And in doing so, I hope I might distract King Eldrik long enough for you to strike, Aaron."

Aaron felt nervous as Karim's and all other eyes fell on him. "Strike?" he asked. "We will save Mom, that's all. No more striking."

"I'm sorry Aaron, but I don't think you will have a

choice. Your mother is an exceptional Giver, and she has almost certainly been placed at King Eldrik's side. To get to her, you will have to fight."

"But, she would never serve him," Aaron objected for the thousandth time.

"Please believe me. They have ways of using Givers, even if they don't serve willingly. Ways of tricking her mind to follow the king's bidding without even realizing what she is doing. And, importantly, if King Eldrik Evermore is using your mother, I am afraid you will only have one chance to free her," Karim continued. "You will have to kill Eldrik."

Aaron felt his heart drop. Kill him? But how does one kill a man who lives forever? And how could he possibly hope to get through this, without Taking again?

"Aaron, will you stay for a moment?" Karim asked as everyone turned to leave the office.

Tobias and Bria both shot Aaron worried glances, but left without a word. Karim might be honest and friendly with them, but he still emitted unquestionable authority when he wanted to. The room emptied, and Aaron turned to face him.

"You are not well," Karim stated matter-of-factly.

"I—"

"Sit down," Karim gestured to a deep chair by the fireplace at the side of the room. Aaron obliged, while Karim filled cups of tea from a pot on the mantelpiece, then sat down, cleared his throat, and spoke in a soft voice. "When looking at the grand scheme of things, it can be hard to tell right from wrong, good from evil. But in the little everyday things, when we have to decide between helping and hurting, it becomes awfully clear."

Aaron nodded.

"So let me ask you. Do you think you are evil?"

Aaron looked up in surprise. "No! Well... Maybe. I killed so many people, I don't know anymore. I cannot trust myself with these powers! I shouldn't be like this!"

"I see..." Karim handed him a steaming hot cup of tea. "Careful, it is hot. It might burn you."

"I know that!" Aaron protested.

"Good. So you know that some things that are not evil can still cause pain."

Aaron looked down at his cup of tea. "I guess so."

"So, why isn't hot tea evil, even though it has the power to scold our mouths if we drink it too fast?"

"How could it be evil? It's just... tea?"

"Quite right." Karim took a sip. "And we are just people. Your powers do not make you evil."

"But I killed all those people!" Aaron protested.

"Right. And I might drink too fast and burn my tongue on the tea today. But I will still dare another cup tomorrow. You need to be better, Aaron, and learn from what happened during the battle. But this is not the end of your path, and for every step you take, you will have another choice—to do good or do bad."

"But... My powers make me do these things!"

"You are what you are, but you must find ways to use your powers for good."

Karim placed a hand on his shoulder. It wasn't comforting, like that of a parent, but supporting. Like a branch to hold on to when pulled away by a river or falling from a tree.

"But... How?"

"You will find ways. In every situation where you think hurting others is the only option, think again. There is always another way."

"But, what if I lose control again?"

"That is what I wish to talk with you about... Here, take this."

Karim took a black ring from his ring finger and handed it to Aaron. It was strangely heavy, and touching it instantly gave him a sense of calm that he couldn't quite place, although he was sure he had felt it before.

"It is a highly condensed alloy of Fero iron. It will suppress the powers of anyone touching it."

Aaron gasped. *Just like Ellie's knife!*

"I believe the Tiranin knew this metal well, and used it for various things. King Eldrik removed all instructions for making it, and forbade researching the matter so no one would use it against his Givers. But, I have been spending some time now on optimizing the alloy. It's not strong enough to completely block the strongest Givers, or Takers for that matter I assume. But it's enough to decrease their powers considerably. You may have it, if it makes you feel safe that you will not misuse your power. You should still be able to Take, but only if you really want to, and even then it will be considerably limited."

Aaron looked at the ring, a hope growing in his chest. This was a *cure* of sorts. Something that could make him normal. "Thank you," he whispered.

"But please, when you face King Eldrik. Do not hold

back. His reign of terror must end for your mother to be free."

Aaron nodded, though the thought or fighting—and killing—anyone, repulsed him. Hopefully, they would find another way. Somehow.

Aaron had a full night's sleep that night, for the first time since the battle. The black metal ring pressed comfortably against his middle finger, reminding him he was safe from his powers. He woke up early, filled his travel pack, and headed toward the docks together with Tobias. They wore normal clothes today, as opposed to the blue robes they had to wear around the school. How amazing it felt to be part of the crowd again. The cool air seemed somehow fresher, and Aaron couldn't help but smile as the sun crept over the roofs as the merchants set up stalls at the market.

"I think I'll miss this place," Tobias remarked.

"I guess I will as well," Aaron replied, thinking back on their many nights roaming the streets and leaping from roof to roof. Roak had been a strange place, the city a playground for him to explore his powers, for better or worse.

They reached the docks, where the sisters were already busy directing a score of men carrying large boxes into the hold of 'The Maiden's Breeze'.

"Hey, about time you two showed up!" Bria's voice sounded. She looked a bit better today, Aaron noted as she walked up to them. Her scars shone in the sunlight, but somehow he barely noticed them now. She just looked like... like Bria, his sister.

The three sisters also approached, and Aaron became painfully aware of his proximity to Ellie. She looked away, casually. Had she really meant he wasn't to talk to her forever? He hadn't dared test it yet.

"So, are you boys ready?" Petra asked, looking at Tobias's and Aaron's travel satchels.

"Yes, we will go light. And, no need to bring much more than Karim's goodbye gift," Tobias replied, rattling a pouch brimming full of gold coins.

"Ever the generous," Ellie said, a skewed smile on her face.

Aaron's heart skipped a beat at the sound of her voice. She hadn't spoken directly to him, but it was close enough.

"Well, then it's time to leave, I guess. Can't have Marcus and his idiot father show up with their army before we are well out of the way," Petra said, and turned to Bria, the sisters hugging her goodbye one after the other.

Then, Bria turned to Aaron. "Be careful, my little brother," she said, pulling him into a tight embrace.

Tears welled up in his eyes. At least this time, they got to say goodbye. "I'll come back."

"Of course you will. And, please, don't make me have to pull you out of any more prison cells," she said, her mouth twisting into a short smile.

She moved over to Tobias and hugged him too. "Please take care of Aaron. Catch him when he falls out of trees and such. And... take care of yourself as well. Some day, we will go home."

Aaron was about to protest how he would certainly

not fall out of any trees, but a firm elbow from Mia caused him to shut up and let Tobias and Bria have their moment.

They boarded the Maidens Breeze, and set off, leaving Roak and the school's black spire behind. Bria stood alone on the pier, waving them off, and Aaron felt tears streaming down his cheeks. He let them come, and didn't look away until she was no more than a line on the distant docks. For a moment, he considered Taking some sight from the others to see her a bit longer, but the thought alone made him nauseous. He hadn't Taken since the battle, and he didn't know if he would ever feel like Taking again. Grateful, he ran his thumb over the smooth metal of the black ring Karim had given him.

"It will be okay. We will find her again," Tobias said, putting a heavy hand on Aaron's shoulder and disturbing his dark thoughts.

"Thank you for coming with me," Aaron said, looking up at Tobias's face.

He smiled, as only Tobias could. Despite everything, he smiled, and Aaron couldn't help but reciprocate it.

A breeze tussled Aaron's hair, which had grown almost as long as Flints. The wind carried the smell of the salty ocean, as well as a hundred other scents Aaron knew he could separate and identify if he used his powers. For now, he let them be, and let the smell fill him with a sense of adventure, foreign, but inviting. An alluring unknown, that lifted his heart. Somehow, they would make it.

Thanks for Reading

Thanks for reading my novel—*Path of the Taker*. I hope you enjoyed it...

If you liked this book, please help out an independent author by rating it on Amazon, Goodreads, or wherever you made your purchase. It would be great if you wrote a little about your feelings, but just adding a few stars helps (obviously the more the better!)

To leave a review on Amazon

- Go to your Amazon order page
- UK: Amazon.co.uk/orders
- US: Amazon.com/orders
- And find your purchase and rate it—simple as that.

Your review means the world to independent authors like me, for whom reviews, and word of mouth, are the difference between life and death in the hectic dog-eat-dog world of self-publishing.

ABOUT THE AUTHOR

Simon is a scientist with an inner storyteller that has finally come out of the closet. He lives in Copenhagen, Denmark, and spends his time as a part-time cancer researcher, part-time backpacker, and part-time author. In his available hours he enjoys playing Dungeons & Dragons, camping in nature, and exercising —all three hobbies serving as inspiration for the travels and challenges in this book. Not to mention, inspiring the powers to Give and to Take.

Simon has been a fantasy nerd his whole life, growing up with books such as The Lord of the Rings, Forgotten Realms, and Harry Potter. Now, he pursues his own adventures as a frequent backpacker and author. His stories emphasize the sense of adventure and following an uncharted path—embracing both the frightening and the inviting.

After all:
no fear, no fun.

To find out more, check Simon's author page
https://www.worldseabooks.com

Printed by Amazon Italia Logistica S.r.l.
Torrazza Piemonte (TO), Italy